pru.

STOLEN PASSION

Windhawk grabbed Joanna by the shoulders and pulled her close.

"You always say no when you mean yes, Joanna," he said. "I have hungered for your lips," he whispered against her mouth.

Joanna felt a sob building in her throat. No, she wouldn't allow Windhawk to make her forget all that was wrong between them.

"Do you think to win me with your soft ways?" she taunted.

She knew in a moment that she had gone too far. Enraged, Windhawk picked her up in his strong arms and carried her kicking and struggling toward the buffalo robe at the back of the lodge.

Joanna began to tremble as Windhawk's eyes moved hungrily over her body. He bent down and removed her moccasins. She closed her eyes and gritted her teeth as his hand moved up her leg. Don't feel, she warned herself, make your mind a blank. When she gained the courage to open her eyes, she saw that Windhawk had removed his clothing!

He pulled her roughly into his arms. She gasped at the warm, wonderful feelings of pleasure that spread throughout her body with the intensity of a raging forest fire. She felt like a puppet in Windhawk's soft, stroking hands, and knew that he had only to pull the strings and she would helplessly respond. . . .

RAPTUROUS ROMANCE BY CONSTANCE O'BANYON

SAVAGE AUTUMN (1457, $3.50)

The white woman Joanna gave a cry of terror when the tall young leader of the Blackfoot tribe carried her away from all she held dear. But when he took her in his arms in his tepee, her soft moans were as rapturous and her kisses as urgent as his own. He knew the heights of passion awaited them in the . . . SAVAGE AUTUMN.

ENCHANTED ECSTASY (1386, $3.75)

Fearless and independent, the Indian princess Maleaha was the most sought-after woman in the New Mexico territory. No man had ever claimed her supple body, but Major Benedict knew she couldn't refuse him, and then he couldn't let her go!

SAVAGE SPLENDOR (1292, $3.50)

Married to the mighty King of the Lagonda tribe, beautiful Mara was respected and admired, but was she truly happy? By day she quesioned whether to remain in her husband's world or with her people. But by night, crushed in the muscular arms of the King, taken to the peaks of rapture, she knew she could never live without him, never let him go . . .

ECSTASY'S PROMISE (978, $3.50)

At seventeen, beautiful Victoria burned the family plantation to keep Sherman's Yankee troops from having it. Fleeing to Texas, meeting handsome, wealthy ranch owner, Edward Hanover, Victoria's passion burst into a raging blaze as his fingers brushed her silky skin. But Hanover had fought for the Union—was an enemy—and the only man she would ever love!

Available wherever paperbacks are sold, or order direct from the Publisher. Send cover price plus 50¢ per copy for mailing and handling to Zebra Books, Dept. 1584, 475 Park Avenue South, New York, N.Y. 10016. DO NOT SEND CASH.

Savage Winter

CONSTANCE O'BANYON

ZEBRA BOOKS
KENSINGTON PUBLISHING CORP.

ZEBRA BOOKS

are published by

Kensington Publishing Corp.
475 Park Avenue South
New York, NY 10016

First printing: May 1985

Printed in the United States of America

Dedication

This is to the unsung heroine and hero of my books, my editor, Leslie Gelbman, who never fails to give me her support and encouragement. I realize when my work is completed on a book, yours has only begun. Thank you for being my mentor and my friend. And to artist Ray Kursár, who creates my beautiful book covers—I thank you.

Savage Winter

When winter covers the land and the trees are stark and bare,
I cry out for my true love with the dark raven hair.
I need to feel him touch me as the heart within me dies.
Oh, cruel fate, you have deceived me as the winter
    snowflakes fly.
When the seeds of doubt are planted, and they begin to grow,
Will he seek the truth from his need to know?
The dark web of silence widens to break love's tender
    embrace.
The signs of love are hidden behind an expressionless face.

Constance O'Banyon

Chapter One

Blackfoot Territory, May, 1840

Sometimes, when Joanna closed her eyes, she could still see her Uncle Howard's hateful face and hear the sound of his voice. He was an actor by trade, and when it had suited him, he had been able to mimic the aristocracy. She could remember all too well the feel of his hot, sweaty palm moving over her arm, and she shivered, remembering how disgusted and degraded she had felt whenever he had touched her.

Joanna was sitting on her horse, Fosset, gazing down at the lush green countryside below. She watched the Milk River as it wound its way lazily over the hills and down through the valleys to be lost among the dense forest. From her vantage point, the river appeared no more than a long, narrow ribbon dividing the canyons and mountains in half.

Her eyes moved to the northern bank of the river, where she could see the Indian village that relied on the life-giving water of the Milk River for its survival.

It was at times like this, when she was alone, that Joanna questioned what she was doing living in that Blood Blackfoot village. How far away her home in Philadelphia seemed to her now!

She dismounted and stood silently gazing toward the rising sun. Each time she looked upon the beauty of this land, it was as if she was seeing it for the first time. The sweet grasses of the prairies fed a multitude of wild game. There were large herds of buffalo, deer, elk, antelope, big horned sheep, and many other game animals that Joanna had never seen before she had come to live with the Blackfoot tribe.

Fosset nudged Joanna's hand, and she absentmindedly stroked his silky white mane. Time had a way of passing here in Blackfoot country without one's being aware of it, she thought.

Joanna plucked a leaf of sweet, green grass and chewed on the stem thoughtfully. She remembered how dramatically her life had changed within the past two years. Her eyes narrowed with hatred and anger when she remembered the cruelties of her father's sister, Margaret, who had been disowned by her family for marrying an actor, and her husband, Howard Landon.

Aunt Margaret and Uncle Howard had arrived one day at her home in Philadelphia. If only Joanna had known that day what the future had in store for her and her brother, Tag, she would never have allowed her aunt and uncle to move into her home, no matter how they had played on her sympathy. At the time, her mother had just died, and Joanna's father had been away on business in the Oregon Country. How was she to know that her uncle was an evil, ambitious man who would soon be in control of her own and Tag's future?

Joanna felt tears in her eyes, remembering the day she had received word that her father had drowned at sea while on his way back to Philadelphia. Howard Landon had lost no time in going to the family lawyer to have himself declared Joanna and Tag's legal guardian. That in itself had been bad enough, but when Howard had threatened to send twelve-year-old Tag to sea and began to shower his unwanted attentions on Joanna, she had realized that she and Tag would somehow have to escape.

In a strange quirk of fate, Joanna, unbeknownst to her aunt and uncle, had later received a letter from her father, who had not drowned, but was gravely ill. In the letter he had instructed Joanna and her brother to come to him in Oregon. Joanna's Uncle Howard had gotten his hands on the letter and had threatened Joanna and Tag. They had been locked in their bedrooms to prevent them from going to their father.

One night, with the help of two faithful servants, Simon and Franny, Joanna and Tag had made good their escape, hoping to reach their father before their Uncle Howard could stop them. At the time, they dared not take a ship to Oregon Country, knowing their uncle would expect it of them and would have men watching the docks to intercept them.

Simon and Franny had helped Joanna and Tag hide out for several weeks. Finally, in desperation, Joanna had realized that the only way to reach her father was to join a wagon train heading for Oregon Country, which was being settled by many Americans, even though the English claimed it belonged to them.

Joanna ran her hand down the front of her soft doeskin gown, remembering a time when she had dressed in silks and velvets and lived in a huge manor house, with

11

servants seeing to her every need. She and her brother had been born and raised on a country estate in England. Her father, Russell James, had built a shipping empire in the Americas and had eventually moved his family to Philadelphia. Joanna had been a happy, carefree young girl. Little had she known that within a few short years her mother would be dead, and she and her younger brother would have to flee for their very lives, to escape their uncle's desperate plans to take over their lives and fortune.

Joanna shook her head. She had thought at the time they joined the wagon train that she was being very clever. That had not been the case, however. The wagon train had been ill-fated from the beginning. Somewhere on the vast, never-ending prairies, the wagon train had been attacked by the Piegan Blackfoot tribe, and most of the families had been killed.

Sometimes, at night, Joanna still had nightmares about the Indian raid on the wagon train when so many people had died, including her beloved Franny. For many months Joanna had thought her brother had been killed in that raid. She hadn't known that he had been taken prisoner by the Piegan Blackfoot and had been forced to endure many cruelties at the hands of their chief, Running Elk.

Running Elk, the chief of the Piegans, had seen Joanna when the wagon train was camped alongside the Platte River. He had wanted her and had attacked the train. During the raid, Joanna's team horses bolted, carrying the wagon she had been riding in down a steep embankment. Running Elk had left her for dead, but took her brother as his captive.

Joanna had lain injured at the bottom of the gully for

12

two days until Windhawk, the chief of the Blood Blackfoot tribe, had found her and nursed her back to health.

Joanna had thought Windhawk responsible for the raid. Thinking her brother was dead, Joanna had blamed him for that, as well. Instead, she learned that Windhawk had rescued Tag from Running Elk so Joanna and her brother could be reunited. Windhawk was like no other man Joanna had ever known. To the people of the Blood Blackfoot tribe he was like a god; to his enemies, he seemed indestructible. The white race thought of him as only an Indian legend, not believing he existed. But to Joanna, he was very real.

Joanna became aware that she was thinking in Blackfoot. It was the most natural thing in the world to her now. How strange it seemed that she seldom spoke in English anymore. She knew she would never have any desire to return to the white world. Her heart was too full of love for the darkly handsome chief of the Blood Blackfoot—Windhawk!

When Joanna had first seen Windhawk, he had made her young heart yearn for something she hadn't understood at the time. Torn as she was between loving and hating him, it had taken a long time for the two of them to overcome the difficulties that kept them apart. But now Joanna was Windhawk's wife, and she wanted nothing more than to stay with him forever.

Joanna knew the time would come when Tag would return to Philadelphia to face his Uncle Howard and reclaim his inheritance. But that time was not now—Tag was still but a boy. She knew, though, that the day he reached his twenty-first birthday, Tag would be leaving her. She would miss him, but she knew deep in her heart that she would have to let him go.

Looking upward, Joanna could feel the warm sun on her face. Her world was here beside the man she loved. She was content to bask in the love of her tall, dark husband, Windhawk!

Seeing the morning was passing, Joanna picked up Fosset's trailing reins and mounted. Turning him toward the village, she nudged him forward into a lope.

Joanna looked about the Indian lodge that had become her home. There were soft buffalo robes for her and Windhawk's bed. The lodge was larger than the others in the village, because Windhawk was chief of the Blood Blackfoot, and many council meetings had to be held in it. On the floor were five huge bearskin rugs, each symbolizing Windhawk's bravery and skill as a hunter. In the middle of the room was a cook-fire. There was a hole at the top of the lodge, which allowed the smoke to escape. At one time, human scalps had hung from the lodgepole, but at Joanna's pleading Windhawk had removed them. The lodgepole now held baskets and Joanna's cooking utensils. Windhawk's weapons hung on the wall, and several spears were stacked neatly beside the entrance.

Joanna hummed happily to herself as she rotated the spit over the cook-fire so the deer roast would brown evenly. The juices from the meat spattered onto the fire, giving off a delicious aroma.

Her mind turned backwards to the time when Windhawk had first brought her to the Blackfoot village. At that time, she had believed herself to be his captive.

She remembered the struggle that had taken place

within her because she had been attracted to the young chief. Against her will, she had been drawn to him. Her attempts to draw away from him had become futile because she loved him so desperately. She remembered the time she had escaped from him, only to have him find her and bring her back. She smiled to herself, thinking that nothing could ever induce her to leave Windhawk again. With him, she had found unbelievable happiness.

She realized that grown men often quaked with fear at the mere mention of Windhawk's name, but she knew him to be a gentle man. He had a deep understanding of a woman's heart and was always loving and tender with her. She was constantly amazed by his patient and generous nature.

She picked up one of his buckskin shirts and held it to her cheek before folding it neatly and putting it in a leather satchel. Windhawk was no legend, as the white men thought, nor a young god, as the Indians believed. He was a man . . . the man who had won her heart.

Glancing about the lodge once more, she felt her heart swell. Like any wife who loved the man she was married to, Joanna felt pride in keeping house for Windhawk. She felt such pleasure in doing the little things that made the lodge their home.

Realizing the hour was late, Joanna moved to the cook-fire. Seeing that the meat was now done, she removed it from the spit and placed it on a wooden platter. Soon Windhawk would be home, and her young heart raced as she thought of her tall, dark husband.

Chapter Two

Taggart James was curled up on one of the bearskin rugs, reading a book. Becoming bored, he laid the book aside and looked up at his sister, hoping she wouldn't scold him. He couldn't understand why Joanna was always so adamant about his continuing his education.

Tag noticed Joanna's face was flushed with an appealing rosy tint as she bent over the fire.

Joanna pushed a loose strand of red-gold hair off her forehead and sat down beside her brother. Tilting his face up to her, she studied him carefully.

"Tag, I believe you are going to need to shave before long."

He looked at her with interest. "Do you really think so?"

"Yes, you are growing up. I will ask Farley to get you a razor the next time he goes to Fort Union."

"I don't think I want to shave. I'd rather be like my friend, Iron Hand. He's sixteen summers and he doesn't have hair on his face."

Joanna smiled. "You could be like Farley instead and

grow a beard," she said, referring to the old trapper who had befriended them. Seeing Tag wasn't amused by her statement, she frowned. "You are not like your Blackfoot friends, Tag. Why do you think I insist that you continue with your lessons? I want you to always remember who you are. Your future is not here in this land. You have a destiny awaiting you in Philadelphia."

"I know, Joanna. Sometimes I wish it did not have to be so, and at other times I wish I didn't have to wait so long to return to Philadelphia."

Joanna's face brightened. "There is no need to dwell on unpleasant matters today. Do you know I'm making your favorite chokecherry cake?"

Tag smiled. "Why do you think I am hanging around? I could smell the cake all the way to Sun Woman's tipi, and I want to be the first to sample it when it's done."

She rested her hand on his shoulder, noticing for the first time that Tag's hair color was changing. Where it had once been red-gold like hers, it was now more golden, as their mother's hair had been.

"Don't you know what today is, Taggart James?"

He looked at her thoughtfully for a moment. "No, I can't say that I do. I sometimes lose track of what month it is."

She laughed softly and kissed his cheek. "I know what you mean—I was thinking the same thing myself only today. It's hard to believe, though, that you would forget something as important as your fourteenth birthday, Taggart James."

He looked astounded for a moment. "I had no idea! How can that be?"

Again she laughed. "That's easy, little brother, you simply grew one year older. You are practically a man now."

Tag jumped to his feet and his eyes lit up with excitement. "Windhawk says that when I become a man I can go on the buffalo hunt with him."

Joanna felt her heart contract with fear. She hated the fact that Tag would be facing dangers like all the other young warriors, but she was wise enough not to voice her fears. She knew that if the Blackfoot were to continue to respect her brother, he would have to prove himself a man in their eyes.

She pushed her fear aside. "Yes, he has said that when you are older you will ride on the buffalo hunt with him . . . but you aren't yet a man."

"Most of my friends have already earned their names, while I remain just plain Tag. Even you were given the Indian name, Flaming Hair."

"Farley is called Crazy One; perhaps you would like him to give you his name," Joanna said, trying to bring humor into their conversation.

Tag set his jaw stubbornly. "I'm not amused, Joanna."

"Yes, I can see that," she replied, trying to control her facial muscles. "If you've noticed, I am very rarely called by my Indian name. Most of the time I'm just plain old Joanna."

Tag's mouth eased into a smile. "I have heard Windhawk call you Flaming Hair several times." His mood turned to teasing. "Of course, when he calls you that, you like it."

"Oh, you think so, do you!" she said, ruffling his hair.

"I know so. Of course, it could be his tone of voice that you like," he said lightly, with mischief dancing in his blue eyes. He then became serious. "Try to understand— I want to be a man, Joanna!"

She put her arms about his shoulder, understanding better than he thought what he was feeling. They both

19

knew that Tag would have to prove himself worthy as a Blackfoot warrior before he could earn his Indian name.

"Try to have patience, Tag. You will be a man soon enough; then you may wish to be a boy again."

At that moment they were interrupted by someone's calling from outside the lodge, asking for admittance. Joanna recognized Gray Fox's voice, and she walked over to the opening, pushing the flap aside so he could enter.

Gray Fox's eyes rested on his best friend's wife for a moment. He felt a strong love for the Flaming-Haired-One, but he could never allow those feelings to show. No one must ever suspect that he loved his best friend's wife.

"Windhawk has sent me for Tag. He wishes him to come to the river at once. I was told to say there is a surprise waiting for your brother."

Tag watched Gray Fox's face expectantly. "What is it? What is the surprise?"

Gray Fox laughed aloud. "Do you remember the horse that you admired from Windhawk's herd?"

"Do you mean Naveron, the brown stallion with the white face, Gray Fox?"

"Yes, that is the one. Today he becomes your horse . . . but Windhawk says you must first prove you can ride the animal before he will belong to you."

Tag beamed. "Can I ride him now?" he asked eagerly.

Gray Fox looked at Joanna's pale face through lowered eyelashes. He knew her well enough to know she was fighting within herself. She feared for her brother's safety, but she was learning to let him go. One of the many things Gray Fox admired about his chief's woman was her spirit. If Joanna could be convinced that something was right, she would give in easily. But on the other hand, if she believed in something, she would make a stand and fight valiantly to the bitter end.

"Come, Tag, I will walk you to the river," Gray Fox said.

Tag looked to Joanna for her permission. He watched as she lowered her eyes.

"I . . . will stay here and have the evening meal ready when you and Windhawk return, Tag," was all she could manage to say.

Gray Fox knew that she couldn't bring herself to watch her brother ride the wild horse. "There will be many who will see to your brother's safety," he told her, trying to give her comfort.

Gray Fox's admiration for her intensified as he watched her push the fear for her brother's safety aside so he could do what was expected of him.

Joanna nodded her head, not trusting herself to speak.

A crowd had gathered on the riverbank to watch Tag break his first horse. The wild stallion was led into the water while Tag rode up beside it on another horse. Windhawk held the horse's head and nodded to Tag to jump onto the animal's back.

Many times Tag had seen the fierce Blackfoot warriors break wild horses. He had always hoped one day to get his chance to prove that he was unafraid, but he was discovering it had been one thing to feel brave while watching from the riverbank, and it was quite another to be on the back of this wild stallion, which would want nothing less than to throw him off.

Tag could feel fear gnawing at his insides as the wild horse pitched its head and rolled its eyes. With stubborn determination, he pushed his fear aside and leaped onto

21

the animal's back.

Immediately, the wild horse reared on his hind legs—he began spinning and thrashing about with hooves flying, trying to rid himself of the rider on his back. Tag felt his legs tremble from the pressure he was applying to the sides of the heaving animal. His muscles were tense and strained to the limit, but he was determined that he would not be shamed in front of the whole tribe. He would ride this horse!

Joanna could no longer stand to remain in the lodge wondering what was taking place at the river. She knew that she couldn't go to the river and watch Tag, so she decided to go for a ride instead.

Fosset raced down the wide valley, and Joanna felt the wind cooling her face. Riding to the top of a small hill, she dismounted and gazed into the distance.

Joanna couldn't stop worrying about Tag. She knew if she had shown her fear it would have shamed Tag in front of the others, so she had allowed him to go, even though in her mind she could see him being thrown by the wild animal and trampled beneath its hooves.

Sighing inwardly, she gathered up Fosset's reins and led him down the hillside. When she reached the bottom of the hill, she paused beside a bubbling pool that was fed by the Milk River and gazed down into the crystal-clear depths.

After allowing Fosset to drink from the cool water, Joanna sat down on the bank and lost herself in thought. She was vaguely aware that Fosset wandered at will, grazing on the sweet green grass along the hillside.

Usually, spring came late to the Blackfoot country, but

Joanna noticed that the wildflowers were now in full bloom. The delicate blossoms of the wild columbine reminded her of nature's perfection, while the bright yellow buttercups seemed to bow their heads in the gentle breeze.

She glanced down into the pool and saw the distant mountains reflected in the mirror-bright depths. How beautiful it was here! The land somehow seemed so untouched by the hand of man. She allowed her hand to trail in the water, and when the ripples settled she saw her own reflection. Windhawk always told her that she was beautiful, but Joanna couldn't judge her own looks. The face that stared back at her was pretty enough, she supposed, but she thought her violet-colored eyes were too large for her face. The features were delicate and soft, but her chin was too stubborn, she reasoned. Her red-gold hair hung almost to her waist and was encircled with a plain leather headband.

Suddenly, another reflection appeared from behind Joanna. She had been so deep in thought that she hadn't heard anyone come up behind her. The Indian who towered above her smiled, and she could feel her heartbeat accelerate. The man in the reflection was extremely tall, and his face was more than handsome. He wore only a leather breechcloth, and she could see the muscles that rippled across his arms and chest. His skin was deeply bronzed, and even in the reflection Joanna could see that his dark, expressive eyes were velvet-soft. Her eyes sought his in the shimmering-bright water, and he could read the unasked question on her face.

"He is fine. You would have been proud of your brother today. He showed very little fear when he mastered the wild horse."

23

Joanna felt overwhelming relief—she had been so sure Tag would be injured by the untamed horse.

Feeling the touch of the Indian's hand on her shoulder, she turned to smile up at him.

"Windhawk, how did you find me?"

He held out his hand, and when Joanna placed her hand in his, he pulled her to her feet to stand beside him.

"I will always find you, Joanna," he said in a deep voice. He reached up his hands and cupped her beautiful face between them. At times, it was still hard for him to realize that the hauntingly beautiful Flaming-Haired-One belonged to him. He had loved Joanna from the first moment he had seen her, and he had known that they would one day be as one, even though it had been hard to convince her that they were destined to walk together.

Her laughter seemed to bubble out, and the sound of it gladdened his heart, as it always had. "I will always make it easy for you to find me, my husband."

Clasping her slender body close to him, Windhawk rested his face against hers. "Stay with me forever, Joanna, and I will love you as no other man ever could."

Joanna could feel his warm breath fan her cheek, and she felt a hunger deep inside. She had heard the uncertainty in his voice and knew he was remembering the time she had run away from him. How long would it take to erase his doubts? When would she be able to convince him that she would never again leave him?

Joanna kissed his cheek. "If one day you were to tire of me and cast me aside, I would still beg you to allow me to stay."

With gentle pressure, he raised her face and looked deeply into her violet-colored eyes. "The day I tire of you will be the day when the sun grows cold; the day I will no longer want you will be the day I close my eyes in death. I think I will desire you even then."

Joanna could see the flames burning in the depth of his dark eyes. It was a bit frightening at times to love and be loved so deeply. Suppose the gods were to become envious of their happiness and rip them apart?

Windhawk swept Joanna into his arms and carried her up the hill to a spot where they would not be seen by anyone who might come to the pool. He laid her down among the wildflowers beneath a tall pine tree.

No words were spoken as he sat down beside her and moved his hand up her arm, allowing it to trail across her breasts. His dark eyes held an expression of love when he gazed into her violet eyes. Joanna drew in her breath as his hands drifted to her hips and he began to push her gown slowly upward.

She tugged playfully at his hair and he arched a dark eyebrow. "Imagine me loving a man whose hair is more beautiful than mine," she teased.

"I can imagine nothing more beautiful than the sun shining on your hair, Joanna," he said, raising a fiery lock to his lips. "I have often wondered how your hair can grow in . . . spirals. When I first saw you, I wondered if you did something to make your hair . . ." he paused, not knowing how to describe the curls. Wrapping a soft curl about his finger, he gave her an inquiring look.

"In English it is called curly hair," she told him.

"Joanna, there is nothing so beautiful as your flaming hair, unless it is your eyes. Sometimes, when I look into your eyes, I feel as if I am drowning."

She touched his lips, and he kissed her fingers one by one. "I think you like my eyes only because they are different from all the Indian maidens you are accustomed to. Had I been born with brown eyes, I doubt that you would have paid the slightest attention to me the day we met."

He leaned forward and kissed each of her eyelids. "That cannot be, Joanna. I have never told you this, but the second time I saw you, I was startled when I could see my own reflection in your eyes. I knew that day that I wanted no man's image but mine to ever be reflected in your eyes."

She smiled sweetly and pulled his head down to rest against her breasts. "I was frightened of you that day. Not because I thought you would harm me, but because I had never before felt so funny inside when a man looked at me."

Windhawk raised his head, and Joanna saw his eyes were shining brightly. "Did you love me even then, Joanna?"

"Oh, yes, my dearest love. I loved you even then," she whispered.

Windhawk pulled her forward and smoothly removed her doeskin gown. Shortly thereafter, her undergarments followed. His eyes moved over her naked body, and he drew in his breath at how perfect she was. Her legs were long and shapely—her hips were well-rounded, and her waist was tiny. Her breasts were firm, with tiny rose tips. His body trembled with anticipation as she raised her arms to him.

Windhawk stripped off his breechcloth and pulled her tightly against him.

Joanna shuddered in delight when his lips caressed her, as he breathed her name over and over. Her fingers laced in his ebony hair, then moved slowly down his shoulder to the corded muscles she felt across his back.

Windhawk's hard flesh fused to Joanna's silken skin, and a sweet longing took over her reasoning. She was more than ready to receive the thrust of his virility. And his body trembled with hunger as he felt the soft, silken sheath of Joanna's inner core.

As they made love beneath the pine tree, Joanna thought the birds had never sung so sweetly. No bed of satin could be as soft as the grass they lay upon. No room in the grandest palace could rival the canopy of bright blue sky above them. Not even the most expensive French perfume could match the scent of the hundreds of wildflowers that were in bloom.

The kiss of the soft, gentle breeze cooled their overheated bodies. As Windhawk whispered words of his undying love in Joanna's ear, she was carried away by his passion. Her desire was boundless as he drove his throbbing manhood into her body again and again.

Joanna's heart soared on wings of love as her husband reintroduced her to the world of beauty and love that the two of them always found in each other's arms. She knew that their love was the deep and lasting kind. Neither time nor distance could ever erase their feelings for each other. From the day they had first met, both Windhawk and Joanna had felt a oneness, as if they had always known each other. At first, it had been an unsettling feeling to Joanna, but she had finally come to accept it.

Joanna closed her eyes, feeling so close to Windhawk that it was almost as if she were an extension of his body. She wondered how they could have been born worlds apart and still be so right for each other.

A sweetness burned deep inside her. It was like pain, and yet beyond pain . . . a raging, sensuous feeling that seemed to rob her of her reasoning power. Windhawk had the ability to make her whole body feel as though it was burning with a slow, warm, lingering fire. She heard him murmuring her name softly, and her body answered his in total satisfaction.

The smile he gave her melted her heart when she curled up in his arms. They both watched the branches of the pine tree overhead swaying gently with the breeze.

"I am so happy, Windhawk," she said, moving her lips across his cheek. "If it is possible for one to obtain total happiness, I have done so."

Closing his eyes, he clasped her tightly against him. "If I have the power, I will see that you never know an unhappy day, Joanna." He picked up the bear-claw necklace which she always wore about her neck. He had given it to her the night he had made her his wife.

Joanna saw him frown and knew instinctively that his thoughts were troubled. She realized he was again remembering when she had left him and wished she knew how to erase all his doubts.

"If I ever leave you again, Windhawk, you will know I no longer want to be with you. But that will never happen. You should know by now that I will always love you."

She noticed when she looked into his dark eyes that they still held a hint of doubt. "You gave up so much to stay with me, Joanna. Perhaps the time will come when you will regret leaving behind the world you knew."

"I left nothing behind, Windhawk. All I will ever want can be found right here in your arms."

"Joanna, if you ever do leave me again, it would be far kinder if you would first take my life. I have this weakness that you have brought into my heart. Before I met you, I feared nothing . . . now I fear the loss of your

28

love more than I fear death itself."

Joanna held him to her, wishing she could erase all his doubts. "Windhawk, my joy is in bringing you happiness. Will you still doubt me when my back is stooped with age and my hair is as white as She Who Heals, the old medicine woman?"

He chuckled and held her close to him. "You sorely tempt me to wait around to watch as your glorious hair changes and fades in color."

She rested her face against his smooth chest. "If God, in his generosity, grants me the time, I will grow old with you, my dearest, dearest love," she told him.

"You have but to hold my hand, Joanna. Together, we will walk this land and find a happiness that has been denied to many."

"I am happy, Windhawk."

He crushed her in his arms, knowing that he wished for nothing more in life than to keep her happy. "If you are happy, then I feel joy, Joanna. When you smile, my heart is gladdened. Help me to know you will not ever leave me."

She pulled back and framed his face with her hands, smiling slightly. "You will never be rid of me, Windhawk. Never!"

He could feel the softness of her skin and it brought a pain to his heart. "I will never want you to be anyplace that I cannot reach out and touch you," he told her.

Chapter Three

It was early August. There had been very little rain and the grasses of the prairie were brown and brittle. The hot wind did little to cool the burning heat of the sun, which beat down on the large group of Blackfoot people, who were riding in a southwestern direction.

The people of the Blood Blackfoot tribe were moving to their summer village on the vast prairies, following the trail of the buffalo. It was a ritual that had taken place for many hundreds of years. In fact, Sun Woman, Windhawk's mother, had told Joanna that in the years before the first white man had brought horses to this country the Blackfoot had followed the restless buffalo trail on foot.

They had been traveling for over a week now, leaving behind the tall mountains and the lush, green valleys of the winter camp. Every once in a while Joanna's eyes would search the distant foothills, and she would wish they were traveling in those mountains so she could find some relief from the grueling, punishing heat. She felt the heat more than the Indians did, and she wondered if she would ever become accustomed to this nomadic life they led.

Her heart swelled with love for this land. Once she had walked here as an intruder and a stranger, wanting nothing more than to return to the world as she had known it. Now she felt she had earned the right to be a part of this land, because she was Windhawk's woman.

She drew rein to slow Fosset's pace, then gazed sideways at Sun Woman. A smile curved Joanna's lips and was returned by the older woman.

"You seem to be happy today, my daughter. I believe you bloom like the wildflowers."

Joanna didn't answer right away, but instead studied Sun Woman's face. Windhawk's mother was still a very attractive woman. Her iron-gray hair was pulled back and bound with a leather strap. She was taller than Joanna, and she always carried herself straight and proud. The Blackfoot people admired and respected Sun Woman. She was a powerful influence on her people. There had been a time when Sun Woman had resented Joanna, but that was before Joanna had proven to the older woman that she was worthy of her friendship and of her son's love. It was often Sun Woman's way to be stern and withdrawn, but Joanna knew that inside she was a very loving woman, and Joanna had come to love her a great deal.

"If I seem to bloom, it is because I am so happy, my mother. My days are filled with useful tasks, and I was just thinking that I am a true Blackfoot now."

Sun Woman nodded. "I would like to see the day you bloom from carrying my grandchild within your body. You and my son have been together for many moons now. I see no reason why you have not conceived."

Joanna looked into her mother-in-law's dark eyes. "What if I am barren and cannot have a child?" she asked, expressing her secret fears. It had been nagging at her that she had not yet conceived. Joanna knew Windhawk wanted a child very badly, and she was troubled that she hadn't, thus far, been able to give him a baby.

Sun Woman very rarely laughed, but she did now because of Joanna's remark. "My son is a very virile man—he keeps you on his mat much of the time. I think it will not be long until I hold my first grandson in my arms."

Joanna blushed at Sun Woman's remark and lowered her head, which only caused Windhawk's mother's laughter to deepen.

Joanna and Windhawk had tried so hard to have a child. What if she did prove to be barren? Would Windhawk turn to another woman to give him the son he wanted so much? It was not unusual for a Blackfoot warrior to take more than one wife. Joanna knew she would never stand idly by while Windhawk brought another woman into their lodge. No, she told herself, Windhawk had told her he would never take another wife, and she believed him.

The dust from the lead horses caused Joanna to cough, and her eyes stung from the particles of dirt that sifted into them. As the morning progressed, the summer heat seemed to intensify. By midday it was almost unbearable.

Joanna was fully aware that She Who Heals kept a watchful eye on her. She knew the old medicine woman was remembering the time when Joanna had lost her sight from snow blindness. How dear these people of the Blackfoot tribe were to her! They had opened their hearts

33

to her, letting her know she was one of them.

Occasionally, Joanna would have to check Fosset's pace, or he would outdistance the other horses with his powerful gait. She could feel rivulets of perspiration running down between her shoulder blades and knew she must look a sight, since her face was streaked with dust. She would be glad when they finally reached the new village site.

Joanna's hair was blowing free, and she lifted the heavy tresses off her neck, hoping she would feel cooler. She was glad she had exchanged her knee-length moccasins for ankle-length ones and was wearing a sleeveless gown. Glancing about her, Joanna noted the women and children who were riding beside her. She knew them all very well—most of them were like family to her. There was She Who Heals, to whom Joanna owed her life and her sight; Gray Fox's two wives, who were both her good friends; and, of course, Windhawk's lovely sister, Morning Song, whom Joanna adored. The young Indian maiden was sweet-tempered and loving. Joanna had rarely heard her raise her voice in anger.

There were many women and children traveling on foot, since some of the poor didn't have horses. The families with horses slowed their progress to match the pace of those who had to walk. The sick and ailing were allowed to ride on a travois horse. The travois were made of wood and rawhide and were pulled by horses, which allowed the Blackfoot to easily transport their belongings from one place to another.

Joanna scanned the distant valley, looking for signs of the other Blackfoot tribes that would be joining the Bloods in their summer camp. Most of the warriors had ridden on ahead, but several had remained with the main body to protect the women and children should they encounter any unforeseen danger. Sun Woman had told Joanna the summer would not only be a season of hard work, but also a time for visiting relatives and friends whom they hadn't seen since the summer before.

Joanna looked forward to the summer camp because she would be reunited with her friend Amanda, who had been captured by the Piegan Blackfoot at the same time as Tag. Windhawk had rescued her along with Tag, but Amanda was now married to Tall Bear, a member of the Blood Blackfoot tribe, and was very happy. Joanna had heard that Amanda was expecting a baby any day, and while she was happy for her, she was also a bit envious.

Joanna shifted her weight, trying to find a comfortable position. Finally, in desperation, she decided to walk beside Fosset for a while to exercise her cramped legs. When she dismounted, Sun Woman followed suit. As they walked along beside the horses, they were soon joined by several of the other women.

"How far is it until we camp for the night, my mother?" Joanna asked.

"I am told that we reach the summer camp just before nightfall."

"I will be glad when we get there. It is hot, and I am weary of riding."

"We are about to have company," Sun Woman said, watching the dust cloud that rose ahead of them. The intruders were still too far away from them to be able to tell whether they were friend or foe.

Joanna noticed that the warriors who rode with them had become alert. Gray Fox, who rode beside his wives, deftly strung his bow and called out for Joanna and Sun Woman to mount their horses. When Windhawk was away, Gray Fox, as war chief, was in charge. As Joanna mounted Fosset, she became aware that all the warriors were now armed and had formed a protective barrier around the women and children.

Tense moments passed as everyone waited to see who the riders were.

Joanna looked at her mother-in-law apprehensively and watched as Sun Woman's worried frown relaxed into a smile. "There is no cause for alarm—it is Windhawk and several of his warriors."

Joanna could now clearly see Windhawk's giant horse, Puh Pom, bearing down on them, and her heart lightened. She hadn't seen him in three days, and she was glad that he would be rejoining her.

When Windhawk drew even with them, instead of coming straight to Joanna, he rode up to Gray Fox. Joanna watched as the two men talked for a moment before Windhawk's gaze rested on her. His face was solemn as he moved to her side.

At first, he said nothing, only scanned her face. Her heart seemed to swell inside her when his dark eyes sent her a silent message of love. How magnificent he looked! Because of the heat, he wore nothing but a breechcloth. The muscles in his body were taut and firm. His hair glistened blue-black in the sunlight.

"I have missed you," she told him.

She noticed his eyes softened before he turned away to speak to Sun Woman. Joanna couldn't hear what he said to his mother, but whatever it was, Sun Woman nodded her head in agreement. Without a word to Joanna, Windhawk reached over and lifted her from her horse and placed her in front of him on his giant horse.

"What are you doing?" she asked, as several of the

women giggled at their chief's daring display, while the men cheered loudly.

Puh Pom reared up on his hind legs, protesting at the extra weight, but Windhawk easily controlled the steed with his powerful leg muscles.

"I am taking you somewhere special so we can be alone," he whispered in her ear. It had been over two weeks since Windhawk and Joanna had been alone together, and she could hear the impatience in his voice.

Joanna leaned her head back against Windhawk's chest and closed her eyes. The powerful horse raced across the prairie and the ground thundered beneath his flying hooves. Soon, the others were left far behind, to be lost from sight.

Joanna looked up into Windhawk's face and saw he was watching her through veiled lashes. "Everyone will know what you have on your mind, Windhawk. Could you not have chosen a less dramatic way of carrying me off?" she asked, feeling embarrassed that the whole tribe had witnessed their chief's antics.

Windhawk smiled at the reproach he heard in her voice. "The women all know what I have in mind for you. They probably wish their husbands would carry them away as I have my wife. As for my warriors, they will think I am a very fortunate man."

Joanna's mouth eased into a smile. "I would like to see Gray Fox perform that deed with his two wives."

Windhawk's lips brushed her forehead. "Let Gray Fox worry about his wives, while I take care of mine." He shifted Joanna's weight so she was sitting across his lap.

"Where are you taking me?" she asked.

"That is a surprise, inquisitive one." His hand drifted down to rest against Joanna's thigh and she felt a deep

37

longing to be with him. His head dipped down and tasted the sweetness of her lips, but Joanna turned her head away and laughed aloud, teasing him. "What you have in mind cannot be performed while riding a horse, Windhawk."

He raised a dark eyebrow inquiringly. "So, woman, you issue me a challenge? I find it hard not to prove to you that the deed could easily be accomplished if we both put our minds to it."

Joanna laughed so hard she felt tears in her eyes. "I think that would be even beyond our skills," she replied between peals of laughter. "Still," she said, smiling mischievously, "the idea does have its merits."

Windhawk's eyes sparkled with amusement. Without ever breaking his mount's stride, he turned Joanna around so she was straddling the horse.

"What are you doing?" she asked, struggling against the firm hand that gripped her waist, pulling her tightly against him.

"I believe I am going to prove to you that I can have you anytime and anywhere I choose," he said, laughing against her ear. He loved the way Joanna's cheeks turned a delicate pink tinge.

He easily raised her doeskin gown and pushed her undergarments aside.

"Windhawk! NO!" Joanna renewed her struggling until he gripped her around the waist and lifted her up, then set her down on his pulsating manhood.

Joanna was unable to do any more than draw a shuddering breath as he penetrated deeply inside her. She threw her head back when his lips settled on her arched neck.

"Shall I stop, Joanna?" he whispered.

"No," her voice was almost a whisper as he plunged deeper into her female core. Windhawk groaned as he lifted Joanna up and pushed her against him in a slow, mind-destroying movement. The movements of the horse were smooth and even, and Windhawk matched his movements to Puh Pom's.

His strong hands gripped Joanna about the waist, and she groaned as he took her to a new plane of delight. With each forward plunge he made into her body, she caught her breath. She wasn't aware of anything but the burning urgency that Windhawk had awakened in her.

For Joanna, this was a new, exciting adventure into the pleasures of the body. Her head fell back against the hard wall of Windhawk's chest, and he sprinkled kisses over her upturned face.

"Jo-anna," he whispered, slipping back into the way he had spoken her name when they first met. Joanna had often noticed that when he was moved by their lovemaking he would call her Jo-anna.

She could feel the excitement building with the tempo of Puh Pom's pounding hooves. Her body quaked uncontrollably. Windhawk's body shuddered, and he clasped Joanna tightly to him until the tremors in both of them subsided. Her head fell forward as she tried to catch her breath. She felt his lips move to her ear.

"You make me feel so alive, Joanna. When I am not with you, I feel this emptiness inside. When I am with you, I want to keep you beneath me."

She smiled and threw her head back, causing her red-gold hair to fan out across his shoulder. Windhawk caught his breath at the sparkle in her eyes. She reached up her hand and touched his cheek.

"I love you so much, Windhawk. I sometimes wish

that we could be alone, with no responsibilities to anyone but ourselves. Do you think that sounds selfish?"

Windhawk noticed that Puh Pom had halted, and he dismounted with Joanna in his arms. He pushed a curl out of her face and looked deeply into her eyes.

"It is not selfish, Joanna, but I have a great many who depend on me for guidance."

She sighed and rested her head against his chest. "Yes, Windhawk, I know what you say is true, but it would be nice if we could spend more time alone."

Windhawk laughed deeply. "Why do you think I carried you away with me today? Did I not tell you I was taking you somewhere special? There is something I want to show you."

"What?"

"You will have to wait and see," he said, placing her back on his horse and climbing on behind her.

As they rode along, Joanna was lulled by a feeling of contentment. She wished that she and Windhawk could ride on like this for eternity—wrapped in the soft warmth of their love. Her head began to nod, and she felt herself getting drowsy. Leaning her head back against Windhawk's shoulder, she fell into a contented sleep.

It was late afternoon when Windhawk shook Joanna to awaken her. She opened her eyes, surprised to find that they were in the mountains.

Windhawk helped her down from his horse before dismounting. She still felt sleep-drugged as she watched him tie the leather rope about Puh Pom's forelegs to hobble him.

"Are we there?" she asked, gazing around the dense pine forest. She couldn't see what was so special about this place. It wasn't unlike the forest where the Blackfoot usually made their winter camp.

"It is very near," he replied, taking her arm and leading her forward. There was no path to guide them, and sometimes Windhawk would have to hack his way through the dense undergrowth of bushes with his knife.

They hadn't gone very far when Joanna heard a roaring sound in the distance. Looking up at Windhawk inquiringly, she smiled brightly, knowing the sound she heard could only have come from a waterfall. She hastened her footsteps, running in the direction of the rushing water. Darting around trees and between thick bushes, she could feel her excitement mounting. Windhawk smiled to himself as he watched her face glow when she reached the waterfall.

Joanna stood for a long moment, silently allowing her eyes to drink in the wondrous sight. As she stood beside the shimmering water, which cascaded down from a high cliff, she felt as though the waterfall must have been there since the beginning of time. Her eyes were bright and shining as she watched the foamy water roll and splash into the river below, before calmly kissing against the shore. Joanna had the feeling she was one of the privileged few who had ever witnessed this magnificent spectacle.

Windhawk laughed when he saw Joanna strip her clothing off and plunge into the river. He watched as she swam toward the falls and climbed onto a rock, allowing the water to wash over her.

The water was cool and invigorating, and Joanna laughed with delight as it seemed to wash away the weariness from her aching muscles. She sighed with pleasure when she felt Windhawk next to her, then she melted against him when he pulled her into his arms.

I have it all, she thought, as Windhawk breathed words of eternal love in her ear.

As their hungry lips met, their bodies fused together like two magnets. Joanna sighed as his magnificent hands moved over her hips, pressing her against him. Her eyes glazed with desire and anticipation when he pushed her backwards behind the cascading water, his hand cushioning her tender skin from the rough cliff wall.

Joanna gasped as his throbbing manhood entered her body. Throwing her head back, she felt his lips caress her long, slender neck. Her hands laced into his ebony hair as he filled her body.

Windhawk groaned, thinking each time he took Joanna it was like the first time. When he was making love to her, he always felt there was no mountain he couldn't climb . . . no feat he couldn't accomplish. She was his life as surely as was the heart that beat within his chest.

Delightful feelings ran like wildfire through Joanna's veins. She tossed her head from side to side as their passion reached its zenith. Windhawk lifted her up, and she locked her arms about his neck while her whole body trembled.

Joanna slid her arms down to his shoulders as he carried her out of the water and laid her on the sweet-smelling grass. When he lay down beside her, he pulled her into his arms.

"When you are in my arms, Joanna, I know what it is to be happy," he said in a passionate voice. "I am a man who has sought and found his destiny."

Joanna closed her eyes, loving him with all her heart. Windhawk and she might come from different worlds, but they had overcome their differences. No matter where the future led her, she knew she would always feel safe and secure as long as he stood beside her.

Gazing up into his dark, handsome face, she gave him a bright smile. "Is there nothing more you want that you do not have, my husband?"

His dark, velvet-soft eyes rested on her lips. "There is nothing I want that I do not have . . . except . . . perhaps, a child."

Joanna touched his face softly, and he turned his head to kiss her hand. "I want that, too, Windhawk."

His hair was wet from the river, and Joanna laced her hands through it, thinking how she loved its dark-midnight color. He gave her a look that melted her heart as he laid his face against her smooth, flat stomach. Moments of silence passed as his hands caressed her body. At last, he raised his head and placed his cheek against hers.

"Soon, Joanna, we will have a child that will be born from our love—then you will never want to leave me."

Joanna closed her eyes. Why did he still have this fear that she would leave him? Hadn't she proven to him by now that she loved him?

"I do not need a child to bind me to you, my dearest love. I think I knew when we first met that we had a destiny to fulfill together."

Joy lit his ebony eyes once more, and it seemed as if a flame burned inside them. "When we have a son, I will teach him to walk in the ways of the Blackfoot, but you will also teach him about the white world. One day, he will be chief, and I want him to be armed with knowledge of both his mother's and father's world."

"What if your son turns out to be your daughter?" Joanna asked, giving him a mischievous grin.

His eyes softened. "I would wish her to have hair and eyes the color of yours. Then I would have two flaming-haired princesses."

Soon they both lay in a soft embrace, while each of them thought of the future when a child would bless their life. Joanna hoped their first child would be a boy. She thought of how patient Windhawk was with her brother. He would be a good father, teaching their child to face life as he did—with courage and hope for the future.

Joanna felt his hands slide lingeringly over her stomach. Closing her eyes, she said a silent prayer that she would soon bear him a child.

As the wildflowers lent their sweet fragrance to the air and the tall pine tree bowed its branches with the breeze, Windhawk made love to Joanna once more. This time she could feel the urgency in him. It was as if he was determined to impregnate her body with his child.

"Who knows, my love?" she whispered. "Perhaps, soon, I will give you the child you want so badly."

Joanna watched him as he lay back and closed his eyes. She noticed the tiredness etched on his face. He had so many responsibilities that he never seemed to be at peace. She pulled him forward and rested his dark head against her silken breasts.

"Sleep, my dearest one," she whispered.

Chapter Four

Captain Harland Thatcher stared disbelievingly at the tall, heavy-set man who claimed to be Joanna and Taggart James's uncle. The man's mode of dress, while expensive, was appalling. The bright green waistcoat and loud yellow vest did not represent good taste. Harland was having a hard time associating Howard Landon with Joanna. It wasn't that the man didn't speak excellent English, it was more the fact that there was a certain coarseness about him. There was also something in his manner that Harland didn't like, but he didn't yet know what it was.

Harland sat back in his chair, crossed his legs, and rested his hand on his booted foot. He thought back to the first time he had seen Joanna. She and her brother had been accompanied by two servants when they had joined the wagon train he had been in charge of. At that time, he had had the distinct impression that Joanna had been running away from something, though he had never learned what it was.

Almost from the beginning, Harland had been drawn to Joanna. At one time he had even asked her to be his wife, but she had turned him down. The fact that she had chosen the legendary Blackfoot chief, Windhawk, over him, had done nothing to stem the love he still felt for her.

"I'm afraid I can't do much to help you find your niece and nephew, Mr. Landon. Joanna chose to go to this Windhawk of her own free will. The army had no jurisdiction over her or her brother."

Howard frowned at the captain's manner. "I think what you mean is you *won't* help me. Isn't that right?"

Harland shrugged his shoulders. "I have no power over what you think—believe what you will," he replied with a certain amount of arrogance.

"Both Taggart and Joanna are under age. I, as their legal guardian, feel it my duty to find them and take them back with me to Philadelphia, where they rightfully belong."

"When I first met Joanna and her brother, I got the distinct impression they were running away from something or someone they were afraid of. Joanna never told me what her trouble was, but I now believe what they were frightened of was you, Mr. Landon," Harland said, eyeing the man closely.

Howard snorted. "What they were running away from was the voice of authority. Neither one of them wanted to follow my direction. They were too headstrong and obstinate to know that I was acting in their best interests. Can you not see into their characters by now? You tell me what sane young lady of breeding would go off to some dirty Indian camp to live like a savage?" Howard's eyes narrowed to slits. "I will find them, and when I do . . . I will take them home, with or without your help, Captain Thatcher!"

46

"I am surprised you would take the trouble, Mr. Landon. Apparently Joanna and her brother didn't want to stay with you, or they wouldn't have run away in the first place. It *was* you they were running away from, am I right?"

Howard's face reddened. "Yes, and for that they will both pay! I have been a patient man in the past—but I will no longer tolerate rebellion from either of them." Howard's dramatic skills came to his aid now. "They were my wife's niece and nephew, God rest her soul. She has been dead these last six months. I owe it to her memory to find Joanna and Tag. Besides, I care deeply about my niece and nephew. If they had been left in your care, Captain, would you abandon them?"

"No," Harland agreed, "I can see what you are saying, but I think I should tell you that Joanna considers herself the wife of Windhawk, the chief of the Blood Blackfoot. She will never agree to leave him."

"So I've been told. Good Lord, how can Joanna turn her back on her own kind to live with some dirty Indian?" Howard asked, unable to believe that Joanna had gone willingly to live with the Indians. "Who is this Indian, this Windhawk, everyone speaks of?"

"To many people he is more fiction than fact. The stories that are told about him are not to be believed. It is said he is a great chief and that none of his enemies will dare attack the Bloods as long as he is their leader. He is respected and almost worshipped by the Blackfoot tribe. I saw him only once, and that was just for the space of a short time. I can tell you, in all honesty, I would not want to be the one to cross him or come up against him in a fight."

Howard looked speculative for a moment. "You say

47

Joanna is this damned Indian's . . . wife?"

"Yes, without a doubt. At least, she considers herself his wife, which amounts to the same thing."

Howard turned white around the mouth. He had coveted the fair Joanna since the first day he had walked into her home in Philadelphia. She had a way of getting into a man's blood and making him forget everything but possessing her. He knew, though, that he would have to concentrate on finding Taggart, since the boy was the whole key to the James fortune. If Tag had died, Howard would have lost everything.

But Howard knew the real reason he had come to this God-forsaken country had been to get Joanna back. He hadn't been able to get her out of his mind. His wife, Margaret, had known about his feelings for her niece. Poor Margaret had met with a most unfortunate accident. She had fallen down a flight of stairs, killing herself instantly. Howard frowned to himself. Before Margaret had expired, he had tricked her into signing papers, giving him power over all her affairs. He had thought he would inherit the James shipping empire through her. He couldn't have been more wrong. The James's lawyer, on learning that Russell James had died, read his will. Howard could still taste his disappointment like a bitter pill in his mouth. The will stipulated that the moneys and estate would be held in trust for Taggart until he reached his twenty-first birthday. While Howard was still allowed to remain in the house in Philadelphia, he received only as much money as it took to pay the servants and run the household. He was also allowed a generous clothes and food allowance, but it could hardly be termed a fortune. So Howard knew he had to get his hands on the boy, since he was still classified as Taggart's legal guardian.

He remembered poor Margaret, and a sinister smile moved over his face. The doctor had said her heart couldn't stand the strain of her fall. What the doctor hadn't known was that Howard himself had given her the shove that sent her tumbling down the stairs. Howard had grown weary of Margaret's constant complaining. She had been aware of his feelings for Joanna and had constantly badgered him with her jealousy.

In the back of Howard's mind, the thought nagged at him that if he didn't get Taggart back, one day, when the boy reached manhood, he would make trouble for him. He *had* to find Tag and take him back to Philadelphia, so he could be in full control again. According to the attorney, he had to bring back proof that Tag was still alive.

But still he knew that the real reason he had traveled so far from civilization was to find Joanna. She had become an obsession with him. Her face had haunted him for two years now. He felt confident that he would have her sooner or later—she wouldn't get away from him this time!

Howard realized his mind had been drifting and that Captain Thatcher was staring at him. "Can you recommend someone to me who might be willing to travel to this Blackfoot village, Captain?" he asked.

The captain raised his eyebrow. "You are either a very brave man or a very foolish one, Mr. Landon. If you think you can just go riding into Windhawk's village, you are badly misinformed. He would kill you first and ask questions later."

"I have no thought of going to this village myself." Howard patted his pocket. "When one has money, one

49

hires others to take risks for them. I am prepared to pay a substantial reward for the return of my niece and nephew. You can pass the word on to anyone you think might be interested."

Harland watched Howard Landon for a moment. His dislike for the pompous, arrogant man grew. There wasn't anything in particular that Harland could pin his dislike on, but Mr. Landon struck him as an interloper and a fraud. He doubted that the man would find anyone who would go against Windhawk to get his niece and nephew back. Although Harland had been ordered by Colonel Jackson, the commander of Fort Leavenworth, to lend his help to Joanna's uncle, Howard Landon had already received all the help he would get from him. There had to be a good reason why Joanna had run away from the man in the first place. Harland had no intentions of helping Mr. Landon get her and her brother back.

Thinking he might throw Mr. Landon off the trail, he decided to give him what he considered a piece of useless advice. In doing so, however, Harland Thatcher had no way of knowing that his good intentions were unwittingly placing Joanna in very grave danger.

"I believe if you are determined to find your niece and nephew, you would be well-advised to go to the fort that belongs to The American Fur Company. It's located much closer to Blackfoot territory than we are here."

"What's the name of this fort?" Howard asked, sensing the captain's dislike for him.

"Fort Union. You shouldn't have any trouble finding someone who will guide you there with your loose purse strings," Captain Thatcher said sarcastically.

Howard's eyes gleamed with a secretive light as he

faced the young captain. "You might want to reconsider going after my charges yourself, Captain. As I told you, I'm offering a substantial reward for their safe return."

Harland frowned. "I have no need for your money, sir, but you might just possibly find some poor, misguided fool who will risk his life for your offer, Mr. Landon. I'll give you a piece of good advice, although, I doubt that you will follow it . . . Windhawk will never allow anyone to get close enough to Joanna and Taggart to take them away!"

Harland's eyes flashed for just a moment. It had nagged at him for months that Joanna had turned down his marriage proposal to return to Windhawk. He was from a very prominent family in Philadelphia, and he would have been willing to lay the world at her feet had she consented to become his wife. He remembered her smile, which could tear a man's heart out. Visions of her red-gold hair had disturbed his dreams many times. And the thought of her sweetly curved body set him on fire even now.

"If you are a betting man, Captain, I will wager that before the summer is out, I shall have both Joanna and Tag."

"You are a fool, Mr. Landon! Even if you do convince some poor simpleton to do your dirty work for you, he won't live past the first week in Blackfoot country. A man would have to be a complete imbecile to go against Windhawk. My God, man, this isn't Philadelphia! Windhawk will see you dead if you don't give up this foolhardy notion!"

Howard gazed out the fort gate to the vast prairie lands beyond the fort. "Joanna is somewhere out there, Captain. I know about some men's greed for gold. I will have little trouble finding such a man. Besides, I don't believe there is some damned Indian chief who strikes terror in everyone's heart."

"Oh, Windhawk's real all right, but you'll find that out for yourself. Lord help you if you do succeed in getting Tag and Joanna away from him. There won't be anywhere on God's green earth you can hide to escape Windhawk's wrath . . . I can promise you that."

Howard laughed contemptuously. "I can see the army has become frightened of a myth. After all that's said and done, Windhawk is still just a man."

"You are deluding yourself if you believe that. You haven't the slightest notion whom you are dealing with. Ask any of the trappers or buffalo hunters about Windhawk when you get to Fort Union. They will be able to tell you stories that will keep you awake at night, Mr. Landon."

Howard shook his head. "If you will excuse me, I think I'll set about finding a guide to escort me to Fort Union. It's for damn sure I'll get no help from the army. I find very little comfort in knowing that men like you, Captain Thatcher, are all that stands between the rest of us and the Indians!"

Harland glared at Joanna's uncle. "You'll need more than just comfort from the army if you ever come up against Windhawk, Mr. Landon."

Windhawk's Blood Blackfoot had made their camp along the Milk River among the Sweetgrass Hills. The summer breezes that blew down from the nearby mountains and across the land brought with them the pleasant odor of blooming wildflowers mixed with the fresh, clean aroma of the pine forest.

The Blackfoot village was thriving with activity. The buffalo were plentiful this year, and there was meat to go around for everyone. Joanna worked tirelessly beside Windhawk's mother and sister. The meat had to be butchered and cured and the skins prepared for later use.

Each night, Joanna would fall asleep almost as soon as she lay down. She was finding the Indian woman's way of life a hard one, but she felt good knowing she was making a home for Windhawk. How far she had come from the girl she had once been!

Joanna could often see pride in Windhawk's mother's eyes as she worked alongside her, and she knew she was truly accepted as Windhawk's wife and Sun Woman's daughter. The Blackfoot were an outgoing and loving people, and they didn't hesitate to show their feelings. Joanna found no difference in the way Sun Woman treated her and the way she treated her own daughter, Morning Song.

Tag was having the time of his life. Windhawk had taken it upon himself to see that Tag learned as much as he could about the Blackfoot ways. He would often take Tag on buffalo hunts and trained him with the bow and lance. Joanna could see Tag growing more confident in his ability under Windhawk's strong guiding hand.

It was early evening as Joanna and Windhawk walked beside the river. The night was dark, with no moon to lend its light to the deep shadows. Thousands of stars seemed to twinkle in the ebony skies.

Windhawk took Joanna's hand and turned her to face him. "You are quiet tonight, Joanna," he said, drawing her into his arms.

She sighed contentedly, laying her head on his shoulder. "I was just thinking how peaceful it is here. I cannot explain to you how I feel. I was thinking today how much I love the people of your tribe."

His chin rested on the top of her head and he smiled. "What about me? Do you also love me?"

She raised her head and touched her lips to his cheek. "You I love more than I can say."

He laughed deeply and hugged her to him. "Sometimes, I wonder why the spirits chose me to be the lover of the Flaming Hair. I have everything I could want when I hold you in my arms, Joanna."

She threw back her head and laughed up at him. "The spirits did not choose you . . . I did! After the first day we met, I was the one who wanted you. I did not know it at the time, but now I do."

"Did I not stand a chance of getting away, then?" Windhawk asked in a light and teasing voice.

Her hand moved up to touch his dark hair. "No, you never stood a chance. Had you but known it then, there was no way for you to get away from me."

Joanna felt his hands span her waist and he lifted her up over his head and then let her slide down the length of his body. "No," he whispered, touching his lips lightly to hers, "I never stood a chance."

Joanna saw that there were now others who walked by the river and she moved away from Windhawk and sat down on the grass. "How is Tag doing, Windhawk? He seems so happy . . . is he being well accepted by the other young boys? It matters to him a great deal that they like him."

Windhawk sat down beside her and took her hand in

his. "I am very proud of your brother, Joanna. When we have a son, I hope he will be like Tag. The others think of him as a Blackfoot. He is daring and brave and is never afraid to test his courage."

"I am glad. Sometimes, I worry about him, but he is happy and that is the most important thing, do you not think?"

"Yes, this is important," he agreed. "I have been wanting to talk to you about Tag, and I think now is a good time." He paused, wondering how to tell her what Tag wanted to do.

"I am listening."

". . . Joanna, four of my warriors are going up into the Canada. It will be a mission where they take several young boys to teach them many things about survival. It is considered a great honor for a young boy to be selected to go . . . Tag has been selected."

Joanna was quiet for a moment. When she spoke, Windhawk could hear the concern in her voice. "What would Tag do and how long would he be gone?" she asked at last.

"He would be gone for several months, and he would learn how to live under the most primitive conditions. I would ask that you think carefully before you decide, Joanna. Tag would be exposed to many dangers, but he would be taught how to meet those dangers. I think it would be good for him to go . . . and he has asked that I talk to you about it. I told him if you said no, he must accept your decision as final, and he has agreed to this."

"Did you go on such a venture when you were a boy?" Joanna wanted to know, wishing she could just say no and get it over with. It was hard for her not to be overprotective where her brother was concerned. She knew that Tag would benefit by such an experience, but still her heart felt heavy.

"Yes, I was younger than Tag when I went on the journey of learning."

"What do you think I should say?"

"I cannot tell you what is best for your brother. This you will have to decide for yourself."

Again, Joanna lapsed into silence. She knew in her heart that she would have to allow Tag to go. Raising her face to Windhawk, she sighed. "You can tell Tag that I have given my consent. He can go on the journey."

Windhawk took her hand and placed it against his cheek. "I somehow knew you would make the right choice. This will be a valuable lesson for your brother. It will get him through many hard times in his life."

"I do not know what Tag would have done had it not been for you, Windhawk. When he needed the guidance of a man, you were always there for him. I am very grateful to you for caring about him."

"It is easy to love the boy; he is very like his sister," Windhawk said, pulling her into his arms.

Joanna's head was resting against Windhawk's chest, and she could hear the drumming of his heart. She thought how greatly this man had touched her life as well as Tag's. Joanna loved him with all her heart. Surely he was a man like no other. She hoped she would always be worthy of him.

"Joanna, I must also tell you that I will be going away for a while," he said softly.

"How long will you be gone?" she asked, feeling a deep sadness that he was leaving.

"I do not know how long I will be away. The buffalo are

moving in a westerly direction, and I must follow them."

Joanna shivered in spite of the hot night, feeling a deep foreboding in her heart. She wanted to beg him not to go, but she knew, as the wife of the chief, she was expected to act the part.

"I will miss you," she said, closing her eyes to keep the tears from seeping through.

"Come," Windhawk said, standing up and pulling her to her feet. "I leave in the morning. I want to be with you before I go."

Joanna's heart was heavy as she realized both Windhawk and Tag would be going away. She managed to smile in spite of her grief as Windhawk led her into their lodge.

That night, as Windhawk lay sleeping beside Joanna, troubled thoughts continued to plague her. She couldn't tell Windhawk that she didn't want him to go away. He would only laugh at her fears. What did she sense? Was it only that she didn't want him to leave her . . . or was it a premonition of disaster . . . a warning of some kind?

Joanna curled up beside Windhawk, and in his sleep he pulled her tightly against him. She tried to push her troubled thoughts aside, but she couldn't. Reaching for Windhawk's hand, she clasped it tightly against her. How would she live if anything should happen to him? She tried to tell herself that she was just being foolish, but it didn't seem to help.

The next morning when she saw Windhawk on his way, she tried to smile, so he wouldn't suspect she was troubled. The feeling of unrest only deepened when Tag left that afternoon. She sighed, thinking a woman's lot in life was to wait and worry about the men she loved.

The uneasy feeling stayed with Joanna for days, until she finally pushed it to the back of her mind.

Joanna went about her daily tasks with a heavy heart. She hadn't seen Windhawk for over a month and she missed him terribly. She was also lonesome for Tag. Had it not been for the fact that she had her friends to talk with, she would have been miserable.

It was apparent that Amanda was happy with Tall Bear, and it gladdened Joanna's heart to see her friend so contented. She remembered all too well when Amanda had been captured by the Piegans and forced to live with their chief, Running Elk, until Windhawk had rescued her.

And she could share Amanda and Tall Bear's joy that they were expecting a baby, because Joanna now knew she was going to have Windhawk's child. She waited each day for him to come home so she could tell him the happy news. She hugged her precious secret to herself, telling no one, since she wanted Windhawk to be the first to know. If her calculations were correct, the child would be born in midwinter.

Joanna was helping Sun Woman hang strips of buffalo meat on a drying rack, while Windhawk's sister, Morning Song, worked nearby, grinding berries to add to the meat for seasoning. Joanna felt a closeness to Sun Woman that she had never felt for her own mother, and she adored Windhawk's lovely, soft-eyed sister. They were her family now.

Sun Woman looked at Joanna with concern. "You must rest, my daughter. You have labored very hard today. Did you not scrape the hair from the buffalo hide, as well as help me butcher and dry the meat? I would not want anything happening to you while my son is away."

"I will rest when you do, my mother," Joanna said with determination. Joanna was one of the few who ever dared disagree with the stubborn Sun Woman.

"Yes, but you are not like the Indian maiden who has been trained to labor hard," Sun Woman argued.

There was a time when Joanna would have been hurt by a statement like that from Windhawk's mother, but that was before the older woman had accepted her. She now knew that Sun Woman loved her and was merely concerned for her health.

"I would have you treat me as any Blackfoot woman, my mother. I am stronger than you believe."

"I know this." Sun Woman's words were stern, but Joanna saw the smile that played about her mouth.

Morning Song took Joanna's hand. "You know when our mother has something on her mind, we can do no more than obey her. It will be best if you rest for a while."

"No," Joanna stated firmly. "I will not rest until the work is finished."

Sun Woman looked as if she might say more, but instead, she clamped her lips tightly together. After a long silence, she turned back to Joanna. "It has been a long day and most of the work is completed. We will all stop now."

Joanna nodded in agreement. She and Morning Song exchanged glances, knowing it had not been easy for Windhawk's mother to relent.

Joanna and Morning Song gathered up the tools and put them away, while Sun Woman disappeared into her lodge.

"Joanna, you are the only one who can come up

59

against my mother in a clash of wills and win. I have never seen her back down with anyone but you . . . except, of course, Windhawk," Morning Song added as an afterthought.

Joanna knew Morning Song was right. As she sat down on a fallen log and looked about the camp, her heart was warmed by the peace and contentment that surrounded her. There were many campfires lit so the women of the Blood tribe could dry the meat their husbands had provided for them. It was the height of the buffalo season, a time for hard work and very little play. The meat must be cured and dried for the long winter months when game would be scarce.

Joanna's eyes traveled to Gray Fox's tipi, where his two wives worked in silent companionship. Gray Fox's son toddled around happily, riding an imaginary horse. She remembered the time she had saved him from a charging wild boar. Her mind reached backwards to the time when the women of the Blackfoot tribe had been hostile toward her. It wasn't until after she had saved Gray Fox's child that the women had accepted her as Windhawk's wife. Before that time, her only friend had been Windhawk's sister, Morning Song.

Joanna's eyes traveled to her sister-in-law. Morning Song was now fifteen summers and of an age when all the young braves were looking at her with interest. So far, Morning Song hadn't shown a preference for any one of them. Joanna wondered why Morning Song never paid any attention to the young braves, as the other maidens did. As the sister of the chief, only the young men from the more prominent families were eligible to pay her court. Joanna knew her bride's price would be high, and no young warrior from one of the poor families would be able to meet it.

Morning Song felt Joanna's eyes on her and smiled sweetly, transforming her lovely face with a warm glow. She was soft-spoken and always had a smile for everyone. Her midnight-colored hair was unbraided and hung down to her waist. Joanna loved the young girl, and she hoped that when Morning Song came of age and it was time for her to wed, she would have a husband who would be kind to her.

Joanna was distracted by a rider coming into the village. She recognized Farley, the grizzly old trapper who had become so very dear to her. She watched him dismount and amble toward her. His shaggy white beard and hair gave him an awesome look. His buckskin trousers and shirt were none too clean, but then that was Farley. At one time, he had tried to help Joanna escape Windhawk. The attempt had ended in disaster, but she had become very close to the old man, and he laughingly told anyone who would listen to him that he was like Tag and Joanna's grandfather. She loved that old man and was glad that Windhawk allowed him to live in the Blackfoot village.

Farley stood over Joanna and studied her closely, then spoke to her in his colorful brand of English. "I seed yore taking it easy, Joanna," he said, sitting down on the log beside her.

She smiled up at him. "I'm just resting for a moment. Are you going to Fort Union today?" she asked, laying her hand on his arm.

He grinned a toothy grin. "Course I am. You got many supplies you want me to fetch back to you?"

"Indeed I do, Farley," she laughed. "You will have to take an extra pack horse just to transport them. How

61

long do you think you will be away?"

"Ifen you don't keep me here jawing, I 'spect I'll be back 'fore too many weeks pass."

"Come back soon, Farley. With Windhawk and Tag gone, I get so lonesome."

The old man looked at Joanna speculatively—he saw the dark circles under her eyes and knew she hadn't been sleeping.

"What's got you in a fret, Joanna?"

"Nothing," she answered wistfully.

"I 'spect your nothing is something. Wanna talk?"

"There is not much to say, Farley. I guess I just miss Windhawk."

"And?"

"I don't know . . . it's a feeling I have. You would probably just say I was being a woman, but I feel as if something bad were about to happen."

"You're just being a woman," he said, laughing aloud at what he thought was witticism on his part.

Joanna's eyes traveled to the distant mountains and she felt a prickle of fear. "Perhaps, Farley. I pray that it is so!"

Chapter Five

Joanna's Uncle Howard paced back and forth across the room. He was remembering the day he had read the notice in the Philadelphia newspaper listing the names of all the people who had died in an Indian raid on an ill-fated wagon train. When he had seen Joanna's and Tag's names on that list, he had lost no time in heading to Fort Leavenworth to find out all the details.

Howard had feared with Tag's and Joanna's deaths that he would lose everything. Russell James's attorney had informed him that if Tag and Joanna were dead, he would be forced to hand the James inheritance over to some distant cousin in England. What Howard hadn't foreseen was what he discovered when Russell James's will was read—that the bulk of the money would be tied up until Taggart reached his twenty-first birthday— neither had he considered that, should anything happen to Tag, the money would pass to the nearest James male relative. Howard had learned too late that he could only control a small part of the estate as long as Tag was alive and under twenty-one.

So he could do nothing to get his hands on the huge shipping empire that had been left to Tag, since the court had appointed a manager to oversee the business. But there was now proof that Tag was alive, and Howard was confident he would soon be in control again.

Now he was at Fort Union, but so far, he had been unable to convince anyone to go to the Blackfoot village to make inquiries about Joanna and Tag, and he was becoming frustrated.

Howard sat down and stared into the fireplace, feeling its warmth creep into his body. Lately, he had felt a chill in his bones—even on the hottest days, he would still feel the cold. He watched the flames lick hungrily at the dry logs . . . somehow, the flames reminded him of Joanna's glorious curtain of hair.

"Joanna, Joanna, because of you I have killed twice," he said aloud. "It's not the money I want the most . . . it never has been just the money . . . it's you."

He felt no remorse that he had been responsible for the deaths of his wife and her brother. He wasn't the least bit sorry that he had killed Margaret or that he had hired a man to go to the Oregon Country to finish off Joanna's father. Russell James had been recovering from a broken back. The man Howard had sent to Oregon had reported that it had been easy to smother the helpless man with a pillow. No, he wasn't sorry for either deed. Howard Landon was a survivor, and he would always do what he had to to acquire what he wanted.

He knew deep inside that it would all have been for nothing if he couldn't have Joanna. She was so hauntingly beautiful, and as elusive and unobtainable as the wealth Howard had always craved.

His face whitened in anger when he thought of

Joanna's giving herself to some damned Indian. "No matter, Joanna, soon, very soon, I will have you!" he vowed.

Claudia Maxwell stared into the hand-held mirror, trying to see her reflection. She was aware that she was pretty, and she was proud of the bright golden color of her hair. Lately, she had been unable to use her looks to their best advantage. There just weren't any eligible men here at Fort Union, at least, not any she was interested in.

She still remembered the humiliation she had suffered last fall when she had been forced to leave Fort Leavenworth because of a scandal involving herself and a certain married sergeant. Having nowhere to go, she had accepted a small-paying job as companion to one of the trapper's wives at Fort Union. The fort belonged to the American Fur Company and, to Claudia's way of thinking, was not the most exciting place in the world. The only people she ever saw were a bunch of old trappers, a few buffalo hunters, and Indians.

Claudia had learned a valuable lesson at Fort Leavenworth and had decided that not the slightest hint of scandal would ever again touch her name. She hadn't allowed any of the men here at the fort to bed her. She had decided to save herself for just the right man—a man who could take her away from this poor existence. Claudia was determined that the next time she allowed a man to make love to her, he would be the man she was going to marry.

Her eyes gleamed brightly. She had heard that Joanna James's uncle was at Fort Union and was offering a high reward to get Joanna and Tag back. She had been told that

65

he was not only wealthy, but his wife had only recently died, making him very eligible in Claudia's eyes.

At times Claudia's hatred for Joanna was the driving force in her life. She remembered the day she had first met Joanna. Joanna and Tag had joined the wagon train that Claudia and her parents had been traveling with. For Claudia it had been hatred at first sight of the beautiful, flaming-haired Joanna. Perhaps it was the fact that all the men on the train seemed to go out of their way to gain Joanna's attention. Perhaps it was because Joanna seemed to have everything that Claudia had always wanted: money, beautiful clothes, and a soft, ladylike manner. Or maybe it was that being with Joanna had always made her feel so inadequate. Whatever the reason, in her twisted way of thinking Claudia felt that Joanna was responsible for everything that had gone wrong in her life in the past two years. Besides Claudia, there had been only four other survivors of the wagon train massacre—and Claudia hadn't been in the least overjoyed when she learned that Joanna had been one of those survivors.

She frowned in distaste when she looked at her faded yellow print gown. Surely, Joanna's uncle was accustomed to women who were well-dressed, powdered, and perfumed. She shrugged her shoulders; if only she could be cunning enough, she would use her charms to her best advantage. Perhaps she would yet find a way out of this no man's land.

In her mind she could see herself driving down the streets of Philadelphia in a fine carriage, thumbing her nose at the people she had once known.

*   *   *

Howard Landon crossed the room to answer the knock at the door. He was astonished to find a young woman standing outside. Her face, while not beautiful, held a certain appeal. It was the bold sparkle in her eyes that caught and held his attention more than anything else.

"Mr. Landon, you don't know me; my name is Claudia Maxwell. I was a friend of your niece, Joanna."

"What can I do for you, Miss Maxwell?"

"May I come in?"

He looked over her shoulder to see if anyone was about, thinking he didn't want to start any loose tongues wagging by having a female in his room. Seeing no one, he moved aside, allowing her to enter.

Claudia gave Howard her most precocious smile as she held her hands out to him. She had heard that he was offering a great deal of money to get Joanna and Tag away from the Indians, and she thought she might just be the one to collect. He wasn't a bad-looking man, she thought, assessing him critically. He did have a certain amount of dignity, which came from having money, she supposed.

Claudia knew she must hide the fact from Mr. Landon that she detested Joanna James more than anyone she knew if she was going to get her hands on the reward money. Again, she reminded herself that if it hadn't been for Joanna Captain Thatcher might now be her husband.

"You said you knew my niece?" Howard asked, raising her hand to his lips. His eyes gleamed as he watched her eyelashes flutter.

"Yes, I was on the same wagon train with Joanna and Tag," Claudia said, as she felt his lips against her fingers. She reminded herself that she must not act too forward and lowered her eyes coyly.

"If that's so, how did you escape the Indian raid?"

67

Howard asked suspiciously, dropping her hand.

"When the Indians struck, I hid in some bushes until it was all over." Claudia sat down in the chair he offered her, while Howard remained standing. His eyes were drawn to Claudia's low-cut yellow gown, which offered him a fair view of her creamy white breasts.

She smiled at the older man, noticing how his eyes were fastened on her breasts.

"I understand you were only recently widowed. May I offer you my sympathies?"

Howard didn't answer right away. Claudia watched him cautiously, hoping she hadn't overplayed her hand.

"Why are you still here at Fort Union, Miss Maxwell? Surely you should have returned to your home by now."

"My folks were killed in the raid, and I had nowhere else to go. One of the trappers, Ebenezer Hankins, brought his wife West. She was lonesome with so few women around, so they allowed me to stay with them." Claudia dabbed at her eyes with a handkerchief. "It's not easy being without a ma and pa, or anyone who cares about you, Mr. Landon."

"Since the wagon train you were traveling with originated in Philadelphia, should I assume that was your home before the tragedy?"

"Yes, my folks were very wealthy, but they sold everything when we joined the wagon train. I lost all I had in the raid, Mr. Landon."

Howard was a shrewd man. He knew instinctively that the girl was lying. What did she wish to gain by her deception? He would judge her to be the daughter of a poor farmer, or perhaps even a tavernkeeper, or a fisherman. She was definitely not from the gentry. He wondered why she was trying to appear to be what she wasn't. What a poor actress she was, he thought—still, she was a pretty girl, and he could feel the heat in his loins when she licked her lips and smiled at him.

"I know Joanna very well. I think I should warn you it won't be easy to get her away from her Indian lover. I have heard some awesome things about this Windhawk. I hear that he is a very dangerous person to cross."

"Is this what you came here to tell me?" Howard asked. He was becoming weary of everyone's telling him about that red bastard.

"Well, yes, in a way. I thought maybe I could be of help to you, Mr. Landon."

"In what way?"

Claudia leaned over in such a way that her breasts almost spilled over her gown.

Howard's eyes seemed to devour her, and she smiled to herself, thinking he wouldn't be too hard to entrap. After all, she was the only pretty white female within hundreds of miles. She must play her hand very carefully, however, or she might drive Mr. Landon away before she obtained her goal. If she was smart, she would soon have all she wanted—power, money, and perhaps even a respectable name. How ironic it would be, she thought, if she were to obtain all she had ever dreamed of because of Joanna James . . . her worst enemy!

Claudia looked shyly up at Howard, veiling her true feelings. "What would you give me if I were to deliver Joanna and Tag to you?"

Howard smiled slightly. "There is nothing I wouldn't give to get them back." He looked doubtful. "What makes you think you can deliver them to me?"

Claudia stood up—her eyes were gleaming as a plan began to develop in her mind. She remembered overhearing a conversation last winter between Captain Thatcher and Joanna's hired man, Simon. It seemed that Simon was to return to Philadelphia where he would keep in touch with Joanna and Tag by sending his letters to Fort Union.

"Mr. Landon, instead of asking some buffalo hunter or fur trader to bring Joanna and Tag to you, it would be better if you put your faith in me. I know just how to get them to come to you. Never doubt that I can do it!"

Howard's little beady eyes narrowed. "If you can deliver them into my hands, then you can name your own price."

Claudia turned her back to him as her eyes filled with hatred. At last, her day had come. Revenge would be so sweet! She had the ways and means to bring the proud Joanna tumbling off her pedestal by separating her from Windhawk. It would be an added bonus if, at the same time, she could acquire a small fortune for herself.

"Before I help you, I must first know what you plan to do with Joanna and Tag, Mr. Landon."

"I see," he studied her with his actor's eye. This girl was no friend of Joanna's! He could read the hatred she tried so hard to conceal in her eyes. "I intend to take them back home with me. What else would you expect me to do with them, Miss Maxwell?"

Claudia knew Joanna wouldn't want to be separated from her Indian lover. She remembered when Joanna had left Fort Leavenworth to return to that Indian. It was beyond her understanding why Joanna, who had all that money could buy, would want to live with the Indians. The thought of striking a blow against Joanna would give her the greatest satisfaction. Her heart seemed to burn with contempt for Joanna, the enchantress, who had stolen the wealthy, handsome Captain Harland Thatcher away from her.

"I would help you get Joanna back for nothing, Mr. Landon. I only want her to have what's best for her, since she is such a good friend of mine."

"What about Tag?" he asked, reading Claudia's thoughts in her eyes. "Don't you want to see him returned to his rightful home?"

"Oh, Tag, too. He is such a dear boy."

"Let's see if you can deliver, Miss Maxwell," he said, watching the gleam in her eyes. "Give me what I want and I will not be stingy with you." He knew Claudia was playing a game, but if she could help him get Joanna and Taggart back, he didn't care how many games she played.

"Tell me how you will help me accomplish what others tell me is impossible, Miss Maxwell," he said, thinking she couldn't possibly be of any help to him.

"First of all, we will need quill and parchment. I can't write, can you?"

"I can write a fair hand. Why?"

"You do the writing, and I'll tell you what to say," Claudia told him. Her eyes were gleaming brightly as Howard nodded his agreement.

The days seemed to pass slowly while Joanna waited restlessly for Windhawk to return. She missed him, badly. Time lay heavily on her hands and she became discontent, wishing she could tell Windhawk about the child she was carrying. She knew that he would share her joy.

Why didn't he come? Many of the other warriors had made several trips back to the village to visit with their

71

families. She tried not to feel hurt by Windhawk's neglect, but she couldn't help but feel sorry for herself.

Sometimes, late at night when Joanna was alone in the lodge and the village was quiet, the strange premonition would return, and she would try to push it from her mind. She was waiting for something to happen, and she didn't know what it was. Only time would prove if she was worrying for nothing, she told herself.

Windhawk rode into the Piegan Blackfoot village with six of his warriors. The chief had sent word he wanted to see him on a matter concerning the Assiniboin tribe, who were getting bolder in their raids into Blackfoot Territory.

He walked solemnly toward the big lodge in the center of the village and was greeted warmly by the new chief, Yellow Wing, who clasped his arm in Indian fashion.

"Come into my lodge, Windhawk, and we will talk," Yellow Wing said, holding the flap aside for Windhawk to enter.

Inside, Windhawk and Yellow Wing sat down, and the women served them food.

"I was glad to hear that you had become chief, Yellow Wing," Windhawk said, taking a bite of the buffalo meat.

"I do not think anyone misses Running Elk. He was a cruel man, and my people are happy that he is dead."

Windhawk nodded, remembering the day he had come to the Piegan village to rescue Tag from Running Elk. Tag had been badly mistreated, and Windhawk still became angry when he remembered the red welts on the boy's back where Running Elk had beat him.

"I am glad to hear that my brothers have a brave and

noble chief."

After they had eaten, Yellow Wing handed Windhawk a pipe and Windhawk took a draw. "I have heard that you are concerned about the Assiniboin, Yellow Wing," Windhawk said, handing the pipe back to him.

"Yes, they have raided our horses and, two moons ago, killed six of my warriors."

"They are brave to raid so deep into our territory. I think they believe we will not retaliate," Windhawk said, watching as one of the women sat down beside him and stared boldly into his eyes. He looked quickly at Yellow Wing to see if this woman was his wife and if he would take offense at the woman's strange actions.

"This is my daughter, Red Bird," Yellow Wing explained. He, too, wondered why his daughter was acting so strangely.

Windhawk nodded to the woman, then dismissed her from his mind. He turned back to Yellow Wing and the problem of the Assiniboin. "So far, they have not come near my village. I will post extra guards to make sure we are not taken unaware," Windhawk said.

He could feel Red Bird staring at him, and he turned once more to look at her. She gave him a smile and then looked at her father with a pleased expression on her face. Windhawk was irritated because the woman was present while he and Yellow Wing were discussing their common enemy. He knew the women of his Bloods would never be so bold as to place themselves near him when he was having a council meeting.

"I have sent for you to warn you to be wary lest you be taken by surprise," Yellow Wing told Windhawk.

Windhawk stood. "I am indebted to you for this information. If you find yourself in trouble, you have but

73

to call on your brothers, and we will come to your aid."

Yellow Wing stood also and nodded his head. "I think that time will not come. The Piegans can easily handle the Assiniboin. I think the time will come when we shall have to make war on them."

"I will say good-bye to you now," Windhawk said. "I have a long ride back to the buffalo camp."

"Do not go until morning, Windhawk. I would be honored if you would stay the night in my lodge," Yellow Wing offered.

"The sun has already set; perhaps I *will* leave in the morning," Windhawk said, moving to the flap and pushing it aside.

Joanna awoke from a deep sleep and sat up. She saw the fleeting shadows on the wall of the lodge that were caused by the flickering cook-fire, and she shivered. It was as if a cold hand had just closed over her heart. Lying back down, she tried to empty her mind so she could go back to sleep, but she found she was unable to rid herself of the uneasy feeling. She closed her eyes and wished that Windhawk would soon come home.

Windhawk was only half awake when he felt something soft brush against his body. For a moment, in his sleep-drugged state, he thought it was Joanna, and he reached out and pulled her to him. He clasped his hand about her waist, then slid it down to her stomach. Suddenly, he became fully awake. It was a woman all right, but it wasn't Joanna! Joanna's waist was tiny, and her stomach was smooth and flat. This woman was much larger.

"Windhawk," Red Bird whispered in his ear. "Long have I seen you from a distance and wanted to feel your hands on me."

Windhawk tried to push Red Bird away, but she laughed and bent her head to find his lips. He stiffened as her mouth covered his.

Chapter Six

The unbearable summer heat continued to parch the land. Rivers that usually ran full to their banks were now dangerously low and mud-colored. The grasses were dry and spindly, causing the herds of buffalo to move out of the area in search of grazing land. The Blackfoot warriors, as always, followed the trail of the buffalo.

Windhawk had been away from the village for almost two months. Joanna continued to feel restless and irritated because he hadn't come home. She had thought that by now he would, at least, have come back for a visit, but that hadn't been the case. She still watched many of the other warriors come and go as they took time out for brief visits to their families, but her husband hadn't come to her.

At one point, Windhawk had sent word to Joanna that he and his warriors were following the trail of the buffalo. That had been over three weeks ago. Since that time she had heard nothing from him.

At first she had felt extremely lonely without Windhawk. That loneliness had now turned to anger. If the other husbands could visit their wives, why then couldn't Windhawk come to see her?

She wanted to tell him about the child she was carrying, but that wasn't the kind of news a woman sent to her husband by a messenger.

Windhawk had sent his kills back to the village with several of his warriors. By now all the meat had either been cured or made into pemmican, which was dried and stored for the winter months when food was scarce. The hides had been tanned and made into soft robes or stored away for future needs. The lodge was spotlessly clean, and Joanna felt time weighing heavily on her hands.

She had been so proud of the fine shirt Sun Woman had helped her make for Windhawk. Sun Woman had given her some blue beads and Joanna had attached them to the front of the shirt. It had been fun embroidering the beads onto the shirt in the shape of a hawk with a wide wingspread, as if the bird was in flight. As the weeks passed and still Windhawk hadn't come home, Joanna had angrily packed the shirt away.

It was a scorching hot day as Joanna and Windhawk's sister walked toward her lodge. Joanna had been suffering from morning sickness and was trying to cover it up, not wanting anyone to know about the baby she was carrying until she could tell Windhawk.

Morning Song watched Joanna out of the corner of her eyes. She could tell Joanna was upset by the way she bit her lower lip, and she wanted to comfort her.

"I am very angry with your brother, Morning Song. Am I his wife or just a convenience that he notices when the mood strikes him?"

"You are upset becase Gray Fox brought you no word from Windhawk?" Morning Song inquired.

Joanna neared her lodge and angrily threw the flap back, then went inside and sat down on a buffalo robe before she answered. "No, I am angry because Gray Fox could come home to see his family and Windhawk stays away from his. He is treating me as if I don't even exist!"

"Joanna, as chief, Windhawk must make many sacrifices. I know he would rather be here with you, but he must put himself last. He feels he must set an example for his warriors to follow," Morning Song defended her brother.

Joanna faced Morning Song angrily. "I doubt that the village would fall into ruin if Windhawk were to come home for at least a day to visit his own wife. It would serve him right if I weren't here when he did return!"

Morning Song sat down and took Joanna's hand. "I know why you are upset. You have heard about the chief of the Piegans giving Windhawk his daughter and that Gray Fox has brought her to our village. I do not think you should worry about this. Windhawk loves you."

Joanna felt her heart contract. "What are you saying? I have heard nothing about Windhawk and another woman!" Joanna could hear her own voice rising hysterically.

"Did not Gray Fox tell you that the Piegan woman was to stay in his lodge until Windhawk comes home?" Morning Song asked, wondering why Joanna was reacting so strangely. Surely, she couldn't be jealous of that woman.

Joanna stood up on shaky legs. "Is this woman to be Windhawk's wife?"

"I do not think Windhawk will take Red Bird as his

wife, but he could not insult the chief of the Piegans by casting his daughter aside. It would have been a very bad thing, would it not?"

"I am beginning to see things much more clearly now!" Joanna cried, feeling as if she had been betrayed. "Windhawk found no time to come to see me, yet he has been with this other woman!" Joanna fought against the angry tears that came to her eyes. She looked upward as they fell from her eyes and rolled down her cheeks.

Morning Song stood up and tried to take Joanna's hand, but Joanna turned away from her. "My sister, do not be hurt. I am sure Windhawk will explain everything to you when he comes home. Have faith in him. He would never turn away from you for this woman."

"I want to see this woman," Joanna said through clenched teeth. Her eyes were blazing and her anger had almost reached its zenith. "Bring her to me at once!"

Morning Song had never seen Joanna so angry. She rushed from the lodge to do as Joanna had told her. She was puzzled by Joanna's reaction. Though Windhawk had the right to take as many wives as he chose, he had promised Joanna he would take no other wife, and he would not break that promise. Morning Song knew her brother was an honorable man and would never break his word. She knew her brother's love was great for Joanna. Whatever his plans were, he would never take Red Bird into his lodge.

Joanna gripped the lodgepole so tightly that her knuckles whitened. Now she knew why Windhawk hadn't come to her. He was waiting until she grew accustomed to the idea of his taking another wife. She looked about the lodge where she had been so happy as his wife. She knew she would never share her husband with another woman.

Her mouth flew open in horror. Dear God, how could he expect it of her? How did he plan to move this other woman in? Did he expect them to sleep three to a bed, or would she be banished to a corner while he made love to the other woman? She wanted to cry out in anguish. How could Windhawk have betrayed her?

Joanna covered her eyes with shaky hands. She had believed Windhawk when he had told her he would never take another wife. Had he meant it at the time? Was he tired of her already? She thought how foolish and naive she had been, believing that happiness could last forever.

Joanna heard movement outside the lodge and dried her eyes, then straightened her shoulders. She would meet this woman whom Windhawk had used to betray her.

Morning Song entered, leading Red Bird by the hand. She looked at Joanna apprehensively. "Joanna, this is Red Bird."

Joanna assessed the woman carefully. She appeared to be some years older than herself—small in stature, but large-boned. Her long dark hair was braided and interwoven with silver beads. Joanna could see why Windhawk would want this woman for his wife, for she was very lovely, and she was of his own kind.

While Joanna was looking the Indian woman over, she was aware that Red Bird was also assessing her. Joanna read something akin to hatred in the woman's dark eyes and realized, at that moment, that they would be bitter enemies.

"I have heard much about the Flaming Hair. Windhawk has said you are of the white skin," Red Bird spat out, giving Joanna a disapproving glare.

"I have heard nothing about you," Joanna said. "It is said that you came to our village at my husband's command. Is this the truth?"

The woman smiled. "I have come to await Windhawk's return. When he comes, he will make me his wife."

Joanna looked at Morning Song and noticed she was frowning at Red Bird. Could she also sense the animosity the woman directed at her?

"I am told that you are the number one wife, Flaming Hair. I am the daughter of a powerful chief. I think you will soon be second to me!"

Joanna's temper flared at the woman's forwardness. How dare she make such outrageous statements? "I am second to no one, Red Bird. You will never see the day you will know Windhawk as your husband." Joanna's voice sounded calm, but she was anything but calm on the inside.

She felt as if she had just been delivered a mortal blow. Windhawk had betrayed their love, and in doing so he had pushed Joanna into a corner. She would take nothing from this woman. After all, Red Bird wasn't Windhawk's wife yet.

Red Bird smiled. "You are a fool if you believe that. I have already known Windhawk as a man and a lover. I will soon know him as a husband."

Joanna bit her lip to keep back her angry retort. She couldn't bear the thought of Windhawk's making love to this woman. If Red Bird was telling the truth, and Joanna saw no reason for her to lie, she would never again allow Windhawk to touch her.

Morning Song could see the heartbreak written on Joanna's face, and it caused a pain within her own heart. She didn't like this woman who was trying to come between Joanna and her brother. Even if Windhawk had decided to take Red Bird for his wife, she had no right to say such things to Joanna. She thought it was time to take the Piegan woman out of Joanna's sight.

"Come, I will take you back to Gray Fox's lodge," she told Red Bird, wanting to get her away from Joanna before she made any other damaging statements.

"I would prefer to stay here. This is where I will wait for Windhawk to return," came the bold reply.

Joanna raised her head and leveled a heated gaze at Red Bird. "This is not your lodge yet. Go from my sight!"

Red Bird merely smiled and shrugged her shoulders—she walked from the lodge without a backward glance.

Morning Song came up to Joanna, wanting to give her comfort, but Joanna backed away from her. "I want to be alone," she whispered. "Please go."

When Morning Song sadly departed, Joanna sank down to the bearskin rug and buried her face in its softness. Hot tears scalded her eyes, and she began to sob uncontrollably. Her worst fears had been realized. Windhawk was tired of her and had cast her aside for one of his own kind. This was why he hadn't come to her. While she had been suffering over his absence, he had been with another woman! She couldn't bear to think that the hands that had caressed her body had also touched Red Bird's body.

Dear Lord, what was she to do? She was carrying Windhawk's baby! Could she just walk away from him? Would she be able to stay and watch Red Bird replace her as Windhawk's love? No! Never!

Sitting up, she dried her eyes. Joanna wasn't one to sit around feeling sorry for herself. Windhawk had betrayed her while he professed to love her. Even though she was carrying his child, it wouldn't stop her from leaving him. If he was hesitant to face her now, she just wouldn't be here when he did return.

Joanna swallowed a sob. Why had she been so foolish as to think their love would overcome the differences of their two cultures? Windhawk wouldn't think it was wrong to take another wife, while she would never accept such an atrocity.

The tears on Joanna's face had dried and the anger in her heart took control. The least Windhawk could have done would have been to tell her about Red Bird himself so she would have been prepared before facing her rival. How cruel he was to let her find out about the Piegan woman from Morning Song. Everyone in the village must have known about him and Red Bird, except her.

What would she do? She couldn't leave just now, since Tag was away. No, she could never leave her brother behind. She would have to wait until Tag's return, and she didn't have the slightest notion when that would be.

"Dear God!" she cried aloud. "How will I bear this alone?" She stood up on shaky legs. Now she knew why Windhawk had pressed her to send Tag away on the journey. He must have foreseen how angry she would be when she learned the truth about Red Bird. He knew she would never leave without her brother and, as a precaution, he had sent Tag away.

"I hate you, Windhawk!" she cried, ripping the bear-claw necklace from about her neck and throwing it across the lodge. "I will hate you until I die!" she sobbed, sinking down to her knees and laying her face against the soft bearskin rug, to cry out her misery.

It was several hours later when Joanna heard a dear, familiar voice call to her from outside the lodge.

"Joanna, it's me, Farley."

She stood up and walked over to the entrance, hoping she had composed herself so he wouldn't suspect anything was wrong. She knew Farley was shrewd, and it wouldn't be easy to fool him.

"It's about time you got back. I began to think you had deserted me, like everyone else."

Farley gave her an inquiring glance but didn't bother to ask what was troubling her. "I got the pack horse loaded down, you want me to bring the supplies in here?"

Joanna shrugged her shoulders. "Yes, of course, bring them in."

"What's wrong with you?" Farley asked, giving her a searching glance. "You look a bit peaked to me."

"I'm just tired, nothing more."

"I got something that might perk you up a bit," Farley said, reaching into his pouch and withdrawing a letter. "This here letter was waiting for you at Fort Union," he said, handing it to her.

"For me?"

"Yep, MacKenzie give it to me, saying I was to see you got it."

Joanna saw her name written across the letter and was curious about whom it was from. The handwriting was unfamiliar to her.

"Who could it be from, Farley?"

"How could I guess? You knowed I can't read. The best way I knowed for you to find out is to open it."

Joanna nodded at Farley's reasoning. She was still too numb to feel anything at the moment. "Yes, that would seem the best way to find out." She broke the seal and began to read to herself.

Joanna,

It is imperative that I see you at once. I need your help. I will wait for you every night the week of the fifteenth across the river just inside the woods. Please come to me as soon as you can and bring Tag with you. Tell no one about this since it is a life-and-death situation for me.

HARLAND THATCHER

Joanna read the letter over several times before she folded it and tucked it into her belt.

"Who's it from?" Farley asked with interest.

"Just a friend. What's the date of today, Farley?" she asked, knowing that he always kept up with what day and month it was.

"Today would be the sixteenth," he told her, looking more curious than ever.

Joanna frowned, wondering what kind of trouble Harland could be in. She remembered the times he had helped her and Tag. There was no question in her mind but that she would meet him tonight. Of course, she couldn't bring Tag since he was away.

She dared not tell Farley or anyone who the letter was from, since Harland had specifically asked her not to. Knowing how jealous Windhawk was of Harland, Joanna knew he would be angry with her when he found out she had met secretly with him. What did it matter? she wondered bitterly. Windhawk had kept his little secret about Red Bird . . . what right did he have to object to her seeing an old friend?

Claudia smiled up at Howard Landon, thinking how

easily she was manipulating him. She hoped her plan would work tonight. If it did, by tomorrow he would be forced to make her his wife. He had been panting after her for over a month now, and tonight she would let him think he had worn down her defenses. She was now ready to entrap him with her body.

She had asked him to come to the Hankins' quarters, knowing she would have to move fast if her plan was to work. If Mr. and Mrs. Hankins returned either too soon or too late, all would be lost. Everything depended on perfect timing.

Howard sat down on the wooden chair and smiled at Claudia. She was a pretty wench, and he imagined she would be a good toss in bed. If she succeeded in helping him get Joanna and Tag back, perhaps he would take her back to Philadelphia with him and set her up in a modest house. He had always envied the men who could afford to keep a mistress. In the past, he had always been forced to rely on tavern wenches and whores for his pleasure.

He still had a fair amount of doubt, though, as to whether Joanna would follow the instructions in the letter Claudia had helped him to write.

"What if Joanna isn't fooled by our letter, Miss Maxwell? Suppose she and Taggart don't show up at the rendezvous point? What will we do then?"

"Oh, she'll show up, all right. Joanna is such a do-gooder. If she thinks Captain Thatcher is in trouble, you can depend on her to go rushing to his side." Claudia bent over Howard and her low-cut bodice slipped even lower. She saw his eyes move greedily over her breasts before he looked into her face suspiciously.

"You don't sound like you're a friend of my niece's. Do I detect a bit of animosity in your tone?"

Claudia realized the hatred and bitterness she felt toward Joanna had crept into her voice. She cautioned herself to be more careful. "I'm just concerned about Joanna living with the Indians. You know I think she should be back with you where she belongs."

Howard's eyes narrowed, and he got a faraway look in them. "Yes, she belongs with me."

For the first time, Claudia noticed how Howard's eyes gleamed when he spoke of Joanna. Was there more to their relationship than she had thought? There were many questions she would like to ask, but now wasn't the time. If her little scheme was to work, she must now set it in motion.

"You must practice patience, Mr. Landon," she said, lowering herself to kneel beside him. She could see his eyes were passion-bright and felt confident that her plan would work. Running her hand up his leg, she gave him her most seductive smile.

Howard rose to his feet, taking her with him. "When will the Hankinses return?" he asked in a thick voice.

Claudia rubbed her body against him. "Not for hours," she purred.

He pushed her back against the settee and quickly raised her gown and petticoats upward. He fumbled with his trousers and then fell on top of her.

When he entered her body, Claudia felt revulsion, and she shuddered as his hot, moist lips fastened on hers. She would endure what she must to see her dreams fulfilled. There was too much at stake to pull back now. Let Howard Landon use her body . . . he would never touch her heart. She heard him grunt, and his body quaked. It hadn't been too bad, she told herself. Thank goodness, it had been over quickly. Now she had to keep him occupied until just the right moment. If he left too soon, her plan would be lost.

"Damned if you aren't the best I ever had," Howard breathed heavily in her ear.

At that moment the front door opened, and Howard froze. Claudia tried to look helpless as she shoved him away from her and quickly pulled her gown down.

Lucy Hankins blushed at the sight that met her eyes. She backed out the door, shaking her head in disbelief, while her husband glared at Howard and Claudia.

"What in the hell is the meaning of this?" he bellowed in a loud voice.

Claudia moved forward and took Howard's hand. "It's not what you think, Mr. Hankins! Howard and I love each other . . . we are to be married."

Howard looked down at her with a startled expression, and she could feel his hand tighten on her fingers painfully. She realized he was trying to hold on to his temper.

"Miss Maxwell, I think you will find that such behavior will not be tolerated by The American Fur Company. I am appalled that you should choose my home for your . . ." he was at a loss for words. "I will ask you to gather your belongings and leave immediately!"

"But where will I go?" she asked in her most helpless little-girl voice. "I have no one to turn to."

Ebenezer Hankins looked at her in disgust. "I will speak to Mr. MacKenzie, and I'm sure he will insist Mr. Landon make an honest woman of you."

Claudia felt Howard stiffen, and she lowered her head. Gazing slowly up into his face, she saw the murderous light in his little beady eyes. He realized by now that she had tricked him, but it didn't matter. He was trapped and he knew it! Claudia was sure the stern-faced Mr. MacKenzie, who was in charge of The American Fur Company, would insist that Howard marry her at once. There wouldn't be a thing that Howard could do about it, she thought happily.

Claudia felt momentary apprehension when Howard's eyes narrowed in on hers. Had she pushed him too far? She could see by the anger on his face he was not a man to cross. Reminding herself of how wealthy he was, she faced him without flinching. She was surprised that he had thus far uttered no words in his own defense. He just stared at her with those cold, beady eyes, and it was unsettling, to say the least. She called on all her courage as she faced him.

"I would be honored to be Howard's wife," she said coyly. Claudia could hardly conceal her joy. Everything she had ever wanted in life was now at her fingertips.

"I can assure you, Mr. Landon, if you are thinking you won't have to marry Miss Maxwell, you are mistaken. If you don't, you will be asked to leave Fort Union posthaste," Mr. Hankins informed him.

Claudia could see the anger in Howard's eyes and knew what he was thinking. If he was forced to leave the fort now, he would never get Joanna and Tag back.

She could almost see the way his mind was working. "I'll make you a good wife, Howard."

His face reddened, and she thought for a moment he was considering striking her. "We shall see, missy," he said in a quiet voice. "I'm on to your little game."

"Take her and leave," Mr. Hankins said, indicating the open door with a nod of his head.

Howard stalked out the door, looking straight ahead. Claudia ran after him, thinking she should try to convince him she hadn't intended this to happen.

"Howard, wait! I want to talk to you! It isn't what you think, I never . . ."

He stopped and looked down at her. "Save your little performance for someone else. You're a poor actress, at best. My anger is directed most at myself for not recognizing your performance earlier."

"No, Howard! Please listen!"

"Out of my way," he said, shoving her aside.

Claudia could do no more than watch his departure, knowing it would be best to allow him some time to cool down. She smiled, knowing she had won. There was no shame in Claudia—she had always believed that the end justified the means!

Chapter Seven

There was no moon to light Joanna's way as she rode
Fosset from the village. She had decided to cross the river
downstream so no one would see her. Still puzzling over
Harland's strange request, Joanna halted her horse just
before she entered the river. What kind of trouble could
Harland be in that he would ask to meet with her in
secret?

Her anger at Windhawk was still smoldering just
beneath the surface. Joanna was now more impatient
than ever for his return. She couldn't wait to confront
him about Red Bird. First things first, she told herself.
She would see what was troubling Harland—later on,
there would be time enough for her to worry about her
own problems.

Urging Fosset into the river, she raised her doeskin
gown so it wouldn't get wet. The horse easily carried her
to the opposite shore and up the steep bank.

It was so dark she could barely make out the dense tree
line in the distance. She felt a prickle of uneasiness and
wondered if she had been foolish not to tell anyone where

she was going. Wishing now that she had asked Farley to accompany her, Joanna urged Fosset toward the woods where Harland had asked her to meet him.

The two buffalo hunters, Chester Boggs and his brother Jim, had been waiting impatiently two nights for the girl and her brother to show up.

Jim, the youngest brother, was beginning to wonder if they had been sent on a fool's mission. It was dangerous having to hide out in the forest during the day so they wouldn't be discovered by any of the Blackfoot. He hadn't been too fond of the notion of coming into Blackfoot country in the first place.

"Supposing they don't come, Chester? It's damned risky hanging about here. If any Injuns come upon us, we're dead men!"

Chester sat with his back against a tree and his eyes glued to the river where the boy and girl would cross if they were coming. His brother stood near the horses, making sure they didn't make any noise.

Chester felt something biting into his thigh. Shifting his weight, he found he had been sitting on a pinecone. They had been waiting for several hours, and he was beginning to think the girl and boy either hadn't gotten the message or weren't coming at all.

"Quit your complaining, Jim. If they do come, you and me won't have to worry about money for the rest of our lives. We can live in style back East."

Jim moved to his brother's side and bent down. "What's the money worth if we get our scalps lifted? In case you've forgotten, this here's Blackfoot country! I'd rather be dead and buried than face just one of them

94

mean devils."

"That's hogwash! There ain't no danger long as we lay low and don't do nothing crazy. You've been listening to too many of them trappers spinning their yarns. Next, you'll be telling me you believe in that Injun Windhawk they was telling us about. Get back over there and keep them horses quiet. You'd be scared of your own shadow."

Jim stood up. "Hell, yes, I'm scared! If you had any sense, you would be, too. Just supposing for a minute this Windhawk is a real person?"

"He ain't real. He's someone the Blackfoot invented to scare little boys and cowards like you." Chester laughed softly. "If he's real, then we'll be dead. If he ain't, and we get our hands on the boy and girl, we'll be well set for life. Now, quit your bellyaching and get back to them horses. If they come, I want to make a quick getaway. We'll need to be long gone before daylight."

Suddenly the brothers heard the sound of a lone rider coming out of the river. They both tensed, straining their eyes to see in the darkness.

Joanna dismounted and stared at the tree line where the dense forest started. It looked dark and foreboding, and she couldn't shake her feeling of uneasiness. There was nothing to be frightened of, she told herself. Harland would be somewhere nearby. More than likely, he was watching her from the forest right this moment.

She gathered up Fosset's reins and led him reluctantly toward the forest. Her nerves were on edge, and she felt the tension building. Her hand went to the hilt of the knife that she had tucked into her belt before leaving camp. Joanna's footsteps were soundless as she approached the forest.

"Harland, are you here?" she called out softly, unsheathing her knife.

Tense moments passed, and all she could hear was the chirping of the crickets and an occasional call of some night bird. Joanna remembered the panther that had once attacked Windhawk, and she felt her legs go weak. She had never thought of herself as a coward, but at the moment she felt totally alone and very terrified. Squaring her shoulders, she entered the forest. The hair on the back of her neck seemed to stand on end, and she had the eerie feeling that she was being watched.

Joanna had to force herself to put one foot in front of the other. Gripping Fosset's reins tightly in her hand, she had almost decided to remount and return to the village when she heard the whinny of a horse. Breathing a sigh of relief, she waited for Harland to appear. Hearing a rustling in the bushes to her left, she turned in that direction.

"Harland?"

"Yes," came the muffled reply.

"Thank goodness," she said in relief. "I began to think you hadn't come."

Joanna saw him move from behind a tree, and she strained her eyes to make out his features, but he was no more than a dark, shadowy outline.

"Tag couldn't come with me; he is away from the village. Has something happened to Simon or Kate Jackson? Is that why you sent for me?"

He was right in front of her now, and she waited for him to speak.

All at once, Joanna was grabbed from behind by a

second man, and at first she was too stunned to react.

"You walked right into this one, Injun lover," an unknown voice said against her ear.

Joanna began to struggle and managed to kick out at the assailant who stood in front of her, catching him squarely in the groin. She had the satisfaction of watching him double over in pain.

Realizing she still held the knife in her hand, she managed to free her arms and slashed out at the man who tried to recapture her. He howled out in pain, loosening his grip long enough for her to get away.

Joanna began running toward Fosset as fast as she could. She bounced onto his back, but before she could nudge him forward strong hands gripped her waist and jerked her off Fosset's back. She gasped out in pain when the man threw her to the ground. A thousand lights seemed to explode in Joanna's head when the man doubled up his fist and struck her a stunning blow that rendered her unconscious.

Chester stood over Joanna's body, breathing heavily. "We was told to bring both of them, but we can't hang around waiting for the boy. Once them Injuns find the girl missing, they'll come looking for her. We gotta get her away from here before that happens."

"I can't go! That gal done went and stabbed me! I'm real bad off, Chester."

"You're gonna be a lot worse off if them red devils find you," his brother warned.

That was all the encouragement Jim needed. He ran for the horses and led them quickly forward, ignoring the pain from his wounded shoulder.

The two brothers rode away at breakneck speed with Joanna's unconscious body resting against Chester's lap and Jim leading the reluctant Fosset, who was pulling against the reins, trying to get free.

Back in the Blackfoot village, the people slept peacefully, not knowing Joanna was in danger.

She Who Heals, the old medicine woman, tossed in her sleep. She was dreaming that Windhawk's woman had been spirited away by two white men. The dream was so real it awakened her, and she sat up, looking about the darkened tipi. She had the urge to go to Windhawk's lodge to make certain Joanna was all right. She Who Heals shook her head. It was no more than a dream . . . Joanna would be asleep now. The old woman lay back down and closed her eyes. She was getting old and having foolish dreams, she thought. But still, her uneasy feeling didn't go away. She told herself she would go to Windhawk's lodge when the first light of day touched the land. That way, she could satisfy herself that Joanna was unharmed.

It was Claudia's wedding night. She looked down at her faded yellow gown and thought bitterly that it hadn't been much of a wedding. Parson Richardson, who had come into the wilderness with the intention of converting the Indians to Christianity, had conducted the short ceremony. The only other person in attendance had been Mr. Hankins, and Claudia knew he had been there only because he thought Howard might balk at the last moment and refuse to marry her.

Howard had been sullen and quiet throughout the whole ordeal, but every so often his eyes would seek

Claudia's, and she could read the anger smoldering beneath the surface. She had to keep reminding herself that she was legally his wife and there was nothing he could do about it.

She was still stinging from the affront of none of the good ladies of the fort's attending her wedding. After the ceremony, several of the men had offered to buy drinks in the common room to celebrate the occasion, but not one of the women had made an appearance at that time, either.

Claudia lost count of how many glasses of wine Howard consumed, but she knew he drank more than his share. He hadn't spoken one word to her since the wedding, but she knew he would have plenty to say when he sobered up. There was no question that she would have to face his wrath sooner or later.

At the party, Howard had become too drunk to stand. Two of the men had helped him to his quarters and helped put him to bed. Claudia thought she was fortunate he had passed out cold. Perhaps she wouldn't have to face his anger until tomorrow.

Claudia looked at the bed where her new husband lay. She couldn't help the strong feeling of distaste that washed over her at the sight of him. Howard was still fully clothed. His mouth was gaping open, and he was snoring loudly. His clothes were rumpled and wrinkled, and there were wine stains on his white shirt.

The whole ordeal had been a strain on Claudia's nerves. Howard was at least some twenty years older than herself. He was certainly not the sort of husband a young woman would yearn for. She allowed her thoughts to go to the handsome Captain Harland Thatcher. If only *he* were her husband, instead of Howard, who was old enough to be her father. How would she bear being married to him?

Howard stirred now, and Claudia held her breath. Should she blow out the candle and lie down, pretending to be asleep? What would he do to her when he awoke?

She clutched her hands tightly together when he sat up in bed, looking about as if he didn't know where he was, until his eyes rested on Claudia. She watched apprehensively as he struggled to his feet and staggered his way toward her. She closed her eyes tightly and mentally braced herself for whatever was to come.

Howard reached out and gripped her painfully by the shoulders. "You little slut," he said, slurring his words. "You think you got the best of me today, don't you?"

"Howard, please! I didn't . . . I only wanted to . . ."

He struck her a heavy blow across the face that sent her reeling into the wall. "I got no bargain in you, but I'm stuck with you for now." He raised his hand, and Claudia cringed, thinking he was going to strike her again.

"You think you got me where you want me," he said, grabbing her by the wrist and dragging her toward the bed. Claudia tried to get away from him when he threw her down on the bed.

"Howard, please, think what you're doing!" she pleaded.

"I might as well enjoy you, since I paid such a high price for that pleasure," he said through thick lips.

Claudia cried out in pain as he began kneading her breasts. When he lowered his body down on top of her, she tried to think of what would be best to do. Probably it would be better if she pretended enjoyment, she reasoned, winding her arms about his neck while his lips moved down her neck. She knew she would just have to make the best of a bad situation.

Seeing the gleam in her eyes, Howard laughed. "You aren't Joanna . . . her memory has tormented me day and night for over two years. I would have given up ten years of my life for just one night in bed with her."

"What are you saying?" Claudia cried, feeling all-consuming jealousy and hatred as Howard taunted her with Joanna. Was Joanna's ghost to haunt her even on her wedding night? It didn't matter to her that Howard was repugnant and she could hardly stand the feel of his hands on her body. She couldn't bear to be compared with Joanna again and come up the loser. She was determined to wipe Joanna's memory from his mind once and for all. Rubbing her body against him, she pulled his head down and kissed him hungrily.

"You aren't her, but you'll do for now," Howard whispered hotly into her ear.

The morning sun found the two Boggs brothers still riding hard. Joanna hadn't regained consciousness, and Chester was beginning to feel worried lest he had hit her too hard.

"Hold up, Jim, we best stop by the river and see to this gal."

Jim dismounted and held his arms up so his brother could hand Joanna to him. He then laid her down on the grass and stood up as his brother approached.

"My God, Chester, she's the prettiest little thing I ever did see!"

Both brothers stared at the beautiful, flame-haired Joanna. Her soft features were enhanced by her creamy white skin. The doeskin gown did nothing to hide the lovely curves of her body. Her face was unbelievably lovely, except for the bruise on her chin where Chester had struck her.

Chester bent down and cupped his hands in the river, then trickled the water over her face.

Joanna moaned and slowly opened her eyes. At first she was confused and disoriented, not knowing why she was lying on the ground. Her eyes widened when she saw the two strange men who were bending over her.

Chester gave her his hand and helped her sit up. "How are you feeling, young lady? I didn't mean to hit you so hard. I don't think I ever did strike a woman before. Do you think you can stand up?"

Joanna shook her head, still in a state of confusion. She noticed both men were wearing buckskin trousers and shirts. One was clean-shaven, and the other wore a beard. "Who are you? Why have you done this to me?"

The clean-shaven man, who appeared to be the younger of the two, took Joanna's hand and helped her to stand. "I'm Jim Boggs, and this here's my brother, Chester."

"What do you want with me?" Joanna asked, seeing nothing in the two brothers' attitude to make her fear them.

"We was hired to bring you to Fort Union. We was told not to say any more than that."

"Who would have hired you to do such a thing? If Captain Thatcher sent you after me, he will not be well pleased that you have forced me to come with you. If you know what's good for you, you'll allow me to return to the Blackfoot village," she said, still not understanding what was going on. Who were these men? Who had hired them to take her away? It had to be Harland . . . but why?

"Well, now, we can't rightly do that," Chester replied, looking into her violet-colored eyes. "You will either agree to come with us peacefully or we will tie you on your horse . . . which is it to be?"

Joanna's eyes went to the younger brother, who had removed his buckskin shirt and was bathing his shoulder with river water.

"Where she stabbed me don't look too deep, Chester, but it hurts like hell!" His eyes went to Joanna. "Why did you go and stick me for?"

Joanna shook her head in confusion. She still wasn't sure what had happened. The last thing she remembered was being dragged from Fosset's back.

Chester paid no attention to his brother; he was waiting for Joanna's answer. "Have you decided if you will come along peaceably, Miss James? Do you come of your own free will, or do we make it hard on you?"

Joanna gave him a heated glance, knowing she had little choice in the matter. Harland would hear about this when she saw him, she decided.

"I will come with you because I am forced to, but I doubt if Captain Thatcher will appreciate your methods. You had better look to your back, because if my husband, Windhawk, catches up with you, I will not be able to stay his hand from harming you."

Joanna noticed that Chester's face whitened. "What did you say?" he asked in an uneven voice.

She raised her head proudly, seeing the shock that registered on the man's face at the mention of Windhawk's name. "You heard me clearly! My husband, Windhawk, will see you both dead for this!"

Jim jumped to his feet and looked at his brother.

"Hell's bells, Chester! Did you hear what she said? You told me this Windhawk ain't no real person!"

Chester was studying Joanna's face. "He ain't real. The girl is just using him to scare us. Tell my brother the truth, little lady."

Joanna smiled, knowing the two men would now be looking over their shoulders, and she doubted they would sleep too well that night. "If it suits your purpose to think Windhawk doesn't exist, so be it. You will find out soon enough that I am telling the truth," she said, amused at the way both brothers' eyes kept darting back to the dense trees.

"You're lying," Chester said, in a voice that showed he was trying to convince himself as well as his brother that the legendary Windhawk didn't really exist.

Joanna merely shrugged her shoulders and bent down to wash her face in the river before cupping her hands to drink thirstily. Too many things had happened to her yesterday for her to sort them all out. She was still hurting because of Windhawk's betrayal, and she had no notion why Harland had gone to such extreme measures to get her away from the village.

She Who Heals had been unable to sleep the night before for worrying about Joanna. She entered Windhawk's lodge, and saw that Joanna was not there. It is early yet, she told herself. Joanna could have gone to the river for water. But why was the cook-fire not lit, and why did Joanna's bed look as if it hadn't been slept in?

She left the lodge, hurriedly walking in the direction of the river. Her fears of last night were becoming a reality, for when she reached the river, she saw no sign of

Flaming Hair. She Who Heals questioned the women who were gathered at the river, but not one of them had seen Joanna, either.

By now, Windhawk's mother was also searching for Joanna. Sun Woman went from lodge to lodge, inquiring if anyone had seen her. By midmorning, the whole village had been alerted, and everyone was frantically searching for Windhawk's missing wife.

Farley mounted his horse and crossed the river, searching for tracks.

Red Bird entered Windhawk's lodge. Seeing the discarded bear-claw necklace, she remembered Flaming Hair had worn it the day before. She smiled to herself as she slipped it over her head. She had the necklace . . . she would soon have Windhawk!

Chapter Eight

An uneasy feeling spread over the Blackfoot village. It was nightfall, and still no one had seen Joanna.

Farley went to the pasture where Fosset was always kept with Windhawk's herd. When he discovered Joanna's horse was missing, he rode back to the village to gather a group of warriors to search for her.

Sun Woman sent word to her son to come at once. The women and children of the village watched and waited in fear, while the warriors made a wide sweep of the countryside in search of their chief's woman.

Joanna was well-loved by the Blackfoot tribe, and everyone was worried about her disappearance . . . all but one. Red Bird felt her heart leap with joy. The Flaming Hair was missing, and she hoped she would never return.

Morning Song was frantic. She remembered how upset Joanna had been the day before when she had learned about Red Bird. She wondered if Joanna had left because of the Piegan woman. She felt that it was her fault, since she had been the one to tell Joanna about Red Bird.

Farley bent down and examined the ground along the river thoroughly. There had been too many horses crossing the river; he couldn't locate Fosset's hoofprints. His heart was heavy, and fear gnawed at his insides. He loved Joanna and was afraid of what might have happened to her.

Sun Woman and She Who Heals looked into each other's eyes. They both loved Joanna as a daughter, and both knew in their hearts that Joanna would never have gone away without telling them. There was no answer to the puzzle of Joanna's disappearance. It was as if she had vanished without leaving a trace.

Joanna turned around to look back over her shoulder. She couldn't believe that no one had come to rescue her. Surely by now someone had discovered she was missing. Farley would find her, she thought confidently. He was a good tracker, and even though the two brothers were taking every precaution to cover their tracks, she was sure Farley would not be easily fooled. She wasn't frightened as much as she was angry. So far, the two men had not mistreated her. In fact, they seemed very concerned about her comfort, and would often stop to offer her food and drink, and to allow her to stretch her cramped legs.

Joanna's strongest emotion was anger. How dare Harland hire these two men to carry her off in such a high-handed manner! Why hadn't he come himself, as he had said he would in his letter? She knew if the chance should present itself, she would get away from her captors and make her way back to the Blackfoot village.

Glancing toward the east, Joanna saw dark clouds

gathering on the horizon. She could see the lightning flashing across the sky, and a loud clap of thunder rolled across the plains. She couldn't help thinking how good it was that the much-needed rain was coming at last. It wasn't until later that Joanna realized the rain would work against her—it would wash away any tracks that might be left behind, making it harder for Farley to follow them.

That night Joanna rolled up in a blanket, while both brothers kept a wary eye on her. She noticed they hadn't lit a campfire and realized they were still afraid of being overtaken by the Blackfoot.

Joanna was so tired and emotionally drained that she decided to rest for just a moment. She was determined not to fall asleep, thinking she would only pretend to be asleep until the two men became lax in their watch, and she would then try to escape. Soon, however, her eyes drifted shut, and she fell into a deep sleep. She wasn't even aware that she was being discussed by the two brothers.

Jim watched the sleeping girl's face in the half-light. Damn, he thought she was beautiful! "What do you suppose her story is, Chester? Do you think the Injuns captured her? Do you reckon Windhawk is real?"

Chester eyed his brother suspiciously. "Hell, how should I know what happened to her? Mr. Landon didn't take me into his confidence. I already told you I don't believe Windhawk's a real person. I'll tell you one thing for sure, though—you stay away from the girl. I'd better not catch you laying a hand on her. We're being paid a lot of money to take her to her uncle. If you start trying to fool around with her, we won't get anything. Do I make myself clear?"

Jim looked away from his brother's searching gaze. "Chances are, if she let some Injun dally with her, most likely she wouldn't mind me rolling her in the grass," Jim said as his eyes fastened on the rise and fall of Joanna's breasts.

"You just try it, Jim. I'm not about to let you spoil this chance for us!"

"You're always bossing me around! Just 'cause you're the oldest don't give you no cause to tell me what to do," Jim replied bitterly.

Chester reached out and gripped his brother by the shirtfront, yanking him forward. "I know how you treat women. As I said before, you lay one hand on the girl, and you'll breathe your last!"

Jim's glance shifted away from the angry gleam in his brother's eyes. He knew about Chester's foul temper—it wasn't wise to rile him. He had once seen his brother strangle a man to death with one hand. "I didn't mean nothing by what I said, Chester. I won't touch the girl. Turn me loose!"

Chester shoved Jim aside. "You would be wise to do what you're told. All my life I been getting you out of scrapes, but I'm warning you, don't touch that girl!"

The light was quickly waning, and Chester looked over to the girl to see if she had been awakened by their loud voices. He was relieved to find she was sleeping peacefully.

Jim's face was sullen as he lay back against his saddle. "We might not get the money that man promised us, anyway. He said we was to bring the girl *and* a boy."

Chester laughed without amusement. "I wasn't about to hang around waiting for the boy. If you want to, you can go back and look for him," he jeered.

Jim lapsed into a sullen silence. He was tired of being pushed around by his older brother. All his life, he'd been forced to do everything Chester's way, and he was getting damned tired of it.

Chester didn't seem to notice his brother's sour mood. He was accustomed to Jim's pouting whenever he didn't get his way. "I sure wish that rain would come to wash away our tracks. Most likely, them Injuns have already started searching for Miss James."

As though wishing for it had made it happen, the first raindrops began to fall from the sky. The thunder rumbled over the valley, and great, jagged bolts of lightning split through the air, lighting up the country-side in their wake.

Chester got up and walked over to Joanna, carrying a waterproof tarp. He spread it over the branches above her to protect her from the rain.

Tall Bear rode into the buffalo camp and dismounted before his horse had come to a halt. Seeing his brother, Gray Fox, he rushed over to him.

"Where is the chief?" he asked.

Gray Fox put his hand on Tall Bear's shoulder. "Have you no greeting for your brother?" he asked, half-amused.

"I have no time to talk—I must see Windhawk at once! I have grave news."

Gray Fox nodded to the tipi that was set apart from the others. "What is wrong?"

"Flaming Hair has disappeared! We have searched everywhere but can find no trace of her!"

Gray Fox's eyes narrowed in disbelief. "How could

such a thing happen?"

Tall Bear didn't wait to answer but hurried toward Windhawk's tipi. Not bothering to announce himself, he entered.

Windhawk was cutting strips from a buffalo hide to lace his moccasins, and he smiled up at Tall Bear. "I thought you had enough of the buffalo hunt and had gone home to be with your woman."

"I have bad tidings, my chief," Tall Bear blurted out. "Flaming Hair is missing!"

Windhawk stood up slowly, feeling himself die a little inside. "You had better tell me what you mean," he said in a quiet voice that didn't reveal his distress. Only his dark eyes gave him away. They were wildly pain-filled and disbelieving.

Gray Fox came up behind his brother. "Where is Joanna? What has happened to her?" he asked, in a voice of concern. He looked at Windhawk and saw his troubled expression.

"It was but five moons ago that we discovered Flaming Hair was not in the village," Tall Bear said hurriedly. "Many warriors searched for her day and night, but we found no sign. There was a big rainstorm, and if there were any tracks they have now been washed away."

Without a word, Windhawk ran from the tipi. He leaped onto his horse and rode swiftly in the direction of the Blackfoot village. Gray Fox and Tall Bear caught their mounts and rode hard to catch up with him.

Windhawk felt unbridled fear. What could have happened to Joanna? he wondered in a frenzy. He thought of the time she had run away from him before, but no, she wouldn't leave him now. She loved him! Were they not happy together? Besides, she would never leave without her brother, Tag, he reasoned. No, she hadn't run away, but what had happened to her?

His heart cried out to her wherever she was. He knew she wasn't dead. He would feel it in his heart if she had come to any harm.

He rode swiftly, sparing neither his horse nor himself. Long into the night, his buffalo runner's powerful legs carried him homeward.

After three days of hard riding, Windhawk was in sight of his village. The most difficult thing he had to bear was the uncertainty of not knowing if Joanna had yet been found. Not once did he voice his fears, but Gray Fox, who knew him so well, could read the fear in his friend's eyes.

Windhawk entered the river with an urgency, noticing a large group of his people waiting for him on the other side. Riding his mount out of the water, his face was solemn as he approached the village.

Sun Woman watched her son dismount, thinking how tired and haggard he looked. His eyes asked her the question he couldn't bring himself to voice.

"We have not yet found Joanna, my son. It is as if she disappeared with the morning mist."

"What could have happened to her?" Gray Fox asked apprehensively.

"We know not . . . there is no sign of her anywhere," Sun Woman told him, shaking her head sadly.

Windhawk turned to Gray Fox. "I want to see everyone who talked to Joanna the day before she disappeared. Have them come to my lodge at once. Send someone to the pasture to get Puh Pom, and have him ready to travel. I want to leave as soon as I have

113

questioned everyone. Select two of my warriors to accompany me."

"I will be one of that number," Gray Fox said.

"No, my friend. You have had no rest in three moons. I would not ask you to go with me."

"I shall go, nonetheless. We can both rest when Joanna is found."

"I will go, too," Farley said, coming up beside Windhawk.

Windhawk was tired, and his temper was on edge. "I was not aware that you were the chief, old man, and could make the decisions," he said in an irritated voice.

Farley did not lower his eyes but stared straight at Windhawk. "Be that as it may, I'm a-going with you," he replied simply. "You might need me to speak to any white men we might meet up with. They would talk to me where they wouldn't to you."

Windhawk knew that the old man was making sense. Not bothering to answer, he simply nodded his head, then walked in the direction of his lodge.

Sun Woman put her hand on Farley's shoulder. "Windhawk is not angry with you, old man. He is worried about Joanna and he tries to hide his fear under a gruff voice."

Farley watched the young chief disappear into his lodge. "I fear we all have much to worry about. I have never known anyone to disappear without leaving a trace, as Joanna has."

"You must trust my son to know what is best. If anyone can find Joanna, he can."

On entering his lodge, Windhawk felt the emptiness like a pain in his heart. How cold it felt without Joanna to come into his arms to greet him as she always had. There

114

was no cheerful cook-fire to light the darkened corners. It suddenly hit him hard. This was what it felt like to lose his love. A cold, empty feeling seemed to seep into every fiber of his body. If he would allow it, he could easily abandon control of his emotions.

He grabbed hold of the lodgepole and bowed his head. "Joanna, Joanna, where are you, my beloved?" he whispered in a painful voice.

Hearing the sound of voices, Windhawk straightened his back and turned just as Morning Song and Red Bird entered. Soon the lodge was filled with many people waiting to talk to him.

"Which one of you was the last to see Joanna?" he asked, searching every face.

"I was, my brother," Morning Song said, stepping forward. "I was the last one to speak to her."

"Did she say anything to you to indicate she was upset?" Windhawk asked.

Morning Song met her brother's eyes. "Yes, Windhawk, she was very distressed because you had sent the Piegan woman to our village."

For the first time, Windhawk looked at Red Bird. He had forgotten all about her! Glancing back to his sister, he looked puzzled. "Why should Joanna be upset because Red Bird has come to our village?"

Morning Song took a deep breath. "She . . . Joanna . . . said she would not stay with you when you took another wife. She was very distressed, Windhawk."

Windhawk swung his dark gaze around to Red Bird. "Why should she think I was to take another wife?"

Red Bird stepped forward. Her heart was drumming at the sight of the handsome chief. She was glad the white woman was gone. Now she could have Windhawk all to herself. "The white-skinned woman was angry because I am to be your wife. She was very unkind to me."

Windhawk's eyes narrowed. "Who told Joanna that I would take you as my wife?"

Morning Song bowed her head. "Red Bird did, my brother, but many others thought that was your intention."

"Why? I do not understand why Joanna would believe such a thing!" his voice boomed out.

"Red Bird told everyone in the village that she was to be your wife . . . she also told Joanna." Morning Song's eyes filled with tears. "I did not think Joanna would run away. It is my fault that she has gone."

Windhawk looked back to Red Bird. "Did you tell my people that you were to be my wife?"

Red Bird looked confused. "Yes, I did not know you wanted it kept a secret. You should have told me, then I would have said nothing."

"She also told Joanna that you had lain with her," Morning Song spoke up accusingly. "Joanna was very upset when Red Bird told her she would replace her as the favorite wife."

Windhawk's eyes seemed to burn with unleashed anger. Those who knew him well could see he was making an effort to keep his anger in check.

Red Bird cringed at the foreboding look the young chief gave her. "Why did you say this to my wife?" his voice was deep and laced with anger.

"As I said, I did not . . ."

Windhawk's eyes fell on the bear-claw necklace, which Red Bird now wore. Reaching out, he jerked it from the Piegan woman's neck. "Where did you get this?" he hissed.

Red Bird's eyes were wide with fright. "I found it where the white woman had cast it aside. I did not think you would mind if I took it as my own."

"Go from my sight, Piegan woman! I will deal with you later," he said.

Windhawk dared not allow his mind the freedom to rule his thoughts. Clasping the necklace so tightly it cut into his palm, he realized Joanna must have run away. Did she not love him enough to wait until he came home so he could tell her the truth about Red Bird? Did she love him so little that she would leave like a thief in the night?

Morning Song approached Windhawk, holding out a letter to him. "The old man said he gave this letter to Joanna the day she left. Should I read it to see if it will tell where she has gone?" Morning Song had found the letter only that morning and had hesitated to read it since it belonged to Joanna.

"What does the paper say?" Windhawk asked in a commanding voice. Morning Song was one of the few who could read the white man's words. Joanna had taught her while she had instructed Tag.

"I cannot read all the words . . . it is from a Captain Thatcher. He says he is in trouble and asked Joanna to meet him in the forest and bring Tag with her."

Windhawk's eyes flamed and jealousy burned in his heart. Joanna had gone away with the long knife! His heart cried out in revenge and bitterness. She *had* betrayed him!

Looking down at the bear-claw necklace, he remembered what it symbolized. She had told him not so long ago that if she ever took it off again it would mean she no longer loved him. Bitterness surrounded his heart.

"I know where Joanna has gone," Windhawk whispered. "She is at the fort of the long knives. I will go there and bring her back."

Pushing past the crowd of people who had entered his lodge, Windhawk went outside. Gray Fox was mounted and waiting for him, and Farley was holding Puh Pom's rein.

"Are we ready to ride?" the old trapper asked.

"You had better keep up, old man," Windhawk said, bounding onto his horse's back. "If you do not keep pace, we shall leave you behind."

Sun Woman watched the three men ride away in a cloud of dust, hoping they would find Joanna.

Windhawk's eyes burned like two hot coals. He could envision Joanna in the arms of the long knife. He would kill the man and make Joanna pay for leaving him.

Gray Fox rode at his friend's side. He remembered another time when Joanna had run away from Windhawk, and when he found her, he had been merciless. That time had almost ended in disaster. This time, he was glad he would be along to stay Windhawk's vengeful hand.

Joanna felt wet and miserable as she huddled beneath a pine tree that offered her very little shelter from the driving rain. Rivulets of water washed down the narrow, needlelike leaves and splashed onto her upturned face. They had been traveling hard for two weeks, and she was bone-weary.

Out of the corner of her eye, Joanna could see Jim Boggs watching her. The two brothers kept such a close watch on her that she was allowed very little privacy.

Once again, she wondered why Captain Thatcher had used such forceful measures to get her to Fort Union. She thought of Windhawk and knew how angry he would be when he found out she was missing. He would probably think she had left him of her own free will.

In the past two weeks she had had plenty of time to reflect on her plight. Now might be a good time for her to put some distance between herself and Windhawk. Perhaps she would ask Captain Thatcher to take her to Fort Leavenworth, where she could visit with Kate and Colonel Jackson. She was still too hurt and angry to face Windhawk. Let him wonder why she had left—it just didn't matter anymore.

By bringing Red Bird into the village, Windhawk had cut her free. She remembered the Piegan woman's telling her that she and Windhawk had already been together. It was incredibly painful to think of Windhawk's holding Red Bird in his arms and touching her the way he had once touched Joanna.

She felt her anger surface. Let Windhawk have his Indian wife! She never wanted to see him again!

In her mind, she began making plans. She had to decide what to do about her situation. There was the baby to consider. Did she have a right to deny Windhawk his child? Yes, he had forfeited all his rights when he had taken the other woman to his bed.

She had seen Windhawk's anger directed at her only once, and that had been the time she had run away from him. She shivered inwardly, thinking how he would react this time if he should find her.

She leaned back against the tree trunk as Jim sat down beside her. "Sure is miserable weather, ain't it, ma'am?"

Joanna was in no mood to pass pleasantries with the

119

man who had taken her away by force. She looked past him, ignoring his presence.

"You sure are an uppity little thing, ain't you?" he said, moving closer to her.

"I have no intention of talking to you, Mr. Boggs," Joanna replied, giving him her haughtiest look.

"Peers to me you ain't too careful who you dally with. Any white woman who prefers an Injun to one of her own kind shouldn't think so well of herself."

Joanna scalded him with a glance that made her violet eyes sparkle. "Who do you think you are that you can speak to me in such a way?" She stood up and turned her back, too angry to say anything more. This man had just stepped beyond the bounds of decency, and she intended to let Captain Thatcher know of her displeasure as soon as they reached Fort Union! She had always thought of Harland as a friend, but that friendship was being tested to the limits at the moment. What right did this man have to speak to her in such a disrespectful manner?

Joanna felt Jim Boggs's hand on her shoulder, and she whirled around to face him. "You dare touch me?" she asked through clenched teeth. Her anger soared when he grinned and reached out to gather a handful of red-gold curls.

"Take your hands off me, sir!" Joanna demanded, backing up, only to come up against the tree trunk.

"I got me a powerful itch, little lady, and you're just the one to scratch it. I been hankering after you for days now. You owe me something for stabbing me in the shoulder with that knife."

Before Joanna could react, he reached out and pulled her against him. She looked up at him unafraid, feeling

120

only repulsion at the smell of his foul breath. When he grinned, she caught a glimpse of his chipped yellow teeth.

"I told you to take your hands off me! Windhawk will kill you for touching me!"

Jim hesitated a moment. Just the mention of Windhawk's name was enough to make the bravest man feel fear. "There ain't no such man as Windhawk! Don't you think I know that?"

"You will know it when he plunges his knife into your black heart," she spat, struggling to gain her release.

His arms tightened, and he pulled her against him. Joanna renewed her struggling, but he stuck out his foot and tripped her, sending them both falling to the ground. Jim landed on top of Joanna, and she felt pain shoot through her body. For the moment, she couldn't breathe. Feeling his hands pushing her gown upward, she tried to throw him off.

His coarse laughter sounded next to her ear. "You're a regular little wildcat! I like my women with a lot of vinegar. I'm going to enjoy getting at you."

Joanna wrenched her arm out of his grasp and swung wide, catching him across the face with a hard blow.

Jim grabbed his stinging cheek and uttered a loud oath. Joanna recognized the danger to herself when she saw his eyes narrow angrily.

"You bitch!" he yelled as he doubled up his fist and caught her beside the temple.

Pain shot through Joanna's head, and she began to feel terror. He was stronger than she, and she would have little chance of getting away from him. A whimper escaped her throat as he began pushing her gown upward. She realized that struggle was futile. When he began fumbling with his breeches, Joanna used her last bit of

121

strength to bring her knees up and catch him in the groin.

Again he mumbled an oath, but by now his anger was unbounded. His hands were biting into her tender flesh as he jerked her under him. Joanna closed her eyes, too weak to move. Her mind cried out against what was about to happen to her.

"Damn you, Jim!" Chester bellowed out, seeing what his brother was about. He ran forward like a charging bull and knocked Jim away from Joanna.

Jim landed in a mud puddle, but scrambled quickly to his feet. "I'll kill you for that, Chester!" he hissed as he raced toward his brother with murder in his heart.

Chester was quicker than his brother and side-stepped him, while bringing the butt of his rifle down against his skull. Jim went limp and fell heavily to the ground to lie motionless.

Joanna sprang to her feet, staring at the blood that trickled down Jim's head mixing with the rainwater. "Is . . . he . . . dead?" she asked.

Chester turned to her for a moment. "No, but he oughta be. Are you hurt?"

Joanna placed her hands on her hips. "Why should you care? I feel sorry for you and your brother because you haven't long to live."

Chester bent over and hoisted his fallen brother onto his shoulders. "Don't bother to threaten me with the mythical Windhawk again, 'cause it won't work!"

"It's no threat, Mr. Boggs. It's a reality." Joanna could see by the look on Chester's face that he didn't really believe her, but there was a hint of fear in his eyes, just the same. Her last hope was to play on his fear.

"Your days are numbered. It would be well if you would watch your back. There is nowhere you can go to escape Windhawk's wrath!"

Chester turned his back so Joanna couldn't see if her words had met their mark. "If that's the case, we won't stay around here any longer. One more week and we will be at Fort Union. I think if your imagined savior does exist, he'll have a hard time facing the armed men at the fort."

Joanna watched the heavy rain fall to the ground. Even Windhawk couldn't find her with the rain washing their trail away. She began to wonder just what would await her when they reached the fort. Something wasn't right. Surely, Harland would never have sent these two despicable men for her. Try as she might, Joanna couldn't understand what was going on. She knew it would do no good to question Chester, because he would tell her nothing.

She felt a deep ache in her heart. In spite of her anger at Windhawk, she found herself wishing he would come for her. I need you, Windhawk! she cried out silently. Please find me!

Chapter Nine

Claudia walked across the compound, lifting the skirt of her gown so it wouldn't get muddy. It had been raining for days, and the gloomy weather seemed to fit her mood. She was finding out that being married to Howard was not all she had hoped it would be. He never spoke a civil word to her. The only time he paid her the slightest attention was at night when they went to bed. He had cursed and abused her, and she wondered if it had all been worth it.

He had threatened her more than once by telling her she would be on her own when they reached Philadelphia. She was determined that he wouldn't cast her aside so easily—no, not yet.

She had silently endured his kisses and his fumbling hands. When he took her body, she felt as if she was more than repaying him for any injury he might have suffered to his pride. If she had used him, wasn't he now using her?

Oh, no, Howard Landon, you will not get rid of me, she thought to herself. Like it or not, I'm your wife. She

125

stepped across a mud puddle and walked up the wooden steps. Claudia had stalled as long as she could. There was nothing for her to do but return to the quarters she shared with her husband.

She knew Howard would either be drunk or off with some of the trappers gambling. She was appalled at the amount of money he lost at cards. Claudia lived for the day when they would go to Philadelphia so she could shop for new clothing. Her head was filled with visions of the beautiful gowns she would buy. She would have a gown for every occasion—with shoes and hats to match. Claudia remembered the beautiful, expensive gowns Joanna had worn. Soon, she too, would have all she wanted, and more.

When Claudia reached the door of their quarters, she stopped dead in her tracks. Howard was gazing out the window at her, and the look he gave her chilled her to the bone. Her hand trembled as she opened the door.

"Where have you been?" he thundered. "Strutting around showing off your wares? Bet you didn't get any takers," he taunted.

"What would you care?" she asked, removing her gloves and noticing they needed mending again.

"I *don't* care. You can go to hell for that matter. I wouldn't lose a moment's sleep if you were to descend into hell right before my eyes."

"When I get there, I have a feeling you will be the first one to greet me."

"Slut!" he bellowed.

"Bastard!" she countered.

Howard moved quickly across the room and grabbed a handful of her hair. Claudia closed her eyes, waiting for the blow to fall, but a rap on the door stayed Howard's hand, and he pushed her roughly aside to answer it.

Joanna pushed Jim Boggs's hand away from her waist while she waited for Captain Thatcher to answer Chester's knock on the door. She was ready to give Harland a piece of her mind, rehearsing mentally what she would say. She watched the door open, expecting to see Harland. Joanna swallowed hard and felt her knees go weak at the sight of her Uncle Howard's face!

Dear Lord, don't let this be happening! Let this be a dream from which I will awaken! she cried silently as she gazed into the beady eyes that she had thought never to see again. Joanna felt the ground come up and hit her in the face as she lapsed into unconsciousness.

Howard rushed forward, pushing Chester Boggs away from Joanna. Bending down, he lifted her tenderly into his arms. His eyes were bright and shining, and the blood was pumping in his veins. At last, after two long years of pure hell, he had Joanna back!

Carrying her into the room, Howard laid her on the bed and stared down at her. He had forgotten how lovely she was. His eyes rested on her red-gold hair, and he felt his heart tighten. Never in his wildest dream had he imagined he would get her back! He had so many plans for her that he couldn't wait to get her back to Philadelphia.

Claudia came up beside Howard and stared at her old enemy with malignant eyes. She watched her husband gently push a tumbled red-gold curl from Joanna's face. It didn't matter that she didn't love Howard, jealousy still burned in her heart, knowing he favored Joanna over her. Claudia flicked the fringe of Joanna's gown with her finger. "She's dressed like an Indian," she spit out.

"No matter," Howard said, in a tender voice that she had never heard him use before. "I will soon have her gowned in silks and velvets, as she should be."

Hatred burned anew within Claudia's breast. Howard hadn't allowed her any money to buy new gowns, yet he was talking about dressing Joanna in grand style.

Howard pushed Claudia aside and faced the two brothers. "Where's the boy?"

Chester shook his head. "The boy didn't come with her. There weren't no way we could get our hands on him. The girl said he wasn't in the Blackfoot village."

Howard's eyes burned into Chester's for a moment. He had wanted them both, but he knew that if he took Joanna back to Philadelphia, sooner or later Tag would show up. "No matter, you have done well by bringing my niece to me. Meet me at the common room tonight, and I'll pay you."

"Why don't you just pay us now, and we'll be on our way," Jim stated.

Howard eyed the younger brother shrewdly. "First, I want to speak to my niece. If either of you has laid a hand on her, it won't be money you'll be getting from me." Howard looked at Jim Boggs and watched as the man dropped his eyes. "As I said, meet me in the common room later, and we will discuss what your payment will be."

Jim's eyes remained downcast when his brother took his arm. "We'll see you tonight then, Mr. Landon. You'll find your niece has been untouched."

When the two brothers went outside, Chester removed his hat and struck his brother across the face with it. "See, what did I tell you? If I hadn't stopped you from messing with the girl, we wouldn't get nothing. If you had succeeded, Mr. Landon wouldn't have to kill you, I'd a done it myself."

Claudia watched Howard sit down on the bed and pick up Joanna's hand.

"What about me, Howard? If I hadn't helped, you would never have gotten Joanna back."

Howard was feeling unusually jovial. "I haven't forgotten the part you played in this, Claudia. I also haven't forgotten the trick you played on me. But I am prepared to be generous with you, all the same. I will take you to Philadelphia and see that you have a small house, nothing elaborate, you understand. My attorney will see to an annulment, and we will see the last of each other."

"If you think I will settle for a mere pittance, you are sadly mistaken. You are a wealthy man, and you can afford to set me up in style. I won't allow you to cast me aside like so much extra baggage. You may have been forced to marry me, but you are my husband, nonetheless."

Howard laughed deeply. "My God, you are a fool! What would you think if I were to tell you I don't have two pennies of my own to rub together?"

"I would say you are lying," Claudia replied, staring at Howard suspiciously.

"Do you think so? Why don't you ask Joanna when she regains consciousness? She will tell you that all the money belongs to her and Tag. I doubt that she will be willing to share any part of it with you." His eyes gleamed at the joke on Claudia. "Since you claim to be such good friends with Joanna, why don't you ask her for all the money you want?"

Claudia sank down on a chair. Her face had lost its color, and she felt as if she were going to be sick. "What are you saying?" she said through parched lips, fearing he was telling the truth.

Howard threw back his head and laughed loudly. "I'm saying, Claudia, that I am only Tag and Joanna's legal guardian until Tag reaches his twenty-first birthday. At one time, I spent six months in Newgate prison in England because I couldn't pay my debts."

Claudia ground her teeth together. "I had envisioned you living in a grand house with servants waiting on you. I don't get the impression that you are poverty-stricken."

"Oh, the house is there all right, and so are the servants, but they aren't mine. They work for Tag and Joanna. I am merely the custodian."

"I'm beginning to see why you wanted Tag and Joanna back so badly. You were afraid you would lose everything. That's the reason, isn't it?"

"And so I still might, Claudia. As you heard the man say, Tag will not be coming."

"How . . . much money do you get?"

Howard smiled, enjoying the joke on Claudia. "I get enough to run the house and buy a few doodads. Nothing on a grand scale, you understand. You see, the business and the bulk of the estate is tied up in Taggart's name. Joanna will come into a small fortune on her twenty-first birthday, but I don't think she will be wanting to give it to you or me."

"You tricked me!" she cried. "You allowed me to think you were very wealthy. I can't believe it was all a front. Why did you let me think you had money?"

He arched an eyebrow. "Who tricked whom, Claudia? I don't recall discussing my financial affairs with you or anybody else."

Joanna began to stir, and Howard turned his attention

to her. He watched her eyes slowly open, and he hated the fear he saw in the violet-colored depths when they focused on his face.

"Hello, Joanna," he said, picking up her hand.

She tried to speak, but her tongue seemed to be rooted to the roof of her mouth.

"I know what you are feeling. I'm not going to hurt you. I am prepared to forgive you for running away. Before long, we shall be on our way home."

"I don't understand," she whispered. "I thought Harland . . . had I known you . . ."

"Shh, don't talk now. Just rest. I'm going to see about getting you something to eat, then you can bathe and get out of those awful clothes."

Joanna was too confused to reply, so she silently watched as he crossed the room and left. She was further astonished when she recognized Claudia standing near the foot of the bed.

"Claudia, can you tell me what's happening?"

The irony of it all hit Claudia full force. "I guess you might say I'm your aunt now, Joanna. Can you imagine anything so ludicrous? Forgive me if I don't insist on you calling me Aunt Claudia."

Joanna closed her eyes, hoping to shut out Claudia's hateful voice. She had no idea what Claudia was talking about, and she didn't care to find out at the moment. She was too tired and emotionally drained. Her worst nightmare had been realized. She was back in the clutches of her Uncle Howard! From what he'd implied, he was taking her back to Philadelphia, and there didn't seem to be anything she could do about it.

Somehow, this all tied in with the letter she had gotten from Harland. She now knew he hadn't written the letter at all. What a fool she had been to go forward so trustfully, like a lamb being led to the slaughter!

Farley left Colonel Jackson's office looking puzzled. There was something not right here. The colonel had said Captain Thatcher had left Fort Leavenworth less than a week ago, heading for Fort Union. Farley had gotten that information without revealing his purpose for asking. Colonel Jackson had also told him that Joanna's uncle had been there a while back and had been asking for information about Joanna and Tag.

Mounting his horse, he rode out the fort gates, heading for the other side of the river. If Captain Harland Thatcher had been at Leavenworth when Joanna disappeared, then where was Joanna?

In less than an hour, he crossed the river and rode into the camp where Windhawk and Gray Fox were waiting for him. Before he could dismount, Windhawk came up beside him with hope in his dark eyes.

"Did you see Joanna, old man?"

"No, she has not been to the fort," Farley said, dismounting and scratching his shaggy white head.

"She did not come here with the long knife?" Windhawk asked.

"No, and here the story gets stranger. Captain Thatcher couldn't have met Joanna like the letter said. He was here at Fort Leavenworth at the time she disappeared."

"Do you know this for a fact?" Gray Fox asked. "Perhaps someone did not tell you the truth."

"The man who told me would not lie. He and his wife are good friends of Joanna's."

Windhawk turned his back and walked down to the river. When Farley would have followed him, Gray Fox motioned for him to stay.

"Allow him to be alone for a time. He is feeling pain and would not like you or me to witness it."

"I have been trying to think what to do. Colonel Jackson said something that bothers me a great deal," Farley stated, speaking in perfect Blackfoot.

"What is that, old man?"

"He said that Joanna's uncle was here a few weeks back searching for her—he went on to Fort Union. Since then, Captain Thatcher was mustered out of the army and was heading for Fort Union as well."

"You must tell this to Windhawk, but not now. It will be soon enough to tell him when he returns."

Windhawk walked beside the river, not knowing what to do next. If Joanna had not gone away with the long knife, then where was she?

He picked up the bear-claw necklace he wore about his neck. He had thought Joanna would never take it off again. He looked up at the sky, watching a hawk circle above him. Joanna was somewhere in this world—she was not dead, or he would know it. Where could he look? How could one just disappear without leaving some trace? Closing his eyes, he could see her face so clearly. He could almost hear the sound of her laughter dancing on the soft wind.

"Why have you done this thing, Joanna? If you no longer want to be my woman, should I give up the search?" No, he would not abandon hope yet.

Feeling the warm breeze on his face, he closed his eyes. "Twice you have left me, Joanna. The other time, I forgave you; this time, I will not!"

133

Windhawk watched the sun setting in the west. It was like a great ball of fire suspended in the heavens. Wherever Joanna was, she could be witnessing the same sunset, he thought.

"I gave you my love and my heart, Joanna. Did you cast it aside as you did the bear-claw necklace?" he whispered to himself.

Claudia held up Joanna's doeskin gown, looking at it with distaste. "How the mighty have fallen. I remember you once paraded around in the latest fashions. Is this what they are wearing in Paris this year?"

Joanna sank lower down in the galvanized bathtub, trying to ignore Claudia. She had suffered her acrid tongue in silence for over a week now, and she had just about had her fill of Claudia's complaining. Ducking her head under water, she rinsed the soap from her hair.

If only she could have some time alone so she could think. Surprisingly, her uncle had been kind and considerate to her, which was more than she could say for Claudia.

Joanna's Uncle Howard had hired the wife of one of the trappers to make her several new gowns. As badly as she hated to admit it, her doeskin gown was beyond repairing. She couldn't very well object to wearing the gowns that had been made for her.

"If you know what's good for you, you had better send for that brother of yours. Howard won't put up with your stubbornness for much longer. If you insist on having your way, you may regret it," Claudia threatened, as her voice seemed to drone on and on.

Joanna reached for a towel and wrapped it about her as

she stepped out of the bathtub. "I can assure you, I will do no such thing. Tag will remain where he is and nothing you or my uncle can do will make me change my mind. I would be a fool to expose my brother to any danger." For days, her uncle and Claudia had been grilling her about Tag's whereabouts. She wasn't about to tell either of them where he was.

"Howard said if you don't tell us where Tag is, we're leaving for Philadelphia early tomorrow morning. How will you like that, miss priss?"

Joanna shrugged her shoulders. "It's all the same to me. My uncle will find I am not so easy to control as I once was. Without my brother, he cannot hold the threat of his safety over my head."

Claudia threw the doeskin gown at Joanna, but it landed on the floor at Joanna's feet. "You just wait and see." Claudia's eyes glinted for a moment. "I bet you would give anything to return to that Indian you've been living with. How do you like the way I tricked you?"

Joanna pulled the gray gown over her head and fastened it at the collar. "I have to hand it to you, Claudia, you had me believing Harland had sent for me. Do you feel proud of yourself for taking me away from my husband?"

"You weren't ever married in a proper wedding ceremony. You were living in sin with that heathen!"

Joanna refused to allow Claudia to goad her into anger. "Just because we weren't joined together in a church or by a presiding minister doesn't mean we aren't man and wife. My becoming Windhawk's wife was more beautiful than you could ever imagine."

Claudia sank down in a chair. "I can't understand you at all, Joanna. You had everything a girl could want—

money, beautiful gowns, and a grand house to live in. I happen to know that Captain Thatcher even asked you to marry him. Why would you throw all that away to be with an Indian?"

Joanna picked up a brush and began brushing the tangles from her hair. "It's very simple, but I don't expect you to understand. I love . . . loved Windhawk."

"Tell me what he looks like?" Claudia asked with interest. "I must confess all Indians look alike to me."

Joanna smiled. "How can I describe his handsomeness? How could I make you understand his gentleness and compassion? He has every quality I would ever want in a husband. He was the kindest, most loving man I have ever met."

Claudia's eyes seemed to glaze over. "Tell me, what does it feel like to have a savage make love to you?"

Joanna paused with the brush halfway through a red-gold curl. "You go too far, Claudia. I would never discuss anything so private with you."

Claudia's lewd laughter filled the room. "My, my, aren't we touchy, though! Does your Indian lover know how to kiss a woman?"

Joanna threw the brush down on the bed. "Isn't there something you should be doing? I have nothing further to say to you now or in the future."

Claudia laughed gleefully, knowing she had finally struck a nerve. "I have nothing to do but keep an eye on you to make sure you don't try to escape."

"Do you think you could stop me if I decided to go through that door right now?" Joanna challenged.

"I might not be able to stop you, but the Boggs brothers are stationed right outside that door. I think they could easily detain you."

"What do you expect to get out of all this, Claudia? You can't tell me you married my uncle out of love. I can tell the two of you don't even like each other. Yours doesn't seem to be a match made in heaven!"

Claudia stood up. "Had it not been for you, I would now be married to Captain Thatcher."

"Don't blame me for your failures, Claudia. It's not my fault that Harland didn't marry you."

Claudia's face became distorted with anger. "What is it about you that causes the men to lust after you? I'm as pretty as you are, and a lot more obtainable."

"Look to yourself for the answers. I'm sure I don't know."

"What will your Indian lover do when he finds out you are missing?" Claudia asked, changing the subject abruptly. "Will he come after you, do you think?"

Joanna closed her eyes for just a moment. "I don't know. Because of your letter he will think that I have gone off with Captain Thatcher. Windhawk is very jealous of Harland."

"For some reason, you don't seem unduly upset to be separated from Windhawk. Why is that?"

Joanna had no intention of telling Claudia that she had been hurt because Windhawk had decided to take another wife. How could she tell anyone about the pain that burned in her heart?

She had become resigned to the fact that her uncle was taking her back to Philadelphia—anyway, there wasn't much she could do about it. Perhaps it was for the best. She could never have stayed with Windhawk and watched him turn to another woman. As far as Tag was concerned, he would be much better off with Windhawk than with her uncle. The one thing she must prevent from happening was allowing her Uncle Howard to get his hands on Tag.

"You didn't answer me, Joanna!" Claudia loudly reminded her.

"I don't want to talk to you anymore, Claudia. I'm not feeling too well." In truth, Joanna was still suffering from morning sickness and had been trying to hide her condition from Claudia and her uncle. She knew she couldn't keep her condition hidden much longer. Already, her stomach was beginning to swell, and her waistline was expanding.

"I would like a breath of fresh air. Could we go for a walk?" Joanna asked, feeling as if the four walls were closing in on her.

"Sure, why not? I'm so bored I would even welcome a walk with you," Claudia answered.

As they walked outside, Joanna observed that Claudia had spoken the truth. The two Boggs brothers were leaning against the porch, standing guard. Apparently, her uncle wasn't taking any chances that she might get away.

Joanna looked away with disgust when she saw the way Claudia swung her hips and batted her eyes at Chester and Jim Boggs. Claudia was just the kind of wife her uncle deserved, she thought bitterly.

As they walked along, Joanna noticed many Indians inside the compound. She could tell by their manner of dress that none of them were Blackfoot. She wished there were some way she could get a message to Tag so he would know she was safe. He would never know what had happened to her. The last thing he would ever expect would be that she was back under their uncle's domination. She hoped he never found out, because she knew if he did he would find a way to come to her in Philadelphia.

Joanna saw her uncle walking toward them, and she tensed as she always did when he was near. She noticed there was a man walking beside him who was wearing a blue army uniform.

"Could that soldier possibly be Captain Thatcher?" she asked Claudia.

"If it isn't, the man could pass for his double," Claudia answered.

They waited for the man to approach near enough so they could see his face more clearly.

"Yes, it is Harland!" Joanna cried, happy to see a friendly face. She started running and threw herself into Harland's arms. "I am so glad to see you!" she said, burying her face against his blue jacket.

"I'm sorry to see you here," he whispered in her ear. "Are you all right?"

Joanna stood back and wiped the tears from her face. "Forgive me for the tears, I was just so happy to see you."

Harland read many things on her face. He was devastated that he had unwittingly sent her uncle to Fort Union, making it possible for Howard Landon to get her back. It had been many months since he had last seen her and, if anything, Joanna was even more beautiful than he remembered.

"I wasn't aware that you were so well acquainted with my niece, Captain," Howard Landon spoke up.

Harland took Joanna's hand. "We are very good friends, Mr. Landon. I once asked your niece to marry me, but she turned me down."

"Mores the pity," Claudia intervened. "How are you, Captain?"

"Actually, I'm not a captain any longer, Miss . . . Mrs. Landon. As a matter of fact, I'm on my way home to Philadelphia."

"Strange, I would have thought Fort Union a bit out of your way, if you were going to Pennsylvania," Claudia purred in a silky-smooth voice.

Harland's eyes rested on Joanna. "It is out of the way, but I came to see a friend."

In that moment, Joanna knew that Harland meant he had come to Fort Union because of her. She gave him a bright smile that told him how much she appreciated his kindness.

"On learning that the captain is headed our way, I have asked him to travel along with us," Howard spoke up. "Of course, the Boggs brothers will be traveling with us as far as Independence, as extra protection."

Joanna felt such relief knowing that Harland would be going with them that it showed on her face. She would have a friend beside her on the way back to Philadelphia.

Harland hadn't realized he was still holding Joanna's hand until her uncle wrenched it away from him.

"We'll see you bright and early tomorrow morning, Captain. I intend to get an early start." So saying, he tucked Joanna's hand under his arm and strolled off, leaving Claudia to come or stay as she wished.

"He'll never allow you to see her alone, you know," Claudia taunted Harland.

Harland bowed stiffly—he had never liked Claudia, and it showed in his eyes now. "Good day, Mrs. Landon," he said curtly, turning on his heels and walking away.

Claudia's eyes clouded over. Joanna still had it all, she thought bitterly. She had struck at her in the worst possible way, by tearing her away from the man she loved, and still Joanna seemed to come out the winner. Was there no way she could mortally wound Joanna, other than by taking her life? If there was a weakness in Joanna, somehow . . . she would find it. Her goal in life had become to hurt Joanna, and before she was finished, she was determined to accomplish just that!

Chapter Ten

In spite of the fact that Joanna's uncle had wanted to get an early start, it was midmorning before the small party of travelers rode out the gates of Fort Union. Joanna rode beside Claudia, while Howard and Harland rode to the rear, and the two Boggs brothers led the way.

As Claudia had predicted, Joanna hadn't yet been allowed to be alone with Harland. There were many questions she wanted to ask him, but her uncle seemed bound and determined to keep them apart.

Joanna turned in her saddle to look back over her shoulder. As she watched the fort fade in the distance, there was a deep ache in her heart that she was leaving everyone she cared about behind.

How long would it be before she would see Tag again? Would Sun Woman and Morning Song believe she had run away? She thought of the tall chief of the Bloods. Would he search for her? She doubted that he would ever find out what had happened to her . . . at least, not for a long time. Sooner or later, Farley would go to Fort Union for supplies, and someone there would tell him that her uncle had taken her back to Philadelphia with him.

When Windhawk returned from the buffalo hunt, would he forget all about her and take Red Bird to his lodge? Again, Joanna felt betrayal and heartbreak. He would never know he was going to be a father. She remembered removing the bear-claw necklace Windhawk had given her—she also remembered telling Windhawk if she ever gave it back to him, it would mean she no longer loved him. She hadn't meant it to happen this way, but perhaps it was for the best.

Howard watched Joanna closely. He noticed that a great change had come over her. Once she would have fought him to the bitter end for her freedom; now she seemed almost passive. It was as if she accepted the fact that he was taking her home. He had always felt exhilarated when the two of them had bandied words in the past. Somehow he almost resented the fact that she had become so submissive. Joanna had been breathtaking when she had challenged him two years ago. Howard had loved the way her violet eyes had sparkled with defiance. He didn't know how to handle her now. She was like a small bird with a broken wing. She was bringing out feelings in him that he had never known he possessed. He would take her home and shower her with kindness. Perhaps, one day, she would begin to bloom again.

Howard shook his head—Joanna wasn't the only one who had changed. He no longer wanted to see her humbled as he once had. He wanted to see her raise her head proudly and defy him or anyone who stood in her way.

His eyes moved to Claudia. He had been acquainted with many types of women in the past, but she was a new breed to him. She was completely devoid of any feeling

144

for anyone except herself. He would know how to handle her when they reached Philadelphia. He refused to have her hanging about his neck like a dead weight.

Howard smiled to himself. Claudia might not feel so smug if she knew how he had rid himself of his first wife, he thought.

Harland Thatcher shifted his weight. He too had sensed the change in Joanna. He wanted to talk to her, but Mr. Landon had thus far kept them apart. He was glad that his army duty was over, so he could return to Philadelphia to be near her. Claudia had told him how they had used him to trick Joanna, and he resented the fact that he had been the bait that had cost Joanna her freedom. Somehow he felt responsible for the plight she was now in. If he hadn't unwittingly sent her uncle to Fort Union, Howard Landon might never have found her.

After his release from the army, Harland had ridden to Fort Union because he had an uneasy feeling about Joanna's Uncle Howard. When he reached the fort, he had found out about her capture. Harland was now more sure than ever that she feared her uncle. He had watched her pull back every time Howard Landon approached her.

Harland felt a deep, burning love for Joanna, and he wanted to reach out to her and give her comfort. Somehow, some way, he had to get her alone so he could talk to her. He would keep a wary eye out and make sure that she came to no harm from her uncle. Harland knew that Claudia hated Joanna, and he would be watching her, as well. He wouldn't put anything past that woman!

Windhawk and Gray Fox waited in the forest for

Farley's return from Fort Union. Windhawk viewed the fort through the thick trees, and his lip curled in contempt. Outside the walls of the fort the land was dotted with tipis of the Assiniboin tribe. The Blackfoot and the Assiniboin had been bitter enemies for many years.

"We must take care, Windhawk. The Assiniboin would like nothing better than to have your scalp dangling from their lance," Gray Fox warned.

Windhawk's eyes moved over the distant tipis. "I have little fear of the Assiniboin. They are as lowly as the dog meat they eat for food," he stated contemptuously.

"What will we do if the old man does not find out anything about Joanna, my chief?"

Windhawk looked down, studying the toe of his moccasin. "If that is the case, I will allow you and the old man to return home. I will never give up hope until I have found her or until I have breathed my last breath."

"Do you think Joanna ran away because of the Piegan woman, Windhawk?"

"Yes."

"Did you not see the trouble you would cause by bringing the Piegan chief's daughter to our village? Joanna does not understand about the double marriages. I know this because she and I have talked about this before."

"I had no intention of making Red Bird my wife. I have told Joanna many times I would take no other wife. She should have believed me instead of that woman. I have never spoken a lie to her!"

"Is it true what Red Bird said about you taking her to your mat?"

"What is true is that she came to me one night when I

146

lay in her father's lodge. I was sleeping, and she lay down beside me."

"Would this make Joanna angry?" Gray Fox asked. "Would she care that you took another to your mat?"

"I did not do the deed. I think her father put her up to coming to me. When I found her beside me, I got up and left the lodge."

"You did not want her?"

"No, I did not want her, and I do not like anyone to think they can trick me."

"What happened after that? Why did you send the woman to our village?"

"The next morning, Yellow Wing said that I took his daughter's innocence from her, and it was right that I make her my wife. I told him I had not touched his daughter, but he said she was shamed in front of her people anyway. I explained to him that I had a wife and wished no other. He asked if I would take her to my village to find a suitable husband for her. I think he believed I would marry her . . . he was wrong."

"What do you intend to do with the Piegan woman? She is trouble, I think."

"I have not decided. When I sent her to your tipi, I did not foresee the trouble she would cause. At the time, I thought only to avoid trouble between the Blackfoots and their brothers, the Piegan."

Gray Fox nodded. "I can see that you did the right thing. Your mistake was in not telling Joanna. What will you do to Joanna if you do find her with the long knife?"

Windhawk's eyes darkened. "First, I shall cut the heart out of the man. Joanna . . . I have not decided what will be her fate."

"My chief, if we do find Joanna, I hope you would hear

what she has to say. This trouble would not have happened had you each talked to the other."

Windhawk's eyes settled on his friend. "I know why you beg for my wife. Do you not think I have seen the way you look at her?"

Gray Fox's eyes didn't waver. "There have never been lies between us, Windhawk. Your woman's beauty and goodness touches my heart, but I would never dishonor you or Joanna by speaking of it to her. I would not say this to you now, but you forced me to."

Windhawk turned his back. "It would seem every man desires my woman. I would slay any man who touches her, be he friend or foe!"

Gray Fox felt his anger rise. "You would say this to me? Have I not been as a brother to you? I would never betray our friendship, and you know this! I think you are a very jealous man, Windhawk. I do not think that a man should accuse his friends falsely!"

Windhawk turned and swept Gray Fox with his dark eyes. "Just remember what I have said. I will have no man look at Joanna with love, not even you, Gray Fox."

"I believe you are not thinking clearly. I will overlook what you have said to me today because I know of your concern for Joanna."

Windhawk flexed his fingers and then doubled them into a fist. His eyes were grief-stricken, and Gray Fox could see that he was suffering.

"Forgive me, Gray Fox. It is true I am not thinking clearly. If I allowed my mind to take over, I would be as crazy as the old man claims to be. I have let a woman do this to me. Never again will I permit anyone to cause this weakness which burns inside me."

At that moment both men heard a rider coming down

the trail. They moved back among the cover of the trees and waited. Several moments passed before they recognized that the intruder was the old trapper.

Farley dismounted and ambled over to Windhawk. "Our search is over! I just found out where Joanna is!" he said, grinning broadly.

"Speak, old man!" Windhawk ordered, unable to curb his impatience.

"It seems she is being taken back to Philadelphia by her uncle and Captain Thatcher."

Windhawk looked confused. "Where will we find this Philadelphia? Where is it?"

"I know which trail they will be traveling. They left but two days ago. We should not have any trouble overtaking them before they reach the first white settlement. I was told there were four men, Joanna, and another woman," Farley replied, feeling happy about the good news he was able to relate to Windhawk.

Joanna was lying on a blanket, watching the mighty Missouri River winding its way across the valley. It wasn't long until sundown. They had been forced to wait until the next day for the barge that would take them across the river.

It would now be less than a week until they reached Independence. Joanna remembered very well when the wagon train she and Tag joined had passed through the streets of Independence. It had been a busy town thronged with trappers, bullwhackers, homesteaders, and mule skinners. It would be the first semblance of civilization as the white man knew it. The people who were traveling West often referred to it as the jumping-off place to the unknown.

Joanna felt neither good nor bad about her plight. She was merely accepting the inevitable. Sometimes, she managed to push thoughts of her life with Windhawk to the back of her mind. It was too painful to remember all that had happened between them. Let the past stay the past, she told herself. What did it matter where she lived? She must put her old life behind her. She couldn't allow herself to think of Windhawk or Tag.

"A king's ransom for your thoughts, Joanna," Harland said, sitting down on the blanket beside her.

"My thoughts aren't even worth a poor man's pittance. I was just watching the river; it has a soothing effect, don't you think?"

"How does it feel to be going home?" he asked, watching her face closely.

She sighed. "It feels like nothing. Philadelphia is no longer my home."

"Joanna, I have been observing the way your uncle treats you. He seems kind and concerned about your well-being. I first had the impression that you feared him, but I see no evidence of fear in you now."

Joanna stared across the river. "It's a strange world we live in, Harland. The ones we love can turn on us, and the ones we fear can become our port in a storm."

"I'm not following you," he replied, puzzled by her statement.

She turned her head and smiled at him. "It doesn't matter; it's not important."

Harland took her hand and raised it to his lips. "I hope you will always think of me as your friend, Joanna. I give you my word . . . I'll never turn on you!"

Her face lit up with a bright smile. "I have always

considered you my friend, Harland."

Suddenly, Harland saw her face pale, and she grabbed her stomach. "Joanna, what's the matter—are you ill?" he asked, reaching out to her.

She started laughing hysterically, and he thought for a moment she was losing her senses. "No, I'm not ill," she said, wiping her eyes on the back of her hand. "It's just my baby. Windhawk will never know that the child he craved so badly will soon be a reality."

Harland felt his heart sink. "You are with child?"

"Oh, yes, I'm very definitely with child."

"Does your uncle know?"

"No one knows but me . . . and now you."

Harland was quiet for a long time. When he spoke, his eyes were shining with an earnest light. "Joanna, I'm sure you will remember I once asked you to become my wife: That offer still stands."

Joanna's soft, violet-colored eyes rested on his face. "It's not possible, Harland. You are, and always will, be my dear friend. I would never put you in the awkward situation of being a father to another man's child."

He took her hand and raised it to his face. "Joanna, I love you. I have never stopped loving you, and I would be proud to be your husband as well as the father of your child. You have only to say yes."

Her hand drifted up to brush against his cheek. "Dear, sweet, Harland . . . don't love me. My love is all used up. I doubt that I will ever know what it feels like to love a man again. In truth, I don't want to."

He could read sadness and disillusionment in her lovely eyes, and he was sorry that she must have suffered a great deal. "Are you saying you no longer love Windhawk?"

151

"I am saying that I have forgotten how to love."

"Who's done this to you, Joanna? Did Windhawk mistreat you in any way?"

"I don't want to talk about me anymore. Tell me, how does it feel to be a civilian again?"

Harland thought it best to go along with her change of mood. "It's too soon to say—as you can see, I am still wearing the uniform."

Suddenly, Joanna stiffened, and Harland thought she had felt the baby again. "He's coming, Harland! I can feel it deep inside. He doesn't want me anymore, but still, he will come!"

"Who's coming, Joanna?"

"Windhawk! My God, I wasn't sure he would come, but I know now he will. We must flee!"

Joanna's uncle heard her raise her voice, and he came over to see what was troubling her. "Have you upset my niece, Captain?" his voice thundered out.

Joanna stood up and grabbed her Uncle Howard's hand. "Please, let's not wait until tomorrow when the barge comes to cross the river. We must go now; he will be here before long." Joanna's voice came out in deep sobs, and Howard shook her, trying to calm her down.

"What in God's name has come over you, Joanna? What are you talking about?"

"Windhawk will come soon, and none of you will escape his vengeance. You don't know him; you can't know what he's capable of!"

Joanna's words caused Howard's eyes to move to the dense tree-lined forest. "How do you know he's coming?" her uncle asked, feeling a prickle of fear like a knot tightening in his stomach.

"I can't explain it," Joanna said, with tears running

down her cheeks. "Just believe what I am saying, and let's leave immediately!"

Howard set her down and knelt beside her. "Joanna, get hold of yourself! We can't leave now—the river is too deep and wide to swim the horses across. If it will make you feel any better, I'll have Chester and Jim stand guard tonight."

Joanna buried her face in her hands. "No one can stop Windhawk. You don't know him like I do . . . you don't know him," she sobbed.

That night, because of Joanna's outburst, everyone felt uneasy. Jim's eyes searched the dark shadows, while his brother's eyes were glued to the shoreline . . . they both wished it was daylight so the barge would come.

Claudia was sitting beside Joanna and, for once, she was strangely quiet, while Howard and Captain Thatcher kept their guns handy.

"What will Windhawk do to us if he comes?" Claudia asked, remembering with horror the Indian raid on the wagon train when her mother and father had been killed.

"I don't know. When he's angry, one cannot anticipate what he might do."

"Did he . . . has Windhawk ever beat you?" Claudia wanted to know.

"No, he won't harm me physically . . . especially when he knows about the baby."

Claudia's mouth gaped open. "Good Lord! You are going to have that savage's baby!" She began to laugh. "Did you hear that, Howard? Your lily-white niece is going to have that heathen Indian's baby! How about you, Captain Thatcher, do you still covet the fair Joanna?"

Howard was on his feet instantly, and he towered over

Joanna. "Is that right? Are you going to have a baby?"

Joanna nodded, watching her uncle's face lose its color. He seemed to be having a hard time digesting what she had told him. Finally, he looked down at her and spoke in a soft voice. "We shall just have to take better care of you, won't we? Had you told me before about the baby, I would have seen that we stopped more often so you could rest."

Joanna was confused by her uncle's attitude. He was different somehow, and she didn't know what to say to him. Before, he had never cared about her comfort or her health.

"My, my! Aren't you the fatherly type, Howard?" Claudia said spitefully. "Perhaps you will want to be grandfatherly to the Indian brat when it's born." Claudia's laughter grated on Howard's nerves, and he gave her a heated glance.

"I'll not have—"

Howard never finished what he was about to say because, at that moment, they heard Jim Boggs let out a bloodcurdling scream!

Chapter Eleven

Windhawk dismounted silently and motioned for Farley to stay with the horses to keep them from making any noise. Moving as quietly as a night shadow, he ducked behind a tree to scan the shoreline. Gray Fox dropped to his knees and parted a bush for a better view.

Windhawk used sign language to point out the two men who were on guard, and Gray Fox nodded in understanding.

Jim Boggs never saw his assailant. A hand reached around him from behind to be clamped over his mouth, silencing him. Windhawk drove his knife into the frightened man's body with no remorse. To him, this man was among the number who had taken Joanna away from him.

Jim Boggs's body slipped to the ground. Windhawk had underestimated the time it would take the enemy to die, however. Removing his hand from the man's mouth, he realized his mistake when the white man screamed out in agony. He knew the scream had alerted the others to his presence.

He and Gray Fox faded into the shadows and watched as Chester Boggs ran toward his horse like a frightened rabbit, bounded onto its back, and rode away into the night. Chester knew Windhawk had found them! Not thinking of his dead brother or caring that he was leaving the others unprotected, he urged his horse to a faster pace. All that was on his mind was escaping Windhawk's wrath!

There was a full moon, and Windhawk's eyes moved to the riverbank where he could clearly see Joanna. His eyes burned with hatred when he saw the long knife push her behind him to protect her and raise his rifle, ready to fire. Windhawk didn't know who the other woman was, but he surmised the heavyset man was Joanna's uncle.

"Harland, run! Save yourself—it's Windhawk!" Joanna cried, knowing that Windhawk would not hesitate to kill Harland, since he had always been jealous of him.

"Stay low, Joanna," Harland warned, as he moved cautiously over to the campfire and kicked dirt on it.

Claudia sank to her knees and clasped her hand over her mouth. Now she was going to die, and it was all Joanna's fault. If she were to die, her last deed would be to cause Joanna's death as well, she thought bitterly. Suddenly, a great calm settled over Claudia. Yes, somehow she would destroy Joanna before she died. Joanna had told her that Windhawk was jealous of Captain Thatcher. She would use that jealousy to destroy Joanna!

Howard Landon hit the ground and began to crawl on his stomach until he reached Joanna. "Get across the river. I'll stay here and hold them off," he told her, raising his rifle and squinting his eyes, trying to see who

156

the attackers were.

Joanna looked at her uncle with a fresh view. He knew he was going to die, and yet his last thoughts were about her safety. He had caused her too much pain for her to forgive his past misdeeds, but Joanna knew she couldn't stand by while Windhawk killed him.

Standing up, she looked toward the forest. "I am here, Windhawk! Let the others go," she called out loudly in the Blackfoot tongue.

Suddenly, Harland was caught from behind, and Joanna spun around to see Windhawk holding a knife at his throat.

"Don't hurt him!" she cried out. "It is me you came after. I will go with you, but allow the others to live!"

"I will drive my knife through the heart of your white lover," Windhawk hissed, applying pressure to the knife. Harland struggled to get free, but he was no match for the formidable Windhawk.

Joanna's Uncle Howard raised his rifle to fire at Windhawk, but before he could take aim he was caught from behind in Gray Fox's vicelike grip.

Joanna walked slowly toward Windhawk. "These people have done you no harm. Allow them to live—I came away with him of my own free will. Are you such a savage that you would punish the innocent?" She could see Windhawk's face very clearly now, and she recognized the murderous glint in his eyes.

Claudia could not understand what Joanna and the Indian were saying to each other, but she watched Windhawk's eyes when he looked at Captain Thatcher and saw the jealousy and hatred that burned in the dark depths. She knew that now might be her only chance to get even with Joanna. Her hatred for Joanna was the uppermost thought in her mind; it took precedence over her fear for her own life. Not only would she get the chance to pay Joanna back for all she had caused her to suffer, but she could get her revenge on Captain Thatcher as well. Claudia only prayed that Windhawk could understand English.

"Joanna, do you plead for Captain Thatcher's life because he is the father of your unborn child?" she called out. Claudia didn't know where her bravery came from when she boldly walked over to Windhawk. When he turned his dark eyes on her, she drew in her breath. Good Lord, he was handsome! she thought. He was like no man she had ever seen before. At the moment, he reminded her of a beautiful savage with all semblance of civilization stripped away. No wonder Joanna loved this man!

His dark eyes raked Claudia's face, and she felt as if her stomach were filled with butterflies.

"What are you saying, white woman?" Windhawk asked in English. He was tensely waiting for her to clarify her statement, hoping he had misunderstood her meaning.

Joanna could see what Claudia was doing, and she held up a warning hand to stop her. Didn't she realize that if Windhawk believed her lies, he would not hesitate for a moment to kill Captain Thatcher?

"Joanna told me she was weary of living with the Indians," Claudia said, giving Joanna a vicious smile. "She wanted to go back to her home, where her and Captain Thatcher's child will be born. Would you be so cruel as to kill the father of Joanna's baby?"

Windhawk was silent for a long moment—suddenly, a loud animal sound ripped from his throat! Joanna saw his hand tighten on the hilt of the knife, and she gasped, watching him raise the knife over his head. She rushed forward and threw herself against him. Windhawk pushed her out of the way, and his eyes burned into hers with unleashed fury.

Everything seemed to happen at once. Joanna's uncle grabbed his heart and went limp in Gray Fox's arms. Windhawk brought the hilt of his knife down on Harland's head, and Joanna grabbed Windhawk's arm. Harland crumpled at Joanna's feet as Windhawk stared at Joanna coldly.

"Kill her! Kill her!" Claudia screamed, running around like a madwoman.

Windhawk's eyes moved to the white woman, then back to Joanna. "If I slay this man, do I kill the father of your baby, Joanna?" he asked in English.

Joanna was afraid that in Windhawk's state of mind he wouldn't believe her. He would kill Harland in an instant if he believed Claudia's lies.

"No," she said, sinking down to her knees.

"She lies!" Claudia screamed. "She lies to save her lover's life. Joanna told me she was going to have Captain Thatcher's baby!"

Suddenly, the air seemed thick, and the only sound that could be heard was Windhawk's heavy breathing.

Joanna raised her head and stared into his dark eyes. "Kill me, Windhawk, but allow him to live. I am the one you hate," she said calmly.

She watched Windhawk slowly raise the hand he held the knife in. Joanna saw blood on his hand and knew that he had already killed tonight. She felt no fear as the knife began to descend toward her. She did regret that she would die with a lie between her and Windhawk.

Gray Fox leaped across the space that divided him from

Windhawk and grabbed his arm. "No! Do not act in haste, my chief! Do not do this thing tonight that will tear your heart out tomorrow!"

There was a power struggle between Windhawk and Gray Fox. Joanna could see the muscles of both men's arms were strained to the limit. Suddenly Windhawk wrenched his arm free of Gray Fox's grip and threw the knife down. It landed right in front of Joanna.

"Bring her along," he said, turning his back and walking off into the night.

Joanna hadn't realized that she was crying until she felt the tears on her face. Windhawk had believed Claudia instead of her. She crawled over to Harland and lifted his head onto her lap.

She did not hear Windhawk return until he jerked her upward. "You will wish many times I had killed you tonight, Joanna," he said, pulling her along behind him.

Joanna remembered another time two years ago when Windhawk had spoken those words to her. On that occasion, they had proven to be true. She knew she would receive no mercy from him, but at least it seemed he was going to allow the others to live.

When they reached the horses, Joanna saw that Farley was waiting for them. He had saddled Fosset and now helped her onto the animal's back.

"I'm mighty glad to see you, Joanna," he said in English.

"Pray that you can still say that in the morning," she answered in Blackfoot.

The four of them rode off into the night. Windhawk was in the lead, and he didn't once look back at Joanna.

Was this some kind of nightmare? What would her life

be like from now on? Apparently, Windhawk had believed Claudia when she had told him she was carrying Harland's baby. When he found out she was indeed expecting a child, he would never believe it was his. How would she ever convince him that Claudia hated her and would do anything to see her suffer? Perhaps it would be futile even to try. When the child was born, he would then know he was the father.

For now Joanna had much to be grateful for. She had feared that Windhawk would kill Harland right before her eyes. No one knew better than she did how fortunate Harland, Claudia, and her uncle were to be alive. She knew that Windhawk could easily have killed them all in his present state of mind.

She felt numb, knowing she would receive no mercy from him.

They rode well into the night and didn't stop to make camp until almost daylight. Joanna was so tired that she slumped down on the grass and fell asleep.

She was unaware that Windhawk stood over her. His burning eyes moved over her body, then came to rest on her face. Napi had given Joanna the face of an angel, he thought, but her heart was false and deceitful. She had the power to make a man think she loved only him. How easily she could rip a man's heart out! Had she lain in the arms of the long knife and professed to love him?

It made him angry that he still felt pain in his heart at her betrayal. He would wait to see if Joanna was with child. If she was, she would know about the fury she had awakened inside him.

"Joanna don't look like she's been hurt none," Farley remarked in English.

161

"If you are speaking to me, do not speak in the language of the white man," Windhawk said, turning away. He moved out of view and spread his blanket on the grass. He was too tired to think, and he needed sleep.

Farley folded up a blanket, tenderly placing it under Joanna's head. She was so sound asleep she didn't even stir. His heart went out to her, knowing what she must be feeling. Shaking his head, he then went over to sit beside Gray Fox. Since he had stayed with the horses, he didn't know what had taken place the night before.

"I thought when Windhawk got Joanna back, they would be happy to see each other. What happened?"

"The other white woman told Windhawk that Joanna was with child, and the father was the long knife."

"What white woman?"

"How should I know, old man?" Gray Fox said, rolling up in his blanket and turning his back.

"I hope Windhawk didn't believe such a lie. Joanna would never have . . ."

"Go to sleep, old man! It does not matter what you and I believe—Windhawk will decide what he thinks the truth is for himself."

"Do you believe it?"

Gray Fox turned over and allowed his eyes to travel over Joanna's face. "No, Joanna would never do such a thing to Windhawk. I do not believe the white woman."

"Neither do I," Farley said, to no one in particular. "Neither do I."

Joanna didn't stir and was unaware that she slept all that day and on into the night.

*   *   *

162

Bertram Shipley watched his barge bump against the shore. Seeing that he had three passengers to ferry across, he thought he would receive a good fare, since they seemed well-dressed.

Tying the lead rope to a post, he noticed two men and one woman—one of the men was a soldier, and the other appeared to be ill.

"Morning. You folks been waiting long?" he asked, stepping ashore. His eyes ran over the pretty blond woman with approval before coming to rest on the captain.

"You folks traveling far?" he wanted to know.

Captain Thatcher led the horses forward and handed the reins to the man. "I'm afraid we will need your help. One of our guides was killed and the other ran off. Mr. Landon seems to have suffered some sort of stroke, and I have suffered a head wound."

"What happened here?" Bertram asked, noticing that the bandage tied about the captain's head was blood-soaked.

"Good Lord, man! Don't you see I don't have time to pass the time of day with you? The Indians might take it in their mind to return," Harland said, staggering forward to lean on the landing post for support.

That was the only prompting Bertram needed. He helped the army captain onto the barge, and then helped the woman carry the other man onboard.

As the barge pulled away, Bertram watched the shore. "We don't get many Indians 'round here. Ifen we do, they's usually friendly."

"You ever heard of an Indian named Windhawk?" Claudia asked.

163

"Sure, ain't everybody? He ain't real, though. Just someone the Blackfoot cooked up out of their imagination. Wishful thinking on their part, I 'spect."

"It wasn't wishful thinking that did this to my husband and Captain Thatcher and killed one of our guides. You can tell your grandchildren that you once ferried some folks across in your barge that met Windhawk," Claudia informed him.

Howard Landon groaned and opened his eyes, trying to remember what had happened. Claudia sat quietly, with her husband's head resting on her lap. The right side of Howard's body seemed to be paralyzed, and when he tried to speak, it was unintelligible.

Claudia smiled down at him. "Don't fret none, Howard. I'll take care of you. Think of it, there will be just you and me in that big house. 'Course, I'll see that you are kept quite comfortable." Her hand brushed his forehead. "I wouldn't want anything to happen to you, because if it did, then I'd be out in the cold, wouldn't I?"

Howard watched her eyes glaze over. "Yes, I will see that you get the best of care."

Howard thought she must be mad. Was this God's punishment to him—that he must spend the rest of his days paralyzed and at the mercy of a deranged woman? He had been unconscious when Joanna had been taken, and he couldn't make Claudia understand that he wanted to know what had happened to her.

Claudia was smiling to herself. Oh, had she fixed Joanna! How long would Windhawk make her suffer before he realized that it was his child she was carrying?

In her mind, Claudia began to plan all the things she would do when she got to Philadelphia. She would hire a nurse to look after Howard. She didn't know much about the law, but she doubted that if Howard died she would be allowed to stay on in Joanna's house.

Howard had said that he didn't receive much money from the estate, but what he thought wasn't much money would be a fortune to her. If she had planned her future herself, she couldn't have made it turn out any better.

I've got it all, she thought happily. Oh, Joanna, you have nothing, and I have everything! She remembered the handsome savage she had seen last night. He had been like a magnificent animal wreaking revenge on his enemies. She felt a thrill go through her body and wondered what it would feel like to have Windhawk love her as much as he loved Joanna.

Claudia glanced down at her husband and found him watching her. Did she really have all she wanted? Would she be able to forget that, from now on, everything she would have would really belong to Joanna? Somewhere deep inside it bothered her that she would soon be living in Joanna's house, waited on by Joanna's servants, and eating Joanna's food.

She felt a prickle of uncertainty. One day, in the not too distant future, Tag would grow up and come to Philadelphia. What would she do then? She shook her head. Tag was still just a boy; it would be a long time until he would be old enough to challenge her or Howard. Still, a feeling of uneasiness moved over Claudia's consciousness—she knew that someday she would have to face Tag and Joanna.

Howard tried to speak again. He wanted to know what had happened to Joanna, but no one seemed to understand him. He felt cut off from everything and everyone, as if he were living in a waking nightmare. Why wouldn't someone tell him what was going on? Why couldn't he move? What had happened to him? He felt Claudia's hand on his forehead, and his eyes locked with hers. He shivered at the gleam in her eyes.

"Don't worry, Howard. As I told you, I will take very good care of you when we reach Philadelphia!"

Chapter Twelve

Joanna seemed to be in a daze as she rode silently beside Farley. Windhawk was taking her back to the Blackfoot village, whether she wanted to go or not. Farley kept watching her out of the corner of his eyes, wondering what she was thinking. He was puzzled by her strange mood. There were many questions he wanted to ask her, but the fast pace they were traveling at limited their conversation.

Joanna glanced up and saw Farley watching her with a quizzical expression on his face. She could tell he was worried about her, and she gave him a reassuring smile.

Later in the afternoon, Windhawk called a halt. He ordered Joanna and Farley to remain hidden in the forest, while he and Gray Fox rode away.

Joanna watched them until they disappeared, wondering where they were going. After Farley secured the horses, he ambled over to her and leaned against the tree she was sitting beneath. He gave her a questioning glance.

"I didn't run away, Farley," she told him, knowing

that must be what he thought.

"I figured you didn't. Wanna talk about it?"

"No, not yet. I don't even want to think about it. Perhaps, in a few days, I will talk to you about what happened."

"I'm just gonna ask you one thing, then. Was you mistreated in any way?" he asked.

Joanna leaned her head back against the tree trunk. "No, nothing like that. I am just getting tired of so many people trying to run my life. My uncle thinks he has the right to take me back to Philadelphia; Windhawk thinks he has the right to take me back to the Blackfoot village. Just once, I wish someone would ask me what I wanted to do."

Farley was quiet as he studied her face. "I'm askin'. Whatcha wanna do?"

Joanna sighed heavily and closed her eyes. "I don't know, Farley. Right now, I just don't know."

"Sometimes I 'spect you gotta stand up for what you want, Joanna."

Opening her eyes, she smiled at the old trapper fondly. "You have seen Windhawk's mood. Would you suggest I stand up to him?"

Farley chewed on his lip thoughtfully. "Sometimes I 'spect you oughta back off."

Joanna laughed for the first time in days. She adored Farley and his sharp wit. "I 'spect your right," she mimicked him playfully.

Farley glanced up at the sun to gauge the time of day. "I'm wondering ifen Windhawk and Gray Fox will be gone long. I don't much like the idea of them being out in the open in broad daylight," Farley said.

"Why?"

"'Cause we're crossing into Sioux territory. That group of warriors we seed this morning was Sioux. That's why Windhawk wants us to hide out here while he and Gray Fox do some scouting on ahead to make sure them Sioux has left the vicinity."

Joanna's face whitened. "Are we in danger?"

"Only ifen them Sioux find us. They wouldn't take too kindly to us intruding on their territory. You don't need to worry none, though. Windhawk ain't 'bout to take no unnecessary chances with you along," Farley told her confidently.

The day wore on. When Windhawk and Gray Fox finally returned, it was late afternoon. Without a word, Windhawk motioned for Joanna and Farley to mount up, and soon they were on their way again.

Windhawk had not spoken one word to Joanna since he had taken her four days earlier. He drew rein and pulled back to ride beside her now. She glanced over at him and thought how unbending his attitude seemed. His face was an expressionless mask.

He must have felt her eyes on him, for he turned his head and stared at her for only a moment before looking away again. Joanna saw the unleashed fury in the depth of his eyes. It was all too apparent from his attitude that he believed she had allowed Harland to make love to her, and it angered her. How could he believe such a thing about her? If he was too stubborn to ask the questions that were troubling him, then she would volunteer no answers!

They were riding in open country, and suddenly Windhawk pulled up his horse and motioned for the others to do likewise. Joanna looked around, trying to determine the reason he had stopped. Off to her left she

169

could see a dust cloud, and she thought it might be the group of Sioux Farley had told her about.

"We are too open here . . . we will ride for that distant plateau. I do not think they have seen us yet," Windhawk said, turning Puh Pom and urging him back the way they had come.

Joanna bent low on Fosset's back, and when they reached the rocky incline she dismounted and led her horse up to the top of the plateau.

Farley gathered up the reins of the horses and led them out of sight behind some scrub bushes. Windhawk and Gray Fox lay down on their stomachs and crawled over to the edge of the cliff, peering down.

Farley motioned for Joanna to get down, and she fell quickly to her knees. She could feel the tension in the air as she watched the dust cloud drawing nearer.

"They have picked up our trail," Windhawk said. "It will not be long until our tracks will lead them straight to us."

Joanna estimated there were more than twenty Sioux warriors. She watched as two of them dismounted and studied the ground, knowing Windhawk was right.

Gray Fox knelt down beside Joanna, and she looked questioningly into his face. "What will they do to us, Gray Fox?" she asked fearfully.

"I do not know, Joanna," he replied. "The Sioux are our old enemies. There are far too many of them for us to make a fight."

Windhawk stood up and motioned for Farley. "Old man, it will not be long until the enemy is upon us. I will try to stall them as long as I can, but if I should fail in that, you must be prepared to take Joanna and ride hard until you reach the forest. Go down the back way; it will

170

be your only chance of escape."

Joanna scrambled to her feet. "Windhawk, do not do this! They will kill you!" she cried.

His eyes rested on her face for just a moment, then he glanced away. "If that is so, then you can return to your white lover," he whispered harshly.

She felt as if he had dismissed her from his mind when he turned to Farley. "Do not let the Sioux take her alive," he said pointedly.

Joanna was stunned by his cruel words. Would he face death with this terrible misunderstanding between them? She had to try one more time to reach him.

"Windhawk, why can we not all ride down the back of the hill and try to get away? You said yourself that would be our only chance."

Windhawk seemed to look right through her, and she knew in that moment that he would be buying time for her to get away. Reaching out, she laid her hand on his shoulder.

"Please, Windhawk, come with us!"

He stared down at her hand for a moment, then pushed her roughly away. "I charge you with her safety, old man. Put her on Puh Pom, since he is the swiftest," he said, turning away.

Joanna wanted to go to him and beg him not to do this thing. She wanted to tell him that there was a wall of lies between them and that she still loved him, but his cold indifference sealed her lips.

Farley took her by the hand and led her toward the horses. She was already up on Puh Pom's back before she realized she could never leave Windhawk. How could she just ride away when there were so many misunder-standings between them?

171

She heard Farley utter an oath when she leaped from the horse's back and ran toward the edge of the plateau. She was too late! Windhawk had already started down the slope toward the group of waiting Sioux warriors.

Gray Fox pulled Joanna down beside him and gave her a heated glance. "Windhawk will be angry that you did not obey him, Joanna. It is still not to late to flee!"

"I won't go, and you can't make me leave Windhawk!" she cried in English.

Gray Fox studied her a moment and then nodded. "I do not understand you, Joanna. Did you not leave Windhawk before when he wanted you to stay? Why do you stay now when he wants you to go?"

Joanna didn't bother to answer. She was watching Windhawk make his way down to the enemy. She noticed that the Sioux had their faces painted, and she couldn't help shivering. Some of them had their lances aimed at Windhawk, while others had drawn their bows.

Farley crawled over to Joanna and raised his rifle. He would have no more than one shot, and she knew that wouldn't save Windhawk's life.

How proud and unafraid her love carried himself! Joanna thought. No one but Windhawk would go to meet death instead of allowing it to come to him.

"Will they kill him? Isn't there something we can do to help him?" she asked through trembling lips.

"Shh, let's see what happens," Farley said as Windhawk's voice carried to them.

"Brothers of the great Sioux nation, I am Windhawk, chief of the Blood Blackfoot. As you see, I have come not to war on you but merely to cross your lands."

One of the men raised his hand in greeting and dismounted. "I have heard of the great, powerful Chief

172

Windhawk—your many brave deeds have reached my ears. Why do you cross the land of the Sioux?"

"My woman was taken by the white eyes—I could do no less than follow them to get her back."

"Did you meet the white eyes in battle?"

"Yes."

"Did you reclaim your woman?"

Windhawk hesitated. "Yes."

"It is good. Too many of the white eyes come to our lands. They search for the gold in our sacred mountains. I will not take your life this day. I have too much respect for the great Windhawk to slay you without even odds. Take your woman and go in peace. Do not again come to the land of the Sioux. Tell this to all your brothers to the south."

Joanna felt relief wash over her. Windhawk had faced his enemies unafraid and, in doing so, had won their respect. They weren't going to harm him! She turned tear-bright eyes to Farley, and he shook his head.

"I'll be damned, he's done 'er! Guess this'll just be one more thing to add to the legend of Windhawk."

Windhawk's voice reached them once more. "When I tell my people of this meeting with you, what name shall I call you by?"

"I am called Sitting Bull of the Hunkpapa Sioux. There will be many in my lodge this night who will speak of my meeting with Windhawk."

The two men stared into each other's eyes with shared admiration—then they clasped arms in farewell.

"If all our red brothers were wise, Sitting Bull, they would bury their anger with one another and concentrate on their common enemy, the white eyes."

"That is true, Windhawk; it is a pity this will not

happen in my lifetime or yours. Perhaps our children will be wiser than we are."

Windhawk nodded his head. "It will be too late then, my friend—the whites will already have overrun us."

"It is so," Sitting Bull said, turning away to mount his horse. Windhawk watched the Sioux warriors ride away before he climbed back up the hill.

When Windhawk saw that Joanna and Farley had not gone as he had ordered them to, his dark eyes showed his displeasure. Joanna was still sitting on the ground staring at him when he gathered up his horse's reins and led him down the steep incline. Knowing it was not wise to anger Windhawk further, she got to her feet and followed him.

That night was the first time Windhawk allowed them to light a campfire. Farley had killed two rabbits, and they were now roasting on a spit. Windhawk had gone off into the woods, and Joanna was glad to be relieved of his disturbing presence for a while. When he was near, she could feel the coldness he directed toward her.

She sat down on a blanket, lost in her own misery. How long would this wall of silence exist between her and Windhawk? Sooner or later, she knew they would have to talk. She was determined Windhawk would come to her, because she certainly wasn't going to go to him! She had done nothing wrong, and she wasn't going to act guilty just to appease his anger.

Gray Fox saw Joanna's misery and wanted to go to her and speak words of comfort, but he dared not. He had never seen Windhawk in such a quiet mood before, and he wasn't sure what to expect.

Farley ambled over to Joanna and offered her a portion of the rabbit. "You haven't eat much lately . . . we don't want you getting sick, now do we?"

174

Joanna took the meat and bit into it, more to please Farley than out of hunger. "What do you think will happen to me when we get home, Farley?"

"I can't say, Joanna. That depends on how mad Windhawk is."

"He has no reason to be angry. It is I who have suffered, not him."

"Well, I don't rightly think he seed it just that way. You and me knowed you didn't go running off, but he thinks you did." Farley looked into her eyes. "Tell me, Joanna, just what did happen?"

"I don't know where to start. You know about the letter I received from Captain Thatcher?"

"Yep, I knowed 'bout that."

"As it turned out, it wasn't from Harland at all, but from my uncle. Stranger than that, Farley, my uncle is now married to Claudia Maxwell, and she helped him scheme to get me and Tag back."

Farley whistled through his teeth. "I don't knowed your uncle, but seems he woulda been better off marrying up with a scorpion."

"You don't know the worst of it. Claudia told Windhawk that I was carrying Harland's baby, and he believed her! You know how spiteful Claudia is. She would do anything to hurt me. What makes me mad is that Windhawk took her word against mine—not once has he come to me and asked if it's true."

Farley shook his head. "That woman can't knowed the trouble she started."

"Oh, she knew all right, Farley. Claudia always knows what she's doing."

"Well, her lie can't last fer long. Windhawk will soon knowed that you ain't gonna have no baby."

"That's where you're wrong, Farley. I knew I was going to have Windhawk's baby before I was ever taken captive by the Boggs brothers."

Farley's shrewd eyes fastened on Joanna's face. "It 'pears to me the thing for you to do would be to tell Windhawk the truth."

"Why should I? He wouldn't believe me, anyway. Besides, I don't care what he thinks." Joanna picked up a fallen leaf and ran a delicate finger across its smooth surface.

"Have you heard about Red Bird, Farley?"

Farley lowered his eyes but not before Joanna saw the truth in them. "One can hear lots of things . . . that don't make them true. You oughta know that."

A shadow fell across Joanna's face as someone walked between her and the campfire. She glanced up to see Windhawk standing over her.

"I will speak to Joanna alone, old man," he said.

Farley gave Joanna an encouraging smile before he got up and ambled away.

The time had come! she thought in a panic. Windhawk was ready to talk. She wasn't aware that she was plucking at her skirt nervously.

"Come," he said. "We will walk."

Joanna suddenly realized she was still holding the uneaten portion of meat and laid it aside. Getting to her feet, she followed Windhawk into the woods. For some reason, she was feeling apprehensive. How could they solve all that had gone wrong between them? She was still hurt because he had brought Red Bird into the village and angry because he had believed the worst about her.

Windhawk was some distance ahead of her, and Joanna had to run to catch up. There had been a time in the past when he had slowed his pace to match hers. Now it seemed he was unwilling to walk beside her.

Windhawk came to a fallen log and stopped, motioning for her to be seated. Joanna automatically obeyed.

There was a long, uncomfortable silence—Joanna refused to look up at Windhawk, but she felt his dark gaze burning into her and knew he was watching her closely.

"I have heard it said, when one is guilty of dishonor, he cannot look into the face of the person he has shamed," Windhawk accused.

Joanna's head snapped up, and she purposely allowed her eyes to fuse to his. "That must *not* be true, because you do not look away from me!" she retorted.

His expression didn't change. "Do you play games with me, Joanna?"

"No, I am dead serious. Who would dare play games with the all-knowing Windhawk?"

"You insult me . . . and I will not speak to you if you talk in the white man's tongue."

"You will have to forgive me, oh mighty one—you see, that was the language I was born into. If it offends you, so be it!" she deliberately replied in English.

He ignored her outburst, giving her the look of indulgence that one would bestow on a rebellious child. "First, I will ask you one thing. Do not speak falsely or I shall know it. Are you with child?"

Joanna closed her eyes for just a moment, wishing she could blurt out that she was now carrying the child he had wanted so badly.

Windhawk mistook her silence for an admission of guilt. "I see. You do not have to answer my question. You are with child."

She raised her head proudly. "Yes, I am going to have

177

a baby."

"Did you lay with the long knife?" This was said in a painful whisper.

Joanna felt her anger climb. "Do you dare ask this of me after you took Red Bird to your mat?"

His eyes narrowed to tiny slits. "Did you do this thing with the long knife because you wanted to punish me for sending Red Bird to my village?"

Joanna was so angry she was shaking all over. "You can think what you will. I shall no longer talk to you. What I do not know is why you came after me in the first place. Why did you not just leave me alone?"

He reached out and drew her up beside him. "I wonder that myself," he hissed. His grip was like a vice, and his face was so near hers she could feel his breath on her cheek.

He didn't tell her that his heart had been ripped apart when he had heard that she was carrying another man's child. He had been in torment the last few days, fearing to ask her about the long knife. Now she stood before him as if she had been the one betrayed.

"I know the Blackfoot custom of cutting off the nose of a woman who has taken a lover over her husband. Perhaps you will want to have that done to me."

Windhawk shoved her away from him. "I will speak to you no more. To me . . . you are dead!"

Joanna clenched her hands tightly together. "Does this mean I am free to go?"

"Go from my sight. I no longer want to look upon your face."

Joanna straightened her back. "I'm sure Farley would . . . take me to the nearest army outpost."

Windhawk grabbed her arm. "You will go nowhere! I

178

shall no longer look upon your face, but you will return with me to my village. You shall move into my mother's lodge, but do not ever seek me out for any reason."

Joanna could feel a sob rising up inside her. "Why are you doing this to me, Windhawk?"

"Leave me in peace," he said, before stalking off into the night.

Joanna bit her lip to keep from crying out to him. How easily he had cast love aside when he took Red Bird. Joanna knew she had no choice but to return to the Blackfoot village. She would be forced to watch Windhawk and Red Bird together.

"I cannot bear this," she said, leaning against the trunk of a tree. It was clear that Windhawk hated the sight of her. Had his love for the Indian woman wiped out the love they had shared?

"I will never allow Windhawk or anyone else to see my pain," she moaned. At that moment, she felt the child within her body move, and it brought tears to her eyes. Poor little baby, she thought; your father doesn't want me, and he will not claim you, either.

Windhawk stood overlooking the valley they would descend into the next day. He felt an urgency to reach his village so he could be rid of Joanna. He wanted to put some distance between them. Even now, he felt a weakness within him. He wanted to go to her and take her in his arms, to feel the silken texture of her skin. Joanna had a hold on his heart that even her deceitfulness couldn't loosen. She had as much as admitted that she was going to have the long knife's baby. He closed his eyes, wishing he had driven his knife into the white man when he had the chance.

He would have sworn that Joanna had loved him! Could he have been so mistaken? He was in no mood to face her again tonight. He needed some time to think.

Joanna, Joanna, he thought in agony. Why do I still want you? He raised his face to the star-bright night. Why can I not let you go?

Chapter Thirteen

Farley noticed Joanna was unusually quiet when she returned to camp. He watched her curl up on her blanket and turn away from the fire.

The old man got up and kicked dirt on the campfire. Spreading his blanket out, he sat down on it and gazed up at the stars. He loved Joanna and didn't like seeing her so unhappy. He was beginning to think it would have been better if Windhawk hadn't found her.

Farley thought of what his life had been like before Joanna and Tag had come into it. He had only a vague memory of his own youth. He had lived in a small coastal town in New Jersey with his mother and stepfather. Farley had never known his own father and had never cared much for his stepfather. He had been twelve when his mother had died. The day after her death, he had decided he would light out on his own. He had always had a hankering for the wilderness, so he had headed West.

He grew up fast in the Indian territory, and had soon learned, if he were going to survive, that he would have to be smarter than the Indians. That was when he decided

181

that he would make the Indians believe he was crazy, knowing they would never harm anyone they thought touched by the spirits. More than once he had saved his life by acting the fool. Once he had convinced the Indians he was touched in the head, he had been allowed to move freely over their land. He had made a good living by trapping on Indian land, since he was allowed to go to places that were denied to the other trappers.

Farley had lived a solitary life until his twenty-ninth year. That was when he had taken She Who Sings as his wife. She had been a young Blackfoot maiden, and they had been happy together for twenty years. They had had no children.

After She Who Sings had died, Farley wandered the wilderness, trapping just enough to get by. His only thought had been to survive. That had changed after Joanna and Tag came into his life. He remembered the first time he had seen Joanna and Tag. They had been traveling with a wagon train, and had seemed to stand out among the other travelers. He remembered thinking that day that he had never seen anyone as fair as Joanna James. When he came to know her, he admired her goodness and spirit. He stayed around the Blackfoot village just to be near her and Tag, sort of an unofficial grandfather.

Farley liked and admired the young chief of the Bloods, but, like everyone else, he knew no one dared cross Windhawk. Farley had once been on the receiving end of Windhawk's anger, and he knew that had it not been for Joanna's intervention that day he would now be walking among the spirits.

He couldn't believe Windhawk would ever take Red Bird for his wife. Surely, deep down, he would know that

Joanna must know that, too. He didn't know how this thing would turn out between Joanna and Windhawk, but he would just hang around and find out. He had gone against Windhawk once before for Joanna's sake and, if he had to, he would do it again.

Joanna slept fretfully that night. Each time she awoke, she noticed that Windhawk wasn't lying on his blanket. He didn't return to camp all night, and she wondered where he could be. She had no way of knowing that he was spending a sleepless night, agonizing over their relationship.

Before sunrise the next morning, when they were ready to move out, Windhawk suddenly appeared. He spoke to no one as he waited for them to mount their horses.

Farley couldn't help but notice that not once did Windhawk look in Joanna's direction. There was bad trouble between them, the old trapper reckoned. He caught Gray Fox's eye and realized that the young warrior realized it also.

The scenery was becoming more familiar to Joanna, and she knew they were nearing the Blackfoot village. She dreaded this homecoming more than she had realized. Windhawk had told her she would be staying with his mother. Did that mean Red Bird had already moved into his lodge?

Glancing over at Windhawk, she saw the scowl on his face. She would live with Sun Woman and Morning Song until her baby was born. She would look the other way whenever Windhawk passed by with his new wife, but she wouldn't spend the rest of her days as a forgotten

woman in the Blackfoot village. As soon as her baby was
born, she would decide what would be the best thing for
her to do.

The only happy part of her return would be seeing Tag
again, she thought. She had no idea how Windhawk's
mother and sister would feel about her homecoming.
Would they believe that she had run away, as Windhawk
did?

When they topped a hill, Joanna pulled Fosset to a halt
and gazed down upon the mighty Missouri River that
stretched on as far as the eye could see. Through the
woods she could see the village nestled on the bank of the
river. There was no joy in her heart that she had come
home as she nudged her horse forward to descend the
hill.

Windhawk rode just ahead of Joanna. She noticed how
stiff and rigid he held his back. He looked so magnificent
with his black hair rippling in the wind.

Her heart cried out at the injustice of his accusations.
He hadn't wanted to hear anything she had to tell him. In
believing Claudia's lies, he had justified his reasons for
taking Red Bird. Not that he needed any justification; he
was free to take as many wives as he chose under
Blackfoot law. He could fill his lodge with a dozen
women, she thought, but she would not be one of them!

Joanna tried not to remember the love they had once
shared. She battled within herself to push aside the
memory of how she had felt when he touched her. His
declarations of love had all been a farce. When he had
sworn eternal love to her and told her he would never
take another woman as his wife, he had only been trying
to appease her. Or perhaps he had meant it at the time.
She would fight within herself to be rid of this deep

184

longing she felt to return to the life they had once shared. In time, she would forget that she had ever been Windhawk's woman, but right now all she could think of was how much she loved him.

She watched Windhawk enter the river at a shallow spot, and she moved forward. No, she reminded herself honestly, she could never forget Windhawk. The baby she carried would be a constant reminder of the love she and Windhawk had shared a lifetime ago.

Sun Woman welcomed her into her tipi with open arms. When she learned that Joanna was having a baby, she could hardly contain her joy and rushed about the village telling everyone she would soon be a grand-mother.

Joanna had been back in the Blackfoot village for three weeks. She hadn't seen Windhawk since the first day they had come home. Sun Woman told her that he had rejoined his warriors in the buffalo hunt. Tag had not yet returned to the village, and Joanna was anxious to see him.

No one bothered to ask Joanna whether she had run away on the night she disappeared. The Blackfoot always accepted people for what they were and rarely pried into others' private affairs.

Morning Song had helped her move all her belongings into Sun Woman's tipi. It had been a painful ordeal for Joanna when she had gone to Windhawk's lodge to pack her clothing. She tried not to think about the times Windhawk had held her in his arms and made her body come alive with his lovemaking. She refused to look at the bed of buffalo robes where they had spent so much time in each other's arms. She was glad when the last article of clothing had been packed and she was able to leave the place where she had known such happiness. She was grateful because, if Windhawk had taken Red Bird as his wife, at least, she hadn't yet moved into his lodge. She was not yet ready to come face to face with the Piegan woman.

For the first few days after returning to the Blackfoot village, Joanna had wanted to remain inside Sun Woman's tipi. She knew it would be very difficult facing her friends' sorrowful glances. Would they pity her when they found out Windhawk had cast her aside? She finally realized that one couldn't hide from life forever. She would have to face her friends sooner or later. When, at last, she found the courage to go among the people, she discovered that they eagerly welcomed her back, and no one referred to the fact that she was no longer living with Windhawk. Joanna felt somewhat relieved when she learned that Red Bird had still not moved into Windhawk's lodge. Of course, she realized it would probably be only a matter of time until Windhawk took Red Bird as his wife.

Joanna walked beside the river, watching it lap against the shore. Looking upward at the branches of a cottonwood tree, she noticed the leaves had begun to change colors. Her mind drifted back to another autumn. She and Windhawk had made love beneath the trees while the brightly colored leaves had drifted down all about them.

Several times she had seen Red Bird, but only at a distance. So far she had been successful in avoiding an encounter with her.

Joanna felt as if her life were going nowhere; she was but waiting for the passing of time. In the daytime she kept busy by helping Sun Woman and Morning Song, but at night, when she lay on her mat alone, her mind would drift back to happier times—the times when she lay in the arms of the tall, handsome chief and felt his love reach out to her. Those times were gone forever, and Joanna realized she would soon have to look to the future.

She knew the time was drawing near when the tribe would be moving to their winter camp beside the Milk River. The winter location was the place she really thought of as her home. It was there among the Sweet Grass Hills that she had first become Windhawk's wife.

By now, Joanna's stomach was beginning to gently swell with the baby she was carrying. She looked forward to the time when the baby would be born, so she could decide what to do about her future. So far, she couldn't make any plans. In the back of her mind she knew she was merely waiting for Tag to return so she could discuss it with him.

Her father's servant, Simon, was still waiting for her and Tag in Philadelphia. If Windhawk would allow her to leave, perhaps she, Tag, and the baby would go there. Joanna could sell the rest of her mother's jewels, and she and Tag could get a small place in the country.

"It was on a day very much like this one that you first came to us, Flaming Hair."

Joanna turned around to find the old medicine woman standing just behind her. "It is good to see you, She Who Heals. You were not here when I returned, my friend, and I have missed you."

187

The old, wrinkled-faced woman sat down and motioned for Joanna to sit beside her. "I have been in the mountains gathering berries and herbs to make my cures. This is the season when the berries are at their best."

Joanna sat beside the old woman, noticing how tired and frail she looked. "You should not go into the mountains alone, She Who Heals. Next time you need to go, tell me, and I will go with you." Joanna loved She Who Heals and was concerned because she was getting too old for the long expeditions she took into the mountains.

"I am an old woman, and if it comes my time to walk among the spirits, it will happen wherever I am."

Joanna smiled. "Has anyone told you that you are a stubborn woman?"

The old woman nodded in agreement. "When one reaches my age, one can do as one pleases and not worry about what others expect of one."

Joanna patted the gnarled hand. "Something tells me you did not have to reach this age to do as you wanted. I would guess you have always had your own way!"

The old woman's crackling laughter rang out. "I might say the same for you, Flaming Hair. You have our young chief dangling by a rawhide rope."

"Not so, She Who Heals. I have cut all my ties with your chief."

The old woman looked deep into Joanna's eyes. "Does he know about the child you carry?"

Joanna returned She Who Heals's scrutiny. "Yes, Windhawk knows about the baby."

"Why, then, are you not in Windhawk's lodge making ready for his return?"

Joanna's eyes flamed. "Let Red Bird cook and clean for him! I will not!"

"Windhawk waited many summers before he took a wife. He chose you—I do not think he will take the Piegan woman to him. Have I not seen him happy with you as his woman? Did I not see his sorrow and rage when he thought you had run away from him? I know Windhawk very well, and I do not believe he would ever take the Piegan woman to his mat."

"You are wrong, She Who Heals. Windhawk has already been with her."

"Many men lie with a woman . . . it does not mean he will take that woman as his wife."

"It is all the same to me. I will never forgive Windhawk for betraying me."

"Ah, I see the direction the wind blows. I, too, have heard the stories the Piegan woman has told. Saying something does not make it so."

Joanna didn't realize her eyes had widened hopefully. "Do you think the woman spoke falsely?"

She Who Heals folded her hands in her lap. "I think it might be possible. You will have to seek the truth from Windhawk himself."

Joanna stood up and looked down at the old woman. "I do not care what Windhawk does. As I told you, I am no longer his wife."

The medicine woman took Joanna's hand. "I know what you are thinking, Flaming Hair. You think, when the baby comes, you will find a way to leave. He will never allow you to leave with his child. Never!"

Joanna withdrew her hand. "He does not think the child is his."

"Then he is a fool!"

Joanna laughed. "I challenge you to tell Windhawk that he is a fool."

She Who Heals lowered her head. "He does not need me to tell him of his shortcomings—in time, he will come to know this for himself."

Joanna decided to change the subject. "I have been helping Sun Woman pack her belongings. When do we move to the winter village?"

"In no more than six moons."

Joanna didn't see Red Bird passing until the woman stopped to speak to her. "I cannot wait until we get to the winter village. Windhawk will come home then, and before the winter season, I shall be his wife!"

Joanna's first instinct was to fly at the woman and scratch her eyes out, but common sense prevailed when She Who Heals put a restraining hand on her arm. She merely glared at Red Bird.

"You reach high, Piegan woman," She Who Heals declared loyally.

Red Bird looked at the old medicine woman with contempt etched on her face. "I am the daughter of a great chief—who else would my father give me to but another great chief? I reach no higher than what I deserve."

Joanna saw the amusement in She Who Heals's eyes. "High for some is no more than the lower branches of a tree to others, Red Bird. I will believe you are the wife of our chief when I see you installed in his lodge. It has not escaped my notice that Windhawk has not yet come to you," She Who Heals stated in amusement.

Red Bird's face became distorted with anger. "I notice that he has moved this white-faced one out of his lodge," she countered. "Why would he do such a thing unless he was preparing for his marriage to me?"

Joanna turned away, unable to listen any longer. She

knew that Red Bird spoke the truth, and it was like an open wound in her heart. All she could think about was returning to the tipi.

"Foolish woman," She Who Heals said contemptuously. "What happens with Windhawk and the Flaming Hair has nothing to do with you. You are as unimportant to our chief as the dust he walks upon!"

"You will see, old woman," Red Bird retorted heatedly, staring at Joanna's retreating back. "I will show you all!"

Joanna was angry with herself because she had allowed Red Bird's words to make her cry again. She walked into the tipi and almost bumped into Morning Song.

"Why are you upset, Joanna?"

"It does not matter, Morning Song. I do not want to talk about it."

Morning Song looked at Joanna with sad eyes. "I have often seen you sad, my sister. I wish it were within my power to make you smile again."

Joanna wiped the tears from her face and, seeing tears in Morning Song's eyes, hugged her tightly. "Do not cry for me, little sister . . . just be my friend."

Morning Song smiled. "I have always been your friend; nothing could ever change that."

Joanna closed her eyes. Sometimes she wished she had Windhawk's sister's outlook on life. Morning Song always seemed to accept that which she couldn't change. Joanna realized she would never be Windhawk's woman again—why couldn't she just accept that fact in her heart?

"No matter what happens, Morning Song, you will always be my little sister."

"Joanna, if only you could see Windhawk's eyes when

he looks at you. He loves you; I have seen this many times. How can you doubt it?"

"I think you see only what you want to see."

"I think you do not see what is before your eyes."

"Whatever we say here does not change anything, Morning Song. I am no longer Windhawk's wife. We no longer share the same lodge. How do you explain that?"

"I think you and my brother should talk to each other. It is not good to have all these bad feelings between you when you love each other so much."

Joanna knew it would do no good to tell Morning Song that she and Windhawk no longer had anything to say to each other. The time for talking to each other had passed!

Chapter Fourteen

The time passed, and soon it was only three days before the Blackfoot were to move to their winter campsite.

Joanna knew that She Who Heals had gone into the mountains on one of her excursions, and she began to worry because she hadn't returned. Everyone was busy packing so they could leave. Joanna knew that She Who Heals would be aware it was time to move, so why hadn't she come back?

Joanna was helping Windhawk's mother pack her belongings, and even though Sun Woman had told Joanna not to worry about She Who Heals, she couldn't help but be concerned. Several times she had gone to She Who Heals's tipi to see if she had returned.

It was just after sundown when she entered the medicine woman's tipi, thinking that if she still wasn't there a search party should be sent out to find her. The inside of her tipi was in darkness, and in the dim half-light coming from the opening, Joanna could see She Who Heals lying on her mat.

Dropping down to her knees, she took the old woman's

hand in hers. "She Who Heals, where have you been? I was so worried about you."

"I went into the mountains, and before I could return this weakness came upon me. It took me a long time to make my way home," the old woman said in a feeble voice.

Joanna placed her hand on She Who Heals's brow and found it hot to the touch. "You are burning up with fever! Why didn't you let me know you were ill?"

The medicine woman's eyes fastened on Joanna. "I do not want to be a bother. I have been ill before, and this, too, will pass."

"I'm going to stay with you and take care of you," Joanna said, moving to the cook-fire. When she lit the fire, she could see how ashen She Who Heals looked. "I am very angry that you didn't come straight to me when you got back to the village. Did you not know I would want to care for you?"

She Who Heals turned her face away. "There is nothing you can do that will help me."

"I do not believe that. I will never forget when you saved my life, and I would now be blind had you not taken care of me."

Joanna poured some water into a wooden bowl and held it to She Who Heals's lips so she could take a drink. Seeing the look of pain in the old woman's eyes, Joanna moved to the opening of the tipi, realizing she would need Sun Woman's help.

Sun Woman and Joanna took turns bathing She Who Heals's face to bring her fever down. When the sun came up, it was apparent to them both that the medicine woman had not improved. Joanna feared She Who Heals would be unable to leave with the rest of the tribe when it was time to move, if she didn't get well soon.

Joanna stayed with She Who Heals for the next three days. By now, she realized the old medicine woman was gravely ill, because, instead of improving, she seemed to grow weaker, and Joanna had to force her to take nourishment.

Joanna sat beside her now, bathing her face with cool water. The old eyes that held so much wisdom were fever-bright as they rested on Joanna's face.

"You are so good to me, Flaming Hair," She Who Heals said in a weak voice.

"Shh, do not talk . . . save your strength so you can get well," Joanna urged her.

She Who Heals tried to sit up, but Joanna put a restraining hand on her shoulder. "You must rest—you know you are very ill."

"The others are moving to the winter camp. I can hear them disassembling the tipis and lodges," She Who Heals said in a faint voice.

"It is nothing for you to be concerned with. I will stay with you until you are recovered."

This seemed to calm the old woman, and she closed her eyes and drifted off to sleep.

Joanna held the gnarled old hand in hers, remembering a time when these hands had nursed her with such tenderness. Joanna knew she would never leave She Who Heals. She would stay with her until she was well enough to travel.

It was a hot day, and there was very little air in She Who Heals's tipi. Joanna placed a cool rag on the old woman's face and pushed back the flaps to allow the breeze to penetrate inside.

There was much activity going on outside. The people were now loading their belongings onto the backs of their horses. Joanna knew that within a few hours there would be little sign that the Blackfoot had lived there.

She decided to take advantage of the time She Who Heals slept to get a breath of fresh air. Walking outside, she coughed because the dust kicked up from the departing horses choked her.

Joanna noticed that Sun Woman was tying her folded tipi onto a travois, so she walked over to help her. "I see that you are ready to leave, my mother," Joanna said, as she tied one of the rawhide strips that attached the travois to the horse.

Sun Woman nodded. "I have packed your belongings for you, my daughter. The crazy trapper will bring your horse in from the pasture."

"I cannot leave with you, my mother. As you know, She Who Heals is much too ill to travel at this time, and I will not go without her."

"Windhawk will not like it if you stay behind," Sun Woman warned, raising her eyebrow and looking very like her son at that moment.

"I no longer have to answer to your son. I am staying here because She Who Heals needs me. Would you have me abandon her?"

Sun Woman placed her hand on Joanna's arm. "No, you cannot do that. I would stay with you, but I must see that our belongings are safely transported to the winter camp. I will have Morning Song stay with you. Perhaps, She Who Heals can travel soon, and you can bring her on a travois. I will ask the crazy old man to stay with you, also."

Joanna hugged Sun Woman tightly. "Thank you for understanding. You remember the time She Who Heals once helped me when I was ill; I can do no less than stay with her now that she needs me."

Sun Woman looked at Joanna. "You have a caring heart, my daughter. It is wrong that you cannot have pity for what my son is suffering."

This was the first time that Sun Woman had made any reference to the trouble between Joanna and Windhawk, and it took Joanna off guard for the moment. "I would expect you to be on your son's side in this, my mother, but I cannot see that he is suffering. If he is . . . let him turn to Red Bird. I am sure she will bring him comfort!"

"That one," Sun Woman said in a contemptuous voice. "She is not the one to bring my son happiness. She is selfish and deceitful. I am told by both Gray Fox's wives that they will be glad when that woman is gone. They say she does nothing but complain."

"I can remember a time when you felt much the same way about me," Joanna reminded Sun Woman. "Perhaps you will come to love Red Bird."

Sun Woman's eyes misted. "I was wrong about you, Joanna. I love you, my daughter, and I feel your pain as well as Windhawk's. The time will come when the two of you will put your differences aside."

"I must return to She Who Heals," Joanna said, quickly changing the subject. She wasn't ready to discuss Windhawk with his mother. Hugging Sun Woman tightly, Joanna turned to leave. "Have a safe journey, my mother. We will see you as soon as She Who Heals is well enough to travel."

*　　*　　*

Later that day, Joanna and Morning Song watched until the last horse had crossed the river. When the distant dust cloud settled, Joanna felt a deep, bone-chilling loneliness. If she had gone with the others, she would be able to see Windhawk in a week's time.

Not liking the way her mind was working, Joanna entered the tipi. She Who Heals was awake, so Joanna fed her some thin deer broth, then gave her a cool drink of water.

"Have the others all gone?" the old woman asked in a weak voice.

"All but Morning Song, Farley, and myself," Joanna answered her.

"You should not have stayed behind for me. You should have gone with the others. It is still not too late for you to catch up with them."

Joanna pushed the white hair from the old medicine woman's wrinkled brow. "I am where I want to be."

"You can lie to Windhawk, and you can lie to me, Flaming Hair, but you cannot lie to yourself. You have not stopped loving the chief, nor has he stopped loving you. Where you want to be is at his side."

"Hush, you need to save your strength," Joanna scolded, not wanting to talk about Windhawk.

She Who Heals looked deep into Joanna's eyes. "My strength is all used up, like water on the sand."

"I will not have you talking like that—you *are* going to get better!"

"You cannot hold back the wind, and you cannot prevent me from dying, Flaming Hair. My last wish before I walk the spirit world is that you will talk to Windhawk and tell him the truth about the child you carry. Give me your word you will do this for me."

"I do not want to talk about Windhawk with you or anyone else," Joanna insisted.

She Who Heals struggled to sit up and grabbed on to the front of Joanna's gown. "Give me your word that you will talk to Windhawk and tell him it is his child you are carrying!" The old medicine woman fell back on the buffalo robe and seemed to be gasping for breath. "I will see you happy before I die. You cannot deny me my last request!"

She Who Heals was in such an agitated state that Joanna could deny her nothing, for fear the old woman would make herself worse by her anxiety.

"I will tell Windhawk if I get the chance. You have my word."

The old medicine woman closed her eyes, seeming to relax. Joanna placed her head against She Who Heals's chest to see if she was still breathing. Her heartbeat was so faint, it could barely be heard. She knew, in that moment, that the dear, sweet woman had not long to live.

Morning Song entered, and Joanna looked up at her with sad eyes. "Watch over her. I want to go for a walk, Morning Song. If she awakens, call me."

"I will stay beside her," Morning Song answered.

Joanna walked in the twilight. The western sky was painted with a splash of deep purple. How quiet it now was, when only hours ago, she had heard the sound of children's laughter, as they looked forward with excitement to moving to the winter camp. There were blackened ashes where campfires had once burned brightly. They were the only visible evidence that this had been home to many families who had laughed, loved, and lived beside the Missouri River.

She walked over to the spot where Windhawk's lodge

had stood. Here, too, all that was left were ashes from the cook-fire. Memories danced fleetingly across Joanna's mind. Was it such a short time ago that she and Windhawk had laughed and loved together on this very spot? She knew that when the tribe reached their winter camp Windhawk would already be there. This time, he wouldn't be waiting for her—he would be waiting for Red Bird!

There was such a dull ache deep inside Joanna's body that she wanted to throw herself on the ground and cry out her anguish. Everything seemed to be changing, and she didn't know what to do to stop it. Windhawk had replaced her with another woman, and She Who Heals was dying. If she had the power to turn time backwards, could she have prevented Windhawk from turning to the Piegan woman? No, she couldn't have—any more than she could keep She Who Heals from dying.

"'Pears to me you been doing some heavy thinking," Farley said, coming up beside her.

"Where have you been, Farley?" she asked, glad for the diversion from her troubled thoughts.

"I been seeing to the horses. I thought it best to tether them close to camp 'stead of leaving them in the pasture."

"Farley, She Who Heals isn't going to last much past tonight. She is gravely ill," Joanna whispered, looking into the old man's eyes.

He could hear the pain in Joanna's voice, knowing she loved She Who Heals. "I knowed she were dying. You had a lot to bear lately, Joanna. Ifen it was within my power, I'd take some of the load off your shoulders."

She smiled at him in spite of her grief. "You have already done that, Farley. Just stay nearby. Help me get through this night."

Farley watched Joanna walk away, feeling a sadness deep inside. He had never known anyone who had a kinder heart than hers. She seemed to take on everyone's problems and make them her own. He was sure people like her would get their rewards; if not in this world, then when they reached the spirit world. She was so young, but already her life had been touched by one tragedy after another.

She Who Heals was stronger than Joanna thought. A week had passed, and still the medicine woman lingered on in torment. At times Joanna wished the end would come quickly for the dear old woman, because she was in such pain.

The night was dark and silent—only a small torch was burning inside the tipi so Joanna could watch over She Who Heals. Morning Song was lying on a buffalo robe sleeping, and Farley was bedded down outside, near enough to hear Joanna should she call out to him.

It was unbearably hot, and Joanna rewet the rag and applied it to She Who Heals's forehead. As she stared down at the dear old face, hot tears came to her eyes. She picked up her gnarled hand, wishing she could transfer some of her youth and strength into She Who Heals's body.

The old woman's eyes snapped open, and she stared at Joanna. "I heard something. Run, Joanna, you are in danger!"

Joanna tried to soothe her, thinking she was hallucinating from the fever. "Go to sleep. There is nothing to fear, I will stay beside you."

"No, no! You must flee!" She Who Heals said, clutching at Joanna's hand. "There is danger for you!"

"There is nothing to fear . . . Farley is just outside. He will watch over us," Joanna said in a soothing voice.

The four young Cree warriors hid in the bushes. They were nervous and unsure of themselves, since this was their first raid. They had been watching the deserted camp all afternoon, waiting for the old man to fall asleep.

"How many do you think are in the tipi?" Stalking Wolf, the eldest, who seemed to be in charge, asked.

"Who can say? We saw only the white girl and the Indian maiden. There could be more. We will have no trouble slaying the white man."

"We cannot slay the old man," one of the young braves said. "I recognize him as the crazy one. The spirits protect him—what will we do with him?"

"If we tie him to a tree, he cannot interfere with us, and no harm will befall us if he is not hurt," the older brave replied.

Several moments passed before the leader, Stalking Wolf, spoke again. "We will split up—Big Hand and I will take care of the old man and gather up the horses."

He turned to the other two and spoke to the youngest, who was his brother. This was their first raid, and he wanted to appear brave since the others seemed to look to him for guidance. He remembered that his father, who was the chief of the Cree, had charged him with the safety of his younger brother, and he didn't want him to come to any harm.

"Long Horse, you and my brother will take the women."

* * *

Farley awoke when someone clamped his hand over his mouth. He tried to struggle free, but was grabbed about the waist by a second Indian. There was bright moonlight, and the old man could see his two assailants clearly. He couldn't tell which tribe they were from, but he knew they hadn't come in friendship. His thoughts went to the three women who depended on him for protection, and he struggled all the harder, but still couldn't break free.

"Stop struggling, crazy one," the young brave ordered harshly. Farley had no time to answer because the Indian brought the hilt of his knife down against the back of his skull, and Farley slumped forward into unconsciousness. He never knew when one of the Indians dragged him over to a cottonwood tree, tied him up, and then stuffed a gag in his mouth.

Joanna scrambled quickly to her feet when the tipi flap was thrown aside. She stared in bewilderment at the two strange warriors who entered.

"Who are you? What do you want?" she asked through trembling lips, noticing that they were just young boys. She could tell by their dress that they were not of the Blackfoot tribe.

One of the warriors grabbed her by the wrist, while the other made a dive for Morning Song. Joanna struggled with all her might and almost got away.

"Take your hands off me!" she ordered, kicking out at her assailant.

At that moment, She Who Heals raised up and saw what was happening. Neither of the young warriors noticed when the old woman reached out a trembling hand and picked up the torch. With what little strength she had left, she threw it at the Indian who held Joanna.

As the flaming torch hit its target, the Indian's hair caught fire, and he released his hold on Joanna, screaming in pain and terror.

Seeing what the old woman had done to his friend, the second warrior released Morning Song, picked up a spear, and threw it at She Who Heals. Joanna screamed as the spear entered the old medicine woman's heart. Crying tears of anger and grief, Joanna saw the old woman's body twitch, and her head fell sideways in death.

Everything seemed to happen at once. Joanna quickly removed the spear from She Who Heals's body and advanced on the warrior who had just killed her dear friend. The other warrior had fallen to the floor with his whole body engulfed in flames.

With no hesitation or regret, Joanna drove the spear into the warrior who now had his hands about Morning Song's throat, trying to choke the life out of her.

Joanna knew there might be more of them, so she grabbed Morning Song by the arm and dragged her out of the tipi. There was no time to grieve for She Who Heals, since she was beyond help . . . the grief would come later. Right now, she must think about her own and Morning Song's safety.

When they were outside, Joanna saw that Farley's bedroll was empty. "Come, Morning Song, we must hurry!" she cried, pushing the young girl ahead of her.

When they reached the horses, Joanna breathed a sigh of relief. She had half-feared that their horses might have been stolen, but she was relieved to find they were still tethered where Farley had left them. The two girls quickly removed the leather ropes from their horses' ankles, fearing, at any moment they would be set upon by other braves.

Morning Song jumped on the back of her horse, and Joanna was about to mount Fosset when she saw an Indian drag Morning Song to the ground. She raced forward to help Windhawk's sister; then she herself was caught from behind.

Fosset reared up on his hind legs and then broke into a run. Joanna was struggling, but the Indian who held her was stronger than the other two had been. With very little trouble, he tied Joanna's hands and feet with rawhide ropes and threw her across Farley's horse, while the other Indian did the same to Morning Song.

As they rode off into the night, Joanna saw that She Who Heals's tipi was engulfed in flames. She didn't know what the Indians had done to Farley, and she dared not allow herself to think what they had in mind for her and Morning Song.

Stalking Wolf felt sadness in his heart that his young brother had died in the burning tipi. He knew his father would hold him responsible for his brother's death, and he dreaded facing him with the news.

He stared at the white woman with the flaming hair. He had never seen beauty such as she possessed. He would give her to his father, hoping he would take the girl in place of his dead son. He would leave the girl untouched and present her to his father!

Chapter Fifteen

Joanna felt stark, raving terror as her captors raced on through the night. The leather rope was cutting into her skin, and the Indian kept such a tight grip about her waist that she felt she was going to be sick.

Dear Lord! she thought, was her whole life going to be one upheaval after another? The Indian who carried Morning Song was riding just ahead of her, and all she could see was his back. Her heart went out to Windhawk's young sister, knowing how terrified she must be.

She Who Heals was dead, and she feared Farley might be, too. Joanna had no notion what tribe her captors belonged to, or where they were taking her and Morning Song.

Farley opened his eyes slowly, feeling disoriented. He was groggy, and the inside of his mouth felt as though he had swallowed a roll of cotton.

"What the hell!" His words came out in a muffled

sound through the gag that had been stuffed in his mouth. He soon discovered he was tied to a tree and couldn't get loose. Farley didn't have the vaguest idea from what tribe the Indians had come who had attacked him, but he would never forget their faces!

Suddenly he thought of Joanna and began to struggle with all his strength. He was rewarded by the gag slipping out of his mouth. "Joanna!" he hollered out. "Joanna!" There was no reply.

He couldn't see the tipi from his vantage point, but he saw flames shooting up into the air. The tipi was on fire! Once more, he strained against the ropes, cussing and yanking as hard as he could, but the bonds would not yield. Seeing it was hopeless to struggle, he slumped back against the tree, wondering what had happened.

It was some time later that Farley heard a rider approaching, and he braced himself, not knowing if it was friend or foe. Watching the tree line, he waited for whomever it was to emerge, knowing he was in no position to defend himself.

"Hell's bells," he muttered when he saw the riderless Fosset. The horse came up to Farley, prancing about and shaking his silky mane. The old man knew there was something very wrong. The Indians who had attacked him must have gone to the tipi where Joanna and Morning Song were. He swore loudly, knowing there wasn't anything he could do to help them. The ropes that bound him to the tree were strong, and no matter how hard he struggled, he couldn't work his hands free.

Windhawk's face was a mask of fury as he rode toward the abandoned village beside the Missouri River. As time

208

had passed, he had begun to reflect on what had happened to him and Joanna. Before, he had been unwilling to talk to her, but now he had a burning need to know what had happened between her and the long knife. He had ridden to join his people on their way to the winter camp, hoping to see Joanna. His anger that she had decided to stay behind with She Who Heals, had still not cooled. Even if the medicine woman was ill, he couldn't see why she hadn't been moved on a travois. In his heart, Windhawk felt Joanna had stayed behind only because she wanted to delay the time when she would have to face him.

His body had a burning need to be near her. He had been too long without a woman, and Joanna was the only one who could quench the flaming desire that gnawed painfully at his insides day and night. He knew now he would take her back as his wife even if she had betrayed him with the long knife. His love and desire for her were so deep, they were stronger than his need for revenge.

Crossing the river, he pulled up his horse—he could see smoke rising into the sky. It was barely dawn, and at first he thought the smoke was from She Who Heals's cook-fire but as he drew nearer, he saw the tipi was a mass of smoldering ashes.

Puzzled, he stared at the remains of what had once been She Who Heals's tipi. He wondered why the old woman had burned her home. Perhaps the old woman had died, and Joanna and Morning Song had burned the tipi. He made a sweeping glance of the camp, looking for a scaffold where the old woman's body would have been placed to be received by the spirits.

Hearing a horse whinny, Windhawk turned toward the nearby woods where the sound came from. He unsheathed his knife and walked cautiously in that direction, realizing something wasn't right.

Farley heard the sound of a horse and knew it wasn't Fosset, since he could see Joanna's horse grazing nearby. Again, not knowing if the intruder was a friend or an enemy, he didn't call out. His keen hearing picked up the sound of a snapping twig, and Farley knew it was a human. Whoever it was would soon be upon him. Straining his eyes, he watched the bushes being pushed aside, and Windhawk appeared!

Windhawk stood motionless for a moment with a bewildered look on his face.

"What is this, old man?" he asked in an uneven voice. "What has happened?"

"Hurry up and cut me loose, Windhawk! I know no more about what is going on than you do. I was attacked by two Indians and woke up to find myself tied to this tree. Did you see Joanna? Is she all right?"

Windhawk tried to push down the feeling of panic that rose in his throat like bile. Dropping to his knees, he sliced through the leather ropes.

"Joanna and my sister better be unharmed, old man, or I will run this knife through you," Windhawk said, getting quickly to his feet. He ran back in the direction of the smoldering tipi.

When Farley reached the burned-out ruins, Windhawk was staring at the ashes. "I see the bones of a human, old man!" Windhawk cried out in agony.

Windhawk seemed dazed as he stared into the ashes. It was as if he were paralyzed.

Farley picked up a long stick and plunged it into the ashes, uncovering other burned bodies.

"There's three of them," he said softly. Dropping to

his knees, Farley raised his head to look up at Windhawk. Tears blinded him and ran unchecked down his wrinkled face. "Joanna's dead, Windhawk! She's gone!"

Windhawk dropped to his knees, feeling as if he had just died inside. Staring at the blackened bones, he felt tears in his own eyes, knowing one of the bodies was his beloved, and the other two would be his lovely little sister and the old medicine woman.

Raising his head to the heavens, an agonizing cry issued from his lips. "Napi, why have you punished me thus? Why did you take Joanna, and leave me to walk alone?"

Farley stood up as his anger replaced his grief. He would find who had done this thing, and they would pay with their life! He was guilt-ridden, knowing he should have prevented this from happening.

Windhawk saw a bright object in the ashes and realized it was an armband. He lifted it up and held it to the sun, reading the engraved markings.

"Cree!" he spat out. "I will make them all pay for this deed!"

Windhawk stood up slowly and crushed the armband in his hand. "The Cree nation will know the power of my wrath for what they have done here tonight," Windhawk said in a ragged whisper. "I will avenge you, my beloved, and my sister!" he vowed softly.

As the day passed, Windhawk and Farley wrapped the bones in a blanket and placed them on the scaffold that they had erected a short distance from the village site.

Windhawk dropped to his knees and raised his face to the heavens. "Napi, take this woman who has brought joy to my heart. Take my sister and the old medicine woman, and I will soon send their murderers for you to

211

judge. When the deed is done, take me to be with my woman, for I do not want to walk this earth without her beside me."

Farley bowed his head in silent prayer, asking God to bless Joanna's spirit.

The old man watched with tears in his eyes as Windhawk took a knife and cut a long gash across his stomach. The blood ran freely from the wound. He knew it was the Blackfoot way of showing grief.

It was almost sundown when Windhawk tied Fosset's reins to the wooden scaffold. A shadow passed across the sun as Windhawk raised his head once more to Napi. "I leave the Flaming Hair's horse so her spirit may ride to the spirit world . . . she has a kind heart and will allow Morning Song and She Who Heals to ride with her."

Since the Cree had taken Farley's horse, Windhawk allowed him to ride on Puh Pom behind him. As they rode off into the night, each was silently lost in his own grief. They had spoken not a word to each other all afternoon. Farley knew that Windhawk had decided to spare his life.

Windhawk felt the tears on his cheek. His life had no meaning, except for the driving force that cried out for revenge. The Cree would feel his wrath! He would send a hundred Cree warriors to the spirit world in payment for Joanna's and Morning Song's lives!

He thought of the child Joanna had been carrying. What if it *had* been his child? He swallowed a lump in his throat, knowing he would lose his reasoning power if he allowed himself to think in that vein. The uppermost thought in his mind, for now, was revenge. When he had sent the spirits of the men who had killed Joanna and Morning Song to the sand hills, he hoped Napi, in his

212

compassion, would take his spirit to join Joanna's.

When Windhawk and Farley were out of sight, Fosset reared on his hind legs trying to get loose. The giant horse spun around and pulled hard until the rope snapped. Tossing his silky mane, the horse pawed at the ground, then walked slowly away from the death scaffold!

Joanna and Morning Song had been captives of the Cree warriors for over two weeks. They had been traveling at a fast pace, and always in a northerly direction.

It was now night, and Joanna felt the hardness of the ground beneath her. She had been tied to one side of a tree, while Morning Song was lashed to the other side. They couldn't see each other, but they both watched the two Indians who slept a few yards away. The moon had risen, and Joanna could clearly make out their faces.

"Joanna, are you still awake?" Morning Song asked in a soft whisper. It was the first time they had been close enough to speak.

"Yes. Are you all right, Morning Song?"

"I . . . am frightened. Are you? I still do not know what they want with us."

Joanna was wondering the same thing herself, but she wanted to reassure Morning Song. "Do not worry, little sister. When it is discovered what has happened to us, someone will come to our rescue," she said, in a voice that sounded much more confident than she actually felt.

"What if our people do not find out what has happened until it's too late?" Joanna could hear the panic rising in Morning Song's voice.

"You must be brave and not allow yourself to give up

213

hope, little sister. From what tribe do these men come . . . do you know?"

"They are of the Cree tribe, from the Canadas," Morning Song answered in a contemptuous voice. "They are like the dung of the earth!"

"Morning Song, you must talk to me only in English; perhaps the Cree will be unable to understand us."

"I will do so, Joanna," Morning Song answered in the white man's language.

Joanna began struggling against her ropes, and finally managed to slip her hand down far enough to touch Morning Song's hands, which were tied just below hers. "Do not worry, little sister; so far, we haven't been harmed."

"This is true," she agreed.

"Listen to me, Morning Song. I can feel the ropes on your wrist . . . I will try to work them free. It may hurt you, but don't cry out."

Joanna could hear a sob break from the young girl's lips, and her heart went out to her, knowing how frightened she must be. Being a captive wasn't a new experience for Joanna. It seemed that most of her recent years she had been someone's prisoner.

Suddenly, Joanna heard one of the Indians stirring. Holding her breath, she watched him stand up and walk toward her.

The Indian was silent as he knelt in front of her and ran his hand down Joanna's leg. She kicked at him and he cried out when her aim made contact with a vulnerable spot.

When he had recovered, he leaped forward and grabbed a handful of red-gold hair, jerked her head back, and slammed it against the tree! Joanna felt pain explode

214

in her head, and a whimper escaped her throat.

"You will not have long to live, white woman," the man said in the language of the Blackfoot.

"You are the one who is dead," she answered him. "My husband, Windhawk, will not rest until he sees you dead!"

She couldn't see his face very clearly, but she felt him tense. "You are the woman of Windhawk?" he asked in a disbelieving voice.

"Yes, and Morning Song is his sister. If you harm either one of us, Windhawk will not rest until you are dead. I am sure you have heard of Windhawk's vengeance!"

Joanna didn't realize what an impact her words would have on the Indian until she heard him waking his friend. She understood enough of their conversation to know both Indians deeply feared the name Windhawk.

Her announcement didn't have the effect she had hoped for. Instead of letting her and Morning Song go, the Indians decided to travel at an even faster pace until they had reached their own lands, and Morning Song and Joanna found themselves once more on horseback, racing into the night.

By morning, their pace slowed as the horses tired from carrying double weight. The Indians stopped only long enough to rest their horses before starting out again.

Midmorning brought a sudden drop in the temperature. A strong, chilling wind was blowing down from Canada, bringing rain in its wake. Joanna felt wet and miserable—she tried to hold herself stiff and rigid so she wouldn't come up against the body of the Indian.

Late that afternoon the Indians stopped to make camp. Joanna watched fearfully as the one who seemed to be the leader approached her. She cringed, not knowing what to expect from him.

"I am known as Stalking Wolf," the Cree said. "Tell me about Windhawk."

Joanna tossed her head back and met the Indian's eyes without flinching. "All you need to know about my husband, Windhawk, is that his will be the hand that will end your life!" She was rewarded by the look of fear that came into the young warrior's eyes.

"I am not afraid of Windhawk." His words denied the message of fright she read on his face.

The two Indians didn't seem very old, Joanna thought. Most probably they were young bucks on their first raid. She decided she would play on their inexperience and fear.

"I fear no man! My father, the chief of the Cree, will be well pleased when I bring Windhawk's woman and sister before him."

"I say he will not be pleased that you will bring death and destruction down on your village," Joanna said, looking unafraid into his dark eyes.

He shoved her out of the way and gestured for her to go over and sit beside Morning Song.

Both girls watched as one of the Indians built a small fire using smokeless willow branches, while the other huddled beneath his blanket.

Joanna and Morning Song were forced to watch the Indians eat, while hunger pangs gnawed at their stomachs. After the Cree had satisfied their hunger, the girls were again lashed to a tree, with no protection from the cold rain.

Joanna was thirsty, and it appeared her captors weren't going to offer her and Morning Song water or food. Since their capture, the Cree had allowed them very little to eat and drink. Today they allowed them nothing.

Joanna raised her head into the rain and felt it running down her face and neck. Although it was raining steadily, she couldn't get enough into her mouth to satisfy her thirst.

Suddenly, she heard Morning Song scream out, and she strained her neck to look around the tree to see what was happening to her. Joanna saw Morning Song had been freed from her ropes, and both of the Indians were dragging her across the ground.

Joanna struggled with all her strength but was unable to loosen the ropes. She knew the Indians were going to rape Morning Song, and she would have to use their fear of Windhawk if she was going to help his sister!

"Before you do this thing, ask the great father to save you—because you are already dead men!" she called out in a loud voice.

The Indian who had told her his name was Stalking Wolf was pushing Morning Song's dress up while the other one held her arms. She saw Stalking Wolf pause and look in her direction.

"Why do you say this to me?" he asked.

"Have you not heard that Windhawk can see with the eyes of the spirits? Has it not reached your ears that he ate the heart of the white buffalo?"

The younger of the two looked at his friend. "I have heard this of Windhawk, Stalking Wolf. His woman speaks the truth. It is said that if one is the enemy of the great Windhawk, he will die."

Joanna could read doubt and fear on both their faces. She knew she must press her advantage. "I have heard my husband call the wrath of the spirits down upon his enemies. Your chief would not be well pleased if he learned that you incurred the wrath of Windhawk!" She now saw unbridled fear on the younger Indian's face and hoped they would leave Morning Song untouched.

"Do not listen to her, Big Hand. She is only trying to gain her freedom," Stalking Wolf told his friend.

"But what if she speaks the truth, Stalking Wolf?"

"Go ahead and do the deed if you believe this. Do you have those that you love in your village?" Joanna taunted. "I am sorry for you, because when you return home you will find no one alive."

Big Hand released his hold on Morning Song and stood up. "You can do what you want to, Stalking Wolf, but I will not touch either one of these maidens. I am going home! I believe that Windhawk's woman speaks the truth. I do not want to see my mother and father dead! You are a fool if you do not heed her warning!"

Stalking Wolf searched Joanna's face. "You have won, Windhawk's woman," he said, standing up and helping Morning Song to her feet.

"What are you going to do with them, Stalking Wolf?" his friend asked.

Stalking Wolf pushed Morning Song toward the tree and lashed her to it once more. "I am going to leave them tied to the tree. If Windhawk has the eyes of the spirits, he will find them. Should they be devoured by wild animals or die of hunger, it will not be at our hands that they perish," he said, throwing a buffalo robe to Morning Song. "Take this to keep you warm; I will offer you nothing more."

Joanna didn't know whether to feel relieved or more frightened than ever. Would she and Morning Song die here in the wilderness and be eaten by wild animals? Already they were weak from hunger and thirst.

Joanna and Morning Song watched the two Cree warriors ride away with a feeling of helplessness. Joanna was glad that she had managed to frighten Big Hand and Stalking Wolf, but she would have liked it better if they had untied her and Morning Song before they left.

Stalking Wolf halted his mount and looked back at Joanna. "Tell Windhawk that you and his sister came to no harm at my hands." He then turned his horse and rode off into the night, leaving deadly silence behind him.

"Joanna, you saved me," Morning Song sobbed. "They were going to . . . to . . ."

Joanna felt around until she found Morning Song's hand. "Do not cry, little sister. Be brave . . . I know we will come out of this yet."

"Joanna, do you think Windhawk will come after us? What if he comes too late, and we are unable to get free?"

"I believe we should look on the bright side, Morning Song. Just think how much better off we are now than we were with Stalking Wolf and Big Hand."

Joanna didn't have the heart to tell Morning Song they might have traded a life of captivity for that of the slow death of starvation. But she knew if she had her choice she would rather die tied to this tree than to have her body degraded by the two Cree warriors.

She couldn't help but think of the baby who depended on her for its survival. If she died now, Windhawk would never know it was his child she carried. Until now, the baby hadn't seemed real to her. She felt a mother's instinct to protect her young, as she felt the child move inside her.

Joanna couldn't resist the shudder that wracked her body when she heard the far-off howl of a wolf pack.

"Did you hear that? It is wolves, and they are getting closer!" Morning Song said in a frightened voice.

"Yes," Joanna whispered through trembling lips.

She renewed her struggle but try as she might, she still couldn't free her hands!

Chapter Sixteen

The Blackfoot village was in deep mourning. The death-chant could be heard for miles across the wide valley. Sun Woman, in her grief at losing two daughters, had rubbed ashes on her face and clothing. She had then whipped herself with a willow branch until her arms and face were covered with deep welts, which bled freely.

"I have lost two daughters," she chanted over and over. Many of her friends had joined her and were chanting the death cry. Amanda sat with her newborn baby on her lap, crying tears of grief for her friend, Joanna. She was glad that Tag was away from the village and didn't yet know of his sister's death. Of course, he would have to be told, and she dreaded his finding out about the horrible way Joanna had died.

Windhawk and most of his braves had left three days ago, heading for the Cree village, seeking revenge. Farley had wanted to go also, but Windhawk hadn't allowed him to take part in the raid.

The only one who didn't seem to be grieving was Red Bird. Her eyes were fever-bright as she thought what the death of Flaming Hair would mean for her. Now she was sure that Windhawk would turn to her! After all, he was a powerful chief who needed a wife to give him children and to cook and clean for him.

It was a cold morning and not yet sunrise when Windhawk and his Blackfoot warriors approached the sleeping, unsuspecting Cree village.

Windhawk topped the hill and waved his lance in the air, urging his braves forward. As the sound of thundering hooves reached the people of the Cree tribe there was mass confusion, since they were still in a sleep-drugged state. Arrows flew, finding their targets, and lances pierced the hearts of the Blackfoot enemies.

Windhawk was driven by a force stronger than himself—the power of grief and revenge caused him to show no mercy to the people whom he blamed for Joanna's and Morning Song's deaths. His hands were covered with the blood of the Cree, and still he charged forward.

Riding to the middle of the village, he stopped before the lodge that he knew would belong to the chief. He dismounted, threw back the flap, and entered with his knife drawn and his senses alert. His eyes fell on the older man who was trying to get his family to safety through the hole he had cut in the back of the lodge.

The chief had pushed the last member of his family through the slit in his lodge, and he turned slowly to face Windhawk, seemingly unafraid.

"Are you the chief of the Cree?" Windhawk asked, circling his enemy.

The old man nodded his head. "I am Horse Runner,

chief of the Cree. Who are you and why have you swooped down upon my people without warning?"

"You are in no position to ask questions, Horse Runner. I will spare your life so you may tell all who asked why you have felt my vengeance this day. Your people killed and burned my woman and my sister. Count your dead, old man, and know that twice as many will die if you ever come to Blackfoot territory again!"

"Who are you?" the old man asked again, thinking he faced some vengeful young god.

"I ask the questions, old man! Do you know which of your warriors has slain my wife and sister? I believe there were no more than four."

"I know of none of my braves who have been in Blackfoot territory," the chief said truthfully, since he had no notion who had killed the young warrior's wife and sister.

Windhawk reached into his pouch and pulled out the armband he had found in the burned-out tipi and handed it to the chief. "Do you recognize this?"

The old man drew in his breath and with a trembling hand took the armband he had once given to his youngest son. He kept his eyes downcast, fearing the vengeful young warrior would read the truth in his eyes.

"I know not who this belongs to. It belongs to no one of my village."

Windhawk's hand shot out, and he jerked the man forward by the shirtfront. "You lie, Horse Runner! I can see by your eyes that you know who this armband belongs to. Deliver these men to me at once."

The guilty truth shone in Horse Runner's frightened eyes. "The ones you seek are not here."

"Are they not among the dead?"

"No, they are not."

Windhawk shoved Horse Runner away from him. "I know you would not tell me their names if I should ask it of you. I will charge you to tell them for me that they should always look over their shoulders . . . for the time shall come when they will feel my revenge for slaying my woman and my sister!"

"Who are you?" the Cree chief asked again.

"Tell your people that you have met Windhawk and lived," he said, turning away and disappearing outside.

The Cree chief stood stunned into silence. He had heard many tales of the young Blood chief, and today he had met the legendary Windhawk in all his fury. He tasted fear and knew he was indeed fortunate that he was still alive.

Walking outside, Horse Runner saw with a heavy heart that the ground was littered with the dead and dying. The fire from the smoldering tipis lit the skies.

"Such a day the world has never known," he said, shaking his head sadly. It was still early morning, and the sun was barely up—yet he knew the Cree would long tell of this day—thus adding to the legend of Windhawk!

Horse Runner clasped his son's armband in his hand and wondered if he were dead. Sadness and a need for revenge burned in his heart. Windhawk and his Bloods must pay for what they did here today! he thought bitterly.

It was later that same day when Stalking Wolf and Big Hand rode into their village. Their eyes were wide with fright at the scene of death that greeted them.

"Windhawk is of the spirit gods," Big Hand told his

friend. "His woman was right—we have brought his wrath down upon our people!"

The two young warriors rode past the burning tipis until they came to the chief's lodge. In the dark recesses of their mind, they knew great fear as they realized, without being told, that Windhawk had done this thing to their people. Each of them felt guilt, knowing the part he had played in causing the death and destruction in their village.

Horse Runner watched his oldest son, Stalking Wolf, dismount with a heavy heart. "Where is your brother?" he asked in a thundering voice.

Stalking Wolf lowered his head, unable to meet his father's eyes. "He is dead," he whispered, feeling shame.

Horse Runner's eyes were piercing as he took his spear and knocked his son to the ground with the handle. "You have much to answer for, Stalking Wolf! The blood of your brother and all who have died here today are on your hands, and they cry out to be avenged!"

The night was dark and cold—a steady, chilling rain was falling. Joanna leaned her head back against the tree trunk, feeling helpless. She was exhausted from trying to free herself. She knew her wrists were cut and bleeding from her struggle to get loose from the leather ropes.

Ominous sounds were coming from the darkened recesses of the dense forest, and Joanna shivered. The sounds of the wolf pack were drawing closer, and Joanna knew it would only be a matter of time before the animals would pick up her and Morning Song's scent.

Joanna felt her child move within her body and again experienced a strong mother's protectiveness toward her unborn baby. She must survive for her child's sake!

"Morning Song, are you awake?" she asked.

"Yes," came the weak reply. "I have a knife in my moccasin, Joanna, and have been trying to get to it."

"Hurry, my sister! I fear we do not have much time," Joanna urged.

Morning Song had heard the wolves getting nearer, and she bent her knees, bringing her legs up as close to her body as she could. Moving her head downward, she unlaced her moccasin with her teeth. Slowly bringing her foot forward, she slid it across her knee. Moments passed slowly, and at last, after a painful struggle, she was able to remove her moccasin. Bending forward once more, she picked up her moccasin with her teeth and dumped the knife into her lap.

Morning Song tried to decide how she could transfer the knife to her hand so she could cut the ropes. "Joanna, if I put the knife between my toes and bring my foot back to your hand, can you reach it?" she asked.

"I'll try, Morning Song, but hurry!"

Anxious moments passed as Morning Song caught the knife between her toes and struggled to get to a kneeling position. The ropes cut deeply into her wrist, but she didn't allow the pain to stop her. Joanna groped for the feel of the knife. Once Morning Song dropped the knife and had to start all over again.

Joanna could hear the wolves coming ever closer, and her heart pounded with fear. If they couldn't free themselves, she prayed her death would come before Windhawk's gentle sister's. She didn't want to be a witness to Morning Song's being torn apart by the wolves' sharp fangs.

Again Joanna groped for the knife, and soon was

rewarded by feeling the sharp point biting into her skin. She grasped it by the tip and could feel it slipping. With a silent prayer to heaven, addressing her God and Windhawk's, she prayed for the strength to hold on to the knife.

Degree by slow degree, she finally managed to transfer the knife to her other hand. Grasping the hilt, she cut into the leather ropes that were bound about Morning Song's wrists, and the young girl jerked her hands free!

Morning Song quickly crawled over to Joanna and took the knife from her. Laughing and crying at the same time, she sliced through the rope, freeing Joanna!

Morning Song helped Joanna to her feet, and the two girls hugged each other tightly.

Joanna looked toward the dark woods and knew their only salvation from the hungry wolves would be to climb a tree. The one they had been tied to had low-hanging branches, so she decided it would be as good as any.

"Grab a branch and swing into the tree, Morning Song. The wolves will be here soon!"

After Morning Song had ascended into the tree, Joanna threw the buffalo robe up to her and then swung into the safety of the branches herself. The two girls climbed onto the higher branches until they felt they would be out of reach of the wolf pack.

They huddled together, quaking from fear as much as from the cold. They were both too tense to relax, and both realized they had a long way to go before they would be safe.

Morning Song looked down below, feeling relief wash over her. "I feel sure the wolves cannot reach us here, Joanna. We are safe!"

Joanna pulled the young girl's head to rest on her

shoulder. "No, they cannot get us now, Morning Song."

Joanna thought the night would never end. The wind seemed to intensify, and the icy rain turned to sleet. She held Morning Song close to her, trying to keep them both warm beneath the buffalo robe. She was afraid to fall asleep herself for fear that one of them might tumble out of the tree.

She knew she loved Windhawk's sweet sister, but she hadn't known how much until the Cree had threatened to rape her. Morning Song had lived a very sheltered and protected life, and Joanna hated the thought that such ugliness had touched her world.

By now, the snarling, hunger-crazed wolf pack had reached the base of the tree and had picked up the girls' scent. The wolves then circled the tree and leaped as high as they could, trying to get to the two girls. Joanna had no fear that the animals could reach their safe haven. She couldn't help thinking that, had they not made it into the shelter of the tree, they would have been ripped apart by the wolves' sharp fangs.

Joanna was cold and hungry, and her body ached all over. She didn't know how they would ever get home—but they were alive, and for that she thanked God!

Morning Song's sleep was disturbed by the sound of the snarling wolves, and Joanna talked to her in a soothing voice, hoping she would fall asleep again. The young girl was so tired she sighed and closed her eyes, drifting off into a dreamless sleep, where she felt warm and protected.

Windhawk rode into his village and went directly to his own lodge. He stripped his bloody garments off and fell down on his buffalo robe. "Do not think about Joanna and Morning Song," he murmured out loud. "Sleep, I need sleep," he whispered in a pain-filled voice. Closing his eyes, he prayed he wouldn't dream of the charred bones of his wife and sister. He fell into such a deep sleep that he didn't hear Red Bird enter his lodge. She stood over him, devouring his magnificent body with hungry eyes. She felt a tightening in her stomach and knew she must have this man!

"Leave the lodge of this chief!" Sun Woman said, taking Red Bird by the arm and pushing her none too gently toward the opening.

When they were outside the lodge, Red Bird shrugged Sun Woman's hand off her arm. "I am the daughter of a great chief—you dare to treat me with such disrespect?"

"As you know, I am the mother of Windhawk. I dare do as I please! Your father, Yellow Wing, was only recently made chief of the Piegans. My son, Windhawk, is not only chief of the Bloods, but his father was also a great chief." Sun Woman was pleased to see the Piegan woman lower her eyes. "My son will not want you. He grieves for Flaming Hair."

"I will help him forget the white-face woman," Red Bird said, tossing her dark hair and facing the older woman with less arrogance now that she realized Sun Woman was a force to be reckoned with.

Sun Woman considered the Piegan woman's words for a moment. She didn't like Red Bird, but perhaps the woman could bring her son peace of mind. He was in torment over Joanna's death. If this woman could bring him a few hours of forgetfulness, she would not object.

"Perhaps if Windhawk finds you in his lodge when he wakes, he will not send you away," Sun Woman said thoughtfully. "Go inside and wait."

Red Bird smiled at Windhawk's mother. If she could win the mother's respect, it might help her win the son over to her side.

When she reentered the lodge, her eyes were fever-bright. She lit the cook-fire, thinking she would first console Windhawk with a good meal, and then . . . then she would allow him to take her to his mat. Red Bird felt her body tremble excitedly when she looked at Windhawk. Never had she seen a man whose body was so magnificently proportioned! His face was so handsome she drew in her breath, wishing she dared touch him. She must have him—there would be no one to stand in her way now that Flaming Hair was dead!

All the next day the wolves stayed near the tree. Sometimes they would snarl and circle the tree, and every so often they would lunge at the branches. Once in a while the animals would tire of their pacing and lie down, their eyes looking menacingly up into the tree. Often one of the more adventuresome wolves would lunge at the tree, trying his best to reach Joanna and Morning Song.

Joanna and Morning Song had been able to satisfy their thirst by scooping up handfuls of sleet and putting it into their mouths. There was nothing they could do, however, to alleviate their growing hunger.

Morning Song grabbed hold of an overhead branch and stood up to ease her cramped leg muscles. "How long do you think the wolves will remain here?" she asked Joanna. "Do you think they will soon tire of watching us?"

"I do not know. They seem to be content to outlast us. If we just had food, we would be much better prepared to outwait them."

"We are not completely defenseless. I still have the knife," Morning Song reminded Joanna.

Joanna smiled. "Little good that will do us. One of our main problems at the moment is making sure we do not fall out of the tree."

"Do you think Windhawk will find us?"

"Who can say, Morning Song? The sleet will have covered our tracks. I fear if we are to be saved . . . we will have to do it by ourselves. I do not even know in which direction the Blackfoot village is located."

Morning Song smiled and pointed in a southwesterly direction. "I know the way home, Joanna. Our village is many days in that direction."

"We will have much against us, Morning Song. It is turning colder—we have the wolves to contend with, and there is no food. We will have to be strong and depend on each other for our very survival. That will be our only chance . . . if we are ever allowed to leave this tree!"

Morning Song sat down and looked at her beautiful sister-in-law. "I will help you all I can, Joanna. Somehow, I know we are going to make it back home."

Joanna smiled at the young girl, feeling years older than her. She thought about trying to make small talk to draw Morning Song's mind away from the wolves and her hunger.

"Tell me, is there some young brave in the village whom you feel will miss you, Morning Song?"

The young girl smiled. "There is no one except . . ." she lowered her head. "I sometimes look at Tag and wish he would notice me as a girl. He always treats me as his sister, and I wish he would not."

Joanna looked at the lovely young girl in surprise. "I had no notion that you felt that way about Tag. How long has this been going on?"

"I have always loved Tag, but he does not notice me. I have seen him look at some of the other girls with interest, but never at me."

Joanna smiled, hearing the jealousy in Morning Song's voice. "I suspect he is too young to notice too many girls. Give him time . . . he will change."

"I do not have much time. Tag will one day go away, and I will never see him again. My mother says that I am foolish to think of him as other than a brother, for he will not stay in our world."

"Your mother is right, Morning Song. One day, Tag will leave us to settle an old debt. I would not want to see you hurt."

Morning Song raised her dark eyes to Joanna. "If Tag would just once look at me as a woman, then I would be able to carry that memory in my heart forever. I have told my mother I will never marry because I . . . love Tag. I believe I shall always love him."

Joanna pulled Morning Song into her arms and hugged her tightly. "Dear sweet, little sister, I see only heartbreak for you if you feel this way about Tag. He could no more stay with you than you could go with him to his world. I tell you this because I do not want you to be hurt; you are very dear to me."

A sob broke from Morning Song's lips. "Let us talk about something else. I get so sad when I think about Tag growing up and going away."

Joanna pushed the tumbled hair from Morning Song's face. "Would you like to talk about the baby Windhawk and I are going to have?"

Morning Song's face brightened, and Joanna saw joy on her face. "I have often wanted to speak to you about the baby, but you did not seem to want to talk about it, so I kept my silence. I have wondered why Windhawk does not show his joy at being a father. He has been so different since he brought you back to our village."

Joanna smiled sadly. "There are many reasons why Windhawk and I are no longer together. One of them is that he prefers Red Bird to me."

"Oh, no, he loves you! I know this to be true. He does not love Red Bird!" Morning Song insisted.

"I once thought he loved me, Morning Song, but I no longer believe that. Windhawk believes the baby I carry belongs to a white man who was a friend of mine. He does not accept this child as his."

"How can this be? I know you would never betray my brother with another man."

"I wish your brother had as much faith in me as you do, little sister."

Morning Song was quiet for a moment. "I know you and Windhawk are . . . apart. I thought it was because you ran away from him. Many times I felt sad in my heart that you and my brother were both suffering, but my mother said I could not speak to you about this. She said that whatever was wrong between the two of you concerned only you and Windhawk."

"I did not run away from Windhawk, Morning Song. I was taken away against my will, but Windhawk does not believe that either."

"When we get back to the village, I will tell him this. I know he will believe me," Morning Song said in a determined voice.

"No, that is what you must not do. If Windhawk is to want me, he must come to me on his own. Do you not see, if he comes because of something you say to him, I will never know if he loves me or not."

"He does not love Red Bird. I myself do not even like her."

Joanna laughed and touched Morning Song's cheek. "You have a loyal heart, little sister. You will grow to love any woman that your brother takes as his wife."

Joanna hadn't realized while they had been talking that the wolves had left in search of a more accessible prey. She strained her eyes, searching the darkness to be sure none of them were lurking in the shadows. Seeing no sign of the animals, she decided if she and Morning Song were going to survive, they would have to leave now. If they stayed any longer, the wolves might return. She felt deep fear at the thought of leaving the safety of the tree, knowing the wolves could return at any time. With mental force, she pushed that fear aside.

"You wait here in the tree while I go down below," Joanna cautioned the younger girl.

"No, let me go. I don't want anything to happen to you or the baby," Windhawk's sister protested.

Joanna didn't stay to argue the point, but grabbed hold of a branch and dropped to the ground. At first she was cautious, holding on to a low-hanging branch so she could swing herself back into the tree in case of danger. Moments passed, and she saw no sign of the wolves, so she let go of the branch. Turning around in a circle, while her eyes scanned the forest carefully, she was relieved to see no further sign of them.

She placed her finger to her lips and motioned for Morning Song to join her on the ground.

Joanna picked up a long stick, and Morning Song clutched her knife in her hand. Moving carefully away from the shelter of the tree, they walked quickly away.

Morning Song pointed Joanna in the right direction, and the two girls ran as fast as they could, not stopping until they felt they were far enough away from where the wolves had held them prisoner.

Chapter Seventeen

Windhawk awoke to the smell of roasting buffalo meat. When he had returned from the raid on the Cree village his lodge had been a mere shell, since most of his belongings were still packed in leather satchels. Now, he noticed someone had unpacked and had straightened the lodge, and his meal was cooking over the open flames.

Thinking his mother had set his lodge in order, he stood up. He felt such an emptiness inside. There was a deep ache left by Joanna's death, and he knew it would never completely go away. His life would be no more than a meaningless, shallow existence without her.

The lodge flap was pushed aside, and he watched Red Bird enter, carrying an armload of firewood. His eyes widened in wonder at the woman's brazen audacity in coming to his lodge uninvited.

"It has grown colder and begins to snow more heavily," Red Bird said, dumping the wood beside the cook-fire and giving him a bright smile. When her eyes sought his, her heart seemed to flutter like some foolish young maiden's. Her glance was drawn to his muscular body, which was clad only in a scant breechcloth, and she felt her heart flutter.

"What are you doing in my lodge?" he demanded. "No woman comes to me unless I summon her."

Red Bird took no offense at his words. Her own father was a chief, and she was accustomed to his thundering orders for others to follow. "Your mother sent me to you. She thought you might need . . . comfort."

Windhawk pulled on his buckskin breeches and shirt. "You can stay or go as you like. I will not be here," he said, grabbing up his heavy buffalo robe and walking outside.

He resented the fact that his mother had sent this woman to him. She should have known that his hurt over Joanna's death was still too new. He felt no desire for this woman or any other. He knew Red Bird had a lot to do with the trouble between him and Joanna, but at the moment he was in no mood to talk to her about it.

"I will wait until you return, Windhawk," she called after him.

Windhawk didn't even hear her; his mind was on other things. He had decided to go in search of Tag and bring him home. He dreaded telling the boy that his sister was dead, but he didn't want him to hear about Joanna's death from anyone but him. Knowing how close Tag and Joanna had always been, his heart ached at having to tell him about his sister. Somehow he felt the need to be with Joanna's brother. Perhaps, in sharing his grief, he could lessen it.

Sun Woman watched her son mount his horse and ride away from the village. She shook her head, knowing she had made a mistake in sending Red Bird to him. She didn't know where Windhawk was going, but she knew he needed to be alone. Perhaps, it would be good if Red Bird remained in Windhawk's lodge until he returned, she reasoned. He would need the sympathy only a woman could give him.

Joanna leaned against a tree to rest for a moment and catch her breath. It was so cold that her breath was coming out like cloudy puffs of fog. Her hands and feet were so cold they felt numb.

Glancing over at Morning Song, she saw her digging in the snow beneath a chokecherry bush and realized she was searching for berries.

Joanna dropped down beside her and helped her dig the snow away. Beneath the snow they found a few scattered berries and crammed them into their mouths, eating them hungrily, seeds and all.

"If the snow were not covering the ground, we would find roots and nuts to satisfy our hunger," Morning Song said, wiping her mouth.

"We are going to need something more substantial than berries if we are going to make it to the village," Joanna reminded her.

"We will freeze to death if we don't find some shelter," Morning Song stated.

"I admit I have no experience in wilderness survival, Morning Song," Joanna said, knowing that a young Blackfoot girl was trained from birth to live off the land. "I will rely on your good judgment to get us through. Tell me what we should do? It is getting colder, and with night coming on the temperature will drop even more. You realize our biggest problem will be keeping warm?"

"I was once told by my father of a time when he was

239

lost in a snowstorm," Morning Song said. "He told me that he had covered himself with snow, and it kept him warm. Perhaps we should try to cover ourselves with snow."

"I am not disputing your father's words, Morning Song, but it does not sound right to . . ." her voice trailed off. "Wait! I remember Farley telling me about when he was buried in snow. Perhaps we should try it!"

Morning Song looked around, trying to find a sheltered place that would help protect them from the cold. Spotting a small hill in the distance, she pointed to it. "If we spend the night there, we will be sheltered from the north wind."

Joanna nodded her agreement, and the two girls made their way slowly to the hill. The wind was biting cold, and Joanna could feel her face stinging from the snow the wind pelted at her with a driving force.

When they reached the hill, Morning Song knelt down and cleared the snow away. Removing the buffalo robe from her shoulders, she placed it on the ground.

"I suppose the best thing to do would be for both of us to roll up in the buffalo robe, Joanna."

"That seems the correct way to me," Joanna said, smiling. "You lie down, and I will cover you."

"No, we will have to lie together. It is snowing very heavily now—in time, we will be covered with snow. One good thing about this is that the wild animals will not be able to pick up our scent."

The two girls wrapped themselves in the buffalo robe. Joanna felt she would never be warm again. Morning Song huddled close to her while they shivered, listening to the howling of the wind.

Joanna pulled the buffalo robe over their heads, trying

to think of anything except how cold she felt. She wanted to find something to talk about with Morning Song, so they could both forget about the hunger that gnawed constantly at their insides.

"Morning Song, what do you think I should call the baby if it is a girl?" Joanna asked. She could hear the young girl's teeth chattering from the cold. Probably they would both freeze to death during the night, she told herself. It was a helpless feeling knowing there was nowhere they could go to escape the cold.

"I . . . do not . . . know," Morning Song whispered. "It would . . . be nice if you had a girl."

"Be thinking about it—remember, she will be the daughter of a chief just as you were and should have a lovely-sounding name, like yours."

"Can I really help you name this baby if it should turn out to be a girl?"

"Yes, you may. I suppose if it is a boy Windhawk will give him a name."

"I will love this child whether it is a girl or boy. May I help you with the baby when it is born?"

Joanna rubbed Morning Song's arms and hands trying to warm them. Right now she felt the responsibility for Morning Song's safety, and realized what it would be like to be the mother of a daughter.

"I will depend on your help when the baby comes, Morning Song. I know very little about babies. I have seldom been around small children."

"I know a great deal about babies. Gray Fox's wives often allow me to help them with their babies."

Joanna snuggled close to Morning Song, thinking she was too young to die. Morning Song hadn't even begun to live yet. Joanna felt herself getting drowsy and began to nod off. She remembered reading somewhere that if one is freezing the one thing he must not do is fall asleep. She tried to pull herself out of her sleep-drugged state, but found she was just too exhausted to fight against the sleep she needed so badly. She was not surprised when her last thoughts turned to Windhawk.

"Morning Song, if you make it back home, and I do not, tell Windhawk that I love him," she whispered, before drifting off to a deep sleep.

Morning Song didn't answer because she had already fallen asleep.

The snow continued to fall heavily during the night, and soon a thick, white blanket covered the two girls.

Windhawk had easily found Tag, since he himself had made the same journey when he had been a boy.

He watched sadly as Tag digested what he had told him about his sister's death.

"You are sure my sister is dead?" the boy said, with unashamed tears running down his face.

"There can be no doubt, Tag. I saw her . . . body." Windhawk thought Tag would suffer enough over Joanna's death; he found no reason to tell him that the body had been burned beyond all recognition.

Tag wiped the tears from his eyes with the back of his hand. "I do not know why you allowed Joanna and Morning Song to remain behind with the others left with only Farley to protect them, Windhawk," Tag said, trying to make sense out of what Windhawk had told him.

Windhawk looked into Tag's face, thinking the young boy had learned much from his journey into the wilderness. He was taller, and his shoulders were broader. His hair was now completely golden in color and had lost its red cast, no longer reminding Windhawk of Joanna's hair. He couldn't bring himself to tell Tag about the trouble between himself and Joanna. Perhaps someday, when the pain wasn't so acute, he would talk to the boy about his sister . . . but not now.

"Looking back with regret does not return the dead to us, Tag. Do you feel that I am responsible for Joanna's and Morning Song's deaths?"

Tag walked out of the tipi. Windhawk followed him, watching as he raised his face to the sky. "No, I know you loved them both. I blame you for nothing."

Windhawk sighed inwardly. "I think, perhaps, I feel responsible for the tragedy, Tag."

"As you said, Windhawk, looking back with regret does not return the dead to us," Tag said, reminding Windhawk of his own words earlier.

"Yes, that is so, Tag."

"I am no longer called Tag. I have earned my name."

"What is your name, Tag?"

"I am called Mountain Wolf."

"How did you earn your name?"

"I slew a wolf with only a knife. The animal had me and Crooked Nose trapped on a mountain ledge. I had to decide whether to kill the wolf or leap to my death in the canyon below. As you see, I decided to slay the wolf."

The change in Tag was becoming more apparent as Windhawk listened to him talk. He had indeed become a man. He felt pride in Tag's accomplishment.

"Come, Mountain Wolf," he said, placing a hand on the boy's shoulder, "it is time for you and me to go home."

*   *   *

Joanna didn't know how much time had passed, but she awoke feeling as though a heavy weight was bearing down on her. She felt very warm and wanted to throw off whatever was on top of her. When she became fully awake, she remembered their desperate situation.

"Joanna, are you awake?"

"Yes, apparently we made it through the night."

"My father and Farley were right, were they not? The snow did keep us warm."

"It would seem so, for, in truth, I am too warm. It must have snowed a great deal, because I can feel something weighing down on us."

Morning Song giggled, pushing upward on the buffalo robe, only to be rewarded by a mound of snow which came tumbling down into their faces.

Joanna stood up and stared about her in amazement. The countryside was so beautiful . . . a winter paradise! She would have enjoyed it more if it hadn't been for her hunger. She picked up the buffalo robe, shook the snow from it, and placed it about Morning Song's shoulders.

"No," Morning Song said, removing the warm robe and holding it out to Joanna. "I will not wear the robe, since you have nothing to keep you warm. You must wear this," she insisted adamantly.

Joanna caught her hand. "We must be sensible if we are to stay alive, Morning Song. The only reasonable thing to do would be to take turns wearing the robe. Does that not make sense to you?"

"Can we not put it about both of us?"

"If need be, but at the moment, I do not want it," Joanna answered, picking up the long stick she had kept with her, thinking she might need it for protection.

They trudged on and on in the snow. Sometimes they

would step into a snowdrift and be buried up to their knees, and at other times they would slip and fall on the icy surface. Nothing deterred them in their need to reach the Blackfoot village.

By midmorning, they were both exhausted and had to stop to rest. Joanna knew they couldn't keep up this grueling pace without food to sustain them.

"Do you see those big mountains in the distance?" Morning Song pointed out. "We must cross them—about six moons on the other side, we will find our village."

Joanna stared at the unyielding face of the mountain. "They do not look passable to me."

"They are our sacred mountains. It is said they have much of the yellow gold that the white man craves. I know the way through them."

"How many moons will it take us to cross the mountains?" Joanna wanted to know.

"On horseback, many moons. Walking, three times as long, I think."

Joanna and Morning Song struggled on through the snow. The way was hard, and many times they fell to their knees, but each time, they rose and pushed onward, setting their sights on the distant mountains as their goal.

In Joanna's heart there burned a flame. She must not die before she saw Windhawk again. How could she die with so many bad feelings still between them?

Later that afternoon, Morning Song cut the bark from a tree, and she and Joanna ate the tender underside. It didn't do much to eliminate their hunger, however, and gave them no added strength.

Joanna knew they were both growing weaker with the passing of time. She realized if they didn't find something to eat soon, they would both perish. All the elements were against them, and yet they both refused to give up!

Eating only berries they found buried beneath the snow, it took them over two weeks to reach the foothills of the tall mountains. Joanna stood at the base of the mountain, thinking it would be an impossible climb up its stone face.

When they started the climb, it was sometimes so steep that they slid back down the icy slopes. Joanna found herself so weary she wanted to give up, but she knew if she did, they would never make it out of the mountains alive.

The first night in the mountains was the worst. It had turned so bitterly cold that the buffalo robe did little to keep them warm. The wind was blowing so strongly it whipped at the robe and several times blew it away, forcing them to chase after it. Joanna and Morning Song huddled beneath the robe with their teeth chattering.

After they had been in the mountains for two days, Joanna began to think they would never find their way out. Each time they reached a steep incline it became a trial to make it to the top—and when they finally did there would always be another hill to climb. It seemed the whole world was made up of one hill after another, and Joanna found she was talking to herself. "Put one foot in front of the other . . . one foot in front of the other," she repeated over and over.

On the fourth morning in the mountains, Morning Song fell to her knees, too weary to rise. "I cannot go on, Joanna, you must try to make it without me."

Joanna sat down beside her. "If you give up, I will also. It will be a pity that my baby will die without ever having known life."

246

Joanna's words caused Morning Song to struggle to her feet, and they pushed onward.

"I know of a cave where we can stay tomorrow night. My father took me and Windhawk there when I was very young. I believe I will be able to find it," Morning Song said weakly. She fell to her knees, and Joanna knew they could not go much farther that day.

Seeing two huge boulders in the distance that came together in a vee, she helped Morning Song to her feet, thinking they might spend the night there, protected from the cold.

It was early the next day when they reached the cave. Morning Song collapsed just inside the entrance. Joanna knelt down beside her and felt her forehead. Her skin was cold to the touch, and she was grateful to find Morning Song had no fever. With considerable effort, she managed to half drag, half carry Windhawk's young sister to the back of the cave and lay her down upon the buffalo robe.

"Forget about me, Joanna," Morning Song said weakly. "I have not the strength to go on."

"You must lie still. I am going to try to build a fire and find us some food. You will grow stronger with the proper nourishment."

Morning Song turned her head to the wall of the cave. She knew that neither of them was going to make it out of the mountains alive. She closed her eyes, no longer caring. If only it wasn't winter, they might have made it, she thought sadly. She fell asleep, thinking she would never feel warm again.

Joanna knew the first and most important thing she

must do was to build a fire. Many times she had seen Windhawk build one, and she knew what she needed was some flint rocks. She wasn't sure if she would know what flint looked like even if she did find it.

Joanna walked along the wall of the cave until she came to a smooth rock formation that reminded her of the flint Windhawk had used for the tips of his arrows and lances. She knew that Morning Song could instruct her on how to build a fire, if only she were awake. She would have to do the best she could on her own, because Morning Song was so weak she was beyond caring about anything.

Picking up a large stone she found on the floor of the cave, she hit it against the wall until several good-sized pieces of stone chipped away. Next, she found some dried pine needles that the wind had blown into the cave. Gathering them into a pile, she began rubbing the flint together. Joanna tried to remember how Windhawk had used the flint to start a fire. She wished she had paid more attention at the time.

Joanna rubbed and rubbed the stones together, but got no more than a spark. After about half an hour at her task, she was almost crying in frustration. Glancing over at Morning Song, she noticed she hadn't moved and began to worry about her.

Finally, in desperation, Joanna tried again. This time she applied more pressure to the flint, and her reward was seeing the dry pine needles catch a spark. Joanna gathered up pine cones and dried branches, placed them on the fire, and blew on the smoldering sparks. She was crying tears of happiness by the time the fire licked at the wood and burst into a bright flame.

She knew she would have to gather more wood so she

could feed the flames. Not only did they need the fire for warmth, but she hoped it would also serve to keep the wild animals at bay.

Joanna walked out of the cave, hugging her arms about her to keep warm. It was a long, tedious process trying to find firewood under the deep snowdrifts. Every move she made was an effort, but she couldn't give up. She quickly learned that the best place to search for firewood was underneath the pine trees.

She made several trips to the cave loaded down with wood. Stacking it against the cave wall, she ventured forth again to find still more firewood.

Once more, Joanna noticed that Morning Song hadn't moved, and she realized she was weaker than she had thought. When, at last, she felt she had enough wood to burn until the next day, she knew the next thing to do would be to try to find food. How, or where, she didn't know.

Joanna took Morning Song's knife and began to cut thin strips off the buffalo robe. When that was accomplished, she attached the knife to the end of a long pole and secured it with the buffalo strips. She was pleased with her makeshift spear. Testing it for sturdiness, she found it to be strong.

Carrying her new weapon, she walked out of the cave, knowing she must find food for Morning Song or she would die.

For hours, Joanna walked about in the snow looking for any sign of animal tracks. Once she spotted a deer, but she knew she would never be able to bring it down with such a primitive weapon.

After a while, when she was ready to admit defeat, she saw the tracks of a small rabbit. As silently as possible, she followed the tracks. After about a hundred yards, she spotted a small cottontail camouflaged against a small snowdrift. Joanna froze, fearing she would frighten the animal away. Slowly she moved her arm backward and aimed the spear. She held her breath as the spear sailed through the air, and to her surprise and delight saw she had hit the target. The cottontail leaped into the air and fell dead!

Joanna was so happy, tears of joy sparkled in her eyes. She shouted, and her voice echoed and reechoed through the mountains. Picking up her kill, she rushed happily back to the cave.

After she had cleaned and gutted the animal, Joanna took the knife and cut a sharp stick for a skewer to roast the meat. Placing it over the fire, her mouth watered as she smelled the delicious aroma of the cooking rabbit. She had no idea if the smell would attract wild animals, and she didn't much care at the moment. All that mattered was that she and Morning Song would have meat to eat tonight. Joanna was proud of her accomplishments, and she knew that two short years ago she would not have had the knowledge or skill to survive one day in the wilderness. She reflected on many things as she watched the dying rays of the sun cast a rosy glow over the falling snow. She knew if she did make it home alive, she would never be the same girl again.

Morning Song was dreaming. In her dream, she smelled meat cooking. Opening her eyes, she sat up slowly, waiting for her vision to clear. It was no dream . . . she hadn't imagined it—she did smell meat!

Joanna placed more wood on the fire and smiled at the young girl. "How is your appetite?"

"How did you . . . how is it possible . . . ?"

"With wit and cunning," Joanna laughed, walking over to Morning Song and helping her to her feet. She then led her over to the warm fire and spread the buffalo robe for them to sit on.

Both girls sat by the fire, waiting for the rabbit to cook. When Joanna began removing the meat from the spit, they were both almost ecstatic in anticipation.

"How did you ever get the rabbit?" Morning Song asked, watching the juice drip from the meat to spatter on the fire.

"It wasn't so difficult. I had the help of Napi and God."

Joanna handed Morning Song a slice of meat, and the young girl didn't wait until it cooled to tear into it. The delicious juices ran down her chin, and she closed her eyes, savoring each mouthful.

Joanna bit into the succulent meat, thinking she had never tasted anything as good. "What more could we want at the moment, Morning Song? We have a warm place to sleep, food, and good company."

"A horse would be nice," Morning Song laughed, licking her fingers.

When they had satisfied their hunger, Joanna took the remainder of the rabbit and buried it in the deep snow just outside the cave, thinking to preserve it until the next day.

It was dark now, and the two girls sat staring into the warm flames. The snow fell heavily outside the cave, but inside the girls were warm and almost happy.

"It is easy to have a brighter outlook when one has a full stomach," Joanna observed.

They decided that they would take turns tending the fire. Morning Song insisted, since she had already slept and Joanna had killed and cooked the meal, that she would take the first watch.

Joanna laid down on the buffalo robe, wondering if some wild animal had been attracted by the smell of the cooking meat. There was always the possibility that some enemy tribe would see their campfire and come to investigate, she supposed, closing her eyes. She could hear the wind howling outside the cave, and the snowstorm had turned into a blizzard, but she didn't care.

We are going to come out of this alive, Windhawk, she thought just before she drifted off.

Morning Song sat by the fire watching the snowflakes swirl past the mouth of the cave. She had always loved Joanna, but now she felt closer to her than anyone else. Together, the two of them had struggled against impossible odds and, if Napi was kind, she was now sure they would make it out of these mountains alive!

The people of the Cree tribe had not yet recovered from the revenge Windhawk and his Blackfoot warriors had rained down upon them. Their village had been moved, and many sentries now manned the nearby hillsides, alert in case Windhawk should take it into his head to swoop down upon them again.

Horse Runner had called a council meeting to determine what would be done about his son and Big Hand.

The lodge was smoke-filled as all the most prominent chiefs passed the medicine pipe around and spoke in hushed tones.

"I say we turn Stalking Wolf and Big Hand over to the Blackfoot," one of the chiefs stated.

"No, whatever they have done, they are still Cree," Horse Runner said, getting to his feet. "Would you ask us to betray our own?"

"They have brought Windhawk's wrath down upon us, and who can say that the Blackfoot will not come at us again," another spoke up.

Horse Runner nodded his head. "Should we punish our young braves when they raid our enemies? I say we should banish them from the tribe until they bring me the scalp of the chief of the Bloods—Windhawk!"

Horse Runner's announcement hung in the air as each man looked to him for guidance. A sudden gust of wind hammered at the tipi, and there was fear in many of the faces of the men present.

"You cannot kill Windhawk," one of the men said. "He is as the morning mist that disappears before the afternoon sun. No one can harm him. I say if you send these two young braves to slay him, he will return and kill us all." There were many who nodded their heads in agreement.

Horse Runner held up his hand for silence. "I say to you, Windhawk is but a man. Did he not speak to me? Did I not hear his voice when he talked to me? Are you all old women who quake in the face of danger? I say we are of the Cree tribe, and our fathers and grandfathers before us call out to avenge our honor!"

There was a great murmuring and shaking of heads until, at last, everyone agreed that Horse Runner spoke wisely. The chief felt sadness in his heart as he sent for his son, Stalking Wolf, and his friend, Big Hand.

When the two young warriors stood before their chief awaiting his judgment, they looked at each other in fear, not knowing what to expect.

"This council has made a decision," Horse Runner said, looking grimly at his son. "You, Stalking Wolf, and you, Big Hand, will be banished from the village."

Stalking Wolf looked at his father. He had expected to be severely punished, but not to be banished. His shame was great as he looked into the troubled eyes of his friend, Big Hand.

"What is the length of the banishment, my father?" Stalking Wolf asked.

Horse Runner pushed the armband of Stalking Wolf's dead brother into his hand. "You will not come back until the day you can bring this to me and tell me you have killed Windhawk! The day I see you again let the Blood chief's scalp be hanging from your lance!"

Stalking Wolf's eyes widened in fright. He had no wish to face Windhawk. No man could come up against the chief of the Bloods and live. He looked for a softening in his father's eyes, but saw only determination.

"It will be as you say, my father. We will not return until we have slain . . . Windhawk!"

The two young warriors left the council lodge, knowing they would never see their people again. They knew in their hearts that no one could kill Windhawk.

Horse Runner watched his son mount his horse and ride slowly out of the village, feeling as if he had looked upon his face for the last time. There was sadness in his heart, but there was also a burning need for revenge against the young chief of the Blood Blackfoot!

Chapter Eighteen

Joanna awoke and, to her surprise, found she had slept straight through the night without waking. Sitting up, she looked about the cave to discover that Morning Song was nowhere to be seen.

She stood up and walked over to place more wood on the fire, wondering where Morning Song could be. As she walked outside, she noticed it was still snowing, but she was grateful that the wind had died down. The large flakes drifted lazily down to the ground, painting the land into a beautiful, wintery-white wonderland.

Glancing down the rocky slope, she smiled when she saw Morning Song waving up to her. She stomped the snow from her moccasins while she waited for the young girl to climb up to her.

"You should have awakened me last night. I did not expect you to stay up all night tending the fire. I thought we had an agreement that we would take turns," Joanna said, in a mildly reproving voice.

"I knew you needed the rest, and I was not tired. As you know, I slept yesterday afternoon. We have to start

255

taking better care of you and the baby. You provided the meal yesterday, so I am providing it this morning," Morning Song told her, dangling some sort of unappetizing-looking roots in front of her face.

"What have you got there?" Joanna asked with interest, noticing that Morning Song was carrying something else in her pouch.

"It is not as good or as exciting as the rabbit you prepared last night, but it will be filling, and we can save the rabbit for later when we start down the mountain. I have nuts, berries, and roots."

Joanna wrinkled her nose in distaste. "I suppose we should be grateful for anything we find to eat. I wonder if one could survive very long without meat?"

"Indeed one can," Morning Song told her. "I once knew a medicine man who never ate meat. He had a vision when he was a young boy and, in that vision, he was told only to eat roots and berries . . . I suppose it finally killed him, though," Morning Song said, with a twinkle in her eyes.

"At what age did the medicine man die?" Joanna asked, rising to the bait.

Morning Song's laughter peeled out. "He died in his eightieth summer."

Joanna yanked playfully at Morning Song's hair. "I can see much of your brother in you. You are going to be a trial for some unsuspecting man one day."

Morning Song giggled. "Like my brother is a trial to you, Joanna?"

Joanna smiled. "Yes, like your brother has been a trial to me."

The girls made their way into the cave and sat beside the fire, warming themselves.

"What should we do?" Joanna asked, chewing on the root that Morning Song handed her and finding it didn't taste at all good. "If we stay here, we are protected from the cold, but we could starve to death, or be prey for wild animals, or even an enemy tribe."

Morning Song's eyes traveled outside, watching the swirling snow falling to earth. "It is but the beginning of the winter season. The weather is much worse in these mountains than it is on the prairies; soon, it will be even more severe. We cannot stay here much longer."

Joanna took another bite of the bitter root and couldn't help wrinkling her nose in distaste.

Morning Song laughed and handed Joanna a different kind of root, urging her to try it. "The taste of this root is not quite as offensive as the other, Joanna. You must eat to keep up your strength, you know."

Joanna noticed the worried frown on Morning Song's face and proceeded to rub away the dirt that still clung to the root. She then bit into it, hoping it wouldn't taste as bitter as the other one had, while Morning Song watched her expectantly. To Joanna's surprise, it had a nutlike flavor. While it was certainly not delicious, she found it to be palatable.

"I suppose we should gather all the nuts and berries we can find, so we can carry them with us when we leave. I think the time will come when we will welcome even these horrible things," Joanna said.

Morning Song nodded. "It would be best if we were to continue our journey in the morning. It will be difficult to leave this shelter, but we dare not linger here any longer than necessary." Morning Song touched Joanna's arm. "I am very concerned about the baby. We do not want it to be born in these mountains. I want to take care of you."

Joanna squeezed her sister-in-law's hand. "We shall look after each other. Do not despair about the baby—I am very strong, and together we will make it out of these mountains, Morning Song. Look how far we have made it already. As a team, we are unbeatable."

Morning Song nodded her head in complete agreement. She bit into the root and frowned at its bitter taste as Joanna had only moments before. "What I would not give for a slice of our mother's buffalo roast or even some pemmican," the young girl said earnestly.

Joanna laughed. "Please, say no more, you are making my mouth water!"

After both girls had eaten, Joanna took Morning Song's knife and used it to sharpen the end of the long pole. When that had been accomplished, they went out of the cave in search of more food. It was difficult to find nuts and berries underneath the thick blanket of snow, and they both knew they would have to rely more and more on the bitter roots.

When each of them had filled their pouches with whatever foodstuff they could find, they returned to the cave. They sat beside the fire trying to get warm, each lost in her own thoughts.

In the late afternoon, Joanna and Morning Song made another trip down the mountainside to gather more firewood. By then, the storm seemed to be intensifying, making it very difficult to climb back up to the cave. When they finally reached the cave, they both huddled close to the fire, trying to get warm.

Joanna felt despondent and wondered if they would ever leave these mountains alive. She feared that neither of them would have the strength to endure the fierce storm that howled outside their cozy haven. It was as though she and Morning Song were cut off from the rest of the world. She had the feeling they would never find their way out of the mountains.

"We are going to get home, Joanna," Morning Song said with conviction, as if she had read her mind. "We have to make it for the baby's sake." Morning Song turned to look at her beautiful flame-haired sister. She could see the gentle swell of Joanna's stomach and vowed silently that she would never give up until Joanna and the baby were safe. Windhawk would expect her to watch over his wife and baby.

Joanna hugged the young girl to her. "We will overcome what we must, Morning Song."

"Are you frightened?"

"Yes, I admit to being scared, but look how far we have come already. The odds were against us, and still we escaped the Cree, as well as a pack of hungry wolves. What can possibly be worse than what we have already been through?"

Morning Song tried to smile, but Joanna could see it was an effort for her. "I had hoped that Windhawk would come after us when he discovered we were missing. Even he could never find us in this snowstorm."

"As I told you, Morning Song, the only help we are going to get will come from ourselves. We must look to each other for strength."

"Joanna, you miss She Who Heals, do you not?"

"Yes, very much. She was a wonderful person and touched my life deeply. I remember my father once telling me that the people who touch one's life never really die, but remain a part of us for as long as we live."

"Yes, that is true. I will always have the vision of my

father in my heart," Morning Song agreed, staring into the flickering firelight, remembering the time when her father and Windhawk had brought her to this sacred cave. She somehow felt as if her father's spirit was looking after her and Joanna. Sitting up quickly, she remembered something else.

"Joanna, I want to show you something! My father told me and Windhawk when he showed it to us that we must tell no one about it, but I know he would not mind if I shared the secret with you."

Standing up, Morning Song picked up one of the sticks of wood that burned in the campfire to use as a torch. She motioned for Joanna to follow her.

Morning Song led her to the back of the cave where there was a tiny opening that Joanna hadn't noticed before.

"We must climb through here," Morning Song told her.

"Suppose it is inhabited by a bear or some other wild animal?" Joanna asked.

"The opening is too small for a bear," Morning Song answered. "Here, you hold the torch while I crawl through, then I'll hold it for you."

Joanna nodded in agreement. When it was her turn to climb through the opening, she looked about in awe at what she saw. There were many Indian drawings on the walls. She drew in her breath when the light from the torch fell on the back wall of the cave. Running her hand over the cold, shimmering surface, she turned to face Morning Song.

"Your father was right—you must never tell anyone about this cave. This is called *gold*, and if any white men ever discovered it, there would be no stopping the number of them who would invade your sacred mountain."

"Why is gold so important to the white man, Joanna? I have never understood why they kill for it. It is just rock, is it not? Perhaps it is of a brighter color than most other rocks, but I see nothing about it which would be worth a man's life."

Joanna's face became grim. "With this gold, you could buy wondrous things in the white world. It would bring you wealth beyond your wildest imagination."

Morning Song shook her head. "We of the Blood Blackfoot have all we could ever desire. This gold rock is of no use to us."

"That is as it should be, Morning Song. Remember to tell no one about this cave!" she warned.

"I once told Tag."

Joanna smiled and took the torch from Morning Song, holding it up so the light fell on the ceiling, showing an even larger vein of gold. "There is more gold here than any one person could spend in a lifetime. It is very strange, Morning Song. We are surrounded by enormous wealth, and yet at this moment, I would trade it all for a full stomach, a good horse, and a warm blanket."

As dark descended, Joanna and Morning Song ate the remainder of the rabbit, knowing they would need all their strength to continue their journey the next day.

After Joanna had eaten her share of the rabbit, she began to feel sick at her stomach. Morning Song watched with a troubled frown on her face as Joanna rushed out of the cave, looking very pale.

She quickly followed Joanna and helped her back to the cave after she had retched. Morning Song helped Joanna lie down by the fire and sat down beside her, holding her hand.

During the night, Joanna developed a fever. At one moment she was cold and her teeth chattered, and the next she would be burning up.

Morning Song stayed beside Joanna all night, wishing she knew how to help her.

When the pale sunlight filtered through the mouth of the cave, Joanna was almost out of her head with the fever. All day, Morning Song bathed Joanna's face and urged her to drink the snow she had melted.

It wasn't until the fifth day that Joanna began to improve. By then, Morning Song had managed to snare a squirrel, and she fed Joanna tiny bits of meat.

"Joanna, I think it would be better if we stayed in the cave until you are completely recovered," Morning Song told her.

"I thought you said we should leave as soon as possible. I am sorry that I caused the delay."

"You must rest, Joanna. We could not leave even if we wanted. There is a terrible blizzard, and we could not see our hands in front of our faces."

"Forgive me, Morning Song. I seem to be so weak."

"There is nothing to forgive. Sleep, Joanna . . . I will stay beside you."

As a result of Joanna's illness and the blizzard that raged on, it was several more days before Joanna and Morning Song could leave the cave to renew their journey.

Windhawk and Tag were caught by the first winter

storm, and it took them two days longer to make it home. When they finally reached their village, Tag went in search of Sun Woman to tell her how saddened he was about Morning Song's death. He knew she would share his grief for Joanna, and somehow he needed the comfort of a woman.

Windhawk walked toward his own lodge, hating the thought of how lonely it would be without Joanna. On nearing the opening, he smelled the aroma of cooking meat. He thought his mother must have been expecting him and had prepared his food. Pushing the flap aside, he entered, seeing Red Bird bent over the cook-fire. He had forgotten all about her staying in his lodge. Feeling irritated, he dropped his warm robe on the floor and faced her.

"What are you doing in my lodge?"

Red Bird noticed his eyes were burning with anger. "I want no more than to look after you. If you will allow it, I will cook and clean for you, asking nothing in return."

"I need no one to look after me!"

She lowered her eyes. "Please, do not send me away and shame me before your people," she said pleadingly.

Windhawk looked at her bowed head and reconsidered. "You may stay if you like, Red Bird, but understand . . . I do not take you as my woman."

She looked up at him smiling, knowing she had just won a great victory. Windhawk was a very virile man—if she played it right, he would not be able to resist taking her to his mat, she thought.

Windhawk noticed the way her black hair streamed down her back and her dark eyes held a burning light . . . he remembered soft flaming hair and violet-colored eyes. Turning away, he left the lodge, wanting to be alone.

Joanna slipped and fell to her knees. Adjusting the pack on her back, she stood up slowly. It had been four days since they had left the shelter of the cave. The wind was blowing against her with such a strong force she felt as if she couldn't take another step.

Morning Song came up beside her and took the heavy pack. "It is my turn to carry the load, Joanna, while you wear the buffalo robe."

Joanna felt the warmth of the robe as it covered her body. She could see no end to this mountain. It seemed to stretch on forever! If only they could reach the valley, it wouldn't be so bitterly cold, and it would be much easier going, she thought wearily.

Morning Song stumbled and fell facedown into the snow; Joanna took her hand and helped her to stand, then brushed the snow away from her face.

"I almost wish we had never left the cave, Morning Song. At least we were warm there."

Morning Song pointed to the steep, icy slope that faced them like an unyielding fortress. "When we reach the top of that last steep mountain, we will then begin our descent into the valley. It will be warmer when we get out of these mountains, and much easier going."

Joanna was so cold and weary, she wished she could just give up. Thinking of her baby gave her the strength she needed to go on. It seemed to be an effort just to put one foot in front of the other. She knew they were making very slow progress. Many times the two girls fell on the ice-slick slope, but each time they got back up, dusted the snow off, and forged ahead, their sights always

264

on the steep mountain just ahead of them.

It was almost dark when Joanna fell to her knees, knowing she hadn't the strength to go another step. They were now at the base of the mountain, and she realized she had neither the will nor the inclination to go on.

Morning Song sensed that Joanna had reached her limit. She looked around until she spotted what she thought was a place that would give them some protection from the wind and snow. Clearing the snow away from around a huge rock that jutted out overhead, she helped Joanna get beneath it. Covering her up with the buffalo robe, she set about cutting limbs from a pine tree.

Joanna leaned back against the rock and closed her eyes. Her teeth were chattering together, and her hands and feet felt numb with cold. She tried to close her mind to the howling wind and the devastating cold.

Morning Song piled the branches from the pine trees about Joanna to form a shelter. She then piled up a stack of dead branches and dropped to her knees, striking the two flint rocks together. Soon she was rewarded by a spark that caught the wood. She was tired and cold, but she forced herself to get up and search for more wood, fearing Joanna would freeze to death. It was very difficult finding wood, since it was buried beneath several feet of snow.

Stumbling forward, she dropped her meager armful of wood and bent to build up the fire. She knew that the fire wouldn't last very long, but it would warm them for the moment, and she was too weary to search for more.

Morning Song climbed beneath the buffalo robe with Joanna. Even though they were both exhausted, neither girl slept that night. They were hungry and cold, and in the distance they could hear the howling of the timber wolves.

The next morning, they each ate a handful of the berries and the last of the bitter root and started off again. Each step was an effort, and when they started climbing the mountain they again began the interminable backsliding, getting up, starting up again.

But by late afternoon they stood on level ground, with the wide valley in front of them! Joanna collapsed on the snow, and tears of frustration washed down her face. Morning Song had never seen Joanna in such a state. She helped her to her feet, only to have Joanna fall again, and this time taking Morning Song with her. Morning Song sighed wearily and stood up, pulling Joanna to her feet.

"We must go on, Joanna. We need to find some kind of shelter before night falls."

"How much farther, Morning Song?" Joanna asked, dropping to her knees, too weary to care.

"I think when the sun circles seven times we will be nearing the winter village."

Joanna heard the distant cry of the wolves echoing down the mountain, and she shivered. Seven more days of hell! she thought. Seven more days, and then they could rest and feel warm again.

As the baby moved within her body, she knew that they would make it. According to her calculations, the baby wasn't due for at least another two months. Windhawk's child must not be born until they reached the safety of the village.

That night, Joanna and Morning Song huddled behind the wide trunk of a cottonwood, its broad base helping to protect them from the wind. It had stopped snowing but was bitterly cold.

The next morning, Joanna and Morning Song ate the last of their berries, which did very little to alleviate their hunger. They were still weak, but they traveled slowly onward. That afternoon they came to the bank of the Milk River, and they both felt renewed hope at the familiar sight.

Joanna knelt down beside the river and began breaking the ice. She could see several fish swimming along the shallows. If only she could spear one of them, she thought, picking up the sharpened stick and plunging it into the river, splashing the icy water into her face.

Morning Song removed the pack and knelt down beside Joanna, looking puzzled. She watched Joanna plunge the stick into the water several more times, then heard her cry out in angry frustration.

"Joanna, are you trying to spear the fish?" she asked with interest.

"Yes, but it is no use! I will never be able to catch them. I had hoped they would not be able to swim so swiftly because of the ice."

"The Blackfoot do not eat fish, Joanna. I have never tasted the meat of the fish."

"In the white world, it is a very common food. I can assure you, it is quite delicious," Joanna said, plunging the spear into the water in desperation. She was near tears, and so hungry and miserable!

Morning Song took the spear from Joanna and both girls lay on their stomachs, gazing down into the water as Morning Song raised the spear over her head. She was poised—ready to strike when a big trout swam by. Joanna was amazed at how quickly Windhawk's young sister plunged the spear into the water. They both laughed when Morning Song withdrew the spear and flopped a trout onto the riverbank. Many times more this deed was repeated, until there were several fish flopping around on the icy riverbank.

Suddenly Joanna heard a rustling in the bushes, and she turned her head and stared in fright as a huge, brown bear emerged from the woods!

She grabbed Morning Song by the arm and dragged her to her feet. Both girls backed away from the river, keeping a wary eye on the advancing bear.

The hideous roar from the bear seemed to echo across the valley when the animal charged forward toward Joanna and Morning Song.

As they had done when they escaped the hungry wolves, they both sought the safety of a high tree branch. Both girls knew the tree wouldn't really protect them from the bear. If he took it in his mind to pursue them, he would have no trouble climbing the tree.

They watched as the animal approached their haven. He stood up on his hind legs and swatted at the branch they were clinging to. Tense moments passed as Joanna looked into the red, bloodshot eyes of the animal. Morning Song was whimpering, and Joanna put an arm about her.

"He . . . th . . . the bear can climb the tree, Joanna," Morning Song whispered.

"I know," Joanna answered, pushing Morning Song behind her. She closed her eyes, not wanting to watch the bear in case it decided to climb the tree.

"Joanna, look! I believe the bear is leaving—he's going away!"

Joanna opened her eyes and watched in overwhelming relief as the huge animal ambled toward the river. She was relieved when the bear sat down on the bank of the Milk River and devoured the fish Morning Song had caught earlier.

Hours passed, and the animal didn't seem inclined to leave. Once it returned to the tree Joanna and Morning Song were crouched in and rubbed its back against the trunk, as if satisfying an itch.

It was almost as if the bear was toying with them, playing on their fear. As night descended and the clouds covered the moon, it became pitch dark. Joanna and Morning Song huddled together, trying to keep warm and wishing it weren't so dark so they could keep an eye out for the bear.

"I wish we had thought to bring the buffalo robe," Joanna said through chattering teeth.

"There was no time," Morning Song answered.

Neither girl slept that night, not knowing where the bear was or if it might decide to climb up the tree where they had sought refuge.

Finally, as the first streaks of morning lit the eastern sky, Joanna looked about for the bear. She saw no sign of it and wondered if it would be safe to leave the tree. Finally she decided that if the bear had wanted to harm them, it would already have done so.

Touching Morning Song's arm, Joanna indicated that they should leave the tree. They swung from the branch and stood on the ground, looking about cautiously for the bear. Seeing that it was nowhere in sight, Morning Song ran to pick up the buffalo robe while Joanna retrieved her spear. They ran through the snow as if their feet had wings, and when they could run no farther they leaned up against a pine tree to catch their breaths. Joanna caught Morning Song's eye, and they both started laughing.

"What a funny sight we must have made huddling in a

269

tree all night," Morning Song observed, laughing.

Joanna couldn't seem to stop laughing. It was the kind of laughter that was half-funny and half-hysterical. The irony of their situation seemed to relieve the tension. "I hope that damned bear gets a stomach ache from eating our fish," she said in English.

Morning Song nodded her head, laughing too hard to reply.

When they could control their humor, they decided it would be best to cross the river. It wasn't very wide at this point, and perhaps the river would separate them from the bear should it return.

Joanna shivered as she entered the icy river. She used her pole to test the depth of the water in front of her so she wouldn't fall into a deep hole. The water was like the prickle of a thousand tiny needles piercing her skin, and she knew they must hurry across or they could suffer from frostbite.

When they reached the other side of the river, Joanna breathed a sigh of relief. Her teeth were chattering, and she felt as if her legs wouldn't support her. "Bear or no bear we will have to build a fire to dry our clothing, Morning Song. It will make very little difference if we freeze to death or are killed by the bear. Let us walk a little way upstream, though," she hastily added.

Soon Joanna had a warm fire going, and she and Morning Song removed their moccasins and hung them on a branch to dry. They would lose a whole day, but neither of them were in any condition to travel farther that day.

That afternoon the sun came out, but it did little to warm the two girls, since a cold wind was blowing down the slopes of the mountain.

Joanna watched as Morning Song slipped into her moccasins and picked up the spear, heading toward the river. Lying back on the buffalo robe, she felt too weary to go with her. Closing her eyes, she soon fell asleep.

Morning Song dropped the fish she had caught onto the ground. Standing over Joanna's sleeping form, she looked at the swell of her stomach. Surely, it wouldn't be too long until Joanna's baby would be born. Pulling the buffalo robe up to Joanna's chin to keep her warm, she set about cleaning the fish. When that tiresome chore was finished, she placed them over the fire to cook. The thought of eating the ugly creatures was very repugnant to her, but she knew they had to have meat if they were to survive; besides, Joanna had eaten the fish before, and she had survived.

Sometime later, Joanna awoke to the smell of the cooking fish. Her mouth watered as she sat up and watched Morning Song remove the fish from the wooden skewer.

Not waiting until it cooled, she tore a piece off and held it to her lips, blowing on it. "You have done well, Morning Song. Tonight, we dine," she said laughingly. "You must take care not to swallow a bone—they are very sharp, and one can easily choke on them," Joanna cautioned.

She watched as Morning Song raised the meat to her lips and then paused. "Eat it . . . it will not hurt you. As I told you, I have often eaten fish."

Morning Song took a bite and chewed it slowly. Joanna smiled when her face lit up. "This is very good! I believe I like it."

Joanna closed her eyes, savoring each bite. If she had ever tasted anything more delicious, she couldn't remember it. For the first time in many weeks, both girls satisfied their hunger. They cooked the remaining fish and packed it in the snow where wild animals couldn't get to it, knowing they would need it later on.

Joanna picked up the stick she had carried with her ever since she and Morning Song had escaped from the wolves. Each morning, she had made a notch on the stick to indicate the passing days. The stick now had thirty-two notches. She and Morning Song had survived for over a month under the most primitive conditions, without warm clothing and with very little food.

The next morning Joanna awoke, feeling stronger. Sitting up, she noticed Morning Song was cutting strips from the buffalo robe and stuffing them in the bottom of both their moccasins, since the soles were worn through.

Being out of the mountains, they made better time, and they covered many miles as they followed the winding course of the Milk River.

That night they built a fire near the riverbank and pulled the buffalo robe about them for warmth. Joanna and Morning Song had talked it over and decided the best thing to do was to stay near the river in case any wild animals should come upon them in the night—they could run into the river should the need arise.

They took turns sleeping and tending the fire, but before daylight, both girls had fallen asleep.

Joanna awoke, feeling something wet against her cheek. Opening her eyes, she stared in shocked silence as Fosset nudged her face. Sitting up slowly, she was afraid she might be dreaming. Reaching out a trembling hand, she touched his face.

"Fosset! It *is* you!" she cried, jumping to her feet and throwing her arms about her horse.

Morning Song heard Joanna's voice and awakened. She rubbed her eyes in disbelief when she saw Fosset.

Joanna smiled brightly at her. "Most probably we will never come to know what Fosset is doing here, but he has found us, Morning Song! We no longer have to walk—we can ride the rest of the way home!"

Both girls patted the white horse while he tossed his tangled white mane, glad for the attention.

"Fosset must have been through a great ordeal, too. He has scratches on his forelegs, and he is little more than a bag of bones," Morning Song observed. "How do you suppose he ever found us, Joanna?"

"If he could talk, he would tell us," Joanna said, laying her face against her horse's matted coat. "I am just grateful that he found us. I believe your god and mine have been guiding our footsteps, and now they have sent Fosset to us when they knew we could go no farther."

"If Fosset can make it, we shall be home in two days!" Morning Song cried.

Later, Morning Song dug the snow away from the base of a tree so Fosset could eat some of the remaining green grass underneath. Joanna and Morning Song each ate one of the cooked trout, and then they both mounted Fosset.

Their hearts were light as they rode swiftly toward the village, which they knew they would find if they followed the winding Milk River.

Windhawk stood outside his lodge with his face raised

to the sky. Inside, he felt dead. How could he go on day after day without seeing his beloved? Even though he had seen her charred remains, he still couldn't accept the fact that she was dead. There was no meaning to life now that the world was void of Joanna's laughter. He thought of his little sister who had brought so much joy into everyone's life. Bitter resentment burned in his heart! He had not fully satisfied his revenge against the Cree.

He glanced across the village and saw Tag talking to Farley. The boy was all he had to remind him of Joanna. He would teach Tag all the things he would have taught his own son. He hoped the time would come when Tag would lose his restlessness and be content to stay with him. He had lost his beloved Joanna; he couldn't bear to think of her brother leaving him, too. He had never understood the thing that pulled at Tag. Perhaps soon, Tag would be at peace within himself.

His mind refused to dwell on the fact that Joanna had been carrying the long knife's child when she had died.

Feeling a tightening in his throat, he walked away from his lodge, thinking he would sleep in the old trapper's tipi that night. He did not want to stay in his own lodge, knowing that Red Bird would be there.

When he reached Tag and Farley, the boy moved aside so Windhawk could sit on the log beside him while Farley handed the chief a hunk of deer meat.

The three males who had loved Joanna the most sat in silent companionship, feeling their shared loss.

Tag watched as the dying rays of the sun painted the sky with a soft, rosy glow. He remembered Morning Song's dark, laughing eyes and felt a sadness deep in his heart. If he closed his eyes, he could hear her voice. It was as if he had lost two sisters instead of one. No,

Morning Song was not his sister. She was . . . she was . . . he loved her not as a sister but as a . . . ? He felt confused. He couldn't imagine a world without Morning Song. She had touched his heart, and he loved her.

He glanced at Windhawk and saw the misery in his dark eyes. He was hurting, Tag thought. Windhawk, who had the strength to lead his fierce warriors and to make his enemies quake in fear, had a lost look about him. Tag wondered if Windhawk would ever get over the loss of Joanna.

Stalking Wolf and Big Hand gazed down at the Assiniboin village. They had several friends among the young braves of the tribe and hoped they would welcome them. Riding down the hillside, they entered the village while many of the braves closed ranks about them.

Big Hand felt fear, not knowing how they would be received. He questioned Stalking Wolf's judgment in coming to the Assiniboin village.

Stalking Wolf dismounted and stood unafraid before the man whom he knew to be the chief. "Greetings to our friends of the Assiniboin tribe. My friend, Big Hand, and I come among you seeking friendship."

River Walker, the chief of the Assiniboin, studied the two young braves for a moment before he spoke. "Why have you come among us?" he asked at last, as his eyes narrowed. Big Hand felt uncomfortable under his close scrutiny.

"My friend, Big Hand, and I were sent away from our tribe, because Windhawk destroyed our village while we were away on a hunt."

River Walker gazed hard at Stalking Wolf before he

spoke. "I have always found your father, Horse Runner, to be a wise and noble chief. He would not banish you for being away on a hunt. You must tell me the real reason you have come among my people," the chief said, knowing Stalking Wolf spoke only half-truths.

Stalking Wolf looked at his friend and saw his eyes were wide with fright. He decided it would be best to tell the truth. "Our village was destroyed because we took Windhawk's wife and sister as our captives."

River Walker's eyes narrowed. "I believe you do not speak the truth. No one would dare take Windhawk's woman if he valued his life."

"I speak the truth. His woman is of the white skin and has hair the color of burning flames."

River Walker nodded his head. "I have heard this. Where is the woman now?"

Stalking Wolf lowered his eyes. "We abandoned her and Windhawk's sister, fearing his revenge."

River Walker was thoughtful for a moment. "Why have you come to my village? Why do you not go home to your own people, the Cree?"

"My father will not allow me to return to my village until I have taken the life of Windhawk to avenge my brother's death. I want only his life . . . if you help me, you will have the scalp of Windhawk to hang from your lodgepole, so you can show everyone that Windhawk is not invincible!" Stalking Wolf lied, knowing he would need the scalp of Windhawk to take back to his father. He would worry about the promise to River Walker when, and if, he took Windhawk's scalp.

River Walker smiled. "What makes you think you can slay Windhawk? I have heard it said that nothing can harm him. Are you such a great warrior that you can do this deed? I do not see anything special about you."

"I *will* kill Windhawk! This I swear on the body of my dead brother!"

River Walker looked from Big Hand to Stalking Wolf. "Avenging your brother has no value to me . . . but I would give much for the scalp of Windhawk. He and his Blood Blackfoot spit upon my people."

"Will you help us, then?" Stalking Wolf asked hopefully, knowing that there were many men who craved the scalp of the mysterious, elusive Windhawk!

Chapter Nineteen

It was the twilight hour, and the sky was aglow with the deep purple of the oncoming night, when Fosset approached the Blood Blackfoot village. Joanna and Morning Song had run out of food two days back. They were barely conscious as the giant white horse walked unimpaired into the village.

As strange as it seemed, not one village dog barked at the appearance of Fosset; instead they walked beside the horse, wagging their tails.

Farley was the first to see the strange sight. He was just coming out of his tipi to empty a pan of water when Fosset walked in front of him. At first he thought he was imagining things when he saw Joanna and Morning Song slumped forward on the horse. He stood as if rooted to the spot, unable to speak or move.

Sun Woman was the next to observe Fosset moving by with his precious burden. The horse passed by her—out of habit and instinct, he was heading toward the chief's lodge. Sun Woman placed her hand over her mouth to keep from screaming out. She saw Joanna and Morning

Song and thought she was seeing their spirits.

Soon many people were gathered outside their tipis to witness the strange phenomenon. They were silently watching, but none would dare approach the horse.

Windhawk was sitting in his lodge stretching a buffalo hide over his shield when he heard his people murmuring just outside. Putting his shield aside, he walked out to see what was happening.

As Fosset approached the young chief, Windhawk stiffened. Great Napi, he thought, Joanna's and Morning Song's spirits had ridden their ghost horse back from eternity! He couldn't see his beloved's face, since she was lying forward with her face buried in Fosset's mane, but he knew her eyes would be closed in death. Had Joanna felt his pain and come back to take him to join her in the spirit world? Windhawk felt silent rage that his beloved's spirit should have to walk the earth without finding her way to the spirit world where she would find peace. A great silence moved over the crowd as everyone watched the awesome spectacle in disbelief.

Fosset almost stumbled, but he quickly recovered, and took the last, few faltering steps that brought him in front of Windhawk.

Tag was the first one to react. He came out of Farley's tipi, curious about the strange way everyone was behaving. His eyes followed Farley's, and he saw Fosset standing in front of Windhawk's lodge. Seeing the two figures slumped forward on Fosset's back, he didn't stop to ponder, but raced across the village and grabbed Fosset's reins. Reaching up, he took Joanna's head and raised it.

Windhawk recovered immediately when he saw that Joanna and Morning Song weren't spirits as he had thought—but were alive! The people began murmuring when Windhawk stepped forward and lifted Joanna's slight body into his arms and held her tightly against him. He had never known such happiness, as his heart lightened and seemed to take wings—his beloved was alive! Napi, in his great compassion, had released the Flaming Hair's spirit and sent her back to him!

He rested his cheek against Joanna's, feeling too choked to speak. He watched happily as Tag lifted Morning Song from Fosset's back.

Sun Woman now rushed forward with tears of joy streaming down her face. She was not yet sure that her eyes weren't deceiving her.

"Bring them to my tipi," she said. Her hand was shaking as she brushed the dark hair out of her daughter's face. She caught Windhawk's eyes and saw the confusion she felt mirrored in her son's glance.

Windhawk stared down at Joanna and watched as her eyes opened slightly, then drifted shut again. She was too weak and exhausted to know that Windhawk held her in his arms or that Fosset had brought her and Morning Song safely home to the Blackfoot village.

Windhawk entered his mother's tipi and laid Joanna down on a soft buffalo robe. Kneeling over her, he pushed the matted red-gold hair out of her face. Laying his head to her chest, he felt the steady rhythm of her heartbeat. Running his hand over her body, he pulled back when he felt the swell of her stomach. Conflicting emotions battled for domination of his mind. He was elated that Joanna was still alive, but he was tormented by the fact that she was going to have the long knife's child.

Standing up, he moved to his little sister and knelt

down beside her, and, taking her hand, raised it to his cheek. He would deal with his troubled feelings later; right now, he was too grateful that Joanna and Morning Song were alive to dwell on anything unpleasant.

Farley pushed his way through the crowd of people at the entrance of Sun Woman's lodge. Once he was inside, he went directly to Joanna. The old trapper gazed down at Joanna, thinking she had been through hell from the looks of her. She was nothing more than skin and bones.

Tag dropped to his knees and gathered Joanna close to him, thinking that once again his sister had cheated death to return to him.

"How can I tend my daughters with all of you getting in my way?" Sun Woman said loudly, feeling overwhelming joy that her daughters were not dead. She shoved the three men toward the door, and Windhawk saw the glow on her face. Sun Woman was her old self again, ordering everyone around and sweeping them out of her way.

Windhawk stood in front of his mother's tipi and raised his head to the sky. Closing his eyes, he sent a prayer of thanks to Napi. Catching Tag's eye, he smiled brightly at the young warrior.

"This is a good day. Your sister and mine have somehow cheated death!"

Tag was too choked up to answer, so he nodded.

"You reckon they'll be all right?" Farley asked, forgetting to speak in the tongue of the Blackfoot.

Windhawk raised a dark eyebrow. "They would not have come so far to die now. Napi is not revengeful," Windhawk answered him in Blackfoot.

"I do not understand how they could be alive, Windhawk," Tag said. "You and Farley both said that you saw their dead bodies."

Windhawk shook his head. "We saw what we thought were their bodies. When Joanna and Morning Song are stronger, they will answer all our questions."

Red Bird stood at the entrance of Windhawk's lodge, her eyes burning with hatred! How was it possible, she wondered, that the white-faced one had returned? She went back inside and stared into space. She would not allow the white woman to move back into the chief's lodge. Did she, Red Bird, not share his lodge now? True, she did not yet share his mat, but she was determined that soon she would go to Windhawk and offer herself to him. She had done everything to get him to notice her, but so far he acted as if she didn't even exist. He would eat the food she prepared for him and sleep on the mat she kept clean for him, but not once did he come to her mat, nor did he ask her to come to his.

Red Bird knew he had been grieving for the white woman, and she had thought that, in time, he would put his grief aside and turn to her. If she didn't do something quickly, the white one would be back in his lodge and she, the daughter of Chief Yellow Wing, would be out!

Her eyes flared hatred for Flaming Hair. Somehow, she would keep Windhawk for herself. She was not her father's daughter for nothing!

That night, Red Bird didn't get to put her plan into action because Windhawk didn't return to his lodge. Several times she went to the opening and saw Windhawk, Tag, and the old trapper sitting before Sun Woman's tipi. She knew they were waiting to find out how the two girls were.

Once Red Bird was overcome with curiosity and went to Sun Woman's tipi, offering to help the old woman, but

Sun Woman sent her away.

Joanna awoke to feel a cool hand on her forehead. Opening her eyes, she saw Sun Woman smiling down at her.

"Are you feeling stronger, my daughter?"

Joanna clutched Sun Woman's hand. "Morning Song! How is Morning Song?" she asked in a weak voice.

"She is at this moment enjoying a slice of deer meat and some of my berry cakes. I will get you some also," Sun Woman said gently, helping Joanna to sit up.

Joanna reached for the wooden bowl her mother-in-law handed her and took a big bite of the delicious meat. She smiled at Morning Song when the young girl came over to her mat to sit beside her.

"We made it, Joanna! The odds were against us, but, together, we survived!"

"Yes, my little sister. Nothing could stop us once we made up our minds to find our way home. We are an unbeatable team, are we not?"

Suddenly the tipi flap was pushed aside and Windhawk entered. His eyes went first to Joanna and then to his sister. "If the two of you are feeling strong enough, I have many questions to ask you."

Joanna feasted her eyes on Windhawk's face. Her heart was pounding so loudly she could hardly breathe. She could tell nothing of what he was feeling by looking into his dark eyes. She wanted more than anything to throw herself into his arms as he moved to her side and sat down. If only he knew how the thought of seeing him again had kept her alive and had given her the strength to go on against impossible odds!

"You are feeling well?" he inquired of both girls, but looking at his sister.

"We are well," Morning Song answered.

He nodded solemnly, without looking at Joanna. Now that Joanna was awake, he could not bring himself to look at her. He didn't want to see her stomach swollen with another man's child.

"Tell me all that occurred," he asked of Morning Song. "I do not yet understand why you are still alive."

His sister began with the night of the raid on She Who Heals's tipi by the Cree warriors and ended with Fosset's finding her and Joanna beside the Milk River, more dead than alive.

Not once while Morning Song was talking did Windhawk look at Joanna. Joanna waited for him to turn to her and really see her. She had been so afraid she would never see him again. She lowered her head sadly. He wasn't glad to see her. She had hoped if she returned safely to the village that she and Windhawk would be able to talk and straighten out all their misunderstandings. Apparently, that was not to be the case. If he truly loved her, he would allow her to explain to him about the baby. If he cared about her, wouldn't he show some sign of joy that she was still alive?

Raising her head, she found Windhawk looking at her. His dark eyes were velvet-soft, and she caught something else in the dark orbs that lasted so fleetingly she couldn't define it. Joanna watched as his eyes moved to her stomach, and then he looked back to his sister.

"I am glad that you are safely home, little sister. I was sorely grieved thinking you were dead. My heart is filled with gladness to see you again." He stood and left abruptly, without once saying anything directly

285

to Joanna.

Joanna caught Morning Song's eye and read the sadness written there.

"My brother is glad you are home, too, Joanna. I do not know why he is acting so strangely, but I saw from his eyes that he still loves you."

"If he was demonstrating his love, it is a love that I can easily do without. I do not need . . . nor will I beg for his love," Joanna said, feeling crushed by Windhawk's coldness toward her.

Tag and Farley entered the tipi, and Joanna pushed her hurt and confusion aside. She hugged her brother tightly. It had been so long since she had last seen him, and she could see a great change in him.

"Joanna . . . I . . . love you," he blurted out after kissing her on the cheek.

"I know, Tag. Words are not necessary. I know how you feel."

"I thought . . . we all thought . . ."

"Yes, I have been told," Joanna broke in.

She saw the mist of tears in his eyes and smiled in understanding. "Tag, I believe you have grown two feet since I last saw you," she said through trembling lips.

"I am almost a man now, Joanna."

"Indeed, you are," she answered, watching him turn to Morning Song. Joanna saw the young girl's eyes light up with admiration as Tag took her hand. Knowing how Morning Song felt about her brother, Joanna knew that she was feeling shy at Tag's attention to her.

Turning her attention to Farley, she laughed at the expression on his face. She knew he was still having a hard time believing she was alive.

"Farley, I feared that you had been killed by the Cree. I

am so glad to see that was not the case, my dearest friend," she said, holding her hand out to him.

"I surely am mighty proud to see you alive. I done thought you had breathed your last," he said in a gruff voice, reaching out and taking her small hand in his.

Joanna laughed, "It would seem that you and I are very hard to get rid of, my friend."

Farley laid her hand against his rough cheek, too choked up to speak, but then words had never been necessary between the two of them.

As the day passed, many of Joanna's and Morning Song's friends came by to visit them. The tale of their daring journey was told and retold many times.

Finally, Sun Woman would admit no more visitors and insisted the two girls rest.

Joanna lay back on the buffalo robe, feeling totally exhausted. She was home, but the reception she had received from Windhawk hadn't been what she had hoped for. He was as cold and distant as he had been before. She wondered if Red Bird had moved into Windhawk's lodge, taking her place as his wife. She couldn't bring herself to ask the question of anyone, fearing to hear the truth.

Morning Song smiled at Joanna, and they both allowed Sun Woman to wait on them, knowing it was bringing her pleasure. Sun Woman wasn't satisfied until both girls had eaten a substantial meal.

The next afternoon, a heavy snowstorm moved over the Blackfoot land. By nightfall the wind was gale force, and visibility was very poor as the wind swirled and whipped the snow about forcefully.

Joanna and Morning Song were feeling so well that Morning Song had gone to visit with her friends and Joanna was helping Sun Woman prepare the evening meal.

Sun Woman took Joanna's hand. Her one wish was that Windhawk and Joanna would get back together. Joanna was carrying her grandchild—it was only right that her son should look after his wife and child. She decided she would take a hand in getting things started in that direction.

"I wonder if you are feeling well enough to go to Windhawk's lodge and get some extra blankets, Joanna? The night has turned cold, and we do not have enough to keep us warm."

"I do not want to go to Windhawk's lodge, my mother. Do not ask it of me."

"I would go myself, Joanna, but I have too much to do. I do not think Windhawk will be there," Sun Woman said, speaking what she knew to be a falsehood. She knew with the blizzard that Windhawk would not have left his lodge, and she knew Red Bird wouldn't be there since she had just seen her entering Gray Fox's tipi. Sun Woman would go to any lengths to help Joanna and her son. She felt guilty because it had been at her urging that Red Bird had gone to Windhawk's lodge in the first place. She, like everyone, knew that Windhawk didn't love Red Bird.

"I will go if you think Windhawk will not be there," Joanna said.

With a shake of his head, Windhawk refused the food

Red Bird set before him. Standing up, he walked out the entrance and stared over to his mother's tipi, which was barely visible in the raging snowstorm. He wanted to go to Joanna and rip the long knife's baby from her body. It hadn't escaped his notice that she had been unusually quiet when he had visited her and Morning Song the day before. Windhawk was sure he had read guilt on Joanna's face. There had been many questions he had wanted to ask her, but he had pushed them to the back of his mind. From the size of Joanna's stomach, it wouldn't be too long until the baby would be born. He dreaded the day she would give birth to the white man's baby!

No matter how Joanna had ripped his heart apart, Windhawk couldn't bear to think of her leaving. He would never allow her to go to her white lover. He didn't yet know what to do with her, but he did know he would keep her in his village so he could see her and be near her. No, perhaps he would send her to the other Blood village to stay with her friend Amanda. She could have her baby there, then he wouldn't be near when the child was born.

Thinking that he couldn't stand being in the lodge with Red Bird any longer, he placed a buffalo robe about his shoulders and went out in the storm.

Red Bird slammed the wooden dishes together and placed them in a leather pouch, knowing it was snowing too hard to take them to the river to wash them. She was tired of Windhawk's looking right through her as if she didn't even exist. Tonight, she would make him want her. She knew very well he hadn't been with another woman since the Flaming Hair. Red Bird was angry that not once had he looked at her with eyes of desire. Tonight, she was determined to change that. She dared not wait any longer to put her plan into motion.

When Windhawk returned, he went straight to his mat without even glancing at the Piegan woman. Lying down, he folded his arms behind his head and stared at the top of the lodge. He heard Red Bird moving about and glanced over at her. He watched with little interest as she walked toward him and dropped down to remove her moccasins. She stood up and raised her gown over her head and dropped it to her feet. His mind wasn't really on her as she moved slowly toward him, completely naked—he was thinking of flashing violet eyes and flaming red hair.

"I stand before you ready to offer myself to you, Windhawk," Red Bird said, dropping to her knees.

Windhawk's eyes ran over her nakedness, and it registered in his mind that Red Bird was very beautiful. Her skin was deeply bronzed and smooth—but his body craved soft, creamy white skin; her breasts were large—while the ones he ached to touch were smaller, with rose tips; her hair was black and hung down to her hips—the hair he longed to bury his face in was red-gold and curled and spiraled as if it were alive; Red Bird's eyes were soft brown—the eyes that haunted his dreams were deep violet-blue, and a man could lose himself in them.

Suddenly, he wanted to rid himself of Joanna's domination. She ruled his every thought and deed. He couldn't still the ache that dwelled deep inside of him. Perhaps Red Bird could drive away his demons, he thought, as he reached forward and jerked her down beside him. He molded her body to his and pushed her curtain of dark hair aside to fasten his lips on hers!

He heard her deep intake of breath as his lips traveled down to nudge her breasts. He felt nothing inside when she moved her body against his, and he cursed the feelings for Joanna that wouldn't allow him to take

Red Bird.

He tried to tell himself that Joanna had betrayed him, but still his manhood would not swell with passion for the Piegan woman. He reminded himself that Joanna was now carrying another man's child within her body, but still no desire flamed to life in his body.

Raising his head up, he looked at Red Bird in confusion. Her eyes were passion-bright, and she was breathing heavily, but it sparked no want in him.

Shaking his head, he pushed her away. "I am sorry, Red Bird. I cannot give you what you want, and you cannot fill the emptiness within me."

He watched her features harden as she sprang to her feet. "You are the great Windhawk! How can you want a woman with the pale white skin? I am the daughter of a powerful Piegan chief—it is not good that you insult me in this way. Have you no thought for my feelings?"

"I have no intention of insulting you, Red Bird. I will send you back to your father, if that is your wish."

"No! You cannot shame me in front of your people and mine. I will not go back to my father in disgrace because I was spurned by you!"

Windhawk stood up. "Then perhaps you should look for a husband among my warriors. I have a wife, and I will take no other."

Red Bird's face became a mask of fury. "You mean you do not want one of your own kind for your wife! You would rather have a weak, white-faced woman. If you love her so much, why do you not bring her to your lodge? I have heard that she carries your child . . . why do you not feel happy about that?"

Windhawk's eyes narrowed. No one knew it was not his child that Joanna carried. He was sure there were many of his people who were wondering why he didn't bring Joanna to his lodge.

"I will speak no more to you of this. I am not your husband that you can ask anything of me. It was not my wish that you come to my village."

Red Bird dropped to her knees, thinking she might have said too much. "Do not send me away, Windhawk. Allow me to stay in your lodge and care for you until I know what to do with my life."

Windhawk didn't want her in his lodge. He knew his people were thinking he would soon take her as his wife. He felt guilty that he couldn't give her what she wanted from him. Pity and guilt caused him to speak more kindly to her.

"You can stay for a time. I will search for a husband for you, if that will please you."

Red Bird lowered her head so he didn't see the hatred in her eyes. The white face would pay for the insult that Windhawk had given her. She would make Flaming Hair pay for this affront to her pride somehow, she thought bitterly.

Windhawk reached down and helped Red Bird to stand. "Come, put your clothing on. It is cold."

Hearing a gasp, Windhawk turned to the entrance to see Joanna cover her mouth with her hand. He could see the tears running down her face, and he knew she was thinking that he and Red Bird had just risen from his mat.

Red Bird moved against Windhawk and gave Flaming Hair a vicious smile, knowing the white woman would draw the wrong conclusion.

Joanna seemed to be glued to the spot. She tried to leave, but her feet wouldn't obey her command. The pain in her heart was so acute she felt as if she had just died inside. She hadn't known one could feel such pain and still live. Her eyes sought Windhawk's, and she saw his dark eyes narrow to sparkling slits.

"What do you want?" Windhawk asked her.

"I . . . I came for . . . your mother asked me to get . . . blankets," she said, backing toward the entrance. "I . . . am sorry . . . for . . . your mother said . . . forgive me," she whispered, turning around and running from the lodge.

Windhawk flung Red Bird away from him. He hadn't done anything wrong. Why did he feel this deep hurt at what Joanna must be thinking? It was not he who was the betrayer. Joanna was the one who had cast their love aside. Why did he want to go after her and take her in his arms, explaining to her that he had not taken Red Bird to his mat? He wanted to hold her next to him and speak of the love that burned in his heart for her.

Shaking his head to clear it, Windhawk knew he had too much pride to allow Joanna to see how much power she had over him. He walked to the entrance and flung the flap aside. He saw Joanna enter his mother's lodge, and the urge to follow had left him. He was Windhawk—chief of the Blackfoot! No woman, not even Joanna, could make a fool of him.

Joanna sat dry-eyed, feeling the heart within her break. She remembered the time Windhawk had whispered words of love in her ear, speaking of his eternal love. Her body began to tremble, and she pulled a warm buffalo robe over her. Now, Windhawk had replaced her with the Piegan woman, and she wondered if the hurt of seeing them together would ever heal.

If I were dying, it would not hurt this much, she thought as she lay down and closed her eyes, trying to shut out the vision of Red Bird in Windhawk's arms.

Sun Woman looked up from her cooking and noticed Joanna's strange behavior. "Did you not get the blankets I sent you after, my daughter?"

Joanna shook her head as tears ran down her cheeks. "Why did you not tell me that Red Bird had moved into Windhawk's lodge?"

Sun Woman walked over to Joanna. "I do not think that woman is important in my son's life. If you wanted Windhawk, you could have him back. A woman knows how to get a man to want her."

Joanna gazed upward as tears washed down her face. "I will never, never, allow your son to touch me again! He has betrayed me and our child. I will never forget the sight of Windhawk and that woman . . . they were . . ."

Sun Woman pulled Joanna into her arms and cradled her as if she were a child. "Cry, my daughter, and I will cry with you. I did not know that you would find my son and that Piegan woman on the mat. It is my stupidity that has caused you hurt tonight."

Joanna sobbed brokenheartedly. "I hurt so badly, my mother. I love him so much."

"Hush, hush," she soothed. "The time will come when my son will come to his senses. A woman can do no more than wait for a man to make up his mind."

"I will not wait for him to decide if he wants me," Joanna said, raising her head. "I will put him out of my mind and out of my heart!"

"Often one says things in hurt and anger that one has cause to regret later on, my daughter. Do not be guilty of speaking in haste."

"My mind is clear, my mother. I know what I saw, and nothing you can say will wipe it from my mind. You and

Morning Song have told me many times that Windhawk loves me. Does it seem like love to you if a woman's husband sends his wife away and takes another woman to his lodge? Does it seem like love if a man does not accept his own child?"

Sun Woman could only shake her head. She had no answers to Joanna's questions!

Chapter Twenty

In spite of the snow and the high winds, Joanna walked down to the river and leaned her head against a tree without really feeling the cold. She was still horrified by what she had witnessed between Windhawk and Red Bird. She had thought that Windhawk might take Red Bird for his wife, but actually watching him holding the Piegan woman's naked body in his arms had been so very painful to her that she couldn't seem to get it out of her mind.

Suddenly Joanna raised her head. She had done nothing wrong that would give Windhawk the right to treat her in such a degrading manner. Her worst fault had been in thinking she was meeting Harland because she thought he was in trouble. Her eyes sparkled, and she felt like the old Joanna again. She would not allow Windhawk or anyone else to push her around! She felt ashamed at how meek she had been acting. Squaring her shoulders, Joanna knew she would never allow him to shame her again.

Suddenly, an intense pain ripped through her body,

and she locked her hands around the tree trunk and bit her lower lip to keep from crying out. The baby was letting her know that it was about to be born.

When the pain subsided, Joanna felt shaken. She made her way slowly to Sun Woman's tipi. Pushing the flap aside, she entered, hoping she could make it to her mat before another pain ripped through her body.

Sun Woman laid her sewing aside when she saw Joanna's face. "You have been gone a long time, my daughter. I began to hope you had returned to Windhawk's lodge so the two of you could talk out your differences."

Joanna eased herself down on the buffalo robe. "Your son has another wife. My visit to his lodge earlier today was the last time I will ever go to him!"

Sun Woman studied Joanna's face and noticed how pale it was. It was her fault that Joanna had caught Windhawk and Red Bird together. She had been so sure that her son had not lain with the Piegan woman. She had thought that if Joanna and Windhawk could talk to each other they would be able to put their bitterness aside and make a home for her unborn grandchild.

Joanna grabbed her stomach and doubled up in pain. "Help me, my mother! I think the baby comes."

Sun Woman came to her and dropped to her knees. "It is not yet time for the child. I had thought it would not be born for another full moon."

Joanna waited for the pain to pass before she could speak. "I thought so too, but I was mistaken. I must have counted wrong, or the baby is coming early."

Sun Woman laid her hand on Joanna's shoulder. "I must tell Windhawk he is about to become a father."

Joanna grabbed her stomach once more and doubled

up as another pain ripped through her body. "No, I do not want Windhawk to know I am having the baby. Stay with me, my mother—please, do not leave me alone!"

Sun Woman watched Joanna with a troubled expression on her face. She knew it was too early for the pains to be coming so close together. "I will be right back, Joanna. I am going for help."

After Sun Woman left, Joanna relaxed as the pain subsided. She remembered that a Blackfoot woman was not supposed to cry out while giving birth—she hoped she wouldn't shame herself when the pains became more severe.

A short time later, Sun Woman returned with Swift Walker, a wife of one of the lesser chiefs. She assured Joanna that Swift Walker had delivered many healthy babies.

Joanna couldn't help but wish for She Who Heals. She knew that if the medicine woman had not died she would be here to attend her. Joanna missed the dear old woman more than ever at that moment, because She Who Heals had always brought her comfort when she needed it.

As the night lengthened, Joanna's pains became much more severe. Her body was drenched with perspiration, and she bit her lip until it bled, trying to keep from crying out. Moaning softly, she tossed and turned as her whole being seemed to be locked in a world of pain. A white-hot flash burned into Joanna's eyes, and she placed her hand over her mouth to keep from crying out.

Hour after hour, one pain followed another. Finally, Sun Woman stood up and looked at Swift Walker.

"The baby is turned wrong. I will go to my son and ask if he wants to save Joanna or his child."

Swift Walker nodded her head in understanding. She

knew the Flaming Hair and the child might both die, but there was a chance that one of them could be saved at the sacrifice of the other's life.

Sun Woman threw back the flap and entered Windhawk's darkened lodge. The fire was smoldering and gave very little light to the darkened corners. She made her way to Windhawk's mat. It crossed Sun Woman's mind that she had been right—Windhawk and Red Bird did not share the same mat. Red Bird's mat was located near the fire, while her son's was against the back wall of the lodge.

Windhawk heard his mother's movements and sat up. He watched her approach, knowing something must be wrong because she would never come to his lodge in the middle of the night unless there was a good reason.

"Joanna is having your baby, my son. She is in much pain . . . I fear it is very bad."

Windhawk stood up and turned his back, lowering his voice so Red Bird wouldn't overhear. "You mean she is having the long knife's baby," he whispered.

Sun Woman took his arm and turned him back to face her. "My foolish son. Joanna never lay with the long knife. The baby she is having is yours."

"That is not true! Did not the white woman tell me that Joanna had been with the white man?"

Sun Woman felt anger at her son's blind pride, but now was not the time to argue the point. "I have come to you to ask if you want me to save Joanna or the child? The baby is turned wrong."

She heard the sharp intake of Windhawk's breath, and he reached out and gripped her by the arm. "Are you saying that Joanna might die?"

"Yes, you must choose which one you want me and

300

Swift Walker to save . . . Joanna or your baby? The choice belongs to you alone. You must tell me what to do."

Windhawk turned his back and lowered his head. He had never faced a more important choice, and he had never felt less able to make a decision. His mother wouldn't understand his reasoning just now; to her, Joanna's unborn child was the grandchild she had long awaited. He would never sacrifice Joanna's life for the long knife's child!

"You know what to do, my mother. Save Joanna," he said in a painful whisper.

"No!" Red Bird cried out, coming up beside Sun Woman. "Save the baby! I will be a mother to the child. Allow the white woman to die!"

Windhawk spun around and grabbed Red Bird by the hair and yanked her forward. "You have no say in this, woman! Go to Joanna and save her life, my mother."

Sun Woman nodded and made a hasty retreat while Windhawk still held Red Bird in a painful grasp. "Never dare to interfere in my life again. I did not want you here. I took pity on you and allowed you to enter my lodge because you said it would cause you shame if I did not. I do not like to look upon your face. Go from me!"

Red Bird was raging inside. "You dare to pity me—Red Bird, daughter of a great chief?"

"I grow weary of hearing what a great chief your father is. I will talk to you no more. Go from my sight," Windhawk said in a deadly calm voice.

Suddenly Red Bird felt fear; she pulled free of Windhawk's grasp and backed away. She had heard about the effect Windhawk could have on people when he was angry with them, but this was the first time she had

301

witnessed it herself. It was strange—he didn't even raise his voice, and still she felt terrified of him.

Windhawk walked out of the lodge and stopped before his mother's tipi. He wanted to enter, and yet he feared to. He was filled with silent rage that the baby of the long knife might be killing his Joanna. He was glad the child wouldn't live, but there was fear in his heart that Joanna might yet die.

He heard footsteps crunching on the frozen snow and looked up to see Farley approaching.

"I have word that Joanna is having your baby," the old man said.

"She is having the white man's baby," Windhawk answered angrily.

Farley's eyes narrowed in on Windhawk. "Come with me . . . I think it is time for you and me to talk."

"No, you have nothing to say that I would want to hear, old man."

"I think you will want to hear this. I am going to tell you the truth about Joanna and the long knife." Farley walked away, knowing Windhawk would follow.

When Windhawk entered Farley's tipi, he saw that Tag was asleep. He sat down beside the old trapper and stared into the fire.

"I want to hear about the long knife," he said without looking at Farley.

Farley placed more wood on the fire and then sat down. "It is not right that I must tell you this. You should know it in your heart. Joanna asked me not to tell you what happened to her, but I cannot keep quiet any longer and watch as the two of you tear each other apart."

Windhawk gave Farley a dark look. "I do not want a sermon, old man. If that is what you brought me here for,

I will not stay. Tell me now about Joanna and the long knife, or I will leave."

Farley let out a long breath. "First, I will have to tell you about Claudia, the white woman. She has hated Joanna for as far back as I know. She is jealous because she wanted the long knife, but he loved Joanna and would not look at her as a woman."

"It would seem to me that the woman had much to be jealous of."

"Now, that's where you are wrong," Farley said, lapsing into his own brand of English. Windhawk gave him a warning glance, and he switched to Blackfoot. "Joanna was friendly to the long knife, Captain Thatcher, but she never loved him. He was good to her and Tag at a time when they needed a friend. If she had loved him, she would have married him at the fort a long time ago. In the white world, Captain Thatcher is very wealthy and has much to offer a woman, but Joanna chose you over him, as you will remember."

Windhawk looked skeptical. "Joanna ran away from me to be with him."

"No, that is not what happened at all. You know about the letter Joanna received, at least, what she thought was a letter from Captain Thatcher telling her he was in trouble and needed her help. The letter was actually from Joanna's uncle. Claudia had written it so Joanna's uncle could get her and Tag back. You know how her uncle controlled their life and caused them to run away in the first place."

Windhawk's eyes veiled in thoughtfulness. "Yes, I know that Joanna was frightened of her uncle. But the long knife was with them when I found her."

"You will not want to accept this, but as I told you, the

303

captain has been very good to Joanna and Tag. When Captain Thatcher feared Joanna's uncle had captured her and Tag, he rode to Fort Union to try and help them. You have my word, he never laid a hand on Joanna, nor would she allow it if he had."

"If what you say is true, why would the white woman tell me Joanna had been with the long knife? Why did she tell me Joanna was going to have his child?" Windhawk asked, beginning to see that he might have been mistaken to believe the worst of Joanna. At the time, he had been so eaten up with jealousy that he had taken the white woman's word as the truth.

"As I told you, Claudia hates Joanna. She would do anything to hurt her. While Joanna was her uncle's prisoner, she told Claudia of the love she had for you, and that she was carrying your baby. Think, Windhawk! Why would Claudia, who thought she was going to die by your hand, bother to tell you such lies? What woman who faced death would weave a web of untruths?"

Windhawk shook his head. "I do not know the way a white woman thinks."

"In this case, I do," the old man said. "Claudia thought she was going to die, and she wanted to punish Joanna. The only weapon she had at hand was Joanna's love for you. It is a sad thing that her lies worked. You have helped Joanna's worst enemy destroy her. You, the man who says he loves her and is supposed to protect her from all hurt, has been the instrument of her downfall."

Windhawk jerked his head back as if the old man had struck him. "I thought . . ."

Farley cut him off. "I know you can count, Windhawk. How many moons does it take for a woman to deliver a baby? This baby can only be yours."

304

Windhawk stood up slowly. "May Napi grant me mercy! It is as you say. I have been the woman's tool to harm Joanna." Windhawk's eyes were dark with grief.

Farley nodded his head. "Joanna never betrayed you, Windhawk. It was you who turned away from her."

Windhawk looked at the old trapper. Everything that Farley said was true—he knew that now. "My punishment will come before this night is out, old man. The child I thought was not mine will die."

Farley stood and placed his hand on Windhawk's arm. "I hope you will not suffer, but I am angry that you have done this to Joanna. It was you, not Joanna, who turned to another. It is you, not Joanna, who is guilty of betrayal. She wanted this child even though you did not claim to be the father. I was told by Swift Walker that Joanna might lose her life. If she does, I feel pity for you." No one had dared speak to Windhawk with such disrespect, and Farley didn't know how the young chief would take his words. He was unafraid as he watched Windhawk's face darken. There was complete silence as Windhawk's eyes rested on the old man.

"I have not taken Red Bird to my mat. I could not . . . I did not want to."

"How was Joanna supposed to know that? Did you tell her?"

Windhawk closed his eyes, then turned and left silently. He knew the old man had spoken the truth. Inside him, shame raged like a fever.

He rushed across the village and entered his mother's tipi, and his eyes fell on Joanna. Her eyes were closed, and she looked terribly pale. Windhawk's eyes went to her stomach, and he saw that she had already delivered the child. He noticed his mother wasn't in the tipi, but

Swift Walker moved aside to allow Windhawk to approach Joanna.

Going down on his knees, he touched her glorious red-gold hair. "Is she well?" Windhawk asked Swift Walker. He couldn't bring himself to ask about the child, knowing the child whose life he hadn't considered worth saving had been his own flesh and blood. He knew the child was now dead.

"She has had a very hard time, my chief. She sleeps to regain her strength."

Windhawk stood up. "I will see the child now." He knew he must see the dead child so he would have final proof of Joanna's innocence. He despised himself because he needed that proof after what the old man had told him.

Suddenly, the tipi flap was thrown aside, and his mother entered, carrying the baby wrapped in a blanket. Her eyes were unreadable as she walked over to him. "I went to your lodge to show you the child, but I did not find you there."

Windhawk felt a sick feeling in the pit of his stomach. He already knew the child was his. He didn't want to know if it had been a boy or girl. He only knew he couldn't bring himself to look on the face of his dead baby.

"You see to the building of the funeral scaffold, my mother," he said, moving to side-step Sun Woman. "Tell Gray Fox what you want, and he will attend to it for you," he said, knowing he must be alone to deal with the emotions that were swelling his heart.

"First, you will look on the face of your child, my son," his mother insisted.

His dark eyes locked with hers. "I cannot, my mother. I

306

will not look on the dead face of . . . my child. Do not ask it of me."

Sun Woman nodded for Swift Walker to leave, and when she did she turned back to her son, blocking his exit. "So, you do admit that the child is yours?"

Windhawk dropped his eyes. "Yes, have I not said so? Move out of my way!"

"No, I will not move aside, my foolish son. It is time for you to face many truths." Sun Woman pushed the blanket aside and, in spite of himself, Windhawk's eyes were drawn to the face of the tiny infant.

He was silent as his eyes moved over the dark hair so like his own. The child was dark-skinned, and its face was so beautiful in death that Windhawk felt tears wash down his face. As he reached out a trembling hand to touch the child, he drew back, not wanting to feel the coldness of death on his own flesh and blood. This was the child he had wanted so badly. This was the child whom he had condemned to death!

His eyes were grief-stricken as he looked at his mother. "I do not ever want to hear if this child was a boy or girl. Never, as long as you live, tell me if this child was my son or my daughter," he said in a painful whisper.

Sun Woman whipped the covers from the child, and before Windhawk could look away he saw that the child was naked, and that it was the son he had always wanted. An agonized cry rose from deep inside him, but he wouldn't allow it to pass his lips. Hot, unashamed tears washed freely down his face. With a trembling hand, he reached out to touch the soft black hair on his son's head, but he drew away, feeling overwhelming grief and guilt. How easily he had condemned his son to death last night. Even now, looking on the face of the dead child, he knew

307

he would have made the same decision. He would never have given the order that would allow Joanna to die.

"This is my punishment," he whispered, as his hand moved down to pick up the small limp hand of his son.

"I do not think so, my son. Though you do not deserve it, I think this child is your reward," his mother said, smiling brightly.

Windhawk's heart contracted when he felt the warmth of the child's tiny hand. His son was not dead!

He picked the child up in his arms and smiled down at him through his tears. The baby stretched and opened his eyes, and Windhawk's heart swelled with fatherly love and pride. His hands were still trembling when he raised his son to his face, feeling the soft skin against his. Unbelievable love washed through his body.

Joanna had given him a son!

Laying the baby down beside the warm fire, Windhawk examined the sturdy little body to make sure the child was perfect. Sun Woman knelt down beside him, looking like the proud grandmother she was.

"My prayers have been answered—Napi was kind. This day I have held the son of my son in my arms and watched him take his first breath."

Windhawk could hear the pride in his mother's voice and knew she was feeling much the same as he.

"I thought you could save but one of them?"

"When I returned from seeing you, Joanna was in constant pain, and I thought we would lose both her and the child. I thought I would try one more time to turn the child, and I was able to do so."

Windhawk saw the tears sparkle in his mother's eyes. The only other times he had seen his mother cry were when his father had died and when she had thought

Morning Song and Joanna had been killed. He wrapped the child up warmly and handed him to his mother.

Sun Woman watched him move across the tipi to kneel beside Joanna.

Windhawk took Joanna's limp hand and held it to his lips. As his eyes moved over every feature of her beautiful face, he felt a tightening in his chest. Her dark lashes rested against her pale cheek, and her flaming hair fanned out about her. His eyes moved down to her breasts, which were swollen with milk to feed his son. He felt such a deep hurt, knowing how he had tormented her.

The old man had been right. Joanna hadn't betrayed him; he was the betrayer for not believing in her. How could he have believed that white woman's lies when he knew Joanna had always been truthful with him?

When he thought of all she had been through alone, he felt ashamed. She had been his woman to love and care for, yet he had abandoned her when she needed him most, and she had been forced to walk alone.

He knew that he would have to prove himself worthy of her before she would ever look at him with the eyes of love. Bending down, he kissed her soft lips and then stood up.

"Take care of them both, my mother," he said, walking out into the early morning sunlight. He felt the newness of the day—it was as if everything had been reborn. He was like a man who was told he was going to die only to find he had been granted life!

The baby began to fret, and Sun Woman rocked it gently in her arms while softly crooning an old Blackfoot lullaby, feeling her heart overflow with love for the child. Soon the baby fell asleep, and she laid him beside Joanna.

Sun Woman saw that Joanna was still in a deep sleep. "Sleep well, my daughter," she whispered. "You have walked a long way alone, but my son will see that your days are happy from now on."

Sun Woman knew that her son would have much trouble winning Flaming Hair, but it would do him good to have to prove his worth to Joanna. Sometimes he was much too arrogant for his own good, she thought.

She felt guilty for the part she had played in sending Red Bird to her son's lodge. Her lips curled into a smile. Red Bird would soon be sent from the chief's lodge. Sun Woman knew Joanna would never turn to Windhawk as long as that woman was in his lodge!

Chapter Twenty-One

Joanna held her tiny dark-skinned son in her arms, smiling at the way he cuddled up to her. She kissed his soft cheek, loving him in the very depths of her heart.

Tag took the small hand in his and looked at it in amazement. "He's so little, Joanna," he said in an awed voice.

Sun Woman looked over Tag's shoulder and grinned. "He might be small, but his cry would awaken the dead."

"May I hold him?" Tag asked hopefully, while Morning Song looked on, waiting her turn to hold her nephew.

Joanna placed the baby in his arms, and Tag smiled brightly. "I guess I never thought about the baby being a real person. It is hard for me to realize I am an uncle," he said, looking at the long black hair that was so soft to the touch. He felt choked up and hoped he wasn't going to cry and shame himself in front of everyone.

Windhawk had entered silently—the others were unaware that he had come into the tipi, but Joanna could feel his presence. She gazed up at him, and their eyes locked. She couldn't read the message in his dark eyes, but she hoped he could read the anger in hers.

He walked slowly toward Joanna, never once taking his eyes off her. "I am glad to see there is color in your cheeks this morning, Joanna," he said.

"Have you seen my son?" she asked pointedly, in a voice that dared him to deny the child was his.

His dark eyes clouded over, and he nodded. "I saw *my* son last night."

She raised an inquiring eyebrow, but said nothing. Watching Windhawk drop to his knees, she held her breath at the soft look that came into his eyes when he looked down at his infant son.

"He looks like you, Windhawk," Tag said, handing the tiny infant to his father.

"This is true," Sun Woman agreed. "This is exactly the way Windhawk looked as a baby."

The proud smile was wiped from Windhawk's face when he caught the frosty chill in the depths of Joanna's violet-colored eyes.

"I will talk to Joanna alone," he said, nodding for the others to leave.

Joanna would have liked to protest when the others began to file silently out of the tipi, one by one.

Windhawk sat down beside her and ran his finger over his son's smooth cheek. "Our son is beautiful, Joanna. I always knew if we had a son, he would be exceptional."

Her eyes burned with unspent anger. "Now that you have seen him, you are willing to admit that he is your son. I am sorry, Windhawk, but neither my son nor I need you now. The time for needing you has passed."

Windhawk could hear the pain and disillusionment in her voice, and he knew she was remembering the scene

312

she had witnessed between him and Red Bird. He knew she had every right to be angry with him and, for the first time in his life, Windhawk didn't know what to say to erase the pain he had caused Joanna. He wanted to reach out to her and pull her into his arms. He wished he had the courage to go down on his knees and beg for her forgiveness, but he was still too proud to beg.

"Joanna, we must talk. I know there is much hurt between us, but if we try, we can wipe it all away."

Joanna threw back her head and met his eyes squarely. "That might be the case, Windhawk, if I wanted to talk to you, but I do not. There is nothing you would have to say that would be of interest to me."

His dark brows met in a frown. "I will not hear this from you. I have come to move you and my son back into my lodge."

Joanna got slowly to her feet, wondering how he dared ask such a thing of her after what she had witnessed between him and Red Bird. "Never, Windhawk! I will never live with you and Red Bird. I do not know what kind of woman you think I am, but I would have thought you knew me well enough to know I would never live with you and your . . . wife!" She lapsed into English. "I don't even like you very well, Windhawk. You aren't the man I thought you were."

He frowned. "Red Bird is not now, nor has she ever been, my wife," he answered her flatly in English, loving the way her eyes blazed when she was angry.

"I care not by what name you call her; you can call her your wife . . . or you can call her your harlot. I would die before I ever allowed you to touch me again after you have been with her!"

His face was a mask of fury. "Red Bird is nothing to

me," he said, disliking the fact that he had to defend himself when he had not touched Red Bird. "You and my son will move to my lodge where you belong, Joanna!"

"I know you cannot force me to live with you as you once did, Windhawk. I have been accepted as a Blackfoot; therefore, I do not have to live in your lodge unless I choose to—and I do not choose to!"

He nodded in agreement. "This is true, Joanna. I hoped you would come back because you wanted to."

"You were mistaken. I can't imagine what gave you the notion that I would want to come back to you."

Windhawk laid the baby down and stood up. Dark eyes locked with violet eyes, and Joanna could feel her heart racing.

"Was I mistaken, Joanna?" he whispered. "Can you deny that when I touch you, you quiver inside as I do?" His hand reached out and touched her lips, and he watched her pull away.

"I will not deny or admit anything to you, Windhawk. You are no longer . . . my husband. I no longer have to answer to you about anything."

His eyes softened. "I still consider that you are my wife, Joanna." He reached up to his neck and removed the bear-claw necklace. "This belongs to you," he said, holding it out to her.

She had never seen Windhawk acting so strangely. It was as if his dark eyes were pleading with her. "No! Never!" She turned her back to him, not wanting him to see her tears. "Do you think I will ever forget the sight of you making love to Red Bird? You are a monster!"

"Joanna, sometimes appearances can be deceiving. I give you my word that I have never taken Red Bird to my body, nor have I been with any woman but you since I first saw you. I am not the monster you believe me to be."

She turned quickly to face him. "Do you think I will believe that after what I saw the other day? Do you take me for a fool, Windhawk?"

He saw no sign of softening in Joanna. She was strong and defiant—two qualities he had always admired in her. Those qualities would now keep her from taking what he offered her.

"I wish you would believe me, Joanna, for I speak the truth—I have never been with Red Bird. I will send her away."

"Even if you are telling the truth, I don't want you, Windhawk. You have killed the love I felt for you. I no longer admire you. I could never love someone I didn't admire. As for sending Red Bird away, I would advise you to keep her. She can help you stay warm through the cold winter."

Windhawk's eyes blazed, and he grabbed her by the wrist, pulling her against him. "You may not love me, Joanna, but I can make you want me!"

Joanna pushed against him, feeling real panic. Oh, yes, she thought, he could easily make her want him! Looking into his face, she felt her heart quicken as he lowered his dark head. "No, please, don't do this, Windhawk!"

His hands moved up and down her back in a caressing motion. "Do not fight me, Joanna. Try to remember what we once were to each other." His voice was deep and soft, and Joanna felt the pull of his magnetism.

She watched helplessly as his lips moved closer to hers, and he muffled her cry when his mouth covered hers. At first she struggled to be free of him, but soon his mouth teased and prodded hers into surrender. Joanna could feel her body tremble violently, and his hands went down to pull her tightly against him to still her quaking.

"You want me, Joanna," he whispered huskily in her ear. "The day you die, you will still want me."

Joanna buried her face against his soft buckskin shirt. Yes, she wanted him. Her body was a traitor to her mind. She could feel a wild sweetness spreading throughout her body at his touch.

Suddenly, she wanted to hit out at him for making her feel desire for him. Pushing herself away from him, she gave him a heated glance. "What does that prove, Windhawk? Many women desire you. Why should I be any different? I have come to know that desire is not love."

He reached out to her. "But you want me, Joanna, and we can build on that," he said, reaching out and touching a red-gold curl.

She backed away from him. "Tell this to Red Bird—she will listen to you—I do not want to hear anything else you have to say!" she replied, knowing that she still loved him deeply, and that, if he persisted, he could easily win her over.

He let his hand drop, knowing what he had destroyed could not be repaired in only one day. "I will wait until you are recovered from the birth of my son, then we will talk again. I am going to be away for a while—take care of my son."

Windhawk picked up his son and kissed the sleeping child. He then handed him to Joanna. "Take care of yourself, also, Joanna," he whispered.

Joanna watched him leave, wishing she dared call him back. She wished she were naive enough to believe all that he had told her, but she wasn't. She believed only what she had seen with her own eyes.

The baby began to fuss, and Joanna kissed him softly on the cheek. Holding him tightly against her, she felt the sting of tears in her eyes. "Your father has changed his mind—he thinks he wants me now that he knows you are his son. What shall I do, my little son? Dare I leave myself open for more hurt?"

As the weeks of winter stretched on, the severe weather seemed to intensify. In spite of the cold and snow that kept most of the Blackfoot tribe close to the village, the sound of children's laughter could be heard as they played their favorite winter games.

Joanna walked toward the river carrying a waterskin. She felt healthy and rested, and she smiled as she watched a group of children sliding down a slope on a sled they had constructed out of buffalo bones.

Her baby was now over a month old and growing stronger each day. Windhawk had ridden away the day after the birth of their son and hadn't yet returned. Sun Woman had told Joanna that Windhawk and some of the warriors had ridden to the Northern Blackfoot country to trade for horses.

Joanna bent down to fill the waterskin from the river. Gazing downstream, she saw the Piegan woman and turned quickly away. She had seen Red Bird from a distance several times and knew she was still living in Windhawk's lodge. She saw the woman walking toward her and quickly got to her feet, not wanting to talk to her.

"Wait, Flaming Hair, do not leave yet. I want to speak to you."

Joanna walked toward the village, ignoring the Piegan woman. She heard Red Bird just behind her and knew she was going to be persistent.

"I was not told that you were hard of hearing," Red Bird challenged.

Joanna turned and gave her a scalding look. "I hear the voices of my friends. I do not listen to the Red Bird who chirps nonsense."

"You think that you are above the rest of us because you have the white skin. Have I not seen the way you walk through the village, gathering people about you as if you were a great ruler, and they your lowly subjects?" Red Bird spat out angrily.

"Indeed. I am glad you are so observant," Joanna said, deciding she would not be drawn into a quarrel with this horrible woman.

"It is because of you that Windhawk has gone away," Red Bird accused.

"Is it?"

"You know it is. I have heard that he left because of you."

"You have the ears of a snake, Red Bird—you should have been named accordingly," Joanna countered, before turning to walk away.

Red Bird decided to try another tactic. Perhaps, if she pretended to be Flaming Hair's friend, she would gain more information. She had never considered that the white race had very much intelligence, and she was sure this Flaming Hair would be no exception.

"I have heard that Windhawk asked you to move back into his lodge. I think we could be friends if we both lived with Windhawk."

"Do you think so?" Joanna asked coolly. "I choose my friends carefully. You, I do not even like."

Red Bird gritted her teeth. There was something about

Flaming Hair that put her at a disadvantage. "Why did you not come back to Windhawk?"

"I am sure if you asked him, he would tell you."

"Is it that you are jealous and do not want to share him with me?"

Joanna's eyes flamed. "My reasons are my own. I have things to do and will not talk to you any longer."

"I would never consider moving back in with Windhawk if I were you. He does not need a white-face wife when he has me."

Joanna laughed in spite of the pain in her heart. "At last, we agree on something."

"I think you realize that Windhawk would not want you if it were not for his son. I will one day give him many sons, and he will forget about you and your son," Red Bird said spitefully.

Joanna had known two hateful and spiteful women so far in her life. Claudia had been one of them, and Red Bird was the other. At last Red Bird had struck Joanna at a vulnerable spot. She felt tears sting her eyes, but she refused to allow them to fall, knowing the Piegan woman would delight in her weakness.

"Go away, troublemaker!" Sun Woman's voice rang out. "Do not again seek out my daughter!"

Red Bird smiled smugly when she walked past Joanna. She knew she had done what she had set out to do. Flaming Hair would remember her words when she saw Windhawk again. Red Bird thought how foolish the white woman was. She couldn't understand why Joanna refused to live with Windhawk. She herself loved him and would do anything to please him, but he would not look at her as a woman. She would yet find some way to get rid of Flaming Hair.

Sun Woman walked beside Joanna. "It does one no good to listen to the croaking of a frog. Red Bird is a jealous and spiteful woman. I have come to believe she does not always tell the truth."

"I have known two such women in my life. One was white; the other was Red Bird. Each of them has taken from me that which I loved most in the world. It seems when they struck I had no defense against them."

"Joanna, I want to tell you something. I hope you will understand a foolish old woman's blunder."

Joanna smiled. "What could you have done that could be bad, my mother?"

"It was I who sent Red Bird to Windhawk's lodge. When he thought you were dead, he was grieving, and I thought she would bring him comfort."

Joanna took a deep breath. "Apparently, you were right, my mother. It would seem she has done well in healing your son's wounds."

"If you believe that, then you are blind."

"What does it matter? Windhawk and I are not right for each other. It seems all we do is hurt each other. I will not challenge Red Bird for a place in his lodge."

"Joanna, sometimes when the love is strong between two people, they will hurt each other without intending to. I believe this is what has occurred between you and my son. You should want to find out the truth."

"It also happens when the love is only on one side. Windhawk is at fault for what is wrong between us, my mother. I shoulder no blame in this."

"No one is above making mistakes, Joanna. You must take your share of the blame. The one great fault in all of this is that you and my son listened to others and not to your own hearts."

"Perhaps, but it no longer matters. Red Bird still lives in Windhawk's lodge, does she not?"

"Not as his wife. Windhawk has no wife . . . but you."

Sun Woman closed her mouth. It would do no good for her to tell Joanna that her son was in torment and loved her with a strong love that most women would never find in a man—Joanna would have to find this out for herself.

It was a cold night, and Joanna could hear the wind howling as she sat beside the fire, nursing her son. Sun Woman and Morning Song had gone to visit Gray Fox's wives, and she cherished this time alone with her son.

She smiled down at the baby, who was growing strong and healthy on her milk. His dear little face peeked out of the blanket, and Joanna touched his hand softly.

Sun Woman tended to be the doting grandmother, and while Joanna realized how Windhawk's mother loved the child, she was afraid she was spoiling him. Every time he cried she would pick him up.

A blast of frigid air announced someone's arrival, and Joanna looked up to see Windhawk! If she had been prepared for him, she could have hidden her startled glance, but she hadn't known he had returned to the village.

Joanna's eyes were drawn to his handsome face. When he removed his buffalo robe and hung it from the lodgepole she saw he wore no shirt, and her eyes wandered fleetingly across the broad expanse of his muscular chest. When she looked at his eyes she saw that they were drawn to her breast, where his son was nursing hungrily.

Joanna felt a tightening in her throat as he walked

321

toward her and dropped down beside her. She watched speechlessly as his hand trembled when he reached out to touch the soft hair on his son's head.

"I have missed you and our son," he said, looking deep into Joanna's eyes.

"I . . . did . . . not know you had returned."

She read so much feeling in his velvet-soft eyes that it frightened her. His desire for her was not disguised, and she wanted to look away, afraid of what other emotion she would discover in those dark eyes.

"I just arrived. I rode hard all day so I could see you before you went to bed."

He reached out his hand and gathered up a tress of red-gold hair, allowing it to sift between his fingers, and Joanna was too stunned to react.

"I have thought of nothing but you and our son, Joanna."

"Why did you go away?" she couldn't help asking.

His hand drifted up to her cheek. "I left so you could have time to think about the things I said to you. I was a coward, Joanna, knowing if I stayed near you I would want to . . ." He dipped his head, and Joanna knew he was going to kiss her. She wanted to pull away, but, instead, her lips parted in eager anticipation.

Windhawk groaned softly as his mouth touched hers. Joanna realized that she was being drawn under his magnetic spell and moved her head to the side.

"No, please!" she cried.

"You always say no when you mean yes, Joanna," he whispered. "I have hungered for your lips," he whispered against her mouth.

"No, Windhawk, do not do this!" she cried, placing her hand over her mouth.

Windhawk took her hands and held them in his. "I can see by your eyes that you want me, too, Joanna."

"N . . . no!"

He looked deeply into her eyes and saw the firelight reflected there. "One of the many things I have always admired about you is your honesty, Joanna. Why do you fear to admit the truth to me, as well as to yourself?"

"Windhawk, your mother and sister will be back soon," she said, in an effort to save herself. She feared that her weakness for him would overrule her good judgment.

"No, Joanna, I saw my mother before I came here. I asked her to give me some time alone with you."

Seeing that her son had fallen asleep, Joanna pulled her gown together. Windhawk reached for the child and raised him into his arms.

"Joanna, there are no words to describe what it feels like to be a father. I find myself wanting to tell everyone about him. I think of the time he will ride his first horse. I can envision when he is older, when he will walk beside me, looking to me for guidance. I am so proud of him, and I thank you for giving him to me."

Joanna felt a sob building in her throat. No, she wouldn't allow Windhawk to make her forget all that was wrong between them. "I am sure these feelings will pass. I think you want something when it is new to you, but once you have it, you will tire of it and cast it aside."

Windhawk's eyes narrowed. "You were my wife, and yet you know so little about me."

"I know all I care to know. I know you tired of me soon enough and replaced me with Red Bird."

"I told you I have never been with Red Bird," he said in a deadly calm voice.

"She tells a different story. Perhaps the two of you should get together and decide what is the truth."

His face became a mask, and she could see a muscle throbbing at his temple. "I will have her punished if she has told you this."

"Do not punish her on my account. All I want from you is for you to leave me alone."

His eyes swept her face. "I will never leave you alone, Joanna. How can I? You are the mother of my son," he said in a deep voice.

Joanna shrugged her shoulders. "Red Bird told me she would give you sons."

Windhawk laid the baby down and grasped Joanna's wrist. When he stood up, he carried Joanna with him. "I will hear no more of this! I have told you the truth, but you choose to not believe me. Will it make you feel better if I send that woman away?"

Joanna saw his face was a mask of fury, but she herself was angry. "I do not care what you do with her—it will not make me change my mind about you. As soon as spring comes, I am leaving."

Her announcement fell like a wave of silence over the tipi. She could see Windhawk's eyes go to his son and then back to her. She flinched when he grabbed her by the shoulders and hauled her against his body.

"I would not try that if I were you, Joanna. I will never allow you to take my son away."

"I will not leave without him!"

"Then you will not go!"

"You cannot hold me here against my will. The moment I became accepted as a Blackfoot you had no power to hold me as a captive."

His lips curled into a snarl. "You may no longer be a

captive, Joanna, but you forget—I am the chief of the Blackfoot—my word is law. If I say you stay, you stay!"

She flung her head back. "Do you think to win me with your soft ways?" she taunted. She didn't realize until it was too late that she had pushed him too far.

Windhawk picked her up in his arms and carried her toward the buffalo robe at the back of the lodge. Joanna kicked and struggled, fearing what he had in mind.

"I will never submit to you willingly, and if you take me by force, I will hate you!" she cried.

His smile had no humor in it. "I know what it takes to make you submit, Joanna. Why should I have to take by force what I can have with the touch of my hand?"

She drew in her breath, more determined than ever not to let him see her weakness for him. Flinging back her head, she struggled all the harder.

Windhawk set her on her feet, and before she knew what was happening, he had lifted her gown over her head. Joanna crossed her hands over her breasts, backing as far away from him as she could get before bumping against the wall of the tipi.

"Do not do this, Windhawk," she whispered through trembling lips.

His eyes moved hungrily over her body, and she knew it would do no good to plead with him. She cautioned herself to remain passive and not to give in to the warm touch of his hand. She knew from past experience that she would never be able to resist him.

He bent down and removed her moccasins, and Joanna did nothing to try and stop him. She felt herself begin to tremble as his eyes traveled up her legs, across her stomach to her breasts, then finally to rest on her face.

She closed her eyes and gritted her teeth as his hand

moved up her leg. Don't feel, she warned herself. Make your mind a blank, she pleaded silently. When she gained the courage to open her eyes, she saw that Windhawk had removed his clothing and was standing before her naked!

She drew in her breath as her eyes wandered over his magnificent body. When she looked at his face, she saw his eyes were filled with passion.

Windhawk pulled her into his arms, and her body melted against his. She had forgotten how good it was to feel his hard, muscular body pressed against hers. As his hands traced tiny patterns across her back and then slid down to her waist, she remembered how he could render her mindless with a caress.

Windhawk was sprinkling kisses over her upturned face. "Remember, Jo-anna, remember how good it was between us?" he asked hotly against her ear.

He had spoken her name the way he had pronounced it before he learned to speak it correctly. She remembered all too well that in the past, at times when he had been making love to her, he would often lapse into the old way of saying her name. That, more than anything else he had done or said thus far, was her undoing.

She felt herself moving backwards as he lowered her onto the soft buffalo robe.

Chapter Twenty-Two

Joanna fought against the warm, wonderful feelings of pleasure that spread throughout her body with the intensity of a raging forest fire. She felt as if she were in a drugged state—a puppet that Windhawk could manipulate merely by pulling the strings. His soft, stroking hands were playing havoc with her peace of mind—reminding her of the times when he had introduced her to sensuous experiences.

There was no question of her remaining passive when she felt so alive for the first time in many months. Her body had been starved for Windhawk's touch for so long, and she seemed to have no control of her own.

Windhawk's lips traveled over her face, and Joanna could feel his warm breath on her skin. His ebony hair slid softly across her lips, and she closed her eyes. Her awareness of him seemed to seep into every pore of her skin.

Oh, my love, my dearest love, she thought, as his burning kiss invoked memories of the times when they laughed and loved together. Joanna knew she was a hopeless prisoner of her feelings for this man. She hadn't stopped loving him, if anything she loved him more than ever. Until now she hadn't realized how much she had missed him. Loving him and watching him with Red Bird had been a physical pain, knifing into her heart. She had tried to push her love for him aside, but she hadn't been in the least successful.

"Jo-anna, Jo-anna," he murmured against her ear, reminding her of the first time he had taken her body. How tender and sweet he had been that autumn day so long ago when he had introduced her to the world of touching and feeling. He had been so patient when he showed her how wonderful it was to be his woman.

When Windhawk pulled back and gave Joanna a questioning look, she threaded her hands through his ebony hair and pulled his head forward to her parted lips, forgetting for the moment that they had hurt each other deeply since that first day when they had become as one.

His mouth seemed to burn her tender lips, and Joanna thought she would die from the intense yearning he invoked in her. She knew she would be sorry tomorrow if she surrendered so easily tonight, but she couldn't pull back now . . . they had gone too far for that! Her body was a mass of quivering flesh, yearning for the touch of Windhawk's hand.

"How far I have traveled to find myself going around in a circle, Joanna," Windhawk breathed in her ear.

Not understanding his words, she looked into his eyes, which were velvet soft. Her breath came out in a sob at the tenderness she saw there.

"What do you mean?" she couldn't resist asking.

He lifted her chin and brushed her satiny cheek with his lips. "No matter where I go, my footsteps always bring me back to you, beloved."

His words hit her in the face like a dash of cold water! Suddenly, Joanna felt great fear. What was she doing? Was she so weak that she allowed Windhawk to pull her under his spell with the touch of his hand and a few soft-spoken words? She pushed against him, feeling a fear so wild that she cried out. To her surprise, he moved back. Rolling away from him, she scrambled to her knees.

Windhawk's burning eyes ran the length of her naked body with the devastating effect of an earthquake. Joanna's whole body was a trembling mass when he smiled slightly.

"I always said that you were the perfect woman . . . I have not changed my mind."

Joanna felt a hot wave wash over her, and she could do no more than stare into his dark, expressive eyes. Her eyes widened as he swung to his knees and knelt beside her.

"You can run, Joanna, but like me, you will find you are running in a circle."

She shook her head in a silent denial.

Windhawk's eyes rested on her flaming hair, and he reached out to touch it. "Must I tell you of this love that burns in my heart for you? Did you think my love for you was such a small thing that it would not endure? Did I not once tell you that my love for you would reach out to you even beyond my death?" His voice was deep with feeling.

Joanna felt herself swaying toward him, but she stopped herself from making contact with his body by placing her hand against his chest. Oh, he was good at using silver words, she thought. He had not become the leader of the fierce Blackfoot warriors without being able to manipulate people. Did he also say these same things

329

to Red Bird? She wouldn't make the mistake of believing him again.

"Go away, Windhawk. Please, leave me alone—I do not want you."

Joanna watched as his dark eyes narrowed; she wasn't prepared for his quick action. When he reached out and jerked her forward, her body slammed against the hard, muscled wall of his chest, and she gasped.

He forced her face up to him. "I will leave you alone, Joanna, because when I take you, it will be because it is what you want. I think the time will come when you will come to me," he said lazily, as his eyes drifted down to her lips, waiting for her to deny his words.

"Never!"

He shoved her away from him and smiled ever so slightly. "Never is a long time, Joanna. I think you will come to me before too many moons have passed," he said, standing up and pulling on his buckskin trousers.

"You must think very highly of your prowess with women, oh mighty chief of the Blackfoot. Do not hold your breath until I come to you, Windhawk . . . I can assure you that day will never come. As far as you and I are concerned, there never was a forever."

He smiled indulgently. "Time will prove which one of us is right, Joanna." He looked past her to where their son lay sleeping.

"I almost forgot the reason I came here. I have come to give my son a name."

Joanna wrapped herself in a buffalo robe and stood up, astounded that he could switch from adoring lover to a cool, businesslike manner so quickly. If he could turn cold and indifferent to her so easily, she would show him

330

she could do the same. Her stomach was tied in knots, and her heartbeat had not yet returned to its normal rate, but she raised her eyes to him, pretending indifference.

"I was wondering if you would get around to my son. Why has it taken you so long?" she asked, in a voice that plainly showed her irritation.

"I suppose because the thought of having a son was too new to me, and I had not chosen a name."

"What you mean is you thought my baby was not your son, so you did not bother to choose his name!"

"I have decided to call him Little Hawk," he said, ignoring Joanna's outburst.

"That will be a strange name when he is as tall as you are," she said, trying to find fault with his choice of name for their son. She knew that whatever he decided to call the child would only be his name until he grew older.

"It will be his name only until he earns his own name," he said, reminding her of what she already knew.

Joanna nodded. She knew she had no say in what her son would be called. Windhawk was not only his father, but he was also the chief of the tribe.

She watched as Windhawk picked up his sleeping son and smiled down at him. "Little Hawk, my son, the time will come when we will ride across the prairies together to hunt the buffalo. For now, I give you into your mother's keeping . . . when you are older, I will see to your training."

Little Hawk yawned and drifted back to sleep, not knowing or caring about the conflict that raged between his mother and father.

Windhawk handed the baby to Joanna and swept out of the tipi with the same swiftness with which he had entered. Joanna stood silently, watching the flap swing to and fro in the wind. She felt as if she had just been released from the destructive grip of a summer hurricane.

Lifting Little Hawk to her face, she kissed his smooth cheek. Joanna had no notion what the future held for her and her son. She only knew that if Windhawk had persisted tonight, she would at this very moment be in his arms. She hadn't realized until tonight how much she had missed his lovemaking. He had taught her the sensuous feelings of her mind as well as her body. How could she pretend indifference to him when her body ached for his? Joanna smiled without humor. She hadn't pretended indifference tonight . . . Windhawk had clearly known what she had been feeling! How could he not when she had practically begged him to make love to her?

Joanna was disgusted with herself that he could so easily sway her to him. Windhawk was more dangerous to her than the pack of wolves who had hounded her and Morning Song, because he had the power to destroy her soul, while the wolves could only have destroyed her body. She knew that if he reached out to her right at that moment she would have had to fight herself to keep from giving in to him.

Joanna had to admit to herself that she had wanted Windhawk to hold her in his arms and whisper words of endearment in her ear; in fact, she had secretly been disappointed when he had relented so easily.

She laid Little Hawk down on the buffalo robe and lay down beside him. She had once loved Windhawk with all her being, but that was before she had discovered what he was really like. Joanna could never love a man who would swear his eternal love to her and then quickly turn to

332

another woman. Windhawk had the power to make her body react to him, but her mind was strong, and she would never forgive his deceptions. She wished with her whole heart that he had been the man she had thought him to be.

Joanna remembered her mother once saying that if you lived with a man long enough, his true self would surface. That was what had happened to Windhawk. Her picture of him had once been distorted by her love for him—she could now see him clearly. It wasn't so much that he had taken Red Bird into his lodge that made her angry . . . although Joanna resented that fact. It was more that he had lied to her by telling her he had never lain with the woman. Had she not seen them together with her own eyes?

She pulled Little Hawk close to her, and the baby curled up snugly against her. How she loved her tiny, dark-skinned baby, but she couldn't afford to let the love she felt for his father touch her heart again.

Joanna's eyes drifted shut, and she was asleep before Sun Woman and Morning Song returned.

Windhawk entered his lodge and walked directly over to Red Bird, who was busy mending one of his shirts. He jerked the shirt out of her hand and threw it aside angrily. "I want you to gather your belongings and leave my lodge at once!"

Red Bird blinked her eyes and looked up at him. "Why would you say this to me? You cannot insult me . . . am I not the daughter of a great chief?"

"Yes, your father is a good man, but his seed is as buffalo dung!"

Red Bird stood up slowly, facing her accuser. "My father will hear of the way you have treated me. There will be blood spilled between the Piegans and the Bloods when he learns of your insult to his daughter."

"I myself have already spoken to your father about you; I told him how you have come between me and my wife. He was sorry for the way you have shamed him. He has asked me to tell you he is willing to take you back if you wish to go home."

Red Bird's face lost its color, and she began to see all her hopes turn to bitter ashes. "I love you! How can you do this to me?"

Windhawk's eyes narrowed. "I have never given you any reason to love me. I will hear no more of this. I took pity on you, and, against what I wanted, allowed you to move to my lodge because you begged it of me. My doing so has cost me the woman I love."

Red Bird's eyes were blinded by tears. "I offered you all I have to give a man, and you cast me aside for that white face. . . ."

Windhawk held up his hand. "Do not speak against her. Leave my lodge now!"

Red Bird saw the anger in Windhawk's dark eyes and knew it wouldn't be wise to say any more. Inside her burned a fire of hatred and revenge, and it was directed not only at the white woman but at Windhawk, as well. She had wanted him more than any man she had ever known, but now she would destroy him when she got the chance.

"You will pay for this," she threatened between clenched teeth.

"I already have. Go, I have asked my friend, Gray Fox, to allow you to stay with his wives until you know what you want to do. I know about the lies you told Joanna—you are fortunate that I allow you to get off so easily. If it were not for the respect I have for your father, I would have you severely punished."

A light not unlike madness burned in Red Bird's eyes. Reaching down to her moccasin, she withdrew a knife and lunged at Windhawk. "If I cannot have you, Flaming Hair will not either!" she cried.

Windhawk grabbed her arm and twisted it behind her, applying pressure until she dropped the knife. He shoved her down and stood over her.

"You are very fortunate that you still live, Red Bird," he hissed. "I will see that you leave my village before the full moon has passed."

Red Bird scrambled to her feet and rushed out of the lodge. She knew it was a miracle she was alive. Windhawk was not known for his leniency to those who crossed him. Hatred and revenge burned in her heart, and it was directed at the Flaming Hair. If Windhawk was going to send her away, she would have very little time to seek her revenge!

Windhawk lay down on his mat and stared upward. He could only imagine what lies Red Bird had told Joanna. If he wasn't guilty of unfaithfulness, he was certainly guilty of being a fool. He knew he could have had Joanna tonight if he had persisted. She might not love him anymore, but he could still control her body. Why had he pulled back tonight when he had her ready to surrender? Because he wanted to see her eyes soften with love when he took her to his body.

Joanna had been all he had hoped for in a wife. She had brightened his days and made his nights exciting and unforgettable. Now, she had given him a son, and he felt

335

the invisible tie that would unite them for eternity. He was confused—how would he go about winning back her love and trust? It didn't matter how loudly he proclaimed his innocence, she wouldn't believe him after seeing him and Red Bird together. How would he prove to Joanna that he had been a victim of circumstance the same way she had? Never had he faced anything that was of such great importance. He must not fail!

Closing his eyes, Windhawk wondered how far he would travel before the circle brought him back to Joanna forever. One thing he was sure of—he couldn't stay in the village where he would see Joanna each day without wanting to take her to his mat. He was restless, and a fire burned in his loins. He had to get away for a time. Why did he keep running away when all he wanted to do was stay?

Windhawk was a man in love who was being denied the fulfillment that his body craved. He knew he could easily find a willing woman to share his mat, but that thought was distasteful to him. No matter what Joanna thought of him, he was a man of principle, and he wouldn't take another woman while he felt he was still Joanna's husband.

Windhawk turned over on his side and stared into the glowing fire. He had only returned to the village today, but he knew that he had to get away again. He would give Joanna more time to think. Perhaps, when she found out that Red Bird had moved out of his lodge, she would be more inclined to listen to him.

Windhawk realized that the whole village was wondering what was going on between him and Joanna. He knew many of his people thought that Red Bird had replaced Joanna as his woman. His mistake had been in allowing the Piegan woman to move into his lodge in the first place. He couldn't very well go around announcing to the whole tribe that he had never taken Red Bird to his mat.

He thought of his little son and smiled . . . Little Hawk was a son to be proud of. He hoped Little Hawk would inherit Joanna's kindness and loving nature. Windhawk remembered his boyhood and how safely and securely he had grown up because he had had a loving mother and father. He wanted that same feeling of security for his own son.

He closed his eyes and drifted off to sleep, knowing his dreams would be of Joanna and when they had laughed and loved in a happier time.

Joanna was dreaming. Her dream was taking her back to the time Windhawk had found her after the raid on the wagon train. At that time, she had thought that Windhawk had executed the raid and was responsible for the death of so many people. She hadn't known then that he was in fact her savior and had rescued her. She was frightened of him and of the devastating effect he had on her . . . she didn't want to love him, but, against her will, she had been drawn to him.

Joanna's dream was so real she could almost feel the touch of his long, sensitive fingers against her skin.

There was a sensation like pain when she felt his hand on her shoulder, and she tried to back away. She wanted to cry out as he lifted her into his arms and carried her to the buffalo robe and laid her down. Her heart was pounding with fear as she tried to scramble to her feet, but Windhawk forced her back against the soft buffalo

337

robe. She was making whimpering sounds as he lay down beside her and pulled her into his arms.

Joanna realized she was still dreaming of the time Windhawk had first taken her body, making her his woman. She had been young and innocent then and hadn't known about the feelings a woman could have for the man she loved.

"There is nothing to fear, Joanna. I will not harm you." Windhawk spoke to her in her dream just as he had on the night he had made her a woman.

Her slight body was trembling, so he ran a soothing hand down her back, while pulling her tighter against him.

For long moments he caressed her, until, at last, her trembling ceased. His hand slid up her back to her glorious hair.

Joanna could feel her fear being replaced by a sensation of contentment. She began to feel safe. This man was not of her kind. Again, Joanna realized she was dreaming, and she didn't want to wake up.

In the dream, Windhawk drew her head toward him, and she did not resist, but rested her face against his smooth, bare chest. He was filling her whole being with his presence.

In her dream, Joanna could feel his breath stirring her hair, and suddenly she felt neither safe nor contented. She knew she must flee or she would be lost forever. She could only think of the strong, sensitive hand that traced the outline of her face.

"Windhawk, please, I don't want—" Joanna pleaded in her dream state.

His finger touched her mouth, silencing her plea. "Jo-anna," he whispered in a pain-filled voice. "Jo-anna, you

338

spoke my name."

It was as if a thousand bright lights exploded in her head as his lips touched hers reverently.

His hand drifted down the front of her gown, and before she was aware of what he was doing Windhawk had unfastened it. Slowly he pushed it off her shoulders as his lips brushed the lobe of her ear, then moved down to nuzzle her neck.

"No, please, no," she moaned, twisting and turning in her sleep, feeling the same wild abandonment that she had that night so long ago.

Windhawk covered her lips with his, closing off her protest. He kissed and caressed her, all the while pushing her clothing downward. That night her virgin body had been no match for his experience. Her body had been ready to obey his slightest command. And now, in her dream, she could feel her heart drumming in her head, and she was unaware of anything but Windhawk and his gentle stroking hands, which caused new and unexplored feelings of delight to course through her body. When his hand slid down her throat to rest against her breast, she wanted to protest, but her body betrayed her. Joanna felt momentary relief when he withdrew his hand, until she realized he was pushing her gown and undergarments downward.

Joanna gasped when she felt his lips on her stomach, tying her insides into tight knots.

"No," she cried, pushing against him with all her strength. She hit out at Windhawk, catching him with a loud slap across the face. She froze, thinking that he would strike her back. Seconds passed and she could feel his intense stare even through the darkened tipi.

"Jo-anna, do not fight me. You know you want to feel

339

the oneness with me. It will do no good to fight those feelings. Would it not be better if you would . . . submit?" he asked in his halting English.

He took her hand and raised it to his lips. "These hands were not meant to bring pain to a man . . . only joy." He then slid his body forward and drew her into his arms once more. She had not been aware that he had removed his breechcloth until he pressed his hot body against her.

In her dream Joanna closed her eyes at the unfamiliar feel of a man's body—which was hard and firm in all the places where she was soft. Her breasts were flattened against the wide wall of his chest, and she wanted to deny the pleasure that coursed through her veins. He slid his body against hers, and Joanna didn't even realize that she inched closer to him. She could feel his pulsing manhood pressed against her inner thigh and felt frightened again.

"Please, don't hurt me," she pleaded.

His lips nuzzled her ear. "I would sooner die than cause you pain, Jo-anna." His hot breath fanned her cheek, and suddenly Joanna had no more desire to fight him. He would win in the end, she vaguely reasoned, knowing that she was beyond resisting. She had no idea what he would do to her body, but his mouth sought hers, forcing her lips apart to receive his kiss. Where his kiss had been gentle before, he now plundered her mouth, and she groaned, surprised that he had so easily overcome her resistance. She might hate herself tomorrow, but tonight she would give him all he demanded of her . . . !

Joanna could feel herself waking up, and she fought to return to the dream. When she opened her eyes, she saw that she was back in the present. Her face was wet with tears, and she felt so empty inside. She wished she could lose herself in her dream and live in the world of the past when Windhawk had loved her!

Joanna buried her face in the buffalo robe, losing herself in total misery. The dream had seemed so real, and she felt such a sense of loss, knowing they could never recapture the love they had experienced that autumn night . . . it was gone forever. It was no longer autumn, but the middle of winter. Their love had not endured, as Windhawk had promised her it would.

Closing her eyes, she wished she could recapture the dream and feel the oneness with Windhawk once more.

I love him—I will always love him, she thought, facing the truth with bitter regret. No matter what happened between them now, or how Windhawk shamed her by flaunting Red Bird in her face, she would never stop loving him. It was a hopeless feeling to know that she had no control over whom she would love. If she had her choice, she surely wouldn't have chosen Windhawk . . . yes, she would have. She would choose him over any living man. He would always be her only love, and nothing on this earth would ever change that!

Windhawk awoke and cried out. He sat up quickly, looking about as if in a daze. His body was trembling and wet from perspiration. He had been having a nightmare, and even though he was now fully awake, he still couldn't shake his feeling of foreboding.

In his dream, he had seen Joanna being stabbed over and over by someone who was no more than a dark shadow. He had struggled to get to her, but hadn't been able to reach her in time!

Covering his face with his hands, he tried to wipe the

341

vision of Joanna, bloody and dying, out of his mind. It had been no more than a dream, he told himself. Joanna was safe in his mother's tipi.

Standing up, he pulled a warm buffalo robe about him, knowing he must see for himself that Joanna was safe.

When he entered his mother's tipi, he walked silently to where Joanna was sleeping. He could clearly see her face in the flickering firelight.

Turning away, he left as silently as he had come, thinking how foolish he had been for allowing a dream to upset him, glad no one was aware that he had entered his mother's tipi, and not knowing that his mother had watched him from her mat.

Sun Woman shook her head sadly at her son's torment. She had wanted to cry out at the tears she had seen on Windhawk's face!

Chapter Twenty=Three

Farley had assured Joanna that Fosset was recovering nicely; he was gaining back the weight he had lost, and the scratches were all but healed. Although Joanna took Farley's word that Fosset was mending, she wanted to see for herself.

Little Hawk had been fed, and Morning Song had readily agreed to watch him while Joanna rode to the pasture where Fosset ran with Windhawk's horses.

Joanna kissed Little Hawk on his soft, chubby cheek and waved to Morning Song before leaving. She thought how nice it would be to get out in the fresh air. The weather had been so bad that she had been forced to stay near the village for too long, and her young spirit yearned for the outdoors.

The sun was shining, and although it was lightly snowing the weather was not too cold. She mounted Tag's horse, Navaron, and headed through the village.

Joanna hadn't seen Windhawk for three weeks. Sun Woman had told her that he and several of his warriors had gone hunting. She tried not to think of him, but he was never far from her thoughts. She couldn't help but dwell on the happiness they had once shared, and her body remembered too well the touch of his hand. Many nights she would dream of the time when Windhawk had held her in his arms. In her dreams she could almost feel his caressing hands moving over her body; when she awoke, she would feel sadly empty inside.

Windhawk had made her a woman, and her heart cried out for what they had once shared but had now lost. She wondered how long it would take her to put these disturbing feelings aside. Joanna realized that her life was going nowhere until she could make a decision about her future.

When she drew even with Windhawk's lodge, her eyes picked up movement there, and she turned to see Windhawk talking to Gray Fox. She hadn't been aware that Windhawk had returned, and she felt a weakness wash over her.

Windhawk's back was to her, and she hoped she could get past him without his seeing her, but that was not to be the case. Gray Fox raised his hand and called out to her, causing Windhawk to turn around to look at her.

"It is good to see that you are getting out in the fresh air, Flaming Hair," Gray Fox said, smiling. "How is that son of yours?"

Unless Joanna wanted to be rude, she had no choice but to stop and speak to Gray Fox. Drawing rein on Navaron, she smiled slightly at him, while she avoided looking at Windhawk.

"It is nice to see you, Gray Fox. You have been away and have not yet seen my son. I would be proud to show him off to you."

He walked toward her and rested his hand on her

344

horse's neck. "You are mistaken. I have seen Little Hawk several times. Windhawk is such a proud father, he takes me to see him every chance he gets. I saw him yesterday, as well as today."

Joanna's eyes shifted to Windhawk, who was staring at her with dark, blazing eyes. So Windhawk had been home since yesterday. She felt anger when she realized he must have chosen the times she was away from the tipi to visit Little Hawk. Did he dislike her so much that he wanted to avoid her at all cost?

Her anger must have shown in her face, because Windhawk's eyes darkened and narrowed.

"If you will excuse me, I am on my way to check on my horse, Fosset. I will wish you a good day, Gray Fox," she said, nudging Navaron forward. When she rode away she could feel Windhawk's eyes burning into her back. When at last she was free of the village, she urged the horse into a gallop, wanting to put as much distance as she could between herself and Windhawk's disturbing presence.

Joanna was seething on the inside. What right did Windhawk have to treat her like some stranger? She felt she was trapped in the life she was now forced to live. If only she had a way, she would leave this place and never look back. She didn't know how Windhawk felt about his son. The fact that he had paid any attention to him at all had come as a complete surprise to her.

Windhawk watched Joanna ride away, then he turned to Gray Fox. "I can see you are still drawn to Joanna," he said to his friend in a biting tone.

Gray Fox caught the anger and jealousy in Windhawk's voice. "Is it your wish that I not speak to Joanna? I admire your wife, and as her friend as well as yours, I feel hurt in my heart at what she has been through. It cannot be easy for her to watch her husband take another woman to his lodge. If she were my woman, I would not treat her so. I think she is worth more than Red Bird."

"She is neither your woman, nor is she your concern. You yourself have two wives. You would do well to look to your own wives and leave Joanna to me."

"It is time someone thought of your wife. She was captured by the Cree, and we may never know the hardships she and Morning Song endured; yet when she returned to you it was to find another woman had taken her place. She almost died giving you a son, and still you treat her as if she were the dirt you walk upon. You can get angry with me if you wish, but it is time someone spoke up for Joanna."

Windhawk's eyes held a murderous light as he turned his back and walked away from Gray Fox. He would have spoken to Joanna if she had spoken to him first, but she still treated him like some stranger. He didn't like that Joanna had been so friendly to Gray Fox while ignoring him. He also resented the fact that his friend felt he needed to defend Joanna to him. He knew he was being jealous and unreasonable, but he couldn't seem to help himself. Windhawk walked to his mother's tipi. Seeing Little Hawk was asleep in Morning Song's arms, he left abruptly. Walking to his horse, he mounted and rode off at a gallop.

He was some distance from the village before he realized he was riding toward the pasture where Joanna had said she was going.

Joanna followed the winding river until she came to the pasture where Windhawk kept his horses. She smiled brightly and waved at the young boy, Crooked Nose, who

346

tended Windhawk's herd. Dismounting, she tied Navaron's reins to the branch of a pine tree.

"I have come to see Fosset, Crooked Nose. I am told he is doing well."

"That is so, Flaming Hair. His wounds are all healed, and he is eating well. Windhawk has asked me to take extra care of him. Would you like me to bring him to you?"

"Yes, I would like that."

She watched as the young boy mounted his pony and rode away.

When he returned, he was leading the reluctant Fosset. Joanna moved her hand over Fosset's smooth coat, noticing that he was indeed recovered. Bending down, she examined his legs and found his wounds were all healed.

"You have done well, Crooked Nose. Thank you for tending Fosset so well."

The young boy basked in her praise. "I used the healing herbs that She Who Heals always used on sores, and it took no time for Fosset to heal."

"Yes, I can see that."

At that moment, Joanna and Crooked Nose heard a rider approach from the direction of the village, and they saw Windhawk emerge from the pine forest. Joanna's first instinct was to mount her horse and ride away. She was not ready to face Windhawk. Her anger and hurt were too deep, and her heart pounded fiercely when she remembered what had happened the last time they had been together.

But somehow she could do nothing but wait for him to approach. She refused to look at him, however. Bending down, she pretended to be examining Fosset's hooves.

She could hear Windhawk's horse pawing the ground. Feeling the heat rising in her body, she knew Windhawk was watching her. Standing up, she patted Fosset's hind quarters and turned to Crooked Nose.

"I must return to the village now, my son will be waking up. Thank you again for taking such good care of Fosset for me, Crooked Nose."

The young boy looked from his chief to the Flaming Hair. Everyone in the village knew there was trouble between the two of them, and he could see that for himself. Flaming Hair had not spoken to Windhawk, and he was staring at her in a most peculiar way.

"Take Fosset back to the herd, Crooked Nose," Windhawk said in a commanding voice.

The young boy didn't hesitate to obey. He gathered up the horse's reins and led him over to his pony. Mounting his horse, he rode away and was soon lost from sight.

Joanna turned away and walked toward Navaron. She held her head high and didn't look back at Windhawk. When she had almost reached her goal, she felt Windhawk's hand on her shoulder, and he whirled her around to face him.

"I will speak to you, Joanna—now!" he said in a raspy voice, while his eyes blazed his displeasure.

She looked down at his hand, which was still on her shoulder, refusing to look into his face. "I believe we have said everything that needs to be said. Take your hand off me, if you do not mind," she whispered.

Instead of removing his hand, his grip tightened, and she looked into his face. Oh Lord, she thought as her eyes locked with his. He still has the power to make me fall apart inside. I cannot allow him to see how much I still love him, she thought in a panic. His eyes seemed to draw

348

her to him, and she felt his hand glide down to her back in an almost caress. Not again, she thought to herself, please, not again!

"I do not believe we ever settled anything. We will talk, Joanna. You can come with me now, or I will carry you. It is up to you."

"I have nothing to say to you, and you could say nothing that I would want to hear," she said, knowing she was telling only a half-truth. Joanna didn't want to talk to him; she wanted him to take her in his arms and say the things to her that she so wanted to hear. She wanted to hear him tell her that Red Bird meant nothing to him, and that he loved her.

Fool, she called herself. All he has to do is touch you, and you are willing to overlook everything.

"You will have to force me, Windhawk, because I can imagine nothing that we have not already said to one another."

His dark brows came together in a frown, and before she could react he lifted her into his arms and carried her to his horse. She struggled as he mounted, and his arms tightened about her like iron bands.

"We will have our talk, Joanna. Had you acted like an adult instead of a child, I would not have to force you to come with me. Do not put the blame on me if you are making it hard on yourself."

Joanna was seething on the inside. What could they possibly have to talk about? She didn't answer him but set her jaw stubbornly. Let Windhawk talk, she thought, she wouldn't have to listen to him, and she had no intention of carrying on a conversation with him. She resented his high-handed treatment of her. She had no notion where he was taking her, but she hoped it would

349

be back to the village.

Joanna looked down at his strong hands and remembered how gentle they could be when they had caressed her body. She felt a tremor shake her as his warm breath fanned the red-gold hair near her ear. His lean, hard legs brushed against hers, and she felt a weakness wash over her. She had the urge to lean back and rest her head on his shoulder, but she didn't dare. She was raging on the inside because he caused this weakness deep inside her.

"Where are you taking me?" she asked in a whisper.

He leaned his head forward and his ebony hair brushed against her cheek. "I am taking you where we can talk undisturbed by anyone."

"I need to get back to the baby, he will be waking soon," she said, reaching for an excuse—any excuse.

"I looked in on my son before I left, and he was sleeping soundly. If he awakens, my sister will know how to care for him."

"So," she said, jerking forward and turning her head to look at him. "Do you often go to see Little Hawk when I am not around?" She was unaware that she had spoken in English. "When will you learn, Windhawk, my son and I don't need you. Take me back to the village this instant!"

She began to struggle, and he held her loosely, knowing he was of superior strength and she would soon tire of her childish antics.

Joanna saw his jaw tighten and knew that he was angry, but she was, too. He was nothing more than a brute imposing his will on her, she thought. Why couldn't he just leave her alone?

Finally, she stopped struggling and held herself rigid so she wouldn't touch him. She decided she would act with dignity and make the best of a bad situation.

Joanna held her temper as he entered the river, and she didn't protest when he rode up the bank and into the forest. She tried to act indifferent when he rode on deep into the woods, nor did she react when he pulled up his horse, placed her on the ground, and then dismounted himself.

He took her arm and led her over to a fallen log and set her down. She looked up at him, expecting to see a startled expression on his face because he had gotten his way, but she saw only sadness in his eyes.

"Why have you brought me here?" she asked.

His eyes moved down her face to rest on her swollen breast, and she thought she detected pain on his face. "I told you . . . I wanted to talk to you without being interrupted."

She raised her head defiantly. "I am listening."

His eyes traveled over her red-gold hair, and he watched as the soft snowflakes drifted down to settle on the flaming mass of curls. He felt uncertainty now that they were alone. What would he say to her? He remembered a time when he could have told her anything. He thought of the nights she had lain in his arms, and he had talked to her for hours while she had listened to him. This was the woman he had loved above all else . . . she had shared his deepest secrets. They had laughed and loved together. When had things begun to go wrong between them?

He looked past her and watched the snow drift down to land on the limb of the pine tree, which seemed to bow down with the added weight of the snow. "I do not like this bad feeling that is between us, Joanna. I want to be able to see my son anytime I want."

"Have I ever said you couldn't see him? I did not think you cared about him."

He glanced back to her. "I care."

"We do not need you, Windhawk. Go back to Red Bird—perhaps she will give you a son. She told me she would."

He reached forward and grabbed her by the shoulders, pulling her to her feet. His face was a mask of fury as she squirmed to get free. She wedged her hands against his chest as he brought her closer to him.

"Red Bird no longer lives in my lodge. You must know she has moved into Gray Fox's tipi."

"I have heard that, but it does not concern me. I suppose you grew tired of her, as you did me. Poor Red Bird . . . she has my sympathy."

He was silent so long that Joanna began to think he wouldn't answer. Raising her head, she saw the anger sparkling in his dark eyes.

"I *am* tired of you, Joanna! I am tired of your temper—I am tired of hearing Red Bird thrown in my face—I am tired of this anger that exists between us!"

The angry words she would have spoken stuck in her throat. His eyes were so soft, and she recognized the passion that flamed in their dark depths. She whimpered as he lay his cheek against hers. No, she thought, don't let this be happening. Don't let me forget to hate him.

Windhawk's hands moved down her back, pulling her tighter against him. Knowing she should protest, all she could think of was how right it felt to be in his arms again. She realized how much she had wanted to be with him. He lifted her chin and looked deeply into her eyes.

"Jo-anna, I have never tired of loving you." He swallowed convulsively. "I have not been able to get you out of my mind. I want you." His voice came out in a husky groan.

Her lips parted, inviting his kiss. He dipped his dark head and brushed her mouth. He had been tormented for so long and had resented the fact that he craved the feel of her body next to his. His nights had been spent in dreams where he took her silken body, and in the daytime she was never far from his thoughts. There were so many things wrong between them, but still he wanted her.

Windhawk's body trembled, and he buried his face in Joanna's soft hair. He half expected her to pull away from him, but instead her body became soft and molded to his.

"Joanna . . . Joanna," he murmured, seeking and finding her eager lips. His mouth settled on hers in a kiss so sweet it stirred old memories. Joanna's hands laced in his hair, and his mouth moved over her face to her eyelids, then moved to nuzzle her ear. His lips moved hungrily over hers with a bruising force. Windhawk couldn't seem to get enough of her. He wanted so much more than just a kiss.

Joanna groaned as his mouth moved down her neck to the pulse drumming there. Soon they both knew that they wouldn't be satisfied with just touching.

When Windhawk released her, Joanna leaned against a tree for support. Her eyes were laced with desire and anticipation as she watched him walk to his horse and remove the blanket. When he returned to her, his dark eyes held a promise of things to come. Joanna knew she should demand that he take her back to the village, but she didn't want him to.

When Windhawk held out his arms, Joanna went readily into them.

"I have missed this," he whispered raggedly in her ear. "It has been as if my life stopped when you left me. Give my life back to me, Joanna."

She wanted to protest as he moved away from her until she realized he was spreading the blanket on the snow. He reached out his hand, and she placed hers in it.

He laid her down and noticed that her eyes were soft and luminous. Dropping to his knees, he pulled her up and pressed her against his body.

Joanna couldn't stop the joy that shot through her body. She wanted to be closer to him, and Windhawk seemed to sense that fact because he crushed her body against him. She felt his swollen manhood pressed against her and felt a weakness wash over her.

Joanna didn't feel the cold when Windhawk lifted her dress over her head because she knew he would keep her warm. She lowered her eyes as he laid her gently back against the blanket and watched as he removed his clothing. She ached for his touch as his eyes moved over her body. He stared at her so long that she wondered if this was some new form of torture. Her eyes moved from his wide shoulders down to his taut stomach. When she saw his swollen manhood, she knew he wanted her as much as she wanted him.

Joanna held her hand out to Windhawk and he took it, raising it to his lips. She closed her eyes as his hand then moved down over her breast, to be followed shortly by his mouth. His mouth encircled the rosy tip until it became hard, then he moved to the other one to work the same magic.

Everywhere his hand touched, Joanna's skin seemed to burn with a wild awareness. When he raised his head, she looked into his darkly handsome face, feeling a prickle of shame because he had awakened her desire so easily.

"Because I want you does not mean that things are right between us, Joanna," he said, knowing they would have to talk about their problems.

Joanna thought he was telling her that nothing would change if he took her body. Would he go from her to Red Bird? Her face reddened, thinking what a fool she had been. She pushed against him and tried to sit up, but he pushed her back down against the blanket.

"I do not want this, Windhawk. Please, let me go."

"You want me, Joanna. Do you not think I know that—I am not a fool."

She crossed her arms over her breasts, trying to cover her nakedness. Never had she felt so ashamed of her body, but somehow Windhawk's words had made her feel like a harlot.

"You are wrong, Windhawk—I do not want you," she sobbed, turning her head away.

He was silent, and suddenly Joanna felt the coldness creep into every pore of her body. Opening her eyes, she saw Windhawk standing over her. He bent down and picked up her dress, then tossed it to her.

Joanna scampered to her feet and quickly pulled her dress over her head. Windhawk quickly dressed, picked Joanna up in his arms, and walked to his horse. Without a word, he lifted her onto his horse and climbed on behind her.

As they rode back to the village, Joanna felt as if her heart had been trampled on. She willed herself not to cry in front of Windhawk.

It seemed the ride would never end. By now she was feeling so ashamed she wanted nothing more than to hide from the world. She never wanted to see Windhawk again!

When they reached the village, he stopped his horse in front of his mother's tipi, and Joanna hurriedly slid to the ground. She ran into the tipi and buried her face in her hands, wishing she could die.

"Joanna, what has happened? Is something wrong?" Morning Song inquired.

"No, I . . . am . . . nothing is the matter," she replied, trying to pull herself together.

"You look so pale, are you sure you are not ill?"

"I feel fine. How is Little Hawk?" she asked, quickly changing the subject while trying to push her jumbled feelings aside.

"He is still sleeping." Morning Song was still looking at her, puzzled.

Joanna tried to laugh, but she didn't quite succeed. "He seems to sleep most of the time; he is such a good baby." Joanna scooped her sleeping son into her arms and held him tightly against her. She had come so close to allowing Windhawk to take her body. She was glad that she had come to her senses in time to save herself.

She thought Windhawk had probably gone to Red Bird, who would give him what she had denied him. She couldn't bear to think of his making love to the Piegan woman. But why should she care? She wasn't Windhawk's wife any longer—why should she care what he did with Red Bird? She smiled bitterly. She cared . . . oh, how she cared!

Chapter Twenty-Four

Farley had told Joanna that it was now January. Although it hadn't snowed in over a week, the previous snows were still piled into high mounds throughout the countryside. The children of the village enjoyed the winter games, and the sound of their laughter warmed Joanna's heart.

Walking outside into the bright sunlight, Joanna smiled as she watched Gray Fox's young son, Small Pony, who was trying to climb onto a sled so he could slide down the small slope. He kept slipping on the snow, and she watched tears gather in his dark eyes. Going over to him, she lifted him in her arms, remembering the time when she had saved his life. She kissed his cheek, and then placed him on the sled, giving him a shove that took him down the slope.

She laughed as he yelled out in delight, thinking her own son would one day be old enough to play in the snow with the other children.

Windhawk's mother came up beside Joanna. "This reminds me of when Windhawk was a small boy. He

357

always loved to play in the snow. I have always found joy in the laughter of children," Sun Woman said.

"Yes, there is something magical about children's laughter. I am reminded of when I was a child, and how much I enjoyed the winter, my mother."

"Your home was very far from here, Joanna. This is now your home."

Joanna looked into Windhawk's mother's eyes. "Sometimes I do not know where I belong. Lately, I have begun to miss England a great deal."

"That is the place where you lived as a child. It is across the big water?"

"Yes, it is a very long way from here."

"If you and my son could put your differences aside, you would not have time to miss anything," Sun Woman observed, eyeing Joanna closely. She took something out of her pouch and held it out to Joanna. "I found this—it belongs to you."

Joanna looked at the bear-claw necklace that Windhawk had given her and shook her head. "It no longer belongs to me. Give it back to your son."

Sun Woman sighed visibly. "It has been my observation that sometimes the ones who are supposed to be grown up act more like children than the young ones do."

Joanna couldn't keep from smiling. "I have noticed the same thing."

"Why do you not do something about it, then? Why do you not go to Windhawk and settle this thing that is wrong between you?"

Joanna took Sun Woman's hand. "I do not know, my mother. Sometimes I no longer know wrong from right."

"Humph, you know, Joanna—you are just too stubborn to admit it. I am sure you have noticed that Red

Bird no longer lives in my son's lodge."

"It has not escaped my notice, but where she chooses to live has nothing to do with me."

Sun Woman's eyes moved to Gray Fox's lodge where the Piegan woman was now living. "I am told by Gray Fox that the Piegan woman causes trouble and discontent in his tipi. He has asked Windhawk to send her back to her people."

"It would seem that Windhawk has not done so."

Sun Woman shook her head. "As you know, he is not in the village. I am sure when he returns he will send her back to her father."

Joanna shrugged her shoulders as if she were indifferent to the outcome of the situation. Small Pony pulled his sled over to her, and she placed him on it again, giving him a shove that sent him speeding down the slope once more. She then returned to stand beside Sun Woman.

"It is such a wonderful day that I had thought I would take Little Hawk for a walk. Would you like to come with us, my mother?"

"No, I am on my way to visit Many Robes—she is not feeling well today. You go ahead, it will be good for you and my grandson to get fresh air. Be sure you bundle Little Hawk up warmly," Sun Woman cautioned.

Joanna smiled to herself, thinking how dear Sun Woman was to her. She had been so kind and patient with her. Even though she disapproved of her and Windhawk living apart, Joanna knew she was making an effort not to interfere.

Tag rode into the village with a group of young

warriors. He felt a close bond of kinship with his friends, and at times it was hard for him to realize that he wasn't really one of them.

He had been away for several weeks on a hunting expedition and was proud of the five deer he had killed, using only a bow and arrow. Although he had enjoyed himself on the hunt, he was glad to be back in the village. He had missed Joanna and was anxious to see his nephew, Little Hawk.

Dismounting, he hobbled his horse and walked toward Windhawk's lodge. Seeing Morning Song talking to some of her friends, his eyes lit up as he stopped beside her.

Tag was not aware that the other young maidens' eyes widened in admiration; nor did he realize that Morning Song's eyes softened with the light of love.

Morning Song could not help staring at Tag's golden hair, which seemed to shimmer in the morning sunlight. It was now shoulder-length, and he wore a wide leather headband just like the other young braves.

"It is good to look upon your face, Morning Song," Tag said, using the customary greeting.

He was startled when the other maidens started giggling and covered their mouths with their hands. He gave Morning Song an inquiring glance, and she merely shrugged her shoulders. She couldn't tell him that the others were laughing because they knew that she loved him.

"Is my sister in the lodge?" he asked.

"Tag, walk with me . . . I think you should know what is going on," Morning Song told him.

He gave her a quizzical glance—taking her arm, he steered her in the direction of the river. "You do not have to tell me, Morning Song. I think I can guess that

360

oanna is still staying with you and your mother."

Morning Song nodded sadly. "Yes, I hurt so badly that he and Windhawk cannot solve their differences. They have so much love to give, and yet they cannot seem to peak of it one to the other."

Tag stopped and looked into Morning Song's face. "I also feel pain that they should be apart . . . but nothing you and I can do will help. They must work this out for hemselves. I do not understand how such a thing could happen. It seems so simple to me—all they have to do is alk. Farley says that wars could be avoided if only people would talk to each other. It is the same with Joanna and Windhawk."

Morning Song nodded. "It is as you say, but I wish here was something I could do to help them."

Suddenly, Tag noticed the way Morning Song's hair eemed to glisten blue-black in the bright sunlight. As his yes moved over her lovely face, he stared at her as if eeing her for the first time. Why had he never noticed hat her face was lovely beyond compare, and that her yes were large, dark pools that one could get lost in? eeling a tightening in his chest, he lowered his eyes.

He was confused by this new stirring within him. Morning Song was like a sister to him. Why was he xperiencing this new emotion that left him feeling haken? He reached for something to say to bring his roubled thoughts under control.

"Your brother should never have brought Red Bird to his lodge. I do not blame my sister for being angry," e said, knowing how defensive Morning Song was where er brother was concerned. He was hoping she would become angry with him to distract his wayward emotions.

"I believe as you do, Tag. Windhawk has made a grave

361

mistake, but I think he realizes that, for he has sent Re[d]
Bird to Gray Fox's tipi. I am told that she will b[e]
returning to the Piegan village very soon."

Tag gazed across the distant valley because he foun[d]
looking at Morning Song much too disturbing for hi[s]
peace of mind. "I am no longer called Tag. I have won m[y]
name," he stated, feeling pride at his accomplishmen[t]
and wanting Morning Song to be proud of him also.

Morning Song placed her hand on his arm. "I know—[I]
had heard this. I . . . we . . . are very proud of you. Wha[t]
is the name you were given?"

His deep blue eyes swung around to rest on her face[,]
and he caught his breath at the pride he saw mirrore[d]
there. She was proud of him, he thought, and wondere[d]
why a warm sensation seemed to circle his heart.

"I am now called Mountain Wolf."

She smiled. "I think you will always be Tag to me.'[']

He decided to change the subject. "How is you[r]
mother?"

"She is in good health."

"That is good. How is the baby?" How strange h[e]
felt—he had never been shy with Morning Song before[.]
He now seemed to be making small talk and wondered i[f]
she could sense his unrest.

Morning Song smiled. "He is beautiful."

"Boys are not supposed to be beautiful."

"Little Hawk is," she answered, wishing she dared t[o]
say that she thought Tag was beautiful, also. His hair wa[s]
the golden color of the corn, and his eyes were the sam[e]
deep violet-blue as Joanna's. He still had the slimness o[f]
youth, but his shoulders were wide, and he was tall for hi[s]
age.

She ducked her head, hoping he hadn't read th[e]
adoration in her eyes. She remembered Joanna's tellin[g]

her that Tag would one day have to return to the white world, and she felt a deep sadness, thinking that when that time came she would never see him again.

"Where will I find my sister?" he asked, thinking it would be best to leave before he made a complete fool of himself. He looked toward Sun Woman's tipi to avoid looking at Morning Song.

"I saw her walking toward the woods with the baby only a few moments before you came. If you would like, I will care for your horse, and you can go to her."

Tag nodded and turned away, rushing toward the woods.

Joanna's father had always been a firm believer in fresh air: He had sworn it was the secret to good health. Joanna could attest to that theory, since the Indian children enjoyed such good health. She had bundled Little Hawk up warmly to take him for a walk.

The warm sun was shining, and the snow was beginning to melt across the valley, so she decided to be more adventurous and walk in the woods.

Little Hawk seemed to be aware of everything that was going on around him; his eyes fastened on his mother's face, and he smiled brightly. Joanna's laughter bubbled out, and she kissed him. How dear he was to her. She was finding out what a delight it was being a mother. She loved having someone depend on her for his health and happiness as Little Hawk did. She hoped she would always be able to fill his life with happy days. Joanna tried not to think about his father, but she wasn't always successful.

*   *   *

Red Bird followed Joanna at a safe distance. She had been told by Gray Fox that Windhawk was sending her back to her father the next day. If she was going to get her revenge on Flaming Hair, it would have to be today.

She looked behind her to see if anyone was watching. Seeing no one about, she gripped the hilt of her knife and darted behind a pine tree. How fortunate she was that Flaming Hair had decided to walk in the woods today. There would be no one around to hear her cry for help!

Red Bird tested the knife blade to make sure it was sharp. She was glad she had thought to bring it with her. Looking once more behind her, she entered the woods cautiously, searching for signs that would lead her to Flaming Hair.

Joanna sat on a log holding Little Hawk on her lap. "You are so wonderful," she said, as he smiled up at her. "When you smile at me like that it just melts my heart."

Little Hawk gurgled and cooed at his mother, and she laughed delightedly, not knowing that they were at that moment being watched by jealous, malignant eyes.

Windhawk rode into the village and dismounted. Seeing Morning Song, he walked over to her, smiling "How are you, little sister?" he inquired.

She smiled brightly and threw herself into his arms. "I am fine now that you are home. Why did you stay away so long? We have all missed you, my brother."

He hugged her tightly, then set her on her feet. "I believe you grow more beautiful each time I go away and come back," he teased lightly.

"You are just saying that. I am not beautiful."

He raised a dark eyebrow. "Have you had no young

braves telling you that you are beautiful?"

"No, Windhawk . . . at least, not anyone who matters."

"They must all be blind to overlook the most beautiful flower of them all."

"There is one more fair than I, Windhawk," she said, watching his face. "Joanna is by far more beautiful."

His eyes darkened, and he looked past her to his mother's tipi. "Where is Joanna?"

"I saw her a short time ago walking with the baby toward the woods. Tag has gone to find her."

Windhawk's eyes swept past the village to the woods. Suddenly, he felt something cold touch his heart. Some instinct told him that Joanna and the baby were in danger! He remembered the dream he had had where Joanna had been stabbed by some unknown person, and he knew it hadn't been a dream, but a premonition.

Morning Song watched her brother running toward his horse with a puzzled expression on her face. She was surprised when he bound onto the animal's back and rode swiftly away from the village, heading toward the woods. She wondered why he was acting so strangely.

Joanna noticed the way the soft snow still clung to the branches of the cottonwood trees. While it was quite warm in the valley where the sun was shining, it was much colder here in the forest. She knew it wouldn't be too many more weeks before spring came to Blackfoot country. She was anxious for winter to be over—she yearned for the time when the countryside would come alive with a burst of spring flowers.

Hearing someone coming through the woods, Joanna

got to her feet holding Little Hawk closely to her and waited for whomever it was to make himself known to her. She was unafraid, because by now she had learned to tell the moccasin footsteps from those of an animal. She felt confident it would be someone from the village.

When Joanna recognized that the intruder was Red Bird, she gathered Little Hawk still closer to her with the intention of returning to the village. She had no wish to talk to the Piegan woman.

Red Bird stepped in front of Joanna. "Wait, Flaming Hair, I want to talk to you."

"You could say nothing I would want to hear, Red Bird," Joanna answered, backing up a pace.

"I know how you must feel toward me, but I am leaving for my village tomorrow. I just wanted to talk to you a moment and tell you good-bye."

"I had heard you are leaving . . . I will not pretend I am sorry," Joanna told her.

Red Bird's eyes fastened on the face of Windhawk's son. It was the first time she had seen the baby up close. "Yes, you have won, Flaming Hair."

"I was not aware that you and I were in a contest—what have I won?"

Red Bird's eyes gleamed. "You are right—it was never a contest. You had Windhawk all the time. I was never anything to him," Red Bird admitted, knowing that Flaming Hair would soon be dead.

Joanna knew she should leave, but she wanted to hear more. "I was not the one living in Windhawk's lodge—you were."

The Piegan woman reached out and touched Little Hawk's face. "I was nothing more than someone to cook and clean for Windhawk. I lied to you when I said that had lain with him; he never touched me." Red Bird smiled. "I wanted you to think that he and I were lovers so you would not want to be with him anymore."

"You forget, I saw you and Windhawk in his lodge— you were undressed, and he was holding you in his arms."

Red Bird laughed bitterly. "What you saw was me offering myself to Windhawk; what you did not see was him turning me away."

Joanna closed her eyes, wishing with all her heart that Red Bird was telling the truth. However, she didn't trust the woman . . . if she had lied before, she could be telling a lie now. "I must get back to the village right away. It is too cold to keep Little Hawk out for very long at a time," she said, stepping forward.

"I wonder if you would allow me to hold Windhawk's son? Since I will never be the mother of his children, surely you will not deny me this one request."

Joanna couldn't stand the thought of Red Bird's holding Little Hawk, nor did she like the way she was staring at her son with such a peculiar glint in her eyes.

"As I said, I am returning to the village." Joanna tried to step around Red Bird, but when she did—the woman grabbed Little Hawk out of her arms!

Joanna reached for the baby, but Red Bird stepped back quickly. She froze in her tracks when the Piegan woman withdrew her knife and held it at the baby's throat!

"I will not hesitate to kill this child if you come one step closer!" Red Bird threatened.

Joanna resisted the urge to rush forward and take her baby from Red Bird. Fearing the woman would make good her threat and harm her son if she made a sudden move in her direction, she tried to act calm. She could see the strange, eerie glow in Red Bird's eyes and knew instantly that the woman must be mad!

"Why are you doing this?" she asked through trembling lips. "Surely you would not harm my baby!"

"I have no quarrel with this child. It is you that I will see dead."

"I do not understand. I have never done anything to you," Joanna said, taking a cautious step forward, thinking it would be well to keep the woman talking.

"Have you not? I offered myself to Windhawk . . . he spurned me! *Me*, the daughter of a powerful chief. All he ever thought about was you. That is why I hate you!" The woman screeched hysterically.

Joanna feared what Red Bird might do should she say the wrong thing to her. She took another step forward, watching Red Bird's face carefully; it was distorted with hatred and anger, and she feared more than ever for her son. Joanna realized she must try to reason with the Piegan.

"I am sure Windhawk cares for you. Why else would he allow you to stay in his lodge?"

"I know what you thought!" Red Bird cried in a loud voice. "What you thought was that Windhawk had replaced you with me. He would have no part of me!" The woman's voice rose, and her eyes were wild. "He wanted you when he could have had me!"

Joanna realized in that moment that Red Bird was past reasoning with. She had to get Little Hawk away from her before she harmed him.

"If it were not for you, I would now be Windhawk's wife. You have the white face and are not worthy of him. You are white!"

"Red Bird, let me have my baby, and we will talk."

The woman looked down at Little Hawk as if she had forgotten she was holding him. The knife in her hand wavered, and she smiled maliciously. "This could have been my son. He does not look like the son of a white face."

Joanna took another step, and Red Bird jerked the baby tighter against her. "Do not come any closer. I have told you I will kill this child!"

"Your quarrel is not with the baby but with me. Put Little Hawk down, and we will talk."

Red Bird's eyes fastened on Joanna's. "Talk! What good would it do to talk to you?"

"I understand how you are feeling. I, too, was spurned by Windhawk. He no longer wants me. Was I not banished to his mother's tipi?"

"You don't speak the truth. If you would hold out your hand to Windhawk, he would take it. Have I not heard him call out your name in his sleep?"

"No!" Joanna cried out. It was too painful for her to hear this woman's lies. "Windhawk did not want me anymore. You are not telling the truth. Windhawk no longer looks at me with love. Give me my baby!"

Red Bird didn't hear the soft moccasin footsteps that came up behind her, but Joanna saw Tag moving cautiously toward her. She wanted to cry out to her brother not to make a sudden move, lest the crazed woman harm Little Hawk.

Everything seemed to happen at once. Tag sprang forward and grabbed the baby, pushing Red Bird out of the way. Red Bird lunged at Joanna and knocked her to the ground. The two women struggled and rolled down a steep slope. Joanna grabbed the hand that held the knife and tried to wrestle the weapon out of Red Bird's hand. It soon became apparent to Joanna that the other woman was much stronger than she was.

Red Bird pushed Joanna over on her back and straddled her, trapping her hands above her head. Joanna watched in a dreamlike state as the knife came close to her throat! She tried to call out, but the words stuck in her mouth. She felt fear like a cold hand on her heart. She was going to die, and there wasn't anything she could do about it!

Turning her head, Joanna saw Tag hurrying down the slope toward her, but she knew he would arrive too late to save her. She had only moments to live!

Red Bird also saw Tag and laughed menacingly. "Nothing can save you, Flaming Hair. Today you will walk the spirit world." Her laughter rang out again, and Joanna tried to get free of her grasp.

"You will die, Flaming Hair. Windhawk will not feel love for a dead woman who rots on the scaffold!"

In that moment, Joanna knew that Windhawk had never betrayed her with this woman. Was she going to die before she could tell him of her love?

Wrenching her hands away from Red Bird's, she tried to push the knife away from her throat. She could see Tag standing helplessly behind Red Bird, and she knew he hesitated to make a move, fearing Red Bird would panic and thrust the knife into her throat.

Joanna could feel her strength waning, and the tip of the knife touched her throat. She closed her eyes, knowing the end was at hand.

Hearing a whirring sound and then a soft thud, Joanna opened her eyes to see the Piegan woman's startled expression. There was an arrow sticking out of the woman's chest, and Joanna watched in horror as blood ran out of Red Bird's mouth and down the front of her doeskin dress!

Red Bird gasped and tried to speak, then fell over on the ground . . . dead!

Joanna was too stunned to react at first. She felt Windhawk kneeling down beside her, and she sobbed when he pulled her into his arms. She was trembling so badly she couldn't speak. She wondered vaguely what he was doing there.

Windhawk had killed Red Bird! she thought in horror. Soft whimpering sounds were coming from Joanna's throat as Windhawk helped her to her feet.

Joanna's eyes were drawn back to the Piegan woman, and she could see the woman's eyes were bulging out, and her mouth was gaping open. Shuddering, Joanna turned her face away and closed her eyes.

"You killed her—you killed Red Bird!" was all she could say.

Tag showed Joanna the baby so she would know he hadn't been harmed. Windhawk lifted her into his arms and carried her to his horse. As they rode back to the village, Windhawk held her tightly, trying to still the tremors that shook her body.

Since Tag didn't have his horse, he followed closely behind on foot, carrying Little Hawk in his arms, wondering why that crazy woman had tried to kill his sister.

Joanna was crying softly as Windhawk carried her into his mother's tipi and laid her down upon the buffalo robe.

"See to her and the baby," Windhawk told his mother. "I must take Red Bird's body back to her people."

Joanna didn't even hear Windhawk leave; she was too

busy checking Little Hawk to make sure he was unharmed.

Later, when Joanna had time to think, her mind was a jumble of truths and half-truths. She was no longer sure what was true. All she could think about was how closely her son had come to being harmed by the deranged Red Bird, and that she herself had come very near dying.

She had no idea how Windhawk and Tag had found her. She couldn't even guess how Windhawk felt about having to kill Red Bird. He hadn't spoken over two words to her before he left to take Red Bird's body home to her village.

Sun Woman fed her some thin broth and ordered her to rest while she sat beside her, crooning softly to Little Hawk. Morning Song and Tag came to kneel beside Joanna, and she smiled weakly at them before closing her eyes.

"What happened?" she heard Sun Woman ask in a low voice.

"I am not sure," Tag whispered. "No one but Joanna can tell us what happened."

"I am glad Joanna and the baby are unhurt," Morning Song said, leaning over and touching the baby's soft face to make sure he was all right.

Joanna's eyes opened, but they felt so heavy they drifted shut again, and she felt as if she were floating on an endless sea. Too much had happened too fast, and she didn't want to think about it right now. She wanted nothing more than to sleep, and perhaps when she awoke tomorrow, she would find it had all been a bad dream.

Red Bird's body had been wrapped in a buffalo robe

and lashed to a travois. Windhawk mounted Puh Pom and gathered up the travois horse's reins and rode out of the village. No one who watched his departure would miss Red Bird. There was much speculation about what had happened, but no one knew for sure.

Windhawk stared straight ahead, feeling a numbness wash over him. Today he had watched as Red Bird had tried to kill his beloved. He had felt so helpless when he had realized what was happening. He had thought he was too far away to help Joanna and had feared she would die before he could reach her.

No one would believe him if he told them that he had been over a hundred horse-lengths away from Red Bird when he had shot his arrow. The shot had caught her in the heart, and he knew Napi must have guided his hand. He had never made such a true shot before, and he doubted that he ever would again.

If Joanna had died because of Red Bird, it would have been his fault for bringing the Piegan woman into his village. He had the urge to turn his horse around and ride back to his mother's tipi to assure himself that Joanna was alive. Joanna had been in a state of shock when he had taken her back to the village, but he had been, too. He had wanted to cry out to her that he loved her, but he had remained silent.

A shudder shook his tall frame, and he nudged Puh Pom into a gallop. He wanted to reach the Piegan village quickly, so that he could return home. He didn't know what Joanna was thinking, but he was riddled with guilt. Perhaps it would be better if he were to let her go. She was no longer happy living with his people. The thought of never seeing her again was so painful to him that he felt a tear roll down his cheek. He thought of his son.

Would he be able to let Joanna leave him and take their son?

Windhawk was an even more extraordinary man than the legends about him suggested. He had strength of character. When he knew something was right, he would do what he had to—and now he knew that he would have to let Joanna go . . . because it was right!

Chapter Twenty=Five

Three months had passed since Windhawk had been forced to slay Red Bird. The Piegan woman's death seemed to stand between him and Joanna like an open wound.

Each day Windhawk would come to his mother's tipi to see his son. At those times, he paid very little attention to Joanna. Sometimes she would feel him watching her, but not once had he spoken directly to her.

Joanna had become restless, wondering what would happen between her and Windhawk. She realized that they couldn't go on indefinitely acting as if there had never been anything between them. For some reason, she had become shy in Windhawk's presence. She thought perhaps her shyness came from knowing she had wronged him, or perhaps it was because of the deep love she carried in her heart for him.

It seemed the whole village watched and waited to see what would happen between their chief and his woman. Joanna often saw the people watching her, but not one of them questioned her about Windhawk, and no one ever spoke about Red Bird's death in front of her.

Joanna had no way of knowing that Windhawk was wrestling with himself, believing it would be best for her if he were to take her back to her own people. He just couldn't seem to bring himself to the final act of allowing her to leave. He was content for now to let things go on as they were, thinking the alternative would be to never see her again. He wasn't ready to deal with that right now. He realized he might only be postponing the inevitable, but each day he would put off making any decision about sending her away.

The weather had turned warmer, and the snow had melted weeks ago. Along the river there were patches of green grass, and Joanna found several scattered wildflowers growing in the woods.

Joanna now had plenty of time to reflect on her situation. She knew that Windhawk had not been unfaithful to her with Red Bird. She remembered Red Bird's telling her that Windhawk still loved her. There was no evidence of that love now. Perhaps it had been just one more cruel way for the Piegan woman to hurt her. She wondered each day where her life would go from here. She loved Windhawk and wanted nothing more than to be his wife.

Two jealous women were responsible for the trouble between her and Windhawk. They had been torn apart not only by Claudia's hateful lies, but also by Red Bird's interference. Joanna realized that it was her fault for allowing outsiders to manipulate her life. If she had insisted on telling Windhawk the truth about the baby when he had rescued her from her uncle, they would both have been spared so much pain. She didn't know how much longer she could go on the way she was living now. Each time she saw Windhawk, her eyes followed him hungrily. She noticed everything about him: how tall and proud he carried himself, the way his muscles rippled across his broad shoulders when he walked. She would feel herself quivering inside when he looked at her with his soft, dark eyes.

Joanna knew what she needed from him; she just didn't know how to go about getting what she wanted. He was a proud man, and he might never come to her. She was an equally proud woman, and she would not be the one to reach out first.

Tag had led his horse down to the river to drink. He glanced upward, and his eyes followed the last dying embers of the sun, which reflected off the restless river and turned it the color of a burning lava flow he had once seen in a book.

He sat down on the riverbank, lost in thought. He was now a member of the Blackfoot tribe in every way that counted. He tried to remember the face of his father, but it was no more than a vague memory. His mother's face was a bit more clear to him, but that, too, was no more than a shadow.

Tag thought of his Uncle Howard and tried to feel the anger he had once felt toward the man who had stolen his birthright from him, but even that was difficult. How little importance he now placed on what was lost to him in Philadelphia.

He watched as his horse raised its head and tossed its mane, shaking off a horsefly. This was where he belonged. Everyone he loved was here in this village. He wanted so much to be like Windhawk and live as a

Blackfoot. He thought of Joanna and her constant drilling, teaching, and reminding him that he was not a Blackfoot, always making sure he remembered he had a destiny to fulfill.

By now, the sky had turned a deep purple and cast a dark glow in the west. He laid his head back on the grass that was just starting to show the first signs of spring. He could feel the river's tranquil effect, and his body began to relax. How could anyone want more than what he had found among the Blackfoot tribe?

His thoughts then transferred to Windhawk's sister, Morning Song. Something was different in the way he felt about her. "I have not changed—I am still the same Tag," he told himself. But he was changing, and so was the way that he looked at Morning Song.

Morning Song walked up beside Tag. It was as if thinking about her had made her appear.

"Why do you sit here alone, Tag?" she asked, dropping down beside him on the grass.

He watched as the soft breeze ruffled Morning Song's long ebony hair and felt a tightening in his chest. "I like to come here when it is quiet as it is now. I do my best thinking when I am alone."

Morning Song got to her feet, thinking Tag was trying to tell her he wanted to be alone. "I am sorry. I did not realize that you wanted your solitude. Please, forgive me for disturbing you."

Tag reached up and took her hand. "I did not mean for you to leave. Stay with me for a while, Morning Song. I would like to talk to you."

She sat back down and gazed at the river. "Were you thinking about the white world, Tag?"

"Yes, in a way . . . I was thinking about how much I

love it here. I feel like this is my home now."

Morning Song's heart was gladdened at his words. She hoped he was saying he would be content to stay with her people and not return to the white world that had once beckoned to him.

"I know there are many in the village who care much about you, Tag."

He sat up and smiled slightly. "Are you one of those who care about me, Morning Song?" he asked in a half-teasing, half-serious voice.

She ducked her head to avoid his eyes. "Yes, I care, Tag," she replied in a soft, quiet voice that hardly reached his ears.

Suddenly, Tag needed to hear her admit that she thought of him as more than a friend. He now knew why he had been feeling so many strange emotions about Morning Song. He loved her . . . not as a friend, not as a sister, but something more! He couldn't explain even to himself what he was feeling. Joanna would probably say he was too young to feel love for a girl, but Tag knew that love was exactly the emotion he was experiencing for Morning Song.

"Do you care about me as a brother, or perhaps a friend, Morning Song?" he asked, leaning closer to her.

"No, Tag. There was a time when I thought of you as a brother, but no more," she said, raising her dark eyes to look at him.

"I do not understand," he said, thinking how all the young braves talked about Morning Song's beauty. He knew they went out of their way to talk to her, each thinking he could win a smile from her. Lately it had begun to bother him that his friends wanted to pay court to her. Now he knew why—he had been jealous!

379

"I . . . think I should go back to my mother, Tag," she said, standing up.

Tag sprang to his feet and stood in front of her. He would settle this thing that had been gnawing at his insides for many weeks. He needed to discover how she felt about him so he would know if he had reason to believe she cared for him as he did for her.

She stood very still as he reached out his hand and softly touched her face. His hand then drifted down to lightly touch her trembling lips. "Do you think of me as a man?" he wanted to know.

"Yes," she whispered.

Tag felt as if his heart would burst with joy. He cupped her face between his hands and pulled her closer to rest his cheek against hers. "That is good, Morning Song, because I think of you as a very beautiful woman." He now felt a new uneasiness, a strange urge from deep inside him. He leaned forward and dipped his head to touch her mouth ever so softly with his own.

It was a sweet, tender kiss: the kiss of love's first innocent awakening.

Morning Song felt a warm glow move throughout her body. She couldn't believe that she was actually in Tag's arms and he was kissing her. She loved him so much it was almost painful to her.

Tag raised his head and stepped back a pace as their eyes met. He would never look at Morning Song as a little girl again, but as the maiden he loved!

Tag lowered his head and looked down into Morning Song's lovely face. He had been totally unprepared for the warm feelings the touch of her soft body had awakened in him. He wanted to stay with her forever, protecting her from harm and keeping all the other young warriors away from her. The realization that he wanted no one else to love her came as a shock to him!

The love of a girl was a new emotion to Tag and had come upon him unexpectedly. Not knowing how to handle this new, all-consuming emotion, he smiled and hugged her tightly to him.

"Do you feel as I do, Morning Song? Do you feel as if the stars are so close you could reach up and touch them with your hand?"

She rested her face against his buckskin shirt. "Yes, Tag . . . oh yes!"

"Come, Morning Song, I will walk you back to the village," he said in a soft voice, thinking he didn't know what else to say to her at this time.

Unknown to Tag and Morning Song, Windhawk stood on the hill above them viewing the scene between the two young people. A smile came to his lips as he realized he had just witnessed love in its purest form. He turned and made his way back to his lodge, feeling he had lost the sweet, innocent love he and Joanna had once shared.

Tag gathered up the reins of the horse and started up the path toward the village, holding Morning Song's hand. "Did you know that tonight I have the honor of watching Windhawk's horses?" he told her, not knowing what else to say.

She nodded. "It is a great honor, Tag."

He was making small talk, afraid to talk about what had happened between him and Morning Song beside the river. Love was too new to him, and he didn't yet know how to deal with the emotion.

"All the warriors are going on the buffalo hunt in the morning. Windhawk said that I may go also."

"I had heard that," she replied, wanting Tag to speak

of the beautiful thing that had just happened between them. She realized he was feeling shy and smiled to herself, thinking there would be other days when they could talk about what had happened to them.

"It is not usual for all the braves to be away from the village at the same time," she said, playing his little game.

"That is true, but we are fortunate—a large buffalo herd has been sighted no more than a short ride to the north. Should there be trouble, we could be here quickly."

When they arrived at the village, Tag walked Morning Song to her tipi. Not wanting to end their time together, he squeezed her hand. "I . . . we . . . I must go. The hour grows late, and I have to watch Windhawk's horses." In a daring act of courage, he leaned forward and quickly brushed her lips with his. He then bounded onto his horse and rode out of the village with his heart pounding in his ears. He would have all night to examine his feelings for Morning Song.

When Tag rode into the village the next morning he was tired. The night before had been long and tedious. A coyote had spooked the herd, and he had spent most of the night rounding up the horses. His eyes felt heavy as he made his way to the tipi he now shared with Windhawk.

His bed seemed to beckon to him, and he thought he would lie down for just a few moments. His eyes drifted shut, and he was soon in a deep sleep.

Windhawk came into the lodge and saw Tag asleep. He smiled at the young boy, thinking it would be well for him to sleep, since he had been up all night. He picked up his spear and left quietly, knowing Tag would be disappointed when he awoke. There would be other days the boy could go on the buffalo hunt.

Windhawk remembered the scene he had witnessed between Tag and Morning Song. The time would come when Tag and Morning Song would realize what had happened between them. Windhawk wondered if it was love . . . or merely a young boy and girl finding out about the attraction that can spark between them. He smiled slightly and mounted his horse.

Farley had left Fort Union a week before. He was tired—these trips to the fort were getting harder on him all the time. He yearned for his own bed and the companionship of his Blackfoot friends.

It was early morning, and his mount was still fresh, since he had just started out. His two pack horses were loaded down with supplies for Joanna. He smiled, thinking Joanna would be pleased with the blue print material he had gotten her as a surprise.

Looking skyward, he gauged the position of the sun thinking he would be home by the noon hour.

Suddenly, the instinct that had kept him alive for so many years told him something wasn't right. He could sense something on the other side of the ridge just ahead of him.

He dismounted and tied his three horses to a tree. Silently, Farley made his way to the top of the ridge where he dropped to his knees behind the protection of a bush and peered down into a deep ravine.

His breath came out in a low hiss when he saw a large number of Assiniboin warriors. What in tarnation were they doing this far west? Farley asked himself. Why had they come to Blackfoot territory?

Suddenly, his eyes narrowed. Sitting near the campfire, he saw what appeared to be two Cree warriors, which puzzled him further. He watched as one of the Cree stood up, and the Indian's voice carried to him.

"River Walker and my friends of the Assiniboin tribe, I say to you that today we will cover ourselves with glory. Before the sun sets, we will have defeated the Blackfoot and will have the scalp of their chief, Windhawk!"

At that moment, Farley recognized the young warrior who had just spoken. He was one of the two Cree warriors whom he would never forget. Everything was clear to the old man now—there could be no mistake: The two Cree traveling with the Assiniboin were the same two who had killed She Who Heals, captured Joanna and Morning Song and tied him to the tree!

He watched as the warriors began painting their faces, and then he hurried down the hill, knowing that time was against him. He had to get to the Blackfoot village to warn Windhawk of the impending danger.

Farley led his three horses away as silently as possible. When he thought he was a safe enough distance away from the Assiniboin camp, he mounted and rode toward the Blackfoot village as fast as he could. He was thankful that his horse was still fresh. The pack horses were slowing him down, but he knew he couldn't let them go just yet for fear the Assiniboin would come upon them. He would have to travel some distance before turning them loose.

When he had ridden for a good distance, he let go of the reins of the pack horses and watched them gallop away. He vaguely regretted that Joanna wouldn't ever see the blue material he had bought for her.

Joanna hesitated before she entered Windhawk's lodge. She hadn't been in his lodge for a long time, but she knew he had ridden away this morning and there was no danger of facing him now. Gathering up her courage, she threw back the flap and entered. She wouldn't allow herself to look about the lodge; it was still painful to be in the place where she and Windhawk had once been so happy together.

Seeing Tag curled up on a buffalo robe asleep, she made her way to him and dropped to her knees.

She shook him by the arm. "Tag, wake up. Do you want to sleep the day away?"

Tag opened his eyes and then closed them again. "I am tired, Joanna. I spent most of the night chasing Windhawk's herd."

"It is almost noon, and you missed going on the hunt with Windhawk."

He sat up quickly. "Why didn't Windhawk wake me? He knew I wanted to go on the buffalo hunt!"

"He told Sun Woman to let you sleep. He said you could join the hunt tomorrow."

Tag stood up, plainly showing his disappointment. "I am the only warrior who didn't get to go. Why should I have to remain behind with nothing but women and children?"

She smiled and ruffled his hair. "Most of the young warriors would be glad to be the only male in camp with so many young maidens."

"I'm serious, Joanna, and all you do is make jokes!"

"Not so, my brother . . . I am deadly serious."

385

He smiled, masking his disappointment. "Perhaps you are right. I—"

Suddenly the sound of a horse galloping into the village interrupted Tag. Joanna walked to the flap and threw it aside to look out.

"It's Farley!" she cried, glad to see the old trapper had returned.

"Windhawk! It's the Assiniboin and them two damn Cree!" Farley yelled out in English. "They're coming! Grab your arms and make ready to defend the village!"

Joanna felt her legs go weak—Tag pushed past her and rushed toward Farley.

"What are you saying, Farley?" the boy asked, unable to grasp the fact that the village was about to be attacked.

"Where's Windhawk?" Farley asked, looking past Tag and noticing that there were only women and children gathering about him.

"Windhawk and the rest of the warriors have gone on a buffalo hunt to the north. There are no men in the village," Joanna said, feeling fear prickle her spine.

Farley let out his breath, realizing the seriousness of the situation. "I 'spect it's up to you and me, Tag. Take a fresh horse and ride like hell to find Windhawk. I'll get things ready here."

"No," Tag said, realizing Farley was a far better tracker than he was. The old trapper would be able to find Windhawk faster than he would. "Farley, you go find Windhawk. I'll take care of the women and children."

Sun Woman appeared at Farley's side with a fresh horse, and the old man didn't hesitate before springing onto the animal's back.

"Do the best you can, Tag, but hurry! I'll be back soon as I can. Them Assiniboin are no more than a couple hours behind me."

Tag sprang into action, amazing everyone with his authority, taking over control of the situation.

"Morning Song, take some of the maidens and ride to the pasture. Bring as many horses as you can. Go quickly!" He turned to his sister. "Joanna, organize the women to bring travois to place the old and the sick on. No one must be left behind!" He then spoke to Sun Woman. "Group the children together and have the women take what weapons they can carry. Build up the campfires so it will look like we are still here. We need to buy all the time we can."

Somehow Tag inspired trust in everyone, and they gathered about him to hear what he had to say, ready to obey his command.

Running into Windhawk's lodge, Tag grabbed up the tomahawk Windhawk had once given him along with several lances, spears, and a bow and arrows.

It was strange, Tag thought, but he felt calm and in control of his emotions. He remembered Windhawk once telling him that a man never knows if he will be brave until he is tested. Today Tag was being tested, and he hoped he would make Windhawk proud of him.

When Morning Song returned with the horses, the travois were quickly attached to them, and Tag and several of the women began placing the sick and the elderly on them.

When everyone was ready to leave, they looked once more to Tag for guidance.

"Windhawk will come down from the north—the Assiniboin are coming from the east—we shall ride to the northwest where Windhawk will be between us and the Assiniboin. Hurry, we have no time to lose!"

He waited until the others rode out of the village, then he turned to Morning Song, who stood beside him.

"Is everyone out of the village?" he asked.

"Yes."

Tag helped Morning Song onto her horse, and then he mounted Navaron. He rode to the head of the group so he could lead them to safety.

Joanna and Morning Song rode at the rear, making sure no one lagged behind. Joanna kept looking behind her, fearing the Assiniboin would soon be upon them. She felt such fear that it seemed to seep into every pore of her skin. Suddenly, she realized that she had left behind something irreplaceable—Windhawk's bear-claw necklace! She saw that Sun Woman had Little Hawk with her, and Joanna knew she would keep him safe. She had to return to the village to get Windhawk's necklace!

Every so often Tag would ride to the back to make sure that everyone was moving. He couldn't help but seek out the ones who meant the most to him. Sun Woman had Little Hawk strapped to her back, and Morning Song was riding beside the children. Joanna was—! Where was Joanna?

Turning his mount back toward the village, he allowed his horse to have its head. Joanna had returned to the village.

Tag realized he had to reach her ahead of the Assiniboin!

Chapter Twenty-Six

Farley had no trouble picking up Windhawk's trail. When he topped a hill he saw the large herd of buffalo, and among them rode many of the Blackfoot warriors. Racing down the hill at a full gallop, he rode toward Windhawk, yelling at the top of his voice. The herd of buffalo became spooked by Farley's yelling and began to stampede.

Windhawk pulled up his buffalo runner and watched as the old trapper rode at top speed toward him. Gray Fox stopped beside Windhawk and pointed at Farley.

"The old man has ruined the day's hunt, my chief. He should know that a man does not stampede the buffalo."

"That old man would never do such a thing without a good reason," Windhawk said, nudging his horse in the flanks and riding to meet Farley.

When he was near enough that he could hear what Farley was saying, he drew rein.

"Windhawk, come quick! The Assiniboin are making ready to attack the village!"

"What of Joanna and my son?" Windhawk asked,

feeling great fear.

"Tag will take care of them. He has stayed behind to arm the village."

Windhawk started to say that Farley hadn't been wise to leave a boy in charge until he remembered there were no men in the village. He hoped Tag didn't try to defend the village. He prayed the boy would realize he must get the women and children away to safety.

By now other warriors had gathered about Windhawk, and they heard what the old man had to say.

"Ride fast, my warriors, we go to protect our families!" Windhawk called out as he kicked his horse in the flanks, praying he wouldn't be too late.

Farley drew even with Windhawk and saw the look of concern on his face. "I seed them two Cree warriors that captured Joanna and Morning Song riding with them Assiniboin," Farley said, forgetting to speak in the tongue of the Blackfoot. He watched the look of concern that had been etched on Windhawk's face turn to a look of hatred and anger.

"They will walk among the spirits before the sun sets today," he whispered, more to himself than to the old man.

Joanna rode into the village and quickly leaped from her horse. How strange and silent the village seemed. She had the feeling that she was all alone in the world. There were no sounds of children's laughter and no sign of life of any kind. Even the village dogs were gone.

Feeling fear so strong it was like a great lump in her throat, she raced into Sun Woman's tipi. Looking about her in confusion, she wondered where Windhawk's mother had placed the necklace. Frantically, she searched among baskets and robes, but she couldn't find the necklace anywhere. Suddenly it became the single most important thing in her life. The bear-claw necklace had once symbolized Windhawk's love for her, and she had to find it! Finally, she emptied Sun Woman's sewing basket, and the necklace fell out in her lap. With grateful tears in her eyes, she picked it up lovingly and held it to her breast.

Hearing the thundering of horses' hooves, Joanna realized she had very little time to get away from the village. Jumping quickly to her feet, she raced toward the opening, but in her haste to get away, her legs became entangled in a buffalo robe. She fell to the ground, hitting her head against the lodgepole. Pain shot through her temple, and she felt her head swimming dizzily.

Now the sounds of war whoops reached her ears, and she knew she would never make it to safety if she didn't hurry. She staggered to her feet and made her way outside just as the enemy entered the far end of the village.

Tag spurred Navaron forward and entered the village from the opposite direction of the Assiniboin. He rode directly to Sun Woman's tipi and spotted Fosset just in front. Everything happened at once then—Joanna ran from the tipi and raced toward Fosset, and Big Hand spotted her at the same time as Tag.

Joanna came up to the left of Fosset and tried to mount, but the horse spooked at the sound of the war whoops and skidded to the side.

"Not now, Fosset!" Joanna cried, knowing the giant horse had always been skittish. Once more she tried to leap onto his back, but Fosset reared up on his hind legs and turned into the horse of Big Hand.

Big Hand reached for his tomahawk. Recognizing Windhawk's woman, he knew if he killed her he would settle an old score with the chief of the Blackfoot. As he neared Joanna, he took aim, ready to throw his tomahawk. At the moment Big Hand would have released the tomahawk, Fosset fell against his horse, knocking it to its knees and sending Big Hand flying through the air to land with a thud on the ground.

Joanna screamed as she watched her precious Fosset fall to the ground. An agonizing sound came from deep inside the giant animal!

She was vaguely aware that the enemy were going from tipi to tipi burning and destroying. Confused and disoriented, she didn't know what to do. It was at that moment that she saw Big Hand spring to his feet, and she recognized him as one of the Cree warriors who had captured her and Morning Song.

Joanna seemed to freeze as he advanced on her with his tomahawk poised to strike. She had cheated death many times in the past, but she realized there would be no way to save herself now. She watched with a certain amount of detachment as the tomahawk was thrown and waited for the impact of it to hit her. Suddenly, she was knocked to the ground from behind, and she glanced back to see Tag. She watched as the tomahawk that had been meant for her fell to the ground.

Tag felt the pain that knifed through his shoulder. He knew he had been hit by the blade of the tomahawk, but he couldn't think of himself if he was to save his sister. Leaping to his feet, he stood ready to meet the enemy.

Big Hand's eyes narrowed as he saw the golden-haired

boy who had cheated him out of his victim. No matter, he thought, he would have not only the Flaming Hair's scalp on his lance, but the golden-haired boy's as well.

Tag reached for his tomahawk and, taking careful aim, threw it at the advancing Indian. The weapon found its target, and Big Hand screamed out in agony as it sliced through his chest. His eyes seemed to glaze over as he fell heavily to the ground.

Tag jerked Joanna to her feet and shoved her into the nearest tipi, which was Windhawk's. He shoved her to the back and unsheathed his knife, standing before the opening, ready to defend her with his life. He had no thought for his own safety, for he knew in his mind that he would die, but he couldn't let the enemy take his sister.

"When they come in, Joanna, you must not allow them to take you alive."

She nodded, reaching up to the lodgepole and removing a lance. Tag turned his back to her, watching the doorway, and Joanna saw the blood that was streaming down his back. She hadn't realized he had been hurt!

"Tag, let me help you. You are hurt!" she cried out.

"It's nothing. Stay where you are," he said in a voice of command.

At that moment, a new sound reached their ears. Tag turned to Joanna, and his eyes were bright. "Windhawk has come, Joanna, you are saved!"

Stalking Wolf and the Assiniboin watched as the Blackfoot swarmed into the village. He felt great fear, knowing that the tall Indian who rode at the head of the Blackfoot warriors could be none other than the

393

legendary Windhawk!

"Let no enemy live through this day but the two Cree! I want them for myself!" he called out.

"The women and children are safely out of the village," Gray Fox called out.

The fierce Blackfoot warriors charged forward beside their chief. In the middle of the village the two forces clashed. There were the sounds of the dead and the dying as arrows and lances found their intended victims.

Windhawk leaped from his horse and dragged an Assiniboin from his mount. With a powerful thrust, he plunged his knife into his enemy's heart. Thrusting the dead warrior aside, he turned to meet another.

Windhawk didn't see the Assiniboin warrior who rode toward him from behind. The man raised his tomahawk and brought it forward just as Windhawk turned. He felt the weapon graze his face just before a shot rang out, and the enemy fell to the ground with a bullet wound in his heart. Windhawk's eyes met the old trapper's, and he sent him a silent message of thanks.

On the battle raged, until it became apparent that the Blackfoot were winning. Windhawk had just withdrawn his knife from a dead enemy when he heard Joanna scream!

Raising his head, he knew that the sound had come from his lodge. How could Joanna be here? She was supposed to be with the other women and children. He began slicing and cutting a path through the enemy to get to Joanna!

Joanna had screamed when the lodge flap was thrown

aside and she saw Stalking Wolf enter. Tag lunged forward to meet the intruder with his knife drawn. Stalking Wolf side-stepped Tag and brought his lance down on the back of his head.

His eyes then went to Joanna, and he smiled as he advanced slowly toward her. "We meet again, Flaming Hair. This time you will die!"

She poised the lance in front of her, and her eyes flashed dangerously. "You!" she cried, recognizing Stalking Wolf. "Why have you done this thing?"

He gave her a menacing smile. "It is not time for questions—it is time for you to die!" He leaped at her, and before she could react he grabbed the lance from her hands and pointed it at her. "Today you walk the spirit world—tonight Windhawk will weep for his woman. I know the battle is lost, so I will wound Windhawk where it hurts him the most. I shall kill his woman!"

Stalking Wolf noticed that the Flaming Hair was not looking at him, but, instead, over his shoulder. Sensing rather than hearing a presence behind him, he turned. He saw the tall Blackfoot warrior whose dark eyes seemed to burn into him, and he knew without being told that he faced . . . Windhawk! Fear seemed to hold him immobile.

"What did you say, dog?" Windhawk hissed between clenched teeth. Windhawk leaped forward and grabbed Stalking Wolf. "Tell me what your name is, so I will know who I send to the spirit world," Windhawk commanded, taking the lance and pointing the blade into Stalking Wolf's throat.

"I meant no harm!" Stalking Wolf cried, falling to his knees. "I would not slay your woman. Did I not allow her to go free before?" He groveled at Windhawk's feet. "I do not want to die. Spare me, I beg of you!"

Windhawk looked down at the man who was sniveling like a coward. "It will not be by my hand that you die, dog. Windhawk does not bother to slay cowards. You will not die the quick death of a brave man, but the slow death of a coward."

Gray Fox came in and Windhawk turned to him. "Take this man and tie him up. Later I will decide what is to be done with him."

Gray Fox looked at Joanna and determined that she was all right. He then looked at Tag, who was lying on the floor in a pool of blood. "The battle is won. The enemy have all either died or have fled to the east, my chief," he said, grabbing Stalking Wolf and pulling him to his feet.

"Allow no man to escape. Follow them and slay them, so all men will know that it means death to raid the Blood Blackfoot village."

Gray Fox nodded and pushed Stalking Wolf toward the entrance. "It will be done, Windhawk."

Joanna's eyes sought Windhawk's, and she wanted to fly into his arms.

"Are you unhurt, Joanna?"

She nodded and went quickly to her brother. Tears were streaming down her face as she touched him. "Help Tag, Windhawk. Save my brother!" she pleaded.

Windhawk lifted the boy in his arms and laid him on the buffalo robe. He then examined the wound and found it was not serious.

Joanna picked up a pan of water and a cloth and began cleaning the wound. She then applied the healing herbs and bathed his face.

"You should have seen him today, Windhawk," she said, teary-eyed. "He would have made you so proud."

Windhawk's eyes rested on Joanna's face. How could he tell her that all he could think of at the moment was that she still lived? How could he tell her of the fear that had been in his heart when he heard her scream out?

"I have always been proud of your brother, as I have of his sister."

Their eyes locked, and Windhawk covered her hand with his. "Joanna, I . . ."

Farley pushed the flap aside and entered. He looked at the boy and then at Joanna. "How is the boy?" he asked.

"He is going to be all right, Farley," Joanna assured him.

"In that case, I think you had better come with me," the old man said.

Joanna was hesitant about leaving Tag, but Farley's eyes told her that something was wrong.

The old man took her hand and helped her stand. "It's Fosset . . . he's in pain. I think we are going to have to put him out of his misery."

"No!" Joanna screamed, running from the lodge. Seeing Fosset lying on the ground, she fell on her knees, running her hand over his smooth flank. Tears of overwhelming grief blinded her as Fosset tried to raise his head and an agonizing sound issued from him.

"Oh, Fosset," she cried laying her face against his. He couldn't die. Her father had given him to her.

Windhawk knelt down beside her and began examining Fosset's two front legs. His expression was grim as he looked at Joanna. "Both legs are broken—we must put him out of his pain, Joanna," he said sadly.

"No, I will not allow you to do this! You do not understand. Fosset saved my life! If it hadn't been for him, I would now be dead!"

Windhawk stood and pulled Joanna up with him. "It is good that the horse that brought you and me together should die saving your life," he whispered, knowing what she was feeling. "Fosset is in pain, Joanna—we must release his spirit."

Joanna wrenched her hand away from Windhawk and knelt down again. "Oh, Fosset, you have served me well," she cried, laying her face against his again.

The horse seemed to look straight into Joanna's eyes, and she saw he was in pain.

"Go inside, Joanna . . . I will attend to Fosset," Windhawk told her. He knew what she was feeling and wished he could spare her.

"No!" she cried. "If it must be done, then I will do it. Farley, give me your gun."

The old man gazed at her doubtfully for a moment, but the look in her eyes told him she meant what she said. He made sure his gun was loaded and then handed it to her. Farley watched Joanna raise the rifle to her shoulder, as she took careful aim.

Windhawk saw Joanna's hand tremble and knew how hard it was for her to kill the magnificent animal that she had loved so well. He remembered that the first time he had seen her she had been watering Fosset at the river.

Joanna took careful aim and then quickly pulled the trigger. Her aim had been good—Fosset twitched, then died instantly. She threw down the gun and raced into Windhawk's lodge, where she fell down on the buffalo robe to cry out her grief.

Windhawk and Farley exchanged glances in their shared concern for Joanna's feelings.

On Windhawk's instructions, Farley had ridden out to bring the women and children back home, while Gray Fox and twenty Blackfoot warriors had come upon the last of Assiniboin braves. Gray Fox reminded the warriors of Windhawk's orders to let no man live.

The two tribes came together for the second time that day. Gray Fox removed his knife from the chest of an enemy and turned, looking for the next foe to engage. Glancing to his left, he saw a warrior sitting atop a black horse. Thinking the man must be the chief of the Assiniboin, he raced toward him. He knew that Windhawk would want the chief alive.

Chief River Walker braced himself as he saw the Blackfoot warrior lunge at him. He had no time to raise his lance as Gray Fox pulled him from his horse and held him in a tight grip until he stopped struggling.

"Are you the chief of the Assiniboin?" Gray Fox asked.

"Yes, I am called River Walker. Kill me, I have no fear of death at the hands of a Blackfoot!"

"Today you will wish you had never heard of the Blood Blackfoot," Gray Fox told him. "I will not kill you, but instead take you to Windhawk. You will face his wrath."

Gray Fox did not miss the fear that leaped into the chief's eyes at the mention of Windhawk. River Walker knew he was defeated, but he would not act the part of a coward.

Gray Fox felt respect for the man when he raised his

head proudly and faced him. "I will see this Windhawk. There will be no shame for my family to bear if I die at the hands of the great chief, Windhawk."

Tag had suffered with ill grace while Joanna bandaged his wounds. There was no time to reflect on what had happened that day, as there were many wounded to attend to.

The injured were all brought into Windhawk's lodge, and Joanna moved from one to another, tending them as best she could.

Soon the women and children returned to the village, and the Blackfoot began to count their dead. There were twenty warriors who had lost their lives, and a gloom settled over the village.

The women came to Windhawk's lodge to remove their wounded warriors and took them to their own lodges to tend them. Several of the tipis had been burned, and the Blackfoot whose tipis were still intact shared their homes with their less fortunate friends.

Joanna sat beside Tag, bathing his face. "It is very sad, Tag, that so many had to die. It was all so useless, and what did it prove?"

Tag took Joanna's hand. "Perhaps it has served one purpose. Our enemies will think twice before they attack our village again."

"What do you suppose Windhawk will do with Stalking Wolf?"

Tag drew in a deep breath. "I don't think you want to know. You should try to get some sleep."

"No, I am going to stay with you tonight. Are you in much pain?"

"No, not much."

"I don't think you are telling the truth."

His hand tightened on hers. "I heard about Fosset . . . I'm sorry, Joanna. He saved your life, you know."

Joanna held back her tears. "Yes, I know, and I shall miss him. He was the last thing I had to remind me of Father."

Tag grinned. "You have me, Joanna."

She smiled. "Yes, thank God, I have you!"

Chapter Twenty-Seven

The next day many scaffolds were erected for the Blackfoot dead. Once again the death chant rolled across the valley.

Windhawk walked among his people, giving comfort where he could. It had been many years since the Bloods had engaged the Assiniboin in warfare, and Windhawk paused to reflect on what he and Sitting Bull of the Sioux tribe had once talked about. Would it not be better for all Indian nations to band together to present a united front to their common enemy—the white man? In his heart, he knew this was right. It was not good for the Indian to fight against his own kind. For that matter, he thought it was not good for any man to take the life of another. He remembered the raid he had led on the Cree village. It had only brought retribution down upon the Bloods. Would the killing ever stop? he wondered sadly. Was man destined always to slay his brothers?

Joanna changed Tag's bandages and brought him a cool drink. "I will leave the water pitcher within your reach, in case you get thirsty. You should try to sleep.

Remember, She Who Heals always said that sleep is the great healer."

"I don't like to stay in bed," Tag said, feeling his sister was treating him like a baby. "I feel well enough to get up."

"Nonsense! If you continue to improve, you can get up in a few days."

Windhawk swept into the lodge at that moment, and as always his eyes went to Joanna. So many things were left unsaid between them, he thought, but now wasn't the time to express their feelings. There would be time enough to speak of what he must when the day of mourning was over.

"Windhawk, will you tell Joanna that I am not a baby and I can get up?"

Windhawk smiled at the boy. "You are not a baby, Tag. I am very proud of what you did yesterday. Yours were the actions of a brave warrior, but . . . even a brave warrior must indulge his women. It would be best for you to do as your sister bids. Give your body time to heal and give Joanna time to realize you are a man."

Tag's eyes gleamed at Windhawk's words of praise. He gave Joanna an "I-told-you-so" look.

"I am going to help Sun Woman tend the wounded," Joanna said, walking to the opening. "Tag, I will expect to find you in bed when I return!"

Both Windhawk and Tag watched Joanna depart silently. When she was gone, Windhawk sat down beside Tag and gave him a long, searching look. "I need to talk to you about what happened yesterday. I know about your getting the women and children safely away from the village. What I do not know about is why you and Joanna came back to the village after you were safely away?"

"I myself do not know why Joanna returned. When I discovered she was missing, I rode back here to find her. That was when the enemy struck. We did not have time to get away . . . the rest you know."

"What would cause her to return to the village knowing the Assiniboin were coming?" Windhawk asked more to himself than to Tag. "What could have been so important that it would have caused her to risk her life to recover it?"

"You will have to ask my sister that, Windhawk. I cannot tell you."

Windhawk stood up. "This will be a long day, Tag. We will bury our dead and repair the damage to the village. There would be many more dead had you not acted as you did. I am very proud of you!"

Tag felt the warmth of Windhawk's words. There was no one in the world whom he admired more than Windhawk. There was no one whose praise he treasured more than that of the chief of the Bloods.

"I had no time to plan, Windhawk. I tried to think what you would have done in my place. I knew it would be better to send Farley to find you, because he is a far better tracker than I."

"I might not have had the good judgment to send the women and children to the northwest, as you did. Had the battle gone against us, our families could have made it safely to the Piegan village before the enemy could have overtaken them."

"I didn't think of that. I thought only to put you and your warriors between us and the enemy."

Windhawk laughed. "So you did, Tag . . . so you did."

"May I enter?" Morning Song called from outside the lodge.

"Enter, little sister," Windhawk answered, smiling at Tag. "As I said, Tag, we have to indulge our women."

Windhawk noticed the worried frown on his sister's face as she dropped to her knees and took Tag's hand. "I have been so worried about you, Tag, but there were so many wounded to care for, and my mother said Joanna would watch over you. Are you in much pain?"

Windhawk smiled to himself as he left the lodge. He had not expected Tag and Morning Song to love each other. He could think of no one he would rather give his sister to than Tag. He would have to remind them that they must wait until they were both older before they could walk as one. He wondered if Joanna knew about her brother and Morning Song. He would have to discuss it with her before long, he thought.

"Are you sure you are not in pain, Tag?" Morning Song asked, touching his forehead to see if he was feverish.

"I am well enough to be up, but Joanna treats me like a child, insisting I stay in bed."

"Joanna is wise, Tag. You must listen to her and do as she says."

He smiled and carried Morning Song's hand to his lips. "I have no choice, have I."

Morning Song shyly ducked her head. It had been one thing to allow Tag to kiss her that night in the moonlight, but now it was day, and he could see her face.

"Morning Song, look at me!"

She raised her head and looked into his beautiful violet-blue eyes.

"I love you, Morning Song. I think I have for a long time . . . but I just did not know it." Tag watched as tears sparkled in her soft, brown eyes.

406

"Oh, Tag, I too have loved you for a long time. I dared not hope you would love me in return." She bent forward and touched her lips to his.

Beautiful, young, innocent love had finally surfaced and been recognized by Tag and Morning Song.

It was three days after the raid, and slowly the Blackfoot began to recover from its effects. The dead had been placed to rest, and the burned-out tipis were being replaced.

As the sun began to set, the council fires were lit, and the warriors began to gather around to see what their chief would do with the two prisoners. Many women whose men had been killed in the battle sat in the shadows, waiting to see what punishment their enemies would receive. Joanna was not among those women. She could not bring herself to watch what she knew would be a gruesome spectacle.

Windhawk held his hand up for silence. Immediately, the murmuring stopped, and all eyes went to their chief.

"Bring the captives forward!" he ordered.

Several warriors led the captives out of the tipi where they had been held. They were quickly tied to a stake to await Windhawk's judgment.

River Walker, the chief of the Assiniboin, looked at the Blackfoot with scorn and contempt. There was no fear in his eyes as he waited to hear how he would die. This wasn't true of Stalking Wolf, however. His eyes held fear, and he cringed inside every time Windhawk turned his dark gaze on him.

"River Walker, Chief of the Assiniboin. The Blackfoot despise you as their enemy, but we respect you as a brave warrior. You will be given the chance to die as only a warrior of courage can. Perhaps you will even live," Windhawk said, raising his voice so all could hear what he had to say.

River Walker looked at Windhawk. "Will I then be allowed to die a warrior's death?"

"As I said, you may even live," Windhawk told him. "The council has decided that in the morning, you shall be set free. You will be given a chance to die in the land of your fathers and your grandfathers."

"What does this mean?" River Walker asked. "I have never heard of a Blackfoot allowing an enemy to go free."

"You may wish many times that we had killed you, River Walker, for you will be set free in the wilderness without benefit of clothing, a horse, or food!"

River Walker's eyes widened in surprise. "Why would you give me the chance to live? I am your enemy—I have killed your warriors."

Windhawk's face held a grim expression. "I allow you to live so you may tell all who hear your voice not to come to the village of the Blood Blackfoot. Tell our enemies that to do so is to die!"

River Walker looked into Windhawk's eyes. He felt a deep respect for the young chief. Surely all he had heard about Windhawk was true. Here was a man who was wise beyond his years. There was no doubt in his mind that Windhawk looked at life through the eyes of the great spirits!

"Windhawk is a warrior to be feared, and a man to be respected. I stand ready to receive the punishment of the wise and noble chief of the Blackfoot," River Walker said, in admiration of the young chief's mercy.

Windhawk's eyes moved to Stalking Wolf. "You,

Stalking Wolf, will not receive the death of a brave warrior. I charge you with being a coward!"

"I did not lead the raid on your village, Mighty Chief of the Blackfoot!" Stalking Wolf cried out in fear. "Allow me to go free with River Walker!"

"No!" Windhawk said. "You have proven yourself unworthy to be called a warrior."

Stalking Wolf cringed visibly. "If you will not allow me to go free, then allow me to die at the hands of one of your warriors."

Windhawk turned his face toward the group of Blackfoot warriors. "Is there one among you who will go against Stalking Wolf so he may die as a warrior?"

There was only silence . . . no one stepped forward to accept the challenge.

"You see how it is, Stalking Wolf. My warriors will not fight against a coward. I will give you to the women who have lost their husbands, fathers, and brothers in the raid. You will die at their hands," Windhawk said.

"Wait!" Stalking Wolf called out. "I will tell you why I came to raid your village. My father banished me from my tribe and told me I could not return until I avenged my brother's death."

"Tell me, what did your father require of you?" Windhawk asked.

Stalking Wolf couldn't meet Windhawk's eyes. "He asked that I slay you, then return the armband I wear to him. The armband was my brother's."

"Why?"

"To avenge my brother's death."

"Did I kill your brother?"

"No, I was responsible for his death. You raided our village and killed many of my people!"

Windhawk walked over to Stalking Wolf and removed the armband from his arm. He recognized the armband as the one he had pulled from the ashes of She Who Heals's burned-out tipi. "I will see that your father gets this back. He will also hear how you died. I will let it be known that you died at the hands of Blackfoot women!"

"No!" Stalking Wolf cried out. "You cannot shame me before my father!"

His pleas fell on deaf ears as Windhawk and his warriors left the council fires. Stalking Wolf screamed out in horror as the women advanced on him.

Joanna had come out of the lodge and listened to Windhawk speak. She was impressed by his compassion for River Walker, and she couldn't find it within her to feel sorry for Stalking Wolf. She turned away and reentered the tipi, not wanting to see the women revenge the death of their loved ones. A shudder wracked her body as she tried not to think about what was in store for the Cree warrior.

She looked about Windhawk's lodge, knowing Tag was well enough that he didn't need a nurse any longer. She knew the time had come for her to return to Sun Woman's tipi. With a heavy heart, she gathered up her belongings and placed them in a leather satchel.

Windhawk had not slept in his lodge in the three nights Joanna had stayed with Tag. Perhaps he just didn't want to be near her, she thought.

She picked up Little Hawk and walked toward the opening. She heard an agonizing scream and knew the women had begun their torture on Stalking Wolf. She was undecided on whether to leave yet. Perhaps it would be best to wait until the women had finished with Stalking Wolf.

She stepped back as the lodge flap was pushed aside and Windhawk entered.

Seeing she carried her satchel, he sought her eyes. "Where are you going?"

"Tag is now recovered—I am returning to your mother's tipi."

"I thought you might remain in my lodge. Have I not stayed away from you? There is no reason for you to fear I will come near you."

Joanna winced at his words. "I feel many things for you, Windhawk, but fear is not one of them."

Dark eyes collided with violet-blue eyes, and Joanna held her breath. "Tell me what *do* you feel for me? Joanna?" he asked pointedly.

Joanna searched her mind for something to say to him. She couldn't tell him that she loved him. She couldn't say that every time he was near her she couldn't think straight. How could she admit that when he touched her she trembled with a deep, unfulfilled longing?

"I . . . watched you at the council meeting tonight. I thought you were a very wise and merciful chief. Your justice was very fair."

"You have told me nothing, Joanna. If you despise . . . me, tell me so; if you hate me . . . say the words that will set me free. Do not keep me in uncertainty any longer."

"I do not know what you are asking of me, Windhawk. When you were dealing with other people's lives tonight, you were so wise and so sure of yourself. Why can you not be the same with me?"

His eyes closed to narrow slits. "Now I do not know what you want of *me*, Joanna."

She shrugged her shoulders, trying to portray an indifference she was far from feeling. "I will say the same

411

words to you that you said to me. 'Set me free, do not keep me in uncertainty any longer.'"

He drew in his breath. "Did I not set you free long ago, Joanna? You are free to come and go as you will."

That wasn't what she wanted to hear. She wanted him to say he could never let her go. She wanted him to admit he loved her.

"I no longer know where I belong, Windhawk. Is it your wish that I leave the Blackfoot village?"

He looked down at the sleeping face of his son and felt pain at the thought of never seeing Joanna or Little Hawk again. "That decision will have to come from you, Joanna. I cannot make the choice for you."

Joanna felt a heaviness around her heart. He didn't love her anymore, otherwise he would never allow her to leave and take his son. "I had not thought you would allow me to go. You will have to give me some time to make my plans," she said, feeling that if she didn't leave at once she might break down in front of Windhawk.

"You can make your plans, and when you have decided, let me know."

Joanna nodded and would have left, but Windhawk's words stopped her. "I wish to speak to you about Tag and Morning Song." He took Little Hawk from her and laid him down on the buffalo robe, then indicated that Joanna should sit. When she was seated, she waited for Windhawk to speak.

He sat down and looked deep into her eyes. "Were you aware that your brother and my sister love each other?"

Joanna's mouth opened in surprise. "I knew that Morning Song loved Tag, but I had no notion that he loved her. How do you know this?"

"I have been observing them together."

"No, no, it's not possible!" Joanna said in English.

"Why do you object to their love?" Windhawk asked in Blackfoot. "Do you not think Morning Song is right for your brother? You married an Indian."

"It is not that. For one thing, they are too young, and for another I do not want Morning Song to be hurt. Tag will one day leave this village to take his place as my father's heir. When that happens, Morning Song will not be able to go with him. She would never survive in the white world."

His eyes darkened. "Are you saying Tag would be ashamed of her in the white world?"

"No, of course not!" Joanna said indignantly. "If my brother loves Morning Song, he would never be ashamed of her. Your sister is a lovely girl and all I could ask for in a wife for Tag. What I was trying to say is that in the white world there are hates and prejudices. Morning Song would never be accepted by them, and she would be hurt by their rejection. Besides, they are both too young to think about marriage."

"I agree that they are too young, and I also agree that Morning Song could not go with Tag should he leave . . . what if your brother decides to remain here?" He watched her face closely, awaiting her answer.

"I . . . if . . . I leave it is assumed that Tag will go, too. He would never stay here without me."

"Joanna, I have been listening to you, and I hear more than you are saying. If my sister would not be accepted in your world . . . what about my son . . . ?"

Joanna opened her mouth to speak, and then closed it tightly. She had never considered Little Hawk . . . but, of course, she hadn't really wanted to go away. He would

413

face the same prejudice and distrust that Morning Song would if she took him away from the Blackfoot village.

"I have to admit that our son would not be . . . he would not . . . they would never . . ."

"I see," Windhawk said, cutting into her confusion. "You might want to consider our son before you make your decision to leave."

Joanna watched as he stood up and moved to the opening. "You are a good mother, Joanna . . . I will expect you to do what is best for Little Hawk."

When she was alone, she leaned her head over against the lodgepole and closed her eyes. Would the hurting ever stop? Would she ever feel at peace again? Had Windhawk been implying that she should leave her baby behind when she left? No, she could never do that! Deep inside, she knew Windhawk would never allow her to take their son with her. He was only waiting for her to realize that, also!

Farley rode into the village leading his two pack horses. He'd had a devil of a time finding them. Most of the supplies had been lost, but he had managed to recover some of them.

Seeing Windhawk talking to some of his warriors, he rode over to him.

"Where have you been, old man?" Windhawk asked.

"I have been many days rounding up my pack horses. When I rode back to the village to warn you that the Assiniboin were about to attack, I had to let my horses go."

Windhawk's eyes narrowed. "That same day you caused the buffalo to stampede, costing us the hunt."

414

Windhawk's face eased into a smile. "We owe you much, old man. I myself owe you my life."

That was the first time the young chief had ever said a friendly word to Farley, and the old trapper grinned. "You have allowed me to live among you. I have known that you only let me stay for Joanna's sake."

Windhawk reached up and touched the old man's hand. "I will now allow you to stay because you have earned the right, Farley."

Windhawk and Farley looked into each other's eyes, knowing they shared a common respect. Farley felt, at last, that he had a home where he would live out his old age.

Joanna carried Little Hawk back to Sun Woman's tipi. Windhawk had given her many things to think about. She was as lost and confused as ever. What she needed was for Windhawk to make the decision for her. He should decide whether she should go or stay.

She reminded herself that he had asked her to stay in his lodge, but she knew that was only because of Little Hawk.

Tears fell down her face as she rested her cheek against her baby's. "If I must go away, I could never leave you, my littlest love," Joanna whispered to her sleeping baby. "I will never go without you!"

Chapter Twenty-Eight

Windhawk stood at the end of the long line of warriors. His face was solemn as the drums beat out a tempo and several voices chanted the song of the brave warrior.

Tag held his head high and looked neither to his left nor to his right as he walked down the path made by the Blackfoot warriors—his eyes were on Windhawk.

Joanna felt tears in her eyes as Tag passed her. She was so proud of him! He was being honored tonight for saving the women and children. She had been told by Sun Woman that no white man had ever received this honor, and it made her doubly proud because Farley was walking just behind her brother, and he was also being honored tonight.

Morning Song watched Tag, and she felt her heart swell with love and pride. Tonight he would be recognized by the whole tribe as a brave warrior.

Joanna watched Morning Song's face and saw the love shining there. She loved the young girl and didn't want to see her hurt. She had mixed emotions about her and Tag's feelings for each other. Would Tag be happier if he stayed with the Blackfoot? Would he never want to return to Philadelphia? Whatever he decided, she knew it would have to be his decision. Secretly, she hoped he would remain with the Blackfoot. He was happy here, and he never had been completely happy in Philadelphia. Had she herself not once found overwhelming happiness here among the Blackfoot?

Her eyes traveled up the long line to where Windhawk stood with his arms folded across his chest. Tag had just reached him, and Windhawk raised his hand for silence.

"My people, tonight we honor two brave men. Had it not been for both of them, many of you might not be here tonight. As you may know, Tag has already been given a name. Tonight, I, too, will give him a name. From this day forward, he shall be called . . . Night Falcon!" Windhawk reached for Tag's hand and extended it over his head. "Let all remember his brave deeds, and know that because of him . . . not one of our women or children lost their life in the Assiniboin raid!"

Windhawk then turned to Farley. "All of you know the part this man played in warning us that the Assiniboin were on their way to our village. What you may not know is that he also saved my life. Many months this man has walked among us, giving us his friendship. Although his skin is white, I say inside him beats the heart of a Blackfoot."

Windhawk smiled at Farley. "I will now give Farley an Indian name. Since many of you call him the crazy one, I say to you he is crazy . . . crazy like the fox. The name I bestow on him is . . . Crazy Fox!"

Joanna stayed to see no more. She knew the celebration would go on well into the night. She followed the well-worn path to the river, thinking it would be nice to be alone.

Tag had received his honors, and Farley was at last recognized for his worth. What about her? Where did she fit into the Blackfoot tribe? She realized she was feeling sorry for herself, but what did it matter . . . no one would know.

The moon was shining brightly, and she could hear the laughter and merriment coming from the village. Bending down, she plucked a wild flower, holding it to her nose and inhaling its delicate fragrance.

"Are you touched by the moon's magic, Joanna?" Windhawk asked, moving out of the shadows to stand beside her.

"I do not know what you mean," she said, trying to still the thundering of her heart.

"I have been watching you for some time, and it appeared that the moonlight shimmers off your hair," he said in a deep voice.

Joanna looked up into his face and saw he was staring at her through half-veiled eyes. "I was not aware that you were watching me. Will you not be missed at the ceremony?"

"Your brother and the old man are the center of attention. I will not be missed."

"I really must get back," she said, trying to step around Windhawk. "The baby might be awake."

"My mother is with him," he said, giving her no excuse to leave.

"It is getting late."

"Come, Joanna, walk with me. I think there is much we should talk about." He took her arm and steered her away from the river toward the woods.

She wanted to go with him, and yet she didn't. She

feared what he had to say to her. Was tonight the time Windhawk would cut her adrift in a world in which she felt she no longer belonged? Would he ask her to leave? She remembered how she had once defied anyone who stood in the way of what she wanted. She was no longer the person she had once been. Now, she was feeling too unsure of herself.

Windhawk led her into the woods to a small glen where the trees had been cut away, allowing the bright moonlight to filter through like a hazy mist.

"Was it necessary to come so far from the village?" she asked.

Windhawk sat down on the grass and motioned for her to do the same. When she was seated he spoke. "Yes, I did not want anyone to interrupt us. It seems we never get to finish a conversation."

Joanna plucked at the fringe on her doeskin gown. "I was proud of Tag and Farley tonight."

She heard Windhawk let out his breath in agitation. "I did not bring you here to talk about your brother and the old man. I want to ask you some questions."

Joanna bristled, suddenly feeling more her old self. "Am I supposed to answer all your questions?"

"I hoped you would clear up some things for me," he said, smiling to himself.

"All right," she said, folding her arms across her chest. "You ask and I will answer . . . if I can."

He lay back on the grass and watched how the moon played across her beautiful face. He couldn't see her eyes, but he knew they would be alive and sparkling with fire. Her red-gold hair seemed to shimmer with a silvery light. He moved a little to his left so he could see her face more clearly, wanting to watch her expression when he spoke to her.

"Have you thought any more about what you want to do, Joanna?" he asked, watching the slow rise and fall of her breast. He felt a warmth in his loins and knew he wanted her.

"I have not. If you are in such a hurry to be rid of me, perhaps you should decide when you want me to leave."

He could plainly read hurt on her face. "I was not the one who wanted you to leave, Joanna. If you will remember, you are the one who left in the first place. I am the one who brought you back."

"That was your mistake, Windhawk. Had you not done so you would not have to worry about sending me away now."

He sat up and touched her hair ever so gently. "I can think of many things I would like to do to you, Joanna. Sending you away is not one of them," he whispered close to her ear.

"No," she said, looking at him with frightened eyes.

"Oh, yes, Joanna. Are you not aware that you have had me squirming? Do you not see what everyone else sees?"

"Wh . . . what?"

His hand trailed down her hair, then across her face to outline the shape of her mouth. "I have tried to put you out of my mind, Joanna, but my body will not allow it. I have this craving that gnaws at me night and day. Allow me to touch you so I may find some release from this torment."

Joanna closed her eyes. "Is this why you brought me here, Windhawk? Is this what you had in mind?"

He tilted her face up to his, and she felt his torment and knew it was very much like her own. "I tried to tell myself that I only wanted to talk to you, but in truth, I

421

think I hoped you would allow me to . . ." his hand drifted behind her head, and he brought her face closer to his. ". . . allow me to kiss you," he whispered, lowering his head so his lips were very near hers. "Have you been in torment, Joanna? Do you ever wish for what only I can give you?" His deep, husky voice seemed to vibrate through her whole body, and a small groan escaped her lips.

"Yes, Windhawk . . . Oh, yes!"

Windhawk's mouth covered hers, and she could feel herself moving backwards to rest her head against the cool grass.

"Joanna, my Joanna. I have wanted this for so long," he murmured against her lips.

Was this another cruel jest he was playing on her, Joanna wondered, remembering the last time he had kissed her. In her heart she wanted so much to believe he was sincere, but this time, like the last, he didn't speak words of love . . . he spoke only of desire. He would shatter her heart into a million pieces again if he was only playing with her. Windhawk was an honorable man, she knew that now, but how did he feel about her? She had to know!

Wedging her hand between them, she pushed him away. "Not now, Windhawk! Please, not now!"

"When, Joanna—when? I am so tied up in knots I cannot think straight!"

"No, you must answer some of *my* questions."

He pulled back from her and looked at her long and hard. "Ask your questions, Joanna."

She tried to reach for something to ask, but he was too near, and she couldn't think clearly "I . . . why did you bring Red Bird into your lodge?" She asked the one that seemed the most important.

"I told you . . . I never took her to my body. Do you believe that?"

"Yes, but . . . why then did you allow her to stay with you? Was it just so you could hurt me?"

"Is that what you think?"

"Yes."

He leaned forward and brushed a stray curl out of her face. "I do not think I would knowingly do anything that would bring you pain."

"How can I believe that when the evidence says otherwise?"

"Did I hurt you, Joanna?"

"Yes."

"It seems we have hurt each other. What went wrong, Joanna? When did we start hurting each other?" He asked the same question she had asked herself over and over.

"I was not the first to bring hurt, Windhawk. I was waiting for you to return from the hunts. All the other women's husbands came to them, but you didn't even send word to me. I wanted to tell you about the baby, but you didn't come."

He could hear the hurt in her voice. "That was my mistake, Joanna. I thought you would understand that, as chief, I had to put everyone else's needs above my own."

"Above mine, Windhawk?"

"Yes . . . even yours."

"You didn't come, Windhawk, but Red Bird did. She taunted me with the fact that you had made love to her. She said you were going to replace me with her."

"Joanna, did you have so little faith in me that you

believed the woman's lies? Did you not feel deep inside the love I had for you?"

"I thought you loved me, but I found out I was wrong."

They both lapsed into silence for a moment, then Windhawk spoke. "Did you try to hurt me, Joanna? Did you go to the long knife to cause me pain for what you thought I had done to you?"

"No, I had no intention of going away. I was so angry with you I made a foolish statement to Morning Song about leaving you. I did not leave you, Windhawk; I was forcibly taken away by two men who were hired by my uncle."

He reached out and pulled her into his arms. "Others interfered in our life, Joanna, but if our love had been stronger then they could not have torn us apart. I never wanted anything as badly as I wanted you. Since the day I first saw you, I wanted only you. I did not want to touch any other woman."

She noticed he was talking in the past tense. Yes, she thought, others had ripped them apart. Did she have the courage to pull them back together again?

"Did you intend to make Red Bird your wife, Windhawk?"

"No."

"You were forced to kill her to save me—have you ever regretted that?"

"Yes, many times. I had never killed a woman before. It was very difficult for me when I had to take her body back to her father and tell him what had happened."

"Sometimes things happen that we do not seem to have any control over, Windhawk. I feel like my life has been dictated by someone else for a long time."

"By me, Joanna?"

"Yes . . . by you . . . Claudia . . . my uncle . . . Red Bird."

"None of this is important, Joanna. Would you like to try and . . ."

She placed her hand over his mouth. "Do not speak it, Windhawk. I do not know what I want right now. I need time to find out who I am. If I ever do, I will come to you and tell you."

Again there was silence. After a while, Windhawk stood up and took Joanna's hand and helped her to her feet. "I will walk you back to the village," he said simply.

As they made their way back along the path, they were both silent. When they reached the river, Joanna pulled her hand away from his and raced toward the village.

She entered the tipi to find Little Hawk awake. Sun Woman handed him to her, and Joanna unfastened her gown to feed him. Nothing had been settled between her and Windhawk tonight, but at least they had talked, and she felt that was important.

The time seemed to pass without Joanna's even realizing it. Her days were filled with taking care of Little Hawk and helping Sun Woman cure meat and prepare hides and skins. Her nights were filled with emptiness and a deep loneliness.

More often than not, Windhawk would be away from the village on a hunt, and at the times when he was present he seemed to pay very little attention to her.

Sometimes Windhawk would ask Morning Song to bring his son to his lodge, and he would keep him there for hours. Joanna didn't know what he did with her son

425

on those occasions because she was never asked to accompany Little Hawk.

Since the night she and Windhawk had walked in the woods he had not approached her, and she knew he was waiting for her to come to him. So far, she hadn't made any decision about her life. All she knew was that she loved Windhawk, but she was finding out that love wasn't always enough.

Since learning about Tag and Morning Song's feelings for each other, Joanna observed them more closely. By now everyone in the village knew that Tag and Windhawk's sister were in love. Joanna knew the day would come when she would have to talk to Tag about his future, but she had been putting it off, not wanting to broach the subject.

The bright sunlight spread its warmth across the land and Joanna breathed in the fragrant aroma of the many wild flowers that were in full bloom.

She was helping Sun Woman dry strips of buffalo meat, and she smiled at Little Hawk who was propped against a tree in his cradleboard, enjoying the outdoors.

"My grandson thrives," Sun Woman observed.

"Yes, he is healthy," Joanna agreed.

Sun Woman added more wood to the cook-fire while Joanna removed some of the meat that was done and placed it in a wooden bowl.

"Have you heard about Tag and Morning Song?" Sun Woman asked, taking the bowl from Joanna.

"Yes, I know they believe themselves to be in love."

"Just because they are young does not mean they cannot experience the same feelings you have."

Joanna sighed. "I suppose you are right, but they are young. How do you feel about them?"

"As you know, I love Tag. He is a fine boy, and he will grow up to be a fine warrior."

"But?"

"But, he has always had this thing in him that would not allow him to be at peace. I know he will not always stay with us."

"I think the time has come for me to talk to him," Joanna said, a troubled frown on her face.

"Do not talk to him yet, my daughter. It will be best if you wait until he comes to you. He will do so before long. When advice is asked for, it can be freely given, but if you offer an opinion unasked, it will not have as much meaning."

Joanna smiled at Sun Woman's wise words. "I will do as you say, my mother."

"Joanna, I have two daughters. First you were happy, and Morning Song was not. Now she is happy, and you are not. This troubles my heart. Why do you not reach out your hand and take my son's hand?"

"I might do so if I thought he wanted me. Sometimes, I believe he thinks of me only as Little Hawk's mother."

"I think you are just making excuses because you fear being hurt again. It is the same with Windhawk. I say if a love is great, it is worth a little pain."

Joanna smiled at her mother-in-law. "You always have wise words. You should have been chief in your son's stead."

Sun Woman smiled. "I would have made a great chief, but instead I became the wife and then the mother of chiefs."

Joanna picked up her son while Sun Woman carried the meat into the tipi. When they were inside Joanna removed Little Hawk from the cradleboard and placed him on a buffalo robe so he could crawl around.

Sun Woman built up the cook-fire and then turned to Joanna. "I have been meaning to ask you something for a long time now, Joanna."

"What?"

"When the Assiniboin were about to raid our village, why did you return? You must have known how dangerous it was to do such a thing."

Joanna turned away from Sun Woman's penetrating gaze. "I discovered that I had forgotten something. Fearing the Assiniboin would burn the village, I came back for it."

"What did you come back for, Joanna?"

"I . . . it was nothing, just a trinket."

"It was the bear-claw necklace, was it not?"

Joanna turned and looked at Sun Woman. "Yes!"

Sun Woman turned back to the cook-fire. "You risked your life for a trinket? I think not, Joanna. The bear-claw necklace was enough for you to risk your life to save it, so I will tell you something about that necklace that you do not know."

Joanna waited for Sun Woman to continue.

"Red Bird found that necklace and put it about her neck. When Windhawk saw it on her, he tore it from her neck in anger. He wanted no one to have the necklace but you."

Joanna lowered her eyes and spoke softly. "I will remind you of your own words, my mother. Advice asked for is cherished, advice not sought is not very effective."

Sun Woman smiled. "This is true, my daughter." It didn't matter what Joanna said, Sun Woman could tell she was pleased by what she had told her about Windhawk. She was weary of Joanna and Windhawk.

428

playing their little games. It was time she took a hand in their affairs, she thought to herself.

It wasn't until the next night that Sun Woman found her son alone. When she followed him into his lodge, Windhawk looked at her with a curious expression on his face.

"I can always tell when you have something on your mind, my mother. Say what you have come to say."

She raised her head and gave him a look that she had often given him as a child. "I just wanted to tell you something that might interest you."

"And what is that?"

"I know why Joanna came back to the village when the Assiniboin were on their way."

Windhawk smiled. "Why was that?"

Sun Woman walked to the opening and then turned back. "She rode back to get the bear-claw necklace. Your father would never have allowed me to vacate his bed as Joanna has yours," she said, before sweeping out of the lodge.

Her announcement seemed to knock the breath from Windhawk. At first it was hard for him to absorb what she had told him. When he thought about it, he started laughing.

Joanna still loved him! She might pretend indifference, but her actions the day of the raid were the proof for which he had been searching. She had come back for the necklace because she knew what it stood for, and, no matter how her lips denied her love, he was now certain she loved him!

His heart was overflowing with joy. Should he go to

her and demand the truth from her lips? No, he would
find another way to make her face the truth. She was the
proudest, most stubborn woman he had ever known, but
he would make her admit to him and to herself that she
loved him.

It was as if a heavy weight had been lifted from his
shoulders; he would have her in his lodge where she
belonged before too long!

Sun Woman smiled to herself. She had always
despised women who interfered in their grown son's and
daughter's lives, but she didn't feel the least bit guilty for
interfering if it would bring Joanna and Windhawk back
together.

She knew her son, and it wouldn't be too long until he
would take matters into his own hands. She laughed out
loud. Poor Joanna, she wouldn't know what was going on
when Windhawk decided to act on the information she
had given him!

Philadelphia

Claudia stood at the second-story window of what had
once been Joanna's bedroom. She looked down on the
front yard noticing that the snow had all melted. As she
let her eyes travel past the huge iron gates which seemed
to hold the world at bay, she reflected on her situation.
She should be happy, because her fondest dream had
come true. Was she not now the lady of a grand house
and was her wardrobe not overflowing with beautiful
costly gowns? There were servants to see to her every
need and she didn't have to worry anymore about what to
do with her life. She thought of Harland Thatcher—wore

had reached her that he had recovered completely from his wounds. Not once had he called on her or Howard since they reached Philadelphia. Claudia was finding out that she and Howard might live on the hill with all the socially elite, but they were certainly not accepted by any of them, and that included the Thatchers. There existed an invisible line that separated her from the old families of Philadelphia, and it couldn't be easily crossed over. It didn't help Claudia's temper any to know Joanna would have been welcomed with open arms by the Thatchers and their kind.

Claudia's eyes sparked fire. One day she would have the money and power to make all of Philadelphia bow down to her. She would hold grand balls and no one would dare decline an invitation for fear of offending her.

Howard had been examined by several different doctors, and it had been each of their opinions that he would never fully regain the use of the right side of his body. He had been installed in one of the bedrooms and he had hired a man to see to his needs, freeing her to do as she pleased. At first it had been like a glorious dream to be able to walk into the finest shops in Philadelphia and buy anything she desired. Lately, however, she had begun to feel at loose ends. She was finding out that Howard had spoken the truth when he had told her that most of the money had been tied up in trust for Tag and Joanna.

She turned around, scanning the bedroom with a critical eye. She had been told by one of the maids that the room hadn't been changed since the night Joanna had left the house. Claudia often found herself in this room, touching the things that had belonged to her hated enemy. Why did she feel the need to punish herself by coming here? she wondered. Deep inside her there burned a hatred so intense that it seemed to overshadow everything else in her life. She picked up a delicate ivory-handled brush and threw it against the wall, finding satisfaction in the fact that it shattered into many small pieces. She walked past the wardrobe that still held many of Joanna's gowns and stood at the window once more. "You may not ever come back, Joanna," she said aloud, "but one day Tag will return to Philadelphia, and I'll be waiting for him." Her eyes looked past the gates once more. What would she do on the day when she was finally confronted by Joanna or her brother? She knew in that moment that she must prepare herself for the inevitable. Now that she had tasted the good life, she had no intention of giving it up. Someway, somehow, she would hold on to what she now had!

Howard watched as Baxter the handyman hung the portrait of the James family over the mantel in his bedroom. He was thankful that at least he was able to make his wishes known by writing out his orders with his left hand. He had written instructions the day before, stating that the portrait should be moved to his room and that Joanna's room should not be disturbed in any way. Later, when he was feeling stronger, he would have Baxter carry him to Joanna's bedroom, where he could feel close to her.

He lifted his eyes to the painting and stared at Joanna's lovely face. If he were able to look at her likeness each day, perhaps it would keep him from losing his mind, he thought. His eyes caressed her face, and he knew in his heart that he would never see her again. One day, when Taggart was older, he would return—but Joanna wouldn't come with her brother. He almost wished the years would fly by so that day would come.

He heard footsteps in the hallway and frowned when Claudia entered the room. She looked up at the portrait and gave him a malevolent smile, and her lip curled into a snarl.

"So, you are still mooning over Joanna," she said, walking over to the bed and plumping up the pillows. "I should be insanely jealous that my husband loves another, but I may just be able to live with that fact. After all, you will need something to keep your mind occupied in the long days and nights ahead, won't you, Howard?"

He turned his face away, not wanting to look at Claudia. He was paying, and paying dearly, for any sins he had committed in the past. He was at the mercy of a deranged woman, and there wasn't anything he could do about it.

When Howard turned back to his wife he found her staring at the portrait. He could read the naked hatred and rage that was so clearly written on her face. She knew the day would come when her position would be challenged by Taggart, he thought. Suddenly he saw fear in Claudia's eyes, and smiled to himself, realizing that she was living in hell the same as he was—he found great satisfaction in that fact. She schemed and manipulated other people's lives, but she hadn't won a complete victory. Every day of her life she would be haunted by the fact that her dreams might decay into dust. Suddenly he had a driving need to live. He wanted desperately to stay alive, in the hopes of one day watching Claudia get what was coming to her!

And it mattered but little to Howard that, when that day did come, he would also be pulled down with her.

Chapter Twenty-Nine

The Blood Blackfoot village

Joanna's feelings of unrest continued to plague her. Although Windhawk did not single her out again, she could feel he was watching her.

Each day he asked Morning Song to bring Little Hawk to his lodge, and Morning Song told Joanna that Windhawk spent those mornings playing with his son.

Whenever Joanna saw Windhawk, her eyes followed him, and she felt an ache deep inside. She was honest enough with herself now to admit that, even if he didn't love her, she still longed for the touch of his hand and the feel of his hard, muscled body next to hers.

As time passed, Joanna found herself waking up in the mornings anxious to see Windhawk. She took particular care with her appearance, hoping he would think she was pretty.

Sun Woman watched her son and Joanna with mixed feelings of amusement and irritation. She was amused because all the village knew that Windhawk and Joanna craved the oneness they had once shared—and irritated that they were both too prideful to take the first step that would bring them together.

Sun Woman lifted up the gown she had been working on and examined it with a critical eye. She smiled, feeling pleased with the green and blue porcupine quills she had worked into the design. The gown was made of soft doeskin, and she thought it might be the best work she had ever done.

Hearing Joanna enter, she quickly hid the garment behind her.

"It is a nice afternoon, my mother, but there are rain clouds moving in from the north. I fear it will rain tonight and perhaps spoil the ceremony."

"No, it will not spoil the ceremony, since it will be held in Windhawk's lodge. Let us hope, though, that the rain holds off until the *assinahpeska* dance is over."

Joanna bent over Little Hawk and saw he was sleeping. "Tell me about the dance, my mother. I know that all the young maidens line up on one side of the lodge and the young warriors line up opposite them."

"That is true. A young maiden may show her feelings for a certain young warrior by dancing up to him. When the ceremony begins, the maidens and young men will dance toward each other and then retreat. This will go on for a time, and then they will stop to feast. After the feast, the dance will begin again. The maiden will choose the man of her choice and throw her robe over him. The young man must give her a kiss, and later a gift. If the young man likes the maiden, he may give her a gift of great value, such as a horse or a fine robe. If she is not the maiden of his choice, he may give her only colored beads or some small trinket."

"It sounds like fun to me."

"Yes, I remember when I was young. I had loved Windhawk's father, but was too shy to show him. I gathered up my courage at the *assinahpeska* dance and threw my robe over him."

"What gift did he give you?" Joanna wanted to know.

Sun Woman smiled as she remembered that night. "He gave me three horses and asked me to be his wife. I did not know that he had loved me, also."

"How wonderful for a maiden to have a chance to show the man she loves her feelings," Joanna said wistfully. "In the society I was brought up in, it would never be allowed."

Sun Woman stood up and walked over to Joanna. "You could go to the dance tonight and throw the robe over Windhawk's head," she said, watching Joanna's face.

Joanna's mouth flew open in horror. "No, I could never act in such a bold way!"

Sun Woman held the dress she had made out to Joanna. "I have made this for you just for the *assinahpeska* dance. You will wear this tonight when you dance for Windhawk."

Joanna's eyes ran over the beautiful dress, and she felt tears sparkle in her eyes because Windhawk's mother had made it for her. "I thank you for the lovely dress, my mother, but I could never join in the dance—I would be too embarrassed!"

"Sometimes, a woman has to take the first step toward the man she loves. Joanna, have I ever spoken an untruth to you?"

"No."

"I will not do so now. Listen to me and hear what I say.

437

Windhawk loves you. If you had seen him when he thought you were dead you would know this for yourself. He has been shamed before the whole tribe because his woman lives with his mother and not with him. I think he has reached out to you several times, but you would not take his hand. Go to the dance tonight—throw your robe over Windhawk so he can once more hold his head up with pride. I know it will be hard for you, but if you love Windhawk, you can do it."

Joanna's eyes were sparkling with tears. "I cannot."

"Why?"

"Because I . . . he does not . . . I fear he will not want me."

"I say that he does want you. I will tell you what to do, and you will do exactly what I say!"

Joanna looked into Sun Woman's eyes. "I want him to love me. But what if he turns me away?"

Sun Woman smiled and hugged Joanna to her. "I do not think Windhawk will give you the beads or trinkets. I think he will give you a horse . . . or a whole herd of horses!" she said, her eyes twinkling with amusement.

The *assinahpeska* dance was about to begin. The drums beat a haunting tempo while the elders of the tribe chanted. The young unmarried men sat on one side of the lodge and the young maidens sat on the other.

There was a festive mood, and much laughter accompanied the young people as they stood up. There seemed to be a feeling of frivolous abandonment as the music became louder and the young people moved toward each other. When they met in the middle, they rose on tiptoes, then dropped to their knees. And so it went, first advancing to each other, and then retreating, while singing and looking into each other's eyes.

After a while the dancing stopped, and a feast was served.

Sun Woman was helping Joanna dress. When she slipped the doeskin dress over Joanna's head, she stood back to observe with satisfaction how lovely her daughter looked.

Joanna ran her hand over the soft doeskin and smiled at Windhawk's mother. "It is lovely . . . I thank you for making it for me."

The dress was sleeveless and had fringe along the bottom, which reached Joanna's ankles. Joanna wore her hair unbraided, with only a beaded headband as adornment.

She could hear the drums had started up again, and she felt nervous. "I do not think I can do this."

"You will do it. It is important that you do this for Windhawk."

Sun Woman took Joanna's hand and led her out of the tipi toward Windhawk's lodge, thinking she would return shortly to stay with her sleeping grandson.

Windhawk was watching the young maidens dance toward the young warrior of their choice. His eyes moved to his sister, Morning Song, who was dancing toward Tag. He smiled, thinking how one could see their love for one another by the way they looked into each other's eyes.

The drumbeat grew louder, and the dance became more intense. Windhawk's eyes were drawn to the entrance of his lodge, and he held his breath as Joanna entered.

His eyes swept her face, and he saw the boldness in her eyes as she looked back at him. His heartbeat seemed to stop when he watched her fall into line beside the young maidens. All eyes turned to her as she danced forward toward him. She looked so beautiful that Windhawk blinked his eyes to clear his vision. Her white skin stood out among so many dark-skinned people, and her red-gold hair shimmered as if it were alive.

What was she doing? he wondered. Why was she here? He looked into her eyes and saw her smile slightly. He was confused and taken off guard as she stopped in front of him and held out her hand!

It seemed his heart had taken wings as he slowly stood up and looked deep into her eyes. He was not mistaken— he could plainly see the love shining in her eyes! She had come to him in a public display of her feelings to show his people that she wanted to be his woman, and, in doing so, was allowing him to save face.

He took her hand, and they bent their knees, then stood up and backed away from each other.

To Joanna, it felt as if her heart were in her mouth. She had been half-afraid that Windhawk would reject her in front of everyone. She had seen the confusion in his eyes and wondered what he was thinking. She knew everyone was watching her and Windhawk.

As they danced toward each other again, she saw his dark eyes sparkle and a half-amused smile on his lips. When she stood in front of him, she took her robe and threw it over both their heads.

Joanna felt his cheek against hers and his warm breath fanned her ear, sending shivers of delight down her spine. It was dark beneath the robe, and she felt his mouth move over her face to find and cover her lips. It was a soft kiss, but it had all the impact of a strong wind, which seemed to sweep through Joanna's body. Wild abandonment raced through her veins as Windhawk deepened the kiss.

"Do you play games with me like some frivolous maiden, Joanna?" he asked in a deeply amused voice.

She moved closer to him and turned her face up to him. "It is not a game I am playing. I am seeking a father for my son."

"Your son has a father," he stated flatly.

"That is true. I suppose I am seeking a husband for my son's mother," she whispered.

She heard his sharp intake of breath. "You had better mean this, Joanna," Windhawk whispered harshly against her ear.

She pulled the robe off their heads and smiled as everyone began to laugh.

"What shall I give this woman?" Windhawk called out, smiling down at Joanna.

Sun Woman was leaning against the lodgepole with her arms folded across her chest. "You could give her a string of brightly colored beads," she called out in an amused voice. Joanna saw the mischief sparkle in her eyes.

"No, I cannot; surely one with the beauty of the Flaming Hair is worth more than a string of beads."

"What will you give her?" many voices called out.

Windhawk looked down at Joanna through half-closed eyelashes. "She already has my heart," he whispered. "What can I give her of equal value?"

Everyone began to laugh, and Windhawk squeezed

Joanna's hand.

Sun Woman smiled to herself as she returned to her tipi to be with her grandson. Her heart was light, and she knew her son and Joanna would again walk as one!

Windhawk pulled Joanna out of his lodge as the dance continued. Lifting her in his arms, he carried her toward his horse.

"Where are you taking me?" she asked, leaning her head against his shoulder.

"I am taking you to a place where we can be alone. Did you think I would take you to my mat with the whole village looking on?"

She could feel the silent laughter vibrate through his chest.

As they galloped away from the village, Joanna thought her heart would burst with happiness. She hadn't known it would be so easy to reach out to Windhawk. She wished she had listened to Sun Woman's words sooner. Joanna knew all it would take to make her happiness complete would be to hear Windhawk admit that he loved her.

Turning her face up to his, she watched the moonlight play across his handsome face. "Windhawk, do you truly love me?"

He pulled her tightly to him and rested his lips against her cheek. "There has never been a day since I first saw you that my love for you did not fill my heart. It was not always easy to love you, but I could not help myself."

She reached up and touched his face. "I love you, Windhawk, my dearest, dearest love!" she cried, sprinkling kisses over his face.

She felt his arms tighten about her and watched as his soft eyes seemed to light up.

"Has the circle led you back to me, Joanna?"

"Yes, my love."

She didn't notice that the horse had stopped until Windhawk dismounted and carried her deeper into the woods. She rested her head against his shoulder as her heart rate accelerated, knowing what he had in mind.

Setting her on her feet, he took the robe from her and spread it on the ground. Turning back to her, he pulled her into his arms.

Joanna quivered as his lips moved over her face while his hands unfastened her doeskin dress. She could sense a impatience in him that matched her own.

Her gown was thrown aside, and Windhawk pushed her back against the robe. She closed her eyes as his hands ran over her body. He touched her and caressed her until she thought she would go slowly out of her mind.

Suddenly she gasped as he covered her body with his. Sweet, aching desire pulsated through her body as she felt Windhawk's throbbing, male hardness enter her body. Joanna arched her body and cried out as her hungry body was at last satisfied.

Windhawk clasped her to him so tightly she thought her ribs would break.

"Jo-anna, my beloved. My body was created to fit with yours." He cried out at the pain that loving her had created.

It was pain, and it was beauty as they finally came together after so many months of being apart. They made love beneath the stars with wild abandonment. And after making love, they held and caressed each other, speaking words of love.

When they were rested, Windhawk again took her

body to him, and Joanna trembled with the wonderful feelings he brought out in her. They forgot all the things that had ripped them apart. Their love would be all the more cherished because it hadn't come easy.

Just before the first flash of sunlight lit the eastern sky, Windhawk took his sleeping wife in his arms and carried her to his horse.

On the ride to his village, Joanna stirred only once. He watched the sleepy smile that lit her face and held her tightly to him. He would love and cherish this woman for the rest of his life. Windhawk vowed that no one would ever come between them again!

He dismounted and carried Joanna into his lodge where he laid her down. She didn't awake, but reached out her hand to him.

Windhawk dropped down beside her and pulled her into his arms. This was his woman, and at last she was home where she belonged.

Her outer beauty was good to look upon, and the goodness of her heart filled his soul.

In her sleep, Joanna moved closer to Windhawk, and his arm went around her waist, pulling her tighter against him. Laying his face against her sweet-smelling hair, he too fell asleep. . . .

Epilogue

It was summer—the prime season for hunting the buffalo. Once again the Blackfoot warriors were on the move, following the restless trail of the buffalo.

Windhawk was on his horse, gazing down below him. He watched Tag skillfully moving among the buffalo. He smiled with pride, thinking the boy was doing well.

His dark, expressive eyes moved over the land that had belonged to the Blackfoot for many generations. The sky was a deep blue, and white fleecy clouds floated lazily by. He watched the winding Milk River moving slowly across the land. In the distance he could see the Sweet Grass Hills and knew his village was just on the other side. His heart swelled with love and pride for this land whose beauty touched his heart.

Sighing inwardly, he nudged his horse forward. There was an urgency in him to see Joanna. When he was troubled, she seemed to calm his restlessness just by her nearness.

As he rode down the hill he thought how sad it was that all men couldn't live as brothers. He had found much to admire in the white man. Could a race be bad that had spawned someone with the sensitivity and love that

Joanna had? Was there no good in a race that could produce a boy with the bravery and courage of Tag?

Windhawk's sadness deepened. There were rumors of the white man's moving westward. He knew the time would come when the white man would challenge the Blackfoot for their right to the land where their grandfathers were buried.

He knew one day there would be war between the two races. He also realized that the white man would win in the end.

Windhawk hoped the white man wouldn't come in his day, or his son's day—but he would come . . . nothing could stop him!

Let the white man come, he thought. For Joanna's sake, he would hold out his hand in friendship to them. If they drew first blood, they would soon feel the wrath of . . . Windhawk!

Where have you gone, O noble lords of the plain?
Time has erased your footprints with the passing seasons' rain.
Your voices have now been silenced to no longer echo in the hills.
The battles are but memories when you watched your lifeblood spill.
It is we who are the losers; it is we who bear the shame.
O mighty Blackfoot warrior, only your legend remains the same.

Constance O'Banyon

THE SAVAGE DESTINY SERIES
by F. Rosanne Bittner

BESTSELLING ROMANCES BY JANELLE TAYLOR

SAVAGE ECSTASY (824, $3.50)

It was like lightning striking, the first time the Indian brave Gray Eagle looked into the eyes of the beautiful young settler Alisha. And from the moment he saw her, he knew that he must possess her—and make her his slave!

DEFIANT ECSTASY (931, $3.50)

When Gray Eagle returned to Fort Pierre's gates with his hundred warriors behind him, Alisha's heart skipped a beat: would Gray Eagle destroy her—or make his destiny her own?

FORBIDDEN ECSTASY (1014, $3.50)

Gray Eagle had promised Alisha his heart forever—nothing could keep him from her. But when Alisha woke to find her red-skinned lover gone, she felt abandoned and alone. Lost between two worlds, desperate and fearful of betrayal, Alisha hungered for the return of her FORBIDDEN ECSTASY.

BRAZEN ECSTASY (1133, $3.50)

When Alisha is swept down a raging river and out of her savage brave's life, Gray Eagle must rescue his love again. But Alisha has no memory of him at all. And as she fights to recall a past love, another white slave woman in their camp is fighting for Gray Eagle!